DATE DUE

THE

RESTORATION STAGE

HOUGHTON MIFFLIN RESEARCH SERIES

Number 8

HOUGHTON MIFFLIN RESEARCH SERIES

1. John I. McCollum, Jr., *The Age of Elizabeth*

2. V. B. Reed and J. D. Williams, *The Case of Aaron Burr*

3. Clarence A. Glasrud, *The Age of Anxiety*

4. Sheldon N. Grebstein, *Monkey Trial*

5. William J. Kimball, *Richmond in Time of War*

6. Joseph Satin, *The 1950's: America's "Placid" Decade*

7. Kelly Thurman, *Semantics*

8. John I. McCollum, Jr., *The Restoration Stage*

9. C. Merton Babcock, *The Ordeal of American English*

THE

RESTORATION

STAGE

Edited by

John I. McCollum, Jr.

UNIVERSITY OF MIAMI

GREENWOOD PRESS, PUBLISHERS
WESTPORT, CONNECTICUT

The Library of Congress has catalogued this publication as follows:

Library of Congress Cataloging in Publication Data

McCollum, John I   ed.
    The Restoration stage.

    Original ed. issued as no. 8 of Houghton Mifflin
research series.
    Bibliography: p.
    1. Theater--England--History. 2. English
drama--Restoration--History and criticism. I. Title.
[PN2592.M25 1973]   792'.0942   72-7812
ISBN 0-8371-6532-6

Copyright © 1961 by John I. McCollum, Jr.

Originally published in 1961
by the Houghton Mifflin Company, Boston

Reprinted with the permission
of the Houghton Mifflin Company, Educational Division

First Greenwood Reprinting 1973

Library of Congress Catalogue Card Number 72-7812

ISBN 0-8371-6532-6

Printed in the United States of America

PUBLISHER'S NOTE

The use of selected research materials no longer needs justification — if indeed it ever did. That they ease the strain on overtaxed libraries and aid the instructor in teaching the heart of the research method by giving him control of material which all his class is using, there is no dispute. But there are other advantages worth noting.

A genuine grasp of research method is of life-long value. The habit of sifting evidence, weighing bias, winnowing fact from opinion, assessing the judgments of others, and reaching an opinion of one's own with due regard for the possibility that new-found evidence may change it tomorrow — this is far more than a means to better grades and better papers; it is a way of mature and responsible thinking which can affect one's competence in every aspect of living. It is the aim of this book, and of the others in the Houghton Mifflin Research Series, to help the student take a stride in this direction.

The aim has been to pack into these pages enough central documentary material to give useful practice in choosing a limited topic within a broader area, scanning a large body of material, and hence in learning to reject that which is not immediately relevant and to select that which is. The major emphasis is thus placed, as it should be, on the selection, evaluation, organization, and synthesis of materials. The mechanics of notetaking, outlining, and footnote and bibliographical form are treated in every handbook and rhetoric and are not discussed here. For accurate documentation, however, the page numbers of original sources are given, when appropriate, in heavy type immediately *after* the material from the page.

Within the limits of these broad aims the book can be used in many ways: (a) for short practice papers stressing the mechanics of research technique; (b) for full-length research papers using only materials here provided; and (c) as a springboard for papers which involve use of the library and additional reading, either historical or literary. Literature as such has been generally excluded, partly for reasons of length and of general student interest, and partly because only the gifted or the specially trained student can at this stage competently handle the very different problems of research and of criticism at the same time. For such students there is ample opportunity to step from the present materials into the literature of special interest to him.

The editor of this book has appended two lists of suggested topics for shorter and longer papers, limited to materials in this book or using additional materials from other sources. It is hoped that these lists will serve as a guide to the instructor and the student and lead to the kinds of reading and thinking essential to competent research in any field.

PREFACE

After the Puritans closed the public theaters in 1642, English drama languished, receiving only sporadic stimulation from the occasional performances of modified plays in the guise of moral and edifying entertainment. A few troupes of actors were able to survive by playing at country fairs and on private estates.

Sir William Davenant was able to keep the theater alive in London by gaining quiet permission from Puritan officials to stage private performances at Rutland House. The most notable presentation during the interim was his *Siege of Rhodes* (1656), reflecting the French influence and representing the beginning of the heroic drama — a form that Dryden and Howard were to employ so successfully after the Restoration. Davenant's contribution to the English theater is a significant one. He was a bridge from the older Elizabethan-Jacobean tradition, as well as a major entrepreneur and a highly imaginative innovator. Whereas men and boys had previously taken the female roles, Davenant introduced women upon the public stage. He also borrowed the use of elaborate scenery from the court masques, and further increased variety in his plays by adding music.

After the Restoration, Charles II granted a patent to Davenant in 1660 to produce plays at the Salisbury Court Theatre as the Duke of York's Company. At the same time Thomas Killigrew was granted a similar patent to form a company as the King's Men at the Theatre Royal. Thus the theater was restored and a stimulating and lively era was under way. During the next twenty-two years these two theaters became rivals for the small London audiences. A capacity audience for one house often meant empty seats in the other. Finally, in 1682, the Duke's Company absorbed the King's Men to form the United Company, and for the next thirteen years it alone provided London's drama. The era was nevertheless a significant one in theater structure and in stage practice, a period of inspired acting and celebrated personalities. Charles II himself provided royal patronage for the theater: often in the audience and intimate with the players, he mediated between conflicting parties, redressed wrongs, and even outfitted the players from his own wardrobe.

The court, the new theaters and scenery, the histrionic power of the actors, the charm and appeal of the actresses — all made the theater a glittering affair. It is no wonder that Pepys was so often drawn to the playhouses in spite of the pressures of business, the pull of ambition, and the restraint and condemnation of his conscience.

Indeed, the playwrights could hardly have asked for more support. If Restoration tragedy seems somewhat strained and its heroism rather noisy, the comedy was flashing, polished, and witty — and often licentious. It did, however, serve as an admirable instrument for satire, seeming to reflect the love of wit and amusement which characterized the audience while at the same time revealing its excesses and affectations.

The "Glorious Revolution" of 1688 brought with it social changes that were to affect the Restoration theater. The nobility was becoming less affluent and powerful socially. Its place was being taken by a rising, wealthy middle class. And a new tone in the theater came in response to this broader, bourgeois audience. While moralizers like Jeremy Collier severely criticized the liberties of the theater, writers like Shadwell, Farquhar, and Cibber reflected the sentiments of this middle-class audience in their plays and provided it with a comedy closer to its own position. This evolved gradually into what became known in the eighteenth century as the sentimental comedy and the "she" tragedy.

The documents reproduced here reveal many of the critical and theoretical tenets on which Restoration drama was built; they also indicate the grounds on which popular practices were both justified and condemned. Memoirs like those of Pepys and Evelyn give candid views of the theater and the audience as seen through native eyes — as do those of Magalotti and Sorbiere from a foreign point of view.

Much of the intellectual and social ferment may be inferred from the contemporary record. These documents are of course ancillary to the drama itself. The beauty of the language, as well as its flamboyance and wit, is to be found only in the lines written to be spoken on the stage. The stage effects are in many cases identified in the directions accompanying the plays; these must be referred to when reconstructing what the Restoration audiences might have seen or heard in their theaters. From the documents reproduced here and the easily available plays, the student may enter the world of the later Stuarts, of Dryden, Congreve, and Cibber. If the theater was sometimes coarse and rowdy, rude and affected, it could also be charming, witty, and stimulating.

For their many courtesies extended to me while I was collecting these materials, I am indebted to the staff of the University of Miami Library, and in particular Mrs. Mildred Selle, who aided me in locating many of the less easily accessible items.

John I. McCollum, Jr.

Coral Gables, Florida

CONTENTS

THE

RESTORATION STAGE

Samuel Butler (1612–80) is known to modern readers as he was to his contemporaries as the author of Hudibras, *a long burlesque poem directed at the Puritans. Little is known of his early life; however, in 1673 he seems to have received the patronage of George Villiers, second duke of Buckingham, with whom he wrote* The Rehearsal, *a satirical play ridiculing the heroic drama so popular at the time.*

He counted among his friends Thomas Hobbes, Sir William Davenant, John Aubrey, and Thomas Shadwell. The popularity of his major work, Hudibras, *brought him a royal pension. Most of his miscellaneous works, however, remained in manuscript until Robert Thyer first edited them in 1759. Among the verse and prose pieces of this collection are some two hundred "characters" and a number of satirical and critical poems, of which the best known is* The Elephant in the Moon, *directed against the* Royal Society. Upon Critics *is a reply to Rymer's* Tragedies of the Last Age Consider'd.

While not a major figure, Butler nevertheless provides a witty commentary on the theatrical practices and critical attitudes of this period.

Samuel Butler. "Upon Critics Who Judge of Modern Plays Precisely by the Rules of the Antients," in *The Genuine Remains in Verse and Prose . . . ,* ed. R. Thyer. London, 1759. I, 161–167.

> Who ever will regard *poetic Fury,*
> When it is once found *Idiot* by a Jury;
> And every pert and arbitrary Fool
> Can all poetic Licence over-rule;
> 5   Assume a barbarous Tyranny to handle
> The *Muses* worse than *Ostrogoth* and *Vandal;*
> Make 'em submit to Verdict and Report,
> And stand or fall to th' Orders of a Court?
> Much less be sentenc'd by the arbitrary
> 10   Proceedings of a witless *Plagiary;*
> That forges old Records and Ordinances
> Against the Right and Property of Fancies,
> More false and nice than weighing of the Weather
> To th' Hundredth Atom of the lightest Feather,
> 15   Or measuring of Air upon *Parnassus*
> With Cylinders of *Torricellian* Glasses;
> Reduce all *Tragedy* by Rules of Art
> Back to its antique Theatre, a *Cart,*

And make them henceforth keep the beaten Roads

20　Of reverend *Chorus's*, and *Episodes;*

Reform and regulate a *Puppet-play,*

According to the true and ancient way;

That not an Actor shall presume to squeak,

Unless he have a Licence for't in *Greek;*

25　Nor *Whittington* henceforward sell his Cat in

Plain vulgar *English*, without mewing *Latin:*

No *Pudding* shall be suffer'd to be witty,

Unless it be in order to raise Pity;

Nor *Devil* in the *Puppet-play* b'allow'd

30　To roar and spit Fire, but to fright the Crowd,

Unless some *God* or *Daemon* chance t' have Piques

Against an ancient Family of *Greeks;*

That other Men may tremble, and take Warning,

How such a fatal Progeny th' are born in.

35　For none but such for *Tragedy* are fitted,

That have been ruin'd only to be pity'd;

And only those held proper to deter,

Who've had th' ill Luck against their Wills to err.

Whence only such as are of middling Sizes,

40　Between Morality and venial Vices,

Are qualify'd to be destroy'd by *Fate*,

For other Mortals to take Warning at.

As if the antique Laws of *Tragedy*

Did with our own Municipal agree;

45　And serv'd, like Cobwebs, but t' ensnare the Weak,

And give Diversion to the Great to break;

To make a less Delinquent to be brought

To answer for a greater Person's Fault,

And suffer all the worst, the worst Approver

50　Can, to excuse and save himself, discover.

No longer shall *Dramatics* be confin'd

To draw true Images of all Mankind;

To punish in Effigy Criminals,

Reprieve the Innocent, and hang the False;

55　But a Club-law to execute and kill,

For nothing, whomsoe'er they please, at will,

To terrify Spectators from committing

The Crimes they did, and suffer'd for unwitting.

These are the Reformations of the *Stage*,

60　Like other Reformations of the Age,

On Purpose to destroy all *Wit* and *Sense*,

As th' other did all *Law* and *Conscience;*

No better than the Laws of *British* Plays,

Confirm'd in th' ancient good King *Howel's* Days,

65　Who made a *general Council* regulate

Mens catching Women by the —— you know what;

And set down in the *Rubric*, at what Time
It should be counted legal, when a Crime,
Declare when 'twas, and when 'twas not a Sin,
70   And on what Days it *went out*, or *came in.*
    An *English* Poet should be try'd b' his Peers,
And not by *Pedants*, and *Philosophers*,
Incompetent to judge poetic Fury,
As *Butchers* are forbid to b' of a Jury;
75   Besides the most intolerable Wrong
To try their Matters in a foreign Tongue,
By foreign *Jurymen*, like *Sophocles*,
Or *Tales* falser than *Euripides;*
When not an *English* Native dares appear,
80   To be a Witness for the Prisoner;
When all the Laws, they use t' arraign and try
The innocent and wrong'd Delinquent by,
Were made b' a foreign *Lawyer*, and his Pupils,
To put an End to all poetic Scruples,
85   And, by th' Advice of *Virtuosi-Tuscans*,
Determin'd all the Doubts of *Socks* and *Buskins;*
Gave Judgment on all past and future Plays,
As is apparent by *Speroni's* Case,
Which *Lope Vega* first began to steal,
90   And after him the *French* Filou *Corneill;*
And since our *English* Plagiaries nim,
And steal their far-fet Criticisms from him;
And, by an Action falsly laid of *Trover*,
The Lumber for their proper Goods recover;
95   Enough to furnish all the lewd Impeachers
Of witty *Beaumont's* Poetry, and *Fletcher's*,
Who, for a few *Misprisions* of Wit,
Are charg'd by those, who ten times worse commit;
And, for misjudging some unhappy Scenes,
100   Are censur'd for't with more unlucky Sense;
When all their worst Miscarriages delight,
And please more, than the best that *Pedants* write.

Samuel Butler. "A Play-Writer," from *Characters*, in *The Genuine Remains in Verse and Prose* . . . , ed. R. Thyer. London, 1759. Vol II.

A Play-Writer

Of our Times is like a *Fanatic*, that has no Wit in ordinary easy Things, and yet attempts the hardest Tusk of Brains in the whole World, only because, whether his Play or Work please or displease, he is certain to come off better than he deserves, and find some of his own Latitude to applaud him, which he could never expect any other Way; and is as sure to lose no Reputation, because he has none to venture.

> Like gaming Rooks, that never stick
> To play for hundreds upon Tick,
> 'Cause, if they chance to lose at Play,
> Th'ave not one halfpenny to pay;
> And, if they win a hundred Pound,
> Gain, if for Sixpence they compound.   page 301 /

Nothing encourages him more in his Undertaking than his Ignorance, for he has not Wit enough to understand so much as the Difficulty of what he attempts; therefore he runs on boldly like a foolhardy Wit, and *Fortune*, that favours Fools and the Bold, sometimes takes Notice of him for his double Capacity, and receives him into her good Graces. He has one Motive more, and that is the concurrent ignorant Judgment of the present Age, in which his sottish Fopperies pass with Applause, like *Oliver Cromwel's* Oratory among *Fanatics* of his own canting Inclination. He finds it easier to write in Rhime than Prose; for the World being overcharged with Romances, he finds his Plots, Passions, and Repartees ready made to his Hand; and if he can but turn them into Rhime, the Thievery is disguised, and they pass for his own Wit and Invention without Question; like a stolen Cloke made into a Coat, or dyed into another Colour. Besides this he makes no Conscience of stealing any Thing that lights in his Way, and borrows the Advice of so many to correct, enlarge, and amend what he has ill-favouredly patcht together, that it becomes like a Thing drawn by Council, and none of his   page 302 /   own Performance, or the Son of a Whore that has no one certain Father. He has very great Reason to prefer Verse before Prose in his Compositions; for Rhime is like Lace, that serves excellently well to hide the Piercing and Coarsness of a bad Stuff, contributes mightily to the Bulk, and makes the less serve by the many Impertinences it commonly requires to make Way for it; for very few are endowed with Abilities to bring it in on its own Accompt. This he finds to be good Husbandry, and a Kind of necessary Thrift; for they that have but a little ought to make as much of it as they can. His Prologue, which is commonly none of his own, is always better than his Play, like a Piece of Cloth that's fine in the Beginning and coarse afterwards, though it has but one Topic, and that's the same that is used by Malefactors, when they are to be tried, to except against as many of the Jury as they can.   page 303 /

Colley Cibber (1671–1757), actor, comic playwright, entrepreneur, *and poet laureate (1730), joined the United Company at the Theatre Royal in 1690. His play* Love's Last Shift, or The Fool of Fashion *was produced in January 1695–96, with Cibber acting Sir Novelty Fashion. Both the play and the author's performance were hailed as great successes. Vanbrugh continued Cibber's plot in* The Relapse *with Sir Novelty ennobled by purchase as Lord Foppington, and Cibber once again played the chief part. So well did he establish the role of the fop that he became in the eyes of the public the vapid, simple-minded dandy he portrayed on the stage. Although he reports of himself that "A giddy negligence always possess'd me," his activities seem to belie this judgment, for he was an extremely successful playwright, a great comedian, and an exceptional critic of the stage. He is generally regarded as one of the most significant persons in the theater of the late seventeenth and early eighteenth centuries. But he was not without critics. Much of his poetry was ridiculed, and Pope made him heir to the Throne of Dulness in the revised* Dunciad. *His most important work by far is the autobiographical* Apology for the Life of Mr. Colley Cibber, Comedian. *Not only does the* Apology *review many of the events associated with the history of the stage, but it admirably sketches such outstanding actors and actresses as Betterton, Mrs. Bracegirdle, Mrs. Barry, Nokes, and Sandford.*

An Apology for the Life of Mr. Colley Cibber, Comedian, and Late Patentee of the Theatre-Royal. With an Historical View of the Stage during his Own Time. Written by Himself. London, 1740.

King *Charles* II. at his Restoration, granted two Patents, one to Sir *William Davenant*, and the other to *Henry Killigrew*, Esq; and their several Heirs and Assigns, for ever, for the forming of two distinct Companies of Comedians: The first were call'd the *King's Servants*, and acted at the Theatre-Royal in *Drury-Lane;* page 53 / and the other the *Duke's Company*, who acted at the Duke's Theatre in *Dorset-Garden*. About ten of the King's Company were on the Royal Houshold-Establishment, having each ten Yards of Scarlet Cloth, with a proper quantity of Lace allow'd them for Liveries; and in their Warrants from the Lord Chamberlain, were stiled *Gentlemen of the Great Chamber:* Whether the like Appointments were extended to the Duke's Company, I am not certain; but they were both in high Estimation with the Publick, and so much the Delight and Concern of the Court, that they were not only supported by its being frequently present at their publick *Presentations*, but by its taking cognizance even of their private Government, insomuch, that their particular Differences, Pretentions, or Complaints, were generally ended by the *King*,

7

or *Duke's* Personal Command or Decision. Besides their being thorough Masters of their Art, these Actors set forwards with two critical Advantages, which perhaps may never happen again in many Ages. The one was, their immediate opening after the so long Interdiction of Plays, during the Civil War, and the Anarchy that follow'd it. What eager Appetites from so long a Fast, must the Guests of those Times have had, to that high and fresh variety of Entertainments, which *Shakespear* had left prepar'd for them? Never was a Stage so provided! A hundred Years are wasted, and another silent Century well advanced, and yet what unborn Age shall say, *Shakespear* has his Equal! How many shining Actors have the warm Scenes of his Genius given to Posterity? without being himself, in his Action, equal to his Writing! A strong Proof that Actors, like Poets, must be born such. Eloquence and Elocution are quite different Talents: *Shakespear* cou'd write *Hamlet;* but Tradition tells us, That the *Ghost* in the same Play, was one of his best Performances as an Actor: Nor is it within the reach of Rule or Precept to complete either of them. Instruction, 'tis true, may guard them equally against Faults or Absurdities, but there it stops; Nature must do the rest: To ex- page 54 / cel in either Art, is a self-born Happiness, which something more than good Sense must be the Mother of.

The other Advantage I was speaking of, is, that before the Restoration, no Actresses had ever been seen upon the *English* Stage. The Characters of Women, on former Theatres, were perform'd by Boys, or young Men of the most effeminate Aspect. And what Grace, or Master-strokes of Action can we conceive such ungain Hoydens to have been capable of? This Defect was so well consider'd by *Shakespear,* that in few of his Plays, he has any greater Dependance upon the Ladies, than in the Innocence and Simplicity of a *Desdemona,* an *Ophelia,* or in the short Specimen of a fond and virtuous *Portia.* The additional Objects then of real, beautiful Women, could not but draw a proportion of new Admirers to the Theatre. We may imagine too, that these Actresses were not ill chosen, when it is well known, that more than one of them had Charms sufficient at their leisure Hours, to calm and mollify the Cares of Empire. Besides these peculiar Advantages, they had a private Rule or Agreement, which both Houses were happily ty'd down to, which was, that no Play acted at one House, should ever be attempted at the other. All the capital Plays therefore of *Shakespear, Fletcher,* and *Ben. Johnson,* were divided between them, by the Approbation of the Court, and their own alternate Choice: So that when *Hart* was famous for *Othello, Betterton* had no less a Reputation for *Hamlet.* By this Order the Stage was supply'd with a greater Variety of Plays, than could possibly have been shewn, had both Companies been employ'd at the same time, upon the same Play; which Liberty too, must have occasion'd such frequent Repetitions of 'em, by their opposite Endeavours to forestall and anticipate one another, that the best Actors in the World must have grown tedious and tasteless to the Spectator: For what Pleasure is not languid to Satiety? It was therefore one of our greatest Happinesses (during my time of being in the Management of the Stage) that page 55 / we had a certain Number of select Plays, which no other Company had the good Fortune to make a tolerable Figure in, and consequently, could find little or no Account, by acting them against us. These Plays therefore, for many Years, by not being too often seen, never fail'd to bring us crowded Audiences; and it was to this Conduct we ow'd no little Share of our Prosperity. . . .

These two excellent Companies were both prosperous for some few Years, 'till their Variety of Plays began to be exhausted: Then of course, the better Actors (which the King's seem to have been allow'd) could not fail of drawing the greater Audiences. **page 56 /** Sir *William Davenant*, therefore, Master of the Duke's Company, to make Head against their Success, was forc'd to add Spectacle and Musick to Action; and to introduce a new Species of Plays, since call'd Dramatick Opera's, of which kind were the *Tempest, Psyche, Circe,* and others, all set off with the most expensive Decorations of Scenes and Habits, with the best Voices and Dancers.

This sensual Supply of Sight and Sound, coming in to the Assistance of the weaker Party, it was no Wonder they should grow too hard for Sense and simple Nature, when it is consider'd how many People there are, that can see and hear, than think and judge. So wanton a Change in the publick Taste, therefore, began to fall as heavy upon the King's Company, as their greater Excellence in Action, had, before, fallen upon their Competitors: Of which Encroachment upon Wit, several good Prologues in those Days frequently complain'd. . . .

. . . Taste and Fashion, with us, have always had Wings, and fly from one publick Spectacle to another so wantonly, that I have been inform'd, by those, who remember it, that a famous Puppet-shew, in *Salisbury* Change . . . so far distrest these two celebrated Companies, that they were reduced to petition the King for Relief against it. . . . *Mohun*, and *Hart* now growing old (for, above thirty Years before this Time, they had severally born the King's Commission of Major and Captain, in the Civil Wars) and the younger Actors, as *Goodman, Clark,* **page 57 /** and others, being impatient to get into their Parts, and growing intractable, the Audiences too of both Houses then falling off, the Patentees of each, by the King's Advice, which perhaps amounted to a Command, united their Interests, and both Companies into one, exclusive of all others, in the Year 1684. This Union was, however, so much in favour of the Duke's Company, that *Hart* left the Stage upon it, and *Mohun* survived not long after.

One only Theatre being now in Possession of the whole Town, the united Patentees impos'd their own Terms, upon the Actors; for the Profits of acting were then divided into twenty Shares, ten of which went to the Proprietors, and the other Moiety to the principal Actors, in such Sub-divisions as their different Merit might pretend to. These Shares of the Patentees were promiscuously sold out to Mony-making Persons, call'd Adventurers, who, tho' utterly ignorant of Theatrical Affairs, were still admitted to a proportionate Vote in the Management of them; all particular Encouragements to Actors were by them, of Consequence, look'd upon as so many Sums deducted from their private Dividends. While therefore the Theatrical Hive had so many Drones in it, the labouring Actors, sure, were under the highest Discouragement, if not a direct State of Oppression. . . . Under this heavy Establishment then groan'd this United Company, when I was first admitted into the lowest Rank of it. How they came to be reliev'd by King *William's* Licence in 1695, how they were **page 58 /** again dispersed, early in Queen *Anne's* Reign . . . will be told in its Place. . . .

In the Year 1690, when I first came into this Company, the principal Actors then at the Head of it were,

Of Men.	Of Women.
Mr. *Betterton*,	Mrs. *Betterton*,
Mr. *Monfort*,	Mrs. *Barry*,
Mr. *Kynaston*,	Mrs. *Leigh*,
Mr. *Sandford*,	Mrs. *Butler*,
Mr. *Nokes*,	Mrs. *Monfort*, and
Mr. *Underhil*, and	Mrs. *Bracegirdle*.
Mr. *Leigh*.	

These Actors, whom I have selected from their Cotemporaries, were all original Masters in their different Stile, not meer auricular Imitators of one another, which commonly is the highest Merit of the middle Rank; but Self-judges of nature, from whose various Lights they only took their true Instruction. . . .

Betterton was an Actor, as *Shakespear* was an Author, both without Competitors! form'd for the mutual Assistance, and Illu- page 59 / stration of each others Genius! How *Shakespear* wrote, all Men who have a Taste for Nature may read, and know — but with what higher Rapture would he still be *read*, could they conceive how *Betterton play'd him!* Then might they know, the one was born alone to speak what the other only knew, to write! . . . Could *how Betterton* spoke be as easily known as *what* he spoke; then might you see the Muse of *Shakespear* in her Triumph, with all her Beauties in their best Array, rising into real Life, and charming her Beholders. But alas! since all this is so far out of the reach of Description, how shall I shew you *Betterton?* Should I therefore tell you, that all the *Othellos, Hamlets, Hotspurs, Mackbeths,* and *Brutus's,* whom you may have seen since his time, have fallen far short of him; This still would give you no Idea of his particular Excellence. Let us see then what a particular Comparison may do! whether that may yet draw him nearer to you?

You have seen a *Hamlet* perhaps, who, on the first Appearance of his Father's Spirit, has thrown himself into all the straining Vociferation requisite to express Rage and Fury, and the House has thunder'd with Applause; tho' the mis-guided Actor was all the while (as *Shakespear* terms it) tearing a Passion into Rags — I am the more bold to offer you this particular Instance, because the late Mr. *Addison*, while I sate by him, to see this Scene acted, made the same Observation, asking me with some Surprize, if I thought *Hamlet* should be in so violent a Passion with the Ghost, which tho' it might have astonish'd, it had not provok'd him? for you may observe that in this beautiful Speech, the Passion never rises beyond an almost breathless Astonishment, or an Impatience, limited by filial Reverence, to enquire into the suspected   page 60 /   Wrongs that may have rais'd him from his peaceful Tomb! and a Desire to know what a Spirit so seemingly distrest, might wish or enjoin a sorrowful Son to execute towards his future Quiet in the Grave? This was the Light into which *Betterton* threw this Scene; which he open'd with a Pause of mute Amazement! then rising slowly, to a solemn, trembling Voice, he made the Ghost equally terrible to the Spectator, as to himself! and in the descriptive Part of the natural Emotions which the ghastly Vision gave him, the boldness of his Expostulation was still govern'd by Decency, manly, but not braving; his Voice never rising into that seeming Outrage, or wild Defiance of what he naturally rever'd. But alas! to preserve this Medium, between mouthing, and meaning too little, to keep the Attention more pleasingly awake, by a temper'd Spirit, than by meer Vehemence of Voice, is of all the Master-strokes of an Actor the most difficult to reach. In this none yet have equall'd *Betterton*. . . .   **page 61 /**

A farther Excellence in *Betterton*, was, that he could vary his Spirit to the different Characters he acted. Those wild impatient Starts, that fierce and flashing Fire, which he threw into *Hotspur*, never came from the unruffled Temper of his *Brutus* (for I have, more than once, seen a *Brutus* as warm as *Hotspur*) when the *Betterton Brutus* was provok'd, in his Dispute with *Cassius*, his Spirit flew only to his Eye; his steady Look alone supply'd that Terror, which he disdain'd an Intemperance in his Voice should rise to. Thus, with a settled Dignity of Contempt, like an unheeding Rock, he repell'd upon himself the Foam of *Cassius*. Perhaps the very Words of *Shakespear* will better let you into my Meaning:

> *Must I give way, and room, to your rash Choler?*
> *Shall I be frighted when a Madman stares?*

And a little after,

> *There is no Terror,* Cassius, *in your Looks!* &c.   **page 62 /**

Not but, in some part of this Scene, where he reproaches *Cassius*, his Temper is not under this Suppression, but opens into that Warmth which becomes a Man of Virtue; yet this is that *Hasty Spark* of Anger, which *Brutus* himself endeavours to excuse.

But with whatever strength of Nature we see the Poet shew, at once, the Philosopher and the Heroe, yet the Image of the Actor's Excellence will be still imperfect to you, unless Language cou'd put Colours in our Words to paint the Voice with.

. . . The most that a *Vandyke* can arrive at, is to make his Portraits of great Persons seem to *think;* a *Shakespear* goes farther yet, and tells you *what* his Pictures thought; a *Betterton* steps beyond 'em both, and calls them from the Grave, to breathe, and be themselves again, in Feature, Speech, and Motion. When the skilful Actor shews you all these Powers united, and gratifies at once your Eye, your Ear, your Understanding. To conceive the Pleasure rising from such Harmony, you must have been present at it! 'tis not be told you!

There cannot be a stronger Proof of the Charms of harmonious Elocution, than the many, even unnatural Scenes and Flights of the false Sublime it has lifted into Applause. In what Raptures have I seen an Audience, at the furious Fustian and turgid Rants in *Nat. Lee's Alexander the Great!* For though I can allow this Play a few great Beauties, yet it is not without its extravagant Blemishes. Every Play of the same Author has more or less of them. Let me give you a Sample from this. *Alexander*, in a full crowd of Courtiers, without being occasionally call'd or provok'd to it, falls into this Rhapsody of Vain-glory.

> *Can none remember? Yes, I know all must!*

And therefore they shall know it agen.   page 63 /

> *When Glory, like the dazzling Eagle, stood*
> *Perch'd on my Beaver, in the Granic Flood,*
> *When Fortune's Self, my Standard trembling bore,*
> *And the pale Fates stood frighted on the Shore,*
> *When the Immortals on the Billows rode,*
> *And I myself appear'd the leading God.*

When these flowing Numbers came from the Mouth of a *Betterton*, the Multitude no more desired Sense to them, than our musical *Connoisseurs* think it essential in the celebrate Airs of an *Italian* Opera. Does not this prove, that there is very near as much Enchantment in the well-govern'd Voice of an Actor, as in the sweet Pipe of an Eunuch? If I tell you, there was no one Tragedy, for many Years, more in favour with the Town than *Alexander*, to what must we impute this its command of publick Admiration? Not to its intrinsick Merit, surely, if it swarms with Passages like this I have shewn you! If this Passage has Merit, let us see what Figure it would make upon Canvas, what sort of Picture would rise from it. If *Le Brun*, who was famous for painting the Battles of this Heroe, had seen this lofty Description, what one Image could he have possibly taken from it? In what Colours would he have shewn us *Glory perch'd upon a Beaver?* How would he have drawn *Fortune trembling?* Or, indeed, what use could he have made of *pale Fates*, or *Immortals* riding upon *Billows*, with this blustering *God* of his own making at the *head* of 'em? Where, then, must have lain the Charm, that once made the Publick so partial to this Tragedy? Why plainly, in the Grace and Harmony of the Actor's Utterance. . . .   page 64 /

When this favourite Play I am speaking of, from its being too frequently acted, was worn out, and came to be deserted by the Town, upon the sudden Death of *Monfort*, who had play'd *Alexander* with Success, for several Years, the Part was given to *Betterton*, which, under this great Disadvantage of the Satiety it had given, he immediately reviv'd with so new a Lustre, that for three Days together it fill'd the House; and had his then declining Strength been equal to the Fatigue the Action gave him, it probably might have doubled its Success; an uncommon Instance of the Power and intrinsick Merit of an Actor. . . . When, from a too advanced Age, he resigned that toilsome Part of *Alexander*, the Play, for many years after, was never able to impose upon page 65 /   the Publick; and I look upon his so particularly supporting the false Fire and Extravagancies of that Character, to be a more surprizing Proof of his Skill, than his being eminent in those of *Shakespear;* because there, Truth and Nature coming to his Assistance, he had not the same Difficulties to combat. . . .   page 66 /

As we have sometimes great Composers of Musick, who cannot sing, we have as frequently great Writers that cannot read; and tho', without the nicest Ear, no Man can be Master of Poetical Numbers, yet the best Ear in the World will not always enable him to pronounce them. Of this Truth, *Dryden,* our first great Master of Verse and Harmony, was a strong Instance: When he brought his Play of *Amphytrion* to the Stage, I heard him give it his first Reading to the Actors, in which, though it is true, he deliver'd the plain Sense of every Period, yet the whole was in so cold, so flat, and unaffecting a manner, that I am afraid of not being believ'd, when I affirm it.

On the contrary, *Lee,* far his Inferior in Poetry, was so pathetick a Reader of his own Scenes, that I have been inform'd by an Actor, who was present, that while *Lee* was reading to Major *Mohun* at a Rehearsal, *Mohun,* in the Warmth of his Admiration, threw down his Part, and said, Unless I were able to *play* it, as well as you *read* it, to what purpose should I undertake it? And yet this very Author, whose Elocution rais'd such Admiration in so capital an Actor, when he attempted to be **page 68 /** an Actor himself, soon quitted the Stage, in an honest Despair of ever making any profitable Figure there. . . . **page 69 /**

. . . What Talents shall we say will infallibly form an Actor? This, I confess, is one of Nature's Secrets, too deep for me to dive into; let us content our selves therefore with affirming, That *Genius,* which Nature only gives, only can complete him. This *Genius* then was so strong in *Betterton,* that it shone out in every Speech and Motion of him. Yet Voice, and Person, are such necessary Supports to it, that, by the Multitude, they have been preferr'd to *Genius* itself, or at least often mistaken for it. *Betterton* had a Voice of that kind, which gave more Spirit to Terror, than to the softer Passions; of more Strength than Melody. The Rage and Jealousy of *Othello,* became him better than the Sighs and Tenderness of *Castalio:* For though in *Castalio* he only excell'd others, in *Othello* he excell'd himself; which you will easily believe, when you consider, that in spite of his Complexion, *Othello* has more natural Beauties than the best Actor can find in all the Magazine of Poetry, to animate his Power, and delight his Judgment with.

The Person of this excellent Actor was suitable to his Voice, more manly than sweet, not exceeding the middle Stature, inclining to the corpulent; of a serious and penetrating Aspect; his Limbs nearer the athletick, than the delicate Proportion; yet however form'd, there arose from the Harmony of the whole a commanding Mien of Majesty, which the fairer-fac'd, or (as *Shakespear* calls 'em) the *curled* Darlings of his Time, ever wanted something to be equal Masters of. There was some Years ago, to be had, almost in every Print-shop, a *Metzotinto,* from *Kneller,* extremely like him. . . . **page 70 /**

The last Part this great Master of his Profession acted, was *Melantius* in the *Maid's Tragedy,* for his own Benefit; when being suddenly seiz'd by the Gout, he submitted, by extraordinary Applications, to have his Foot so far reliev'd, that he might be able to walk on the Stage, in a Slipper, rather than wholly disappoint his Auditors. He was observ'd that Day, to have exerted a more than ordinary Spirit, and met with suitable Applause; but the unhappy Consequence of tampering with his Distemper was, that it flew into his Head, and kill'd him in three Days, (I think) in the seventy-fourth Year of his Age. . . .
page 71 /

CHAP. V

*The Theatrical Characters of the Principal Actors,
in the Year 1690, continu'd.
A few Words to Critical Auditors*

Tho', as I have before observ'd, Women were not admitted to the Stage, 'till the Return of King *Charles*, yet it could not be so suddenly supply'd with them, but that there was still a Necessity, for some time, to put the handsomest young Men into Petticoats; which *Kynaston* was then said to have worn, with Success; particularly in the Part of *Evadne*, in the *Maid's Tragedy*, which I have heard him speak of; and which calls to my Mind a ridiculous Distress that arose from these sort of Shifts, which the Stage was then put to. — The King coming a little before his usual time to a Tragedy, found the Actors not ready to begin, when his Majesty not chusing to have as much Patience as his good Subjects, sent to them, to know the Meaning of it; upon which the Master of the Company came to the Box, and rightly judging, that the best Excuse for their Default, would be the true one, fairly told his Majesty, that the Queen was not *shav'd* yet: The King, whose good Humour lov'd to laugh at a Jest, as well as to make one, accepted the Excuse, which serv'd to divert him, till the male Queen cou'd be effeminated. In a word, *Kynaston*, at that time was so beautiful a Youth, that the Ladies of Quality prided themselves in taking him with them in their Coaches, to *Hyde-Park*, in his Theatrical Habit, after the Play; which in those Days, they might have sufficient time to do, because Plays then, were us'd to begin at four a-Clock: The Hour that People of the same Rank, are now going to Dinner. — Of this Truth, I had the Curiosity to enquire, and had it   page 72 /   confirm'd from his own Mouth, in his advanc'd Age: And indeed, to the last of him, his Handsomeness was very little abated; ev'n at past Sixty, his Teeth were all sound, white, and even, as one would wish to see, in a reigning Toast of Twenty. He had something of a formal Gravity in his Mien, which was attributed to the stately Step he had been so early confin'd to, in a female Decency. But ev'n that, in Characters of Superiority had its proper Graces; it misbecame him not in the Part of *Leon*, in *Fletcher's Rule a Wife, &c.* which he executed with a determin'd Manliness, and honest Authority, well worth the best Actor's Imitation. He had a piercing Eye, and in Characters of heroick Life, a quick imperious Vivacity, in his Tone of Voice, that painted the Tyrant truly terrible. There were two Plays of *Dryden* in which he shone, with uncommon Lustre; in *Aurenge-Zebe* he play'd *Morat*, and in *Don Sebastian, Muley Moloch;* in both these Parts, he had a fierce, Lion-like Majesty in his Port and Utterance, that gave the Spectator a kind of trembling Admiration! . . .   page 73 /

. . . But *Kynaston* staid too long upon the Stage, till his Memory and Spirit began to fail him. . . .

Monfort, a younger Man by twenty Years, and at this time in his highest Reputation, was an Actor of a very different Style: Of Person he was tall, well made, fair, and of an agreeable Aspect: His Voice clear, full, and melodious: In Tragedy he was the most affecting Lover within my Memory. His Addresses had a resistless Recommendation from the very Tone of his Voice, which gave his Words such Softness, that, as *Dryden* says,

    —— *Like Flakes of feather'd Snow,*
    They melted as they fell!

All this he particularly verify'd in that Scene of *Alexander*, where the Heroe throws himself at the Feet of *Statira* for Pardon of his past Infidelities. There we saw the Great, the Tender, the Penitent, the Despairing, the Transported, and the Amiable, in the highest Perfection. In Comedy, he gave the truest Life to what we call the *Fine Gentleman;* his Spirit shone the brighter for being polish'd with Decency: In Scenes of Gaiety, he never broke into the Regard, that was due to the Presence of equal, or superior Characters, tho' inferior Actors play'd them; he fill'd the Stage, not by elbowing, and crossing it before others, or disconcerting their Action, but by surpassing them, in true and masterly Touches of Nature. He never laugh'd at his own Jest, unless the Point of his Raillery upon another requir'd it. — He had a particular Talent, in giving Life to *bons Mots* and *Repartees:* The Wit of the Poet seem'd always to come from him *extempore*, and sharpen'd into more Wit, from his brilliant manner of delivering it; he had himself a good Share of it, or what is equal to it, so lively a Pleasantness of Humour, that when either of these fell into his Hands upon the Stage, he **page 76 /**   wantoned with them, to the highest Delight of his Auditors. . . .

  He had besides all this, a Variety in his Genius, which few capital Actors have shewn, or perhaps have thought it any Addition to their Merit to arrive at; he could entirely change himself; could at once throw off the Man of Sense, for the brisk, vain, rude, and lively Coxcomb, the false, flashy Pretender to Wit, and the Dupe of his own Sufficiency: Of this he gave a delightful Instance in the Character of *Sparkish* in *Wycherly's Country Wife.* In that of Sir *Courtly Nice* his Excellence was still greater: There his whole Man, Voice, Mien, and Gesture, was no longer *Monfort*, but another Person. There, the insipid, soft Civility, the elegant, and formal Mien; the drawling Delicacy of Voice, the stately Flatness of his Address, and the empty Eminence of his Attitudes were so nicely observ'd and guarded by him, that he had not been an entire Master of Nature, had he not kept his Judgment, as it were, a Centinel upon himself, not to admit the least Likeness of what he us'd to be, to enter into any Part of his Performance, he could not possibly have so completely finish'd it. . . .
page 77 /

  This excellent Actor was cut off by a tragical Death, in the 33d Year of his Age, generally lamented by his Friends, and all Lovers of the Theatre. . . .

  Sandford might properly be term'd the *Spagnolet* of the Theatre, an excellent Actor in disagreeable Characters: For as the chief Pieces of that famous Painter were of Human Nature in Pain and Agony; so *Sandford*, upon the Stage, was generally as flagitious as a *Creon*, a *Maligni*, an *Iago*, or a *Machiavil*, could make him. . . . Poor *Sandford* was not the Stage-Villain by Choice, but from Necessity; for having a low and crooked Person, such bodily Defects were too strong to be admitted into great, or amiable Characters; so that whenever, in any new or revived Play, there was a hateful or mischievous Person, *Sandford* was sure to have no Competitor for it: Nor indeed (as we are not to suppose a Villain, or Traitor can be shewn for our Imitation, or not for our Abhorrence) can it be doubted, but the less comely the Actor's Person, the fitter he may be to perform them. . . . **page 78 /** And so unusual had it been to see *Sandford* an innocent Man in a Play, that whenever he was so, the Spectators would hardly give him credit in so gross an Improbability. Let me give you an odd Instance of it, which I heard *Monfort* say was a real Fact. A new Play (the Name of it I have forgot) was brought upon the Stage, wherein *Sandford* happen'd to perform the Part of an honest Statesman: The Pit, after they had sate three or four Acts, in a quiet Expectation, that the well-dissembled Honesty of *Sandford* (for such of course they concluded it) would soon be discover'd, or at least, from its Security, involve the Actors in the Play, in some surprizing Distress or Confusion, which might raise, and animate the Scenes to come; when, at last, finding no such matter, but that the Catastrophe had taken quite another Turn, and that *Sandford* was really an honest Man to the end of the Play, they fairly damn'd it, as if the Author had impos'd upon them the most frontless or incredible Absurdity. . . . **page 79 /**

This actor, in his manner of Speaking, varied very much from those I have already mentioned. His Voice had an acute and piercing Tone, which struck every Syllable of his Words distinctly upon the Ear. He had likewise a peculiar Skill in his Look of marking out to an Audience whatever he judg'd worth their **page 82 /** more than ordinary Notice. When he deliver'd a Command, he would sometimes give it more Force, by seeming to slight the Ornament of Harmony. In *Dryden's* Plays of Rhime, he as little as possible glutted the Ear with the Jingle of it, rather chusing, when the Sense would permit him, to lose it, than to value it.

Had *Sandford* liv'd in *Shakespear's* Time, I am confident his Judgment must have chose him, above all other Actors, to have play'd his *Richard the Third:* I leave his Person out of the Question, which, tho' naturally made for it, yet that would have been the least Part of his Recommendation; *Sandford* had stronger Claims to it; he had sometimes an uncouth Stateliness in his Motion, a harsh and sullen Pride of Speech, a meditating Brow, a stern Aspect, occasionally changing into an almost ludicrous Triumph over all Goodness and Virtue: From thence falling into the most asswasive Gentleness, and soothing Candour of a designing Heart. These, I say, must have preferr'd him to it; these would have been Colours so essentially shining in that Character, that it will be no Dispraise to that great Author, to say, *Sandford* must have shewn as many masterly Strokes in it (had he ever acted it) as are visible in the Writing it. . . . **page 83 /**

Nokes was an Actor of a quite different Genius from any I have ever read, heard of, or seen, since or before his Time; and yet his general Excellence may be comprehended in one Article, *viz.* a plain and palpable Simplicity of Nature, which was so utterly his own, that he was often as unaccountably diverting in his common Speech, as on the Stage. . . . It seems almost amazing, that this Simplicity, so easy to *Nokes*, should never be caught by any one of his Successors. *Leigh* and *Underhil* have been well copied, tho' not equall'd by others. But not all the mimical Skill of *Estcourt* (fam'd as he was for it) though he had often seen *Nokes*, could scarce give us an Idea of him. . . .

The Characters he particularly shone in, were Sir *Martin Marr-al*, *Gomez* in the *Spanish Friar*, Sir *Nicolas Cully* in *Love in a Tub*, *Barnaby Brittle* in the *Wanton Wife*, Sir *Davy Dunce* in the *Soldier's Fortune*, *Sosia* in *Amphytrion*, &c. &c. &c. . . . **page 85 /**

He scarce ever made his first Entrance in a Play, but he was received with an involuntary Applause, not of Hands only, for those may be, and have often been partially prostituted, and bespoken; but by a General Laughter, which the very Sight of him provok'd, and Nature cou'd not resist; yet the louder the Laugh, the graver was his Look upon it; and sure, the ridiculous Solemnity of his Features were enough to have set a whole Bench of Bishops into a Titter. . . . In the ludicrous Distresses, which by the Laws of Comedy, Folly is often involv'd in; he sunk into such a mixture of piteous Pusillanimity, and a Consternation so rufully ridiculous and inconsolable, that when he had shook you, to a Fatigue of Laughter, it became a moot point, whether you ought not to have pity'd him. When he debated any matter by himself, he would shut up his Mouth with a dumb studious Powt, and roll his full Eye, into such a vacant Amazement, such a palpable Ignorance of what to think of it, that his silent Perplexity (which would sometimes hold him several Minutes) gave your Imagination as full Content, as the most absurd thing he could say upon it. . . . **page 86 /**

His Person was of the middle size, his Voice clear, and audible; his natural Countenance grave, and sober; but the Moment he spoke, the settled Seriousness of his Features was utterly discharg'd, and a dry, drolling, or laughing Levity took such full Possession of him, that I can only refer the Idea of him to your Imagination. In some of his low Characters, that became it, he had a shuffling Shamble in his Gait, with so contented an Ignorance in his Aspect, and an aukward Absurdity in his Gesture, that had you not known him, you could not have believ'd, that naturally he could have had a Grain of common Sense. In a Word, I am tempted to sum up the Character of *Nokes*, as a Comedian, in a Parodie of what *Shakespear's Mark Antony* says of *Brutus* as a Hero.

> *His Life was Laughter, and the* Ludicrous
> *So mixt, in him, that Nature might stand up,*
> *And say to all the World — This was an* Actor.　**page 87 /**

·　·

Mrs. *Barry* was then in possession of almost all the chief Parts in Tragedy: With what Skill she gave Life to them, you will　**page 93 /**　judge from the Words of *Dryden*, in his Preface to *Cleomenes*, where he says,

> Mrs. Barry, *always excellent, has in this Tragedy excell'd herself, and gain'd a Reputation, beyond any Woman I have ever seen on the Theatre.*

I very perfectly remember her acting that Part; and however unnecessary it may seem, to give my Judgment after *Dryden's*, I cannot help saying, I do not only close with his Opinion, but will venture to add, that (tho' *Dryden* has been dead these Thirty Eight Years) the same Compliment, to this Hour, may be due to her Excellence. And tho' she was then, not a little, past her Youth, she was not, till that time, fully arriv'd to her Maturity of Power and

Judgment: From whence I would observe, That the short Life of Beauty, is not long enough to form a complete Actress. In Men, the Delicacy of Person is not so absolutely necessary, nor the Decline of it so soon taken notice of. The Fame Mrs. *Barry* arriv'd to, is a particular Proof of the Difficulty there is, in judging with Certainty, from their first Trials, whether young People will ever make any great Figure on a Theatre. There was, it seems, so little Hope of Mrs. *Barry*, at her first setting out, that she was, at the end of the first Year, discharg'd the Company, among others, that were thought to be a useless Expence to it. I take it for granted that the Objection to Mrs. *Barry*, at that time, must have been a defective Ear, or some unskilful Dissonance, in her manner of pronouncing. . . . **page 94 /**

Mrs. *Barry*, in Characters of Greatness, had a Presence of elevated Dignity, her Mien and Motion superb, and gracefully majestick; her Voice full, clear, and strong, so that no Violence of Passion could be too much for her: And when Distress, or Tenderness possess'd her, she subsided into the most affecting Melody, and Softness. In the Art of exciting Pity, she had a Power beyond all the Actresses I have yet seen, or what your Imagination can conceive. Of the former of these two great Excellencies, she gave the most delightful Proofs in almost all the Heroic Plays of *Dryden* and *Lee;* and of the latter, in the softer Passions of *Otway's Monimia* and *Belvidera.* In Scenes of Anger, Defiance, or Resentment, while she was impetuous, and terrible, she pour'd out the Sentiment with an enchanting Harmony; and it was this particular Excellence, for which *Dryden* made her the above-recited Compliment, upon her acting *Cassandra* in his *Cleomenes.* . . . She was the first Person whose Merit was distinguish'd, by the Indulgence of having an annual Benefit-Play, which was granted to her alone, if I mistake not, first in King *James's* time, and which became **page 95 /** not common to others, 'till the Division of this Company, after the Death of King *William's* Queen *Mary.* This great Actress dy'd of a Fever, towards the latter end of Queen Anne. . . .

Mrs. *Betterton*, tho' far advanc'd in Years, was so great a Mistress of Nature, that even Mrs. *Barry*, who acted the Lady *MacBeth* after her, could not in that Part, with all her superior strength, and Melody of Voice, throw out those quick and careless Strokes of Terror, from the Disorder of a guilty Mind, which the other gave us, with a Facility in her Manner, that render'd them at once tremendous, and delightful. Time could not impair her Skill, tho' he had brought her Person to decay. She was, to the last, the Admiration of all true Judges of Nature, and Lovers of *Shakespear*, in whose Plays she chiefly excell'd, and without a Rival. When she quitted the Stage, several good Actresses were the better for her Instruction. She was a Woman of an unblemish'd, and sober Life; and had the Honour to teach Queen *Anne*, when Princess, the Part of *Semandra* in *Mithridates*, which she acted at Court in King *Charles's* time. After the Death of Mr. *Betterton*, her Husband, that Princess, when Queen, order'd her a Pension for Life, but she liv'd not to receive more than the first half Year of it. **page 96 /**

. . . .

Mrs. *Bracegirdle* was now, but just blooming to her Maturity; her Reputation, as an Actress, gradually rising with that of her **page 100 /** Person; never any Woman was in such general Favour of her Spectators, which, to the last Scene of her Dramatick Life, she maintain'd, by not being unguarded in her private Character. This Discretion contributed, not a little, to make her the *Cara*, the Darling of the Theatre: For it will be no extravagant thing to say, Scarce an Audience saw her, that were less than half of them Lovers, without a suspected Favourite among them: And tho' she might be said to have been the Universal Passion, and under the highest Temptations; her Constancy in resisting them, serv'd but to increase the number of her Admirers. . . . It was even a Fashion among the Gay, and Young, to have a Taste or *Tendre* for Mrs. *Bracegirdle*. She inspired the best Authors to write for her, and two of them, when they gave her a Lover, in a Play, seem'd palpably to plead their own Passions, and make their private Court to her, in fictitious Characters. In all the chief Parts she acted, the Desirable was so predominant, that no Judge could be cold enough to consider, from what other particular Excellence, she became delightful. . . . The most eminent Authors always chose her for their favourite Character. . . . There were two very different Characters, in which she acquitted herself with uncommon Ap- **page 101 /** plause: If any thing could excuse that desperate Extravagance of Love, that almost frantick Passion of *Lee's Alexander the Great*, it must have been, when Mrs. *Bracegirdle* was his *Statira*: As when she acted *Millamant*, all the Faults, Follies, and Affectation of that agreeable Tyrant, were venially melted down into so many Charms, and Attractions of a conscious Beauty. In other Characters, where Singing was a necessary Part of them, her Voice and Action gave a Pleasure, which good Sense, in those Days, was not asham'd to give Praise to.

She retir'd from the Stage in the Height of her Favour from the Publick, when most of her Cotemporaries, whom she had been bred up with, were declining, in the Year 1710, nor could she be perswaded to return to it, under new Masters, upon the most advantageous Terms, that were offered her; excepting one Day, about a Year after, to assist her good Friend, Mr. *Betterton*, when she play'd *Angelica*, in *Love for Love*, for his Benefit. . . . **page102 /**

Jeremy Collier (1650–1726) was a political pamphleteer and a debater of some note. He was most widely known for his attack against the corruptions of the theater in A Short View of the Immorality and Profaneness of the English Stage *(1697–98). While the work is to some extent concerned with English dramatists in general, it deals most pointedly with such writers as Dryden, Congreve, Wycherley, Otway, Vanbrugh, and D'Urfey. Objecting to the use of profanity in dialogue, unfavorable portrayals which ridiculed the clergy, and a general encouragement of immorality, he urged that comedy be made an instrument "to recommend Virtue, and discountenance Vice." Congreve and Vanbrugh refuted Collier's argument; then Collier in turn made his final rebuttal. Although Collier was an extremist, Dryden admitted that there was some truth in his criticism, and Cibber commented that "his calling dramatick writers to this strict account had a very wholesome effect on those who writ after this time."*

Jeremy Collier. *A Short View of the Immorality and Profaneness of the English Stage*. London, 1738.

The Introduction.

The Business of *Plays* is to recommend Vertue, and discountenance Vice; To shew the Uncertainty of Humane Greatness, the suddain Turns of Fate, and the unhappy Conclusions of Violence and Injustice: 'Tis to expose the Singularities of Pride and Fancy, to make Folly and Falsehood contemptible, and to bring every Thing that is Ill under Infamy, and Neglect. This Design has been odly pursued by the *English Stage*. Our *Poets* write with a different View, and are gone into another Interest. 'Tis true, were their Intentions fair, they might be *Serviceable* to this *Purpose*. They have in a great Measure the Springs of Thought and Inclination in their Power. *Show, Musick, Action,* and *Rhetorick,* are moving Entertainments; and, rightly employ'd, would be very significant. But Force and Motion are Things indifferent, and the Use lies chiefly in the Application. These advantages are now in the Enemies Hand, and under a very dangerous Management. Like Cannon seized, they are pointed the wrong way; and by the Strength of the Defence the Mischief is made the greater. That this Complaint is not unreasonable, I shall endeavour to prove by shewing the Misbehaviour of the *Stage*, with respect to *Morality,* and *Religion.* Their *Liberties* in the following Particulars are intolerable, *viz.* Their *Smuttiness* of *Expression;* their *Swearing, Profaneness,* **page 1 /** and *Lewd Application of Scripture;* Their *Abuse* of the *Clergy,* Their *making* their *top Characters Libertines,* and giving them *Success* in their *Debauchery.*

This Charge, with some other *Irregularities*, I shall make good against the *Stage*, and shew both the *Novelty* and *Scandal* of the *Practice*. And first, I shall begin with the *Rankness* and *Indecency* of their *Language*.

CHAP. I.

The Immodesty of the Stage.

. . . Now among the Curiosities of this kind we may reckon Mrs. *Pinchwife*, *Horner*, and Lady *Fidget* in the *Country Wife;* Widow *Blackacre* and *Oliva* in the *Plain Dealer*. These, though not all the exceptionable *Characters*, are the most remarkable. I'm sorry the Author should stoop his Wit thus Low, and use his Understanding so unkindly. Some People appear Coarse, and Slovenly out of Poverty: They can't well go to the Charge of Sense. They are Offensive, like Beggars, for want of Necessaries. But this is none of the *Plain* **page 2 /** *Dealer's* Case; He can afford his Muse a better Dress when he pleases. But then the Rule is, where the Motive is the less, the Fault is the greater. To proceed. *Jacinta, Elvira, Dalinda,* and Lady *Plyant*, in the *Mock Astrologer, Spanish Fryar, Love Triumphant* and *Double Dealer*, forget themselves extremely: and almost all the *Characters* in the *Old Batchelor*, are foul and nauseous. *Love* for *Love*, and the *Relapse*, strike sometimes upon this *Sand*, and so likewise does *Don Sebastian*.

. . . Here is a large Collection of Debauchery; such *Pieces* are rarely to be met with: 'Tis sometimes painted at length too, and appears in great Variety of Progress and Practice. It wears almost all sorts of Dresses to engage the Fancy, and fasten upon the Memory, and keep up the Charm from languishing. Sometimes you have it in Image and Description; sometimes by way of Allusion; sometimes in disguise; and sometimes without it. And what can be the Meaning of such a Representation, unless it be to tincture the Audience, to extinguish Shame, and make Lewdness a Diversion? This is the Natural Consequence, and therefore one would think 'twas the Intention too. . . . **page 3 /**

. . . .

In this respect the *Stage* is faulty to a scandalous Degree of Nauseousness and Aggravation. For

1. The *Poets* make *Women* speak Smuttily. Of this the Places before mention'd are sufficient E- **page 5 /** vidence: And if there was occasion they might be multiplied to a much greater Number. Indeed the *Comedies* are seldom clear of these Blemishes: And sometimes you have them in *Tragedy*. For Instance. The *Orphans Monimia* makes a very improper Description; And the Royal *Leonora*, in the *Spanish Fryar*, runs a strange Length in the History of Love. . . . And do Princesses use to make their Reports with such fulsom Freedoms? Certainly this *Leonora* was the first Queen of her Family. Such Raptures are too Luscious for *Joan* of *Naples*. Are these the *Tender Things* Mr. *Dryden* says the Ladies call on him for? I suppose he means the *Ladies* that are too modest to show their Faces in the *Pit*. This Entertainment can be fairly design'd for none but such. Indeed it hits their Palate exactly. It regales

their Lewdness, graces their Character, and keeps up their Spirits for their Vocation: Now to bring Women under such Misbehaviour, is Violence to their Native Modesty, and a Misrepresentation of their Sex. . . . **page 6 /**

. . . Modesty is the distinguishing Virtue of that Sex, and serves both for Ornament and Defence: Modesty was design'd by Providence as a Guard to Vertue; and that it might be always at Hand, 'tis wrought into the Mechanism of the Body. 'Tis likewise proportion'd to the Occasions of Life, and strongest in Youth when Passion is so too. 'Tis a Quality as true to Innocence, as the Senses are to Health; whatever is ungrateful to the first, is prejudicial to the latter. The Enemy no sooner approaches, but the Blood rises in Opposition, and looks Defiance to an Indecency. It supplies the Room of Reasoning, and Collection: Intuitive Knowledge can scarcely make a greater Impression; and what then can be a surer Guide to the Unexperienced? It teaches by sudden Instinct and Aversion; This is both a ready and a powerful Method of Instruction. The Tumult of the Blood and Spirits, and the Uneasiness of the Sensation, are of singular Use. They serve to awaken Reason, and prevent Surprize. Thus the Distinctions of Good and Evil are re- **page 7 /**   fresh'd, and the Temptation kept at a proper Distance.

2. They represent their single Ladies, and Persons of Condition, under these Disorders of Liberty. This makes the Irregularity still more Monstrous, and a greater Contradiction to Nature, and Probability: But rather than not be Vitious, they will venture to spoil a Character. This Mismanagement we have partly seen already. *Jacinta*, and *Belinda* are farther Proof: And the *Double Dealer* is particularly remarkable. There are but *Four* Ladies in this *Play*, and Three of the biggest of them are Whores. A great Compliment to Quality, to tell them there is not above a Quarter of them Honest! . . .

Mock Astrologer Old Batchellor.

3. They have oftentimes not so much as the poor Refuge of a double Meaning to fly to. So that you are under a Necessity either of taking Ribaldry or Nonsence. And when the Sentence has two Handles, the worst is generally turn'd to the Audience. The Matter is so contrived that the Smut and Scum of the Thought now rises uppermost; And, like a Picture drawn to *Sight*, looks always upon the Company.

4. And which is still more extraordinary, the *Prologues*, and *Epilogues* are sometimes Scandalous to the last Degree. . . . Now here, properly speaking, the *Actors* quit the *Stage*, and remove from Fiction into Life. Here they converse with the *Boxes*, and *Pit*, and address directly to the Audience. These Preliminary and concluding Parts, are design'd to justify the Conduct of the *Play*, and bespeak the Favour of the Company. Upon such Occasions one would imagine, if ever, the Ladies should be used with Respect, and the Measures of Decency observ'd. But **page 8 /**   here we have Lewdness without Shame or Example: Here the *Poet* exceeds himself. Here are such Strains as would turn the Stomach of an ordinary Debauchee, and be almost nauseous in the *Stews*. And to make it the more agreeable, Women are commonly pick'd out for this Service. Thus the *Poet* courts the good Opinion of the Audience. This is the Desert he regales the Ladies with at the Close of the Entertainment: It seems, he thinks, they have admirable Palates! **page 9 /**

Mock Astrologer Country Wife Cleomenes Old Batchellor.

•   •

Chap. II.

The Profaneness of the Stage.

Another Instance of the Disorders of the *Stage*, is their *Profaneness;* This Charge may come under these two Particulars.

I. *Their Cursing and Swearing.*

II. *Their Abuse of Religion and Holy Scripture.*

I. *Their Cursing and Swearing.*

What is more frequent than their Wishes of Hell and Confusion, Devils and Diseases, all the Plagues of this World, and the next, to each other. And as for Swearing; 'tis used by all Persons, and upon   page 36 /   all Occasions; by Heroes and Paltroons, by Gentlemen and Clowns, Love and Quarrels, Success and Disappointment, Temper and Passion, must be varnish'd, and set off with *Oaths.* At some times, and with some *Poets,* Swearing is no ordinary Relief. It stands up in the room of Sense, gives Spirit to a flat Expression, and makes a Period Musical and Round. In short, 'tis almost all the Rhetorick, and Reason some People are Masters of: The Manner of Performance is different. Some- *Gad for* times they mince the Matter, change the Letter, and keep the Sense, as if they *God* had a mind to steal a Swearing, and break the Commandment without Sin. At another time, the Oaths are clipt, but not so much within the Ring, but that the *Image and Superscription* are visible. These Expedients I conceive are more for Variety than Conscience: For when the Fit comes on them, they make no Difficulty of Swearing at length. Instances of all these kinds may be met with in the *Old Batchelour, Double Dealer,* and *Love for Love.* And to mention no more, *Don Quixot,* the *Provok'd Wife,* and the *Relapse,* are particularly Rampant and Scandalous. . . .   page 37 /

. . . The *Poets* are of all People most to blame. They want even the Plea of *Bullies* and *Sharpers.* There's no Rencounters, no Starts of Passion, no sudden Accidents to discompose them. They swear in Solitude and cool Blood, under Thought and Deliberation, for Business and for Exercise: This is a terrible Circumstance; It makes all *Malice Prepense,* and enflames the Guilt, and the Reckoning.

And if Religion signifies nothing, (as I am afraid it does with some People) there is Law, as well as Gospel, against *Swearing.* 3 *Jac.* 1. *cap.* 21. is expressly against the *Play-House.* It runs thus.

> For the preventing and avoiding of the great Abuse of the holy Name of God, in Stage-Plays, Enterludes, &c. Be it enacted by our Sovereign Lord, &c. That if at any time, or times, after the End of this present Session of Parliament, any Person or Persons do, or shall, in any Stage-Play, Enterlude, Shew, &c. jestingly or profanely, speak or use the Holy Name of God, or of Christ *Jesus,* or of the Holy Ghost, or of the Trinity, which are not to be spoken, but with Fear and Reverence; shall forfeit for every such Offense, by him or them committed, Ten pound: The one Moiety thereof to the King's Majesty, his Heirs and Successors; the other Moiety thereof to him, or them, that will sue for the same in any Court of Record at *Westminister.* . . .

By this *Act* not only direct Swearing, but all vain Invocation of the Name of God is forbidden. This *Statute* well executed would mend the *Poets,* or **page 38 /** sweep the *Box:* And the *Stage* must either reform, or not thrive upon Profaneness. . . .

II. A *Second* Branch of the Profaneness of the *Stage* is their Abuse of Religion, and *Holy Scripture.* And here sometimes they don't stop short of Blasphemy. To cite all that might be collected of this kind would be tedious. I shall give the *Reader* enough to justify the Charge, and I hope to abhor the Practice.

To begin with the *Mock-Astrologer.* In the First *Act,* the *Scene* is a *Chapel.* And that the Use of such Consecrated Places may be the better understood, the Time is taken up in Courtship, Raillery, and Ridiculing Devotion. *Jacinta* takes her Turn among the rest. She interrupts *Theodosia,* and cries out: *Why Sister, Sister — will you pray? What Injury have I ever done you that you should pray in my Company? Wildblood* swears by *Mahomet,* rallies smuttily upon the other World, and gives the Prefe- **page 39 /** rence to the Turkish Paradise. This Gentleman, to encourage *Jacinta* to a Compliance in Debauchery, tells her, *Heaven is all Eyes and no Tongue.* That is, it sees wickedness but conceals it. He courts much at the same rate a little before. *When* **Hebr. xii.** *a Man comes to a great Lady, he is fain to approach her with Fear, and Reverence, methinks there's something of Godliness in it.* Here you have the Scripture burlesqu'd, and the Pulpit Admonition apply'd to Whoring. . . .

In the Close of the *Play,* they make Sport with Apparitions and Fiends. One of the Devils sneezes, upon this they give him the Blessing of the Occasion, and conclude *he has got Cold by being too long out of the Fire.* . . .

Thus the Stage worships the true God in Blasphemy. . . . **page 40 /**

In the *Old Batchelour, Vain-love* asks *Belmour, Could you be content to go to Heaven?*

Bell. *Hum, not immediately in my Conscience, not heartily.* —— This is playing I take it, with Edge-Tools. To go to Heaven in jest, is the way to go to Hell in earnest. . . . **page 41 /**

Chap. III.

The Clergy abused by the Stage.

The Satyr of the *Stage* upon the *Clergy* is extremely Particular. In other Cases, they level at a single Mark, and confine themselves to Persons. But here their Buffoonry takes an unusual Compass: They shoot Chain'd-shot, and strike at Universals. They play upon the *Character,* and endeavour to expose not only the Men, but the Business. 'Tis true, the *Clergy* are no small rub in the *Poet's* way. 'Tis by their Ministrations that Religion is perpetuated, the other World refresh'd, and the Interest of Virtue kept up. Vice will never have an unlimited Range, nor Conscience be totally subdued, as long as People are so easy as **page 63 /** to be Priest-ridden! As long as these Men are look'd on as the Messengers of Heaven, and the Supports of Government, and enjoy their old Pretensions in Credit and Authority; as long as this Grievance continues; the *Stage* must decline of Course, and Atheism give Ground, and Lewdness lie under Censure, and Discouragement. Therefore that Liberty may not be embarrass'd, nor Principles make Head against Pleasure, the *Clergy* must be attack'd, and rendred ridiculous.

To represent a Person fairly and without disservice to his Reputation, two Things are to be observ'd. First, he must not be ill used by others: Nor, Secondly, be made to play the Fool himself. This latter way of Abuse is rather the worst, because here a Man is a sort of *Felo de se;* and appears ridiculous by his own Fault. The Contradiction of both these Methods is practiced by the *Stage.* To make sure work on't, they leave no Stone unturn'd, the whole *Common-place* of Rudeness is run through. They strain their Invention and their Malice: And overlook nothing in ill Nature, or ill Manners to gain their Point.

To give some Instances of their Civility: In the *Spanish Fryar, Dominick* is made a Pimp for *Lorenzo;* He is call'd *a Parcel of holy Guts and Garbage,* and said *to have Room in his Belly for his Church-steeple.*

Dominick has a great many of these Compliments bestow'd upon him. And to make the railing more effectual, you have a general Stroke or two upon the Profession. Would you know what are the *Infallible Church-Remedies?* Why 'tis to *lie impudently, and swear devoutly.*. . . . **page 64 /**

At last *Dominick* is discover'd to the Company, makes a dishonourable *Exit,* and is push'd off the *Stage* by the Rabble. This is great Justice! The Poet takes care to make him first a Knave, and then an Example. . . . 'Tis not the Fault which is corrected, but the Priest. The Author's Discipline is seldom without a Bias. He commonly gives the *Laity* the Pleasure of an ill Action, and the *Clergy* the Punishment. **page 65 /**

. . . .

. . . In the *Provok'd Wife* Sir *John Brute* puts on the Habit of a Clergyman, counterfeits himself drunk, quarrels with the *Constable,* and is knock'd down and seiz'd. He rails, swears, curses, is lewd and profane to all Heights of Madness and Debauchery: The *Officers* and *Justice* break Jests upon him, and make him a sort of Representative of his Order. . . . **page 71 /**

Thus we see how hearty these People are in their ill Will! How they attack Religion under every Form, and pursue the Priesthood through all the Subdivisions of Opinion. Neither *Jews* nor *Heathens, Turks* nor *Christians, Rome* nor *Geneva, Church* nor *Conventicle,* can escape them. . . . Nay, Talking won't always satisfy them: They must ridicule the *Habit,* as well as the *Function* of the Clergy. 'Tis not enough for them to play the Fool, unless they do it in *Pontificalibus.* The Farce must be play'd in a Religious Figure, and under the Distinctions of their Office! **page 72 /**

. . . .

CHAP. IV.

The Stage-Poets make their principal Persons vicious,
and reward them at the End of the Play.

. . . To put *Lewdness* into a thriving Condition, to give it an Equipage of Quality, and to treat it with Ceremony and Respect, is the way to confound the

Understanding, to fortify the Charm, and to make the Mischief invincible. Innocence is often owing to Fear, and Appetite is kept under by Shame; but when these Restraints are once taken off, when Profit and Liberty lie on the same Side, and a Man can debauch himself into Credit; what then can be expected in such a Case, but that Pleasure should grow absolute, and Madness carry all before it? The *Stage* seems eager to bring Matters to this Issue; they have made a considerable Progress, and are still pushing their Point with all the Vigour imaginable. If this be not their Aim why is *Lewdness* so much consider'd in Character and Success? Why are their Favourites Atheistical, and their fine Gentlemen debauched? To what Purpose is *Vice* thus prefer'd, thus ornamented, and caress'd, unless for Imitation? That Matter of Fact stands

Mock
Astrologer.
Spanish
Fryar.
Country
Wife.
O'd
Batch.
Double
Dealer.

thus, I shall make good by several Instances. To begin then with their Men of Breeding and Figure. *Wild-blood* sets up for *Debauchery*, ridicules Marriage, and swears by *Mahomet*. *Bellamy* makes sport with the Devil, and *Lorenzo* is vicious, and calls his Father *Bawdy Magistrate*. *Horner* is horridly Smutty, and *Harcourt* false to his Friend who used him kindly. In the *Plain Dealer Freeman* talks coarsely, cheats the Widow, debauches her Son, and makes him undutiful. *Belmour* is lewd and profane, and *Mellefont* puts *Careless* in the best Way he can to debauch Lady *Plyant*. These *Sparks* generally marry the top Ladies, and those that do not, are brought to no Penance, but go   **page 92 /** off with the Character of fine Gentlemen: In *Don Sebastian*, *Antonio*, an Atheistical Bully, is rewarded with the Lady *Moraima*, and half the *Mufti's* Estate. *Valentine* in *Love* for *Love* is (if I may so call him) the Hero of the

Love for
Love.

Play; this Spark the *Poet* would pass for a Person of Virtue, but he speaks too late. 'Tis true, He was hearty in his Affection to *Angelica*. Now without question, to be in Love with a fine Lady of 30000 Pounds is a great Virtue! But then abating this single Commendation, *Valentine* is altogether compounded of Vice. He is a prodigal Debauchee, unnatural and profane, obscene, sawcy, and undutiful, and yet this Libertine is crown'd for the Man of Merit, has his Wishes thrown into his Lap, and makes the happy *Exit*. I perceive we should have a

Love for
Love.

rare set of *Virtues* if these *Poets* had the making of them! How they hug a vicious Character, and how profuse are they in their Liberalities to Lewdness? In the *Provok'd Wife Constant* swears at length, solicits Lady *Brute*, confesses himself lewd, and prefers Debauchery to Marriage. He handles the last Subject very notably and worth the hearing. *There is* (says he) *a poor sordid Slavery in Marriage, that turns the flowing Tide of Honour, and sinks it to the lowest Ebb of Infamy. 'Tis a corrupted Soil, ill Nature, Avarice, Sloth, Cowardice, and Dirt, are all its Product——But then Constancy (aliàs Whoring) is a brave, free, haughty, generous Agent.* This is admirable Stuff both for the Rhetorick and the Reason! The Character of *Young Fashion* in the *Relapse* is of the same Staunchness. . . .

To sum up the Evidence. A fine Gentleman, is a fine Whoring, Swearing, Smutty, Atheistical Man. . . . This is the *Stage-Test* for *Quality*,   **page 93 /** and those that can't stand it, ought to be disclaim'd. The Restraints of Conscience and the Pedantry of Virtue, are unbecoming a Cavalier. . . . The *Stage* seldom gives Quarter to any Thing that's serviceable or significant, but persecutes Worth and Goodness under every Appearance. He that would be safe from their Satyr must take care to disguise himself in Vice, and hang out the

Colours of Debauchery. How often is Learning, Industry, and Frugality, ridiculed in Comedy? The rich Citizens are often Misers and Cuckolds, and the *Universities*, Schools **page 94 /** of Pedantry upon this Score. In short, Libertinism and Profaneness, Dressing, Idleness, and Gallantry, are the only valuable Qualities. As if People were not apt enough of themselves to be Lazy, Lewd, and Extravagant, unless they were prick'd forward, and provok'd by Glory and Reputation. Thus the Marks of Honour and Infamy are mis-apply'd, and the Ideas of Virtue and Vice confounded. Thus Monstrousness goes for Proportion, and the Blemishes of humane Nature make up the Beauties of it.

The fine Ladies are of the same Cut with the Gentlemen. . . . **page 95 /**

John Downes (fl. 1662–1710) was a member of the Duke's Servants, a theater company organized by Sir William Davenant, who under a patent from Charles II opened a theater in Lincoln's Inn Fields in 1662. Downes notes that his own career as an actor was spoiled when, as one of the characters in the Siege of Rhodes *in 1662, he suffered stage fright before a brilliant audience of notables including Charles II and the Duke of York. He then became the "book-keeper" or prompter for the company. His duties involved writing out the parts of the plays owned by the company and attending both morning rehearsals and afternoon performances.*

His Roscius Anglicanus, or an Historical Review of the Stage *(1708) is based on his own recollections and on information supplied by Charles Booth, book-keeper to the company headed by Thomas Killigrew, to whom Charles II had granted a patent for a second theater in 1660.*

Although the account is somewhat meager and often inaccurate, Roscius Anglicanus *is nevertheless an invaluable source of information concerning the Restoration stage. Especially important are the lists of actors and actresses who made up the companies, the casts of particular plays, references to the reception accorded to certain plays, and in some instances Downes' personal comments on the merits of both plays and players.*

John Downes. *Roscius Anglicanus, or, an Historical Review of the Stage From 1660 to 1706.* Reprinted by Joseph Knight, London, 1886.

To The READER.

The Editor of the ensuing Relation, being long Conversant with the Plays and Actors of the Original Company, under the Patent of Sir William Davenant, *at his Theatre in* Lincolns-Inn-Fields, *Open'd there 1662. And as Book-keeper and Prompter, continu'd so, till* October 1706. *He Writing out all the Parts in each Play; and Attending every Morning the Actors Rehearsals, and their Performances in Afternoons; Emboldens him to affirm, he is not very Erronious in his Relation. But as to the Actors of* Drury-Lane *Company, / under Mr.* Thomas Killigrew, *he having the Account from Mr.* Charles Booth *sometimes Book-keeper there; If he a little Deviates, as to the Successive Order, and exact time of their Plays Performances, He begs Pardon of the Reader, and Subscribes himself,*

His very Humble Servant,
John Downes.

In the Reign of King *Charles* the First, there were Six Play Houses allow'd in Town: The *Black-Fryars* Company, His Majesty's Servants; The Bull in St. *John's-street;* another in *Salisbury Court;* another call'd the *Fortune;* another

28

at the *Globe;* and the Sixth at the Cock-Pit in *Drury-Lane;* all which continu'd Acting till the beginning of the said Civil Wars. The scattered Remnant of several of these Houses, upon King *Charles's* Restoration, Fram'd a Company who Acted again at the Bull, and Built them a New House in *Gibbon's Tennis Court* in *Clare-Market;* in which Two Places they continu'd Acting all 1660, 1661, 1662 and part of 1663. In this time they Built them a New Theatre in *Drury Lane:* Mr. *Thomas Killigrew* gaining a Patent from the King in **page 1 /** order to Create them the King's Servants; and from that time, they call'd themselves his Majesty's Company of Comedians in *Drury-Lane.*

Whose Names were, *viz.*

Mr. *Theophilus Bird.*	Mr. *Robert Shatterel.*
Mr. *Hart.*	Mr. *William Shatterel.*
Mr. *Mohun.*	Mr. *Duke.*
Mr. *Lacy.*	Mr. *Hancock.*
Mr. *Burt.*	Mr. *Kynaston.*
Mr. *Cartwright.*	Mr. *Wintersel.*
Mr. *Clun.*	Mr. *Bateman.*
Mr. *Baxter.*	Mr. *Blagden.*

Note, these following came not into the Company, till after they had begun in *Drury-Lane.*

Mr. *Hains.*	These Four were Bred up from Boys, under the Master ACTORS.
Mr. *Griffin.*	
Mr. *Goodman.*	
Mr. *Lyddoll.*	Mr. *Bell.*
Mr. *Charleton.*	Mr. *Reeves.*
Mr. *Sherly.*	Mr. *Hughs.*
Mr. *Beeston.*	Mr. *Harris.*

Women.

Mrs. *Corey.*	*NOTE,* these following came into the Company some few Years after.
Mrs. *Ann Marshall.*	
Mrs. *Eastland.*	
Mrs. *Weaver.*	Mrs. *Boutel.*
Mrs. *Uphill.*	Mrs. *Ellin Gwin.*
Mrs. *Knep.*	Mrs. *James.* **page 2 /**
Mrs. *Hughs.*	Mrs. *Verjuice*
Mrs. *Rebecca Marshall*	Mrs. *Reeves.*
Mrs. *Rutter.*	

The Company being thus Compleat, they open'd the New Theatre in *Drury-Lane,* on *Thursday* in *Easter* Week, being the 8*th,* Day of *April* 1663, With the Humorous Lieutenant.

Note, this Comedy was Acted Twelve Days Successively. **page 3 /**

. . . .

. . . [Plays] were Acted by the Old Company at the Theatre Royal, from the time they begun, till the Patent descended to Mr. *Charles Killigrew,* which in

1682, he join'd it to Dr. *Davenant's* Patent, whose Company Acted then in *Dorset* Garden, which upon the Union, were Created the King's Company: After which, Mr. *Hart* Acted no more, having a Pension to the Day of his Death, from the United Company.

I must not Omit to mention the Parts in several Plays of some of the Actors; wherein they Excell'd in the Performance of them. *First*, Mr. *Hart*, in the Part of *Arbaces*, in King and no King; *Amintor*, in the Maids Tragedy; *Othello*; *Rollo*; *Brutus*, in *Julius Caesar*; *Alexander*, towards the latter End of his Acting; if he Acted in any one of these but once in a Fortnight, the House was fill'd as at a New Play, especially *Alexander*, he Acting that with such Grandeur and Agreeable Majesty, That one of the Court was pleas'd to Honour him with this Commendation; That *Hart* might Teach any King on Earth how to Comport himself: He was no less Inferior in Comedy; as *Mosca* in the Fox; *Don John* in the Chances, *Wildblood* in the Mock Astrologer; with sundry other Parts. In all the Comedies and Tragedies, he was concern'd he Performed with that Exactness and Perfection, that not any of his Successors have Equall'd him. **page 16 /**

Major *Mohun*, he was Eminent for *Volpone*; *Face* in the *Alchymist*; *Melantius* in the Maids Tragedy; *Mardonius*, in King and no King; *Cassius*, in *Julius Caesar*; *Clytus* in *Alexander*; *Mithridates*, &c. An Eminent Poet seeing him Act this last, vented suddenly this Saying; Oh *Mohun, Mohun! Thou little Man of Mettle, if I should Write a 100 Plays, I'd Write a Part for thy Mouth;* in short, in all his Parts, he was most Accurate and Correct.

Mr. *Wintersel*, was good in Tragedy, as well as in Comedy, especially in Cokes in *Bartholomew-Fair*; that the Famous Comedian *Nokes* came in that part far short of him.

Then *Mr. Burt, Shatterel, Cartwright* and several other good Actors, but to Particularize their Commendations wou'd be too Tedious; I refer you therefore to the several Books, their Names being there inserted.

Next follows an Account of the Rise and Progression, of the Dukes Servants; under the Patent of Sir *William Davenant* who upon the said Junction in 1682, remov'd to the Theatre Royal in *Drury-Lane*, and Created the King's Company.

In the Year 1659, General *Monk*, Marching then his Army out of *Scotland* to *London*. Mr. *Rhodes* a Bookseller being Wardrobe-Keeper formerly (as I am inform'd) to King *Charles* the First's, Company of Comedians in *Black-Friars*; getting a License from the then Governing State, fitted up a House then for Acting call'd the *Cock-pit* in *Drury-Lane*, and in a short time Compleated his Company. **page 17 /**

Their Names were, *viz.*

Mr. *Betterton.*	*Note*, These six commonly Acted
Mr. Sheppy.	Womens Parts.
Mr. *Lovel.*	Mr. *Kynaston.*
Mr. *Lilliston*	*James Nokes.*
Mr. *Underhill.*	Mr. *Angel.*
Mr. *Turner.*	*William Betterton.*
Mr. *Dixon.*	Mr. *Mosely.*
Robert Nokes.	Mr. *Floid.*

The Plays there Acted were,

The Loyal Subject.
Maid in the *Mill.*
The Wild Goose Chase.
The *Spanish* Curate.
The *Mad* Lover.
Pericles, Prince of *Tyre.*
A Wife for a *Month.*
Rule Wife and have a Wife.
The *Tamer* Tam'd.
The Unfortunate Lovers.
Aglaura.
Changling.
Bondman. *With divers others.*

Mr. *Betterton,* being then but 22 Years Old, was highly Applauded for his Acting in all these Plays, but especially, For the Loyal Subject; The Mad Lover; *Pericles;* The Bondman: *Deflores,* in the Changling; his Voice being then as Audibly strong, full and Articulate, as in the Prime of his Acting. **page 18 /**

Mr. *Sheppy* Perform'd *Theodore* in the Loyal Subject; Duke *Altophil,* in the Unfortunate Lovers; *Asotus,* in the Bondman, and several other Parts very well; But above all the Changling, with general Satisfaction.

Mr. *Kynaston* Acted *Arthiope,* in the Unfortunate Lovers; The Princess in the *Mad* Lover; *Aglaura; Ismenia,* in the *Maid* in the *Mill;* and several other Womens Parts; he being then very Young made a Compleat Female Stage Beauty, performing his Parts so well, especially *Arthiope* and *Aglaura,* being Parts greatly moving Compassion and Pity; that it has since been Disputable among the Judicious, whether any Woman that succeeded him so Sensibly touch'd the Audience as he.

Mr. *James Nokes* Acted first, The *Maid* in the *Mill;* after him Mr. *Angel; Aminta* in the same Play was Acted by Mr. *William Betterton* (who not long after was Drown'd in Swimming at *Wallingford*) They Acted several other Womens Parts in the said Plays, very Acceptable to the Audience: *Mosely* and *Floid* commonly Acted the Part of a Bawd and Whore.

In this Interim, Sir *William Davenant* gain'd a Patent from the King, and Created Mr. *Betterton* and all the Rest of *Rhodes's* Company, the King's Servants; who were Sworn by my Lord *Manchester* then Lord Chamberlain, to Serve his Royal Highness the Duke of *York,* at the Theatre in *Lincoln's-Inn-Fields.*

Note, *The three following, were new Actors taken in by Sir* William, *to Compleat the Company he had from Mr.* Rhodes. **page 19 /**

Mr. *Harris.*   Mr. *Richards.*
Mr. *Price.*   Mr. *Blagden.*

The Five following came not in till almost a Year after they begun.

Mr. *Smith*.   Mr. *Young*.
Mr. *Sandford*.   Mr. *Norris*.
Mr. *Medburn*.

Sir *William Davenant's* Women Actresses were,
Note, These Four being his Principal Actresses, he Boarded them at his own House.

Mrs. *Davenport*.   Mrs. *Davies*.
Mrs. *Saunderson*.   Mrs. *Long*.
Mrs. *Ann Gibbs*.   Mrs. *Holden*.
Mrs. *Norris*.   Mrs. *Jennings*.

His Company being now Compleat, Sir *William* in order to prepare Plays to Open his Theatre, it being then a Building in *Lincoln's-Inn Fields*, His Company Rehears'd the First and Second Part of the Siege of *Rhodes;* and the Wits at *Pothecaries-Hall:* And in Spring 1662, Open'd his House with the said Plays, having new Scenes and Decorations, being the first that e're were Introduc'd in *England*. Mr. *Betterton*, Acted Soly-man the Magnificent; Mr. *Harris*, *Alphonso;* Mr. *Lilliston*, *Villerius* the Grand Master; Mr. *Blagden* the Admiral; Mrs. *Davenport*, *Roxolana;* Mrs. *Sanderson* Ianthe: **page 20 /**   All Parts being Justly and Excellently Perform'd; it continu'd Acting 12 Days without Interruption with great Applause.

. . . .

The Tragedy of *Hamlet; Hamlet* being Perform'd by Mr. *Betterton*, Sir *William* (having seen Mr. *Taylor* of the *Black-Fryars* Company Act it, who being Instructed by the Author Mr. *Shaksepeur*) taught Mr. *Betterton* in every Particle of it; which by his exact Performance of it, gain'd him Esteem and Reputation, Superlative to all other Plays *Horatio* by Mr. *Harris;* The King by Mr. *Lilliston;* The Ghost by Mr. *Richards*, (after by Mr. *Medburn*) *Polonius* by Mr. *Lovel; Rosencrans* by Mr. *Dixon; Guilderstern* by Mr. *Price;* 1st, Grave-maker, by Mr. *Underhill:* The 2*d*, by Mr. *Dacres;* The Queen, by Mrs. *Davenport; Ophelia*, by Mrs. *Sanderson:* No succeeding Tragedy for several Years got more Reputation, or Money to the Company than this.

Love and Honour, wrote by Sir *William Davenant:* This Play was Richly C[l]oath'd; The King giving Mr. *Betterton* his Coronation Suit, in which, he Acted the Part of Prince *Alvaro;* The Duke of *York* giving Mr. *Harris* his, who did Prince *Prospero;* And my Lord of *Oxford*, gave Mr. *Joseph Price* his, who did *Lionel*   **page 21 /**   the Duke of *Parma's* Son; The Duke was Acted by Mr. *Lilliston; Evandra*, by Mrs. *Davenport*, and all the other Parts being very well done: The Play having a great run, Produc'd to the Company great Gain and Estimation from the Town.   **page 22 /**

. . . .

King *Henry* the 8*th*, This Play, by Order of Sir *William Davenant*, was all new Cloath'd in proper Habits: The King's was new, all the Lords, the Cardinals, the Bishops, the Doctors, Proctors, Lawyers, Tip-staves, new Scenes: The part of the King was so right and justly done by Mr. *Betterton*, he being Instructed in it by Sir *William*, who had it from Old Mr. *Lowen*, that had his

Instructions from Mr. *Shakespear* himself, that Idare and will aver, none can, or will come near him in this Age, in the performance of that part: Mr. *Harris's*, performance of Cardinal *Wolsey*, was little Inferior to that, he doing it with such just State, Port and Mein, that I dare affirm, none hitherto has Equall'd him: The Duke of *Buckingham*, by Mr. *Smith; Norfolk*, by Mr. *Nokes; Suffolk*, by Mr. *Lilliston;* Cardinal *Campeius* and *Cranmur*, by Mr. *Medburn;* Bishop *Gardiner*, by Mr. *Underhill;* Earl of *Surry*, by Mr. *Young;* Lord *Sands*, by Mr. *Price;* Mrs. *Betterton*, Queen *Catherine;* Every part by the great Care of Sir *William*, being exactly perform'd; it being all new Cloath'd and new Scenes; it continu'd Acting 15 Days together with general Applause.

Love in a Tub, Wrote by Sir *George Etheridge;* Mr. *Betterton*, performing Lord *Beauford; . . .* **page 24 /**

The clean and well performance of this Comedy, got the Company more Reputation and Profit than any preceding Comedy; the Company taking in a Months time at it 1000*l. . . .* **page 25 /**

These being all the Principal, which we call'd Stock-Plays; that were *Acted* from the Time they Open'd the Theatre in 1662, to the beginning of *May*, 1665, at which time the *Plague* began to Rage: The Company ceas'd *Acting;* till the *Christmass* after the Fire in 1666. Yet there were several other Plays *Acted*, from 1662, to 1665, both Old and Modern. . . . The Company ending . . . with *Mustapha*, in *May* 1665, after a Year and Half's Discontinuance; they by Command began with the same Play again at Court: The *Christmass* after the Fire in 1666: And from thence continu'd again to Act at their Theatre in *Lincoln's -Inn-Fields.* **page 26 /**

The first new Play that was Acted in 1666, was: *The Tragedy* of Cambyses, *King* of Persia. Wrote by Mr. *Settle: . . .* Succeeded six Days with a full Audience.

After this the Company Reviv'd Three Comedies of Mr. Sherly's, *viz.*

The Grateful Servant.	These Plays being perfectly well Per-
The Witty Fair One.	form'd; especially *Dulcino* the Grate-
The School of Complements.	ful Servant, being Acted by Mrs.
The Woman's a Weather Cock.	*Long;* and the first time she appear'd
	in Man's Habit, prov'd as Beneficial to
	the Company, as several succeeding
	new Plays. **page 27 /**

. . . .

Sir *Martin Marral*, The Duke of *New-Castle*, giving Mr. *Dryden* a bare Translation of it, out of a Comedy of the Famous *French Poet* Monsieur *Moleiro:* He Adapted the Part purposely for the Mouth of Mr. *Nokes*, and curiously Polishing the whole. . . . All the Parts being very Just and Exactly perform'd, 'specially Sir *Martin* and his Man, Mr. *Smith*, and several others since have come very near him, but none Equall'd, nor yet Mr. *Nokes* in Sir *Martin:* This Comedy was Crown'd with an Excellent Entry: In the last Act at the Mask, by Mr. *Priest* and Madam *Davies;* This, and Love in a Tub, got the Company more Money than any preceding Comedy. . . . **page 28 /**

The Impertinents, or Sullen Lovers, Wrote by Mr. *Shadwell;* This Comedy being Admirably Acted: Especially, Sir *Positive At-all*, by Mr. *Harris:* Poet

Ninny, by Mr. *Nokes: Woodcock,* by Mr. *Angel: Standford* and *Emilia;* the Sullen Lovers: One by Mr. *Smith,* and the other by Mrs. *Shadwell.* This Play had wonderful Success, being Acted 12 Days together, when our Company were Commanded to *Dover,* in *May* 1670. The King with all his Court, meeting his sister, the Dutchess of *Orleans* there. This Comedy and Sir *Solomon Single,* pleas'd Madam the Dutchess, and the whole Court extremely. The *French* Court wearing then Excessive short Lac'd Coats; some Scarlet, some Blew, with Broad wast Belts; Mr. *Nokes* having at that time one shorter than the *French* Fashion, to Act Sir *Arthur Addle* in; the Duke of *Monmouth* gave Mr. *Nokes* his Sword and Belt from his Side, and Buckled it on himself, on purpose to Ape the *French:* That Mr. *Nokes* lookt more like a Drest up Ape, than a Sir *Arthur:* Which upon his first Entrance on the Stage, put the King and Court to an Excessive Laughter; at which the *French* look'd very Shaggrin, to see themselves Ap'd by such a Buffoon as Sir *Arthur:* Mr. *Nokes* kept the Dukes Sword to his Dying Day. . . . **page 29 /**

The *Man's* the *Master,* Wrote by Sir *William Davenant,* being the last Play he ever Wrote, he Dying presently after; and was Bury'd in *Westminster-Abby,* near Mr. *Chaucer's* Monument, Our whole Company attending his Funeral. This Comedy in general was very well Perform'd, especially, the *Master,* by Mr. *Harris;* the *Man,* by Mr. *Underhill:* Mr. *Harris* and Mr. *Sandford,* Singing the Epilogue like two Street Ballad-Singers. **page 30 /**

Note, Mr. Cademan *in this Play, not long after our Company began in* Dorset-Garden; *his Part being to Fight with Mr.* Harris, *was Unfortunately, with a sharp Foil pierc'd near the Eye, which so Maim'd both his Hand and his Speech, that he can make little use of either; for which Mischance, he has receiv'd a Pension ever since* 1673, *being 35 Years a goe.* . . . .

The new Theatre in *Dorset-Garden* being Finish'd, and our Company after Sir *William's Death,* being under the Rule and Dominion of his Widow the Lady *Davenant,* Mr. *Betterton,* and Mr *Harris,* (Mr. *Charles Davenant*) her Son *Acting* for her) they remov'd from *Lincolns-Inn-Fields* thither. And on the Ninth Day of *November,* 1671, they open'd their new Theatre with Sir *Martin Marral,* which continu'd *Acting* 3 Days together, with a full Audience each Day; notwithstanding it had been *Acted* 30 Days before in *Lincolns-Inn-Fields,* and above 4 times at Court. **page 31 /**

. . . .

The Tragedy of *Macbeth,* alter'd by Sir *William Davenant;* being drest in all it's Finery, as new Cloath's, new Scenes, Machines, as flyings for the Witches; with all the Singing and Dancing in it: THE first Compos'd by Mr. *Lock,* the other by Mr. *Channell* and Mr. *Joseph Preist;* it being all Excellently perform'd, being in the nature of an Opera, it Recompenc'd double the Expence; it proves still a lasting Play.

Note, That this Tragedy, *King Lear* and the *Tempest,* were *Acted* in *Lincolns-Inn-Fields; Lear,* being *Acted* exactly as Mr. *Shakespear* Wrote it; as likewise the *Tempest* alter'd by Sir *William Davenant* and Mr. *Dryden,* before 'twas made into an Opera. . . . **page 33 /**

The Jealous Bridegroom, Wrote by Mrs. *Bhen,* a good Play and lasted six Days; but this made its Exit too, to give Room for a greater. *The Tempest.*

Note, *In this Play, Mr.* Otway *the Poet having an Inclination to turn Actor;*

Mrs. Bhen *gave him the King in the Play, for a Probation Part, but he being not us'd to the Stage; the full House put him to such a Sweat and Tremendous, Agony, being dash't, spoilt him for an Actor. Mr.* Nat. Lee, *had the same Fate in Acting* Duncan *in* Macbeth, *ruin'd him for an Actor too. I must not forget my self, being Listed for an Actor in Sir* William Davenant's *Company in* Lincolns-Inn-Fields: *The very first Day of opening the House there, with the Siege of* Rhodes, *being to Act* Haly; (*The King, Duke of* York, *and all the Nobility in the House, and the first time the King was in a Publick Theatre*) *The sight of that* August *presence, spoil'd me for an Actor too. But being so in the Company of two such Eminent Poets, as they prov'd afterward, made my Disgrace so much the less; from that time, their Genius set them upon Poetry: The first Wrote* Alcibiades; *The later, the Tragedy of* Nero; *the one for the Duke's, the other for the King's House.*

The Year after in 1673. The Tempest, or the Inchanted Island, made into an Opera by Mr. *Shadwell,* having all New in it; as Scenes, Machines; particularly, one Scene Painted with *Myriads* of *Ariel* Spirits; and another flying away, with a Table Furnisht out with Fruits, Sweetmeats and all sorts of Viands; **page 34 /** just when Duke *Trinculo* and his Companions; were going to Dinner; all things perform'd in it so Admirably well, that not any succeeding Opera got more Money. . . .

In *February* 1673. The long expected Opera of *Psyche,* came forth in all her Ornaments; new Scenes, new Machines, new Cloaths, new *French* Dances: This Opera was Splendidly set out, especially in Scenes; the Charge of which **page 35 /** amounted to above 800*l.* It had a Continuance of Performance about 8 Days together it prov'd very Beneficial to the Company; yet the *Tempest* got them more Money. . . . **page 36 /**

The Orphan, or the Unhappy Marriage; Wrote by Mr. *Otway: Castalio* Acted by Mr. *Betterton: Polidor,* Mr. *Williams: Chamont,* Mr. *Smith: Chaplain,* Mr. *Percival: Monimia,* Mrs. *Barry: Serina,* Mrs. *Monfort.* All the Parts being Admirably done, especially the Part of *Monimia:* This, **page 37 /** *and Belvidera in* Venice preserv'd, *or a Plot Discover'd;* together with *Isabella, in the Fatal Marriage:* These three Parts, gain'd her the Name of Famous Mrs. *Barry,* both at Court and City; for when ever She *Acted* any of those three Parts, she forc'd Tears from the Eyes of her Auditory, especially those who have any Sense of Pity for the Distress't.

These 3 Plays, by their Excellent performances, took above all the Modern Plays that succeeded. . . .

Theodosius, or the *Force of Love,* Wrote by Mr. *Nathaniel Lee: Varanes,* the *Persian* Prince, *Acted* by Mr. *Betterton: Marcian* the General, Mr. *Smith: Theodosius,* Mr. *Williams,* Athenais, Mrs. *Barry:* All the Parts in't being perfectly perform'd, with several Entertainments of Singing; Compos'd by the Famous Master Mr. *Henry Purcell,* (being the first he e'er Compos'd for the Stage) made it a living and Gainful Play to the Company: The Court; especially the Ladies, by their daily charming presence, gave it great Encouragement.

The *Lancashire Witches, Acted* in 1681, made by Mr. *Shadwell,* being a kind of Opera, having several *Machines* of Flyings for the Witches, and other Diverting Contrivances in't: All being well perform'd, it prov'd beyond Ex- **page 38 /** pectation; very Beneficial to the Poet and *Actors.*

All the preceding Plays, being the chief that were *Acted* in *Dorset-Garden*, from *November* 1671, to the Year 1682; at which time the Patentees of each Company United Patents; and by so Incorporating the Duke's Company were made the King's Company, and immediately remov'd to the Theatre Royal in *Drury-Lane*.

Upon this Union, Mr. *Hart* being the Heart of the Company under Mr. *Killsgrew's* Patent never *Acted* more, by reason of his Malady; being Afflicted with the Stone and Gravel, of which he Dy'd some time after: Having a Sallary of 40 Shillings a Week to the Day of his Death. But the Remnant of that Company; as Major *Mohun*, Mr. *Cartwright*, Mr. *Kynaston*, Mr. *Griffin*, Mr. *Goodman*, Mr. *Duke Watson*, Mr. *Powel* Senior, Mr. *Wiltshire*, Mrs *Corey*, Mrs. *Bowtell*, Mrs *Cook*, Mrs. *Monfort*, &c. . . . **page 39** /

The Squire of *Alsatia*, a Comedy Wrote by Mr. *Shadwell*: Sir *William Belfond*, DONE by Mr. *Leigh*: Sir *Edward*, Mr. *Griffin*: The Squire by Mr. *Nokes*, afterwards by Mr. *Jevon*: Belfond Junior, Mr. *Mounfort*: Mrs *Termigant*, Mrs. *Boutel*: *Lucia*, Mrs. *Bracegirdle*. This Play by its Excellent Acting, being often Honour'd with the presence of Chancellour Jeffereies, and other great Persons; had an Uninterrupted run of 13 Days together.

Note, *The Poet receiv'd for his third Day in the House in* Drury-Lane *at single Prizes* 130*l. which was the greatest Receipt they ever had at that House at single Prizes.* . . . **page 41** /

Some time after, a difference happening between the United Patentees, and the chief *Actors*: As Mr. *Betterton*; Mrs. *Barry* and Mrs. *Bracegirdle;* the latter complaining of Oppression from the former; they for Redress, Appeal'd to my Lord of *Dorset*, then Lord Chamberlain, for Justice; who Espousing the Cause of the Actors, with the assistance of Sir *Robert Howard*, finding their Complaints just, procur'd from King *William*, a Seperate License for Mr. *Congreve*, Mr. *Betterton*, Mrs. *Bracegirdle* and Mrs. *Barry*, and others, to set up a new Company, calling it the New Theatre in *Lincolns-Inn-Fields;* and the House being fitted up from a Tennis-Court, they Open'd it the last Day of *April*, 1695, with a new Comedy: Call'd, **page 43** /

Love for Love, Wrote by Mr. *Congreve;* this Comedy was Superior in Success, than most of the precedent Plays; *Valentine*, *Acted* by Mr. *Betterton; Scandall*, Mr. *Smith; Foresight*, Mr. *Sandford; Sampson*, Mr. *Underhill; Ben* the Saylor, Mr. *Dogget; Jeremy*, Mr. *Bowen;* Mrs. *Frail*, by Madam *Barry; Tattle*, Mr. *Boman; Angelica*, Mrs. *Bracegirdle:* This Comedy being Extraordinary well Acted, chiefly the Part of *Ben* the Sailor, it took 13 Days Successively. . . . **page 44** /

The Way of the World, a Comedy wrote by Mr. *Congreve*, twas curiously *Acted;* Madam *Bracegirdle* performing her Part so exactly and just, gain'd the Applause of Court and City; but being too Keen a Satyr, had not the Success the Company Expected. . . . **page 45** /

Note, In the space of Ten Years past, Mr. *Betterton* to gratify the desires and Fancies of the Nobility and Gentry; procur'd from Abroad the best Dances and Singers, as Monsieur *L'Abbe*, Madam *Sublini*, Monsieur *Balon*, *Margarita Delpine*, *Maria Gallia* and divers others; who being Exorbitantly Expensive produc'd small Profit to him and his Company, but vast Gain to themselves; Madam

Delpine since her Arrival in *England*, by Modest Computation; having got by the Stage and Gentry, above 10000 Guineas. . . . **page 46 /**

About the end of 1704, Mr. *Betterton* Assign'd his Licence, and his whole Company over to **page 47 /** Captain *Vantbrugg* to *Act* under HIS, at the Theatre in the *Hay Market*.

And upon the 9*th*, of *April* 1705. Captain *Vantbrugg* open'd his new Theatre in the *Hay-Market*, with a Foreign Opera, Perform'd by a new set of Singers, Arriv'd from *Italy;* (the worst that e're came from thence) for it lasted but 5 Days, and they being lik'd but indifferently by the Gentry; they in a little time marcht back to their own Country. . . . **page 48 /**

After this Captain *Vantbrugg* gave leave to Mr. *Verbruggen* and Mr. *Booth*, and all the Young Company, to Act the remainder of the Summer, what Plays they cou'd by their Industry get up for their own Benefit; continuing till *Bartholomew-Eve*, 23*d*, of *August*, 1706, ending on that Day, with *The* London *Cuckolds:* But in all that time their Profit Amounted not to half their Salaries, they receiv'd in Winter.

From *Bartholomew* day 1706, to the 15*th*, of *Octob.* following there was no more *Acting* there.

In this Interval Captain *Vantbrugg* by Agreement with Mr. *Swinny*, and by the Concurrence of my Lord Chamberlain, Transferr'd and Invested his License and Government of the Theatre to Mr. *Swinny;* who brought with him from Mr. *Rich*, Mr. *Wilks*, Mr. *Cyber*, Mr. *Mills*, Mr. *Johnson*, Mr. *Keene*, Mr. *Norris*, Mr. *Fairbank*, Mrs. *Oldfield* and others; United them to the Old Company; Mr. *Betterton* and Mr. *Underhill*, being the only remains of the Duke of *York's* Servants, from 1662, till the Union in *October* 1706. Now having given an Account of all the Principal Actors and Plays, down to 1706. I with the said Union, conclude my History. **page 50 /**

John Dryden (1631–1700), clearly the outstanding literary figure of the late seventeenth century, was one of the most versatile writers in English literary history. A professional man of letters, he was a master of satire as well as a successful craftsman in every other genre *popular in his lifetime: critical and polemic prose, lyric and narrative poetry, tragic and comic drama. Alexander Pope felt that he could discover in Dryden's poetry better specimens of every mode than could be found in the works of any other English writer. Samuel Johnson called him "the father of English criticism."*

Dryden's earliest plays were The Wild Gallant, *the first to be performed (1663) though it was not published until 1669, and* The Rival Ladies, *the first to be printed though it was not acted until 1664. He first gained fame as a dramatist with* The Indian Emperor *(1665), in which Nell Gwyn at the age of fifteen made her stage debut. Between 1668 and 1681 he wrote fourteen plays, among them Almanzor and Almahide, or the Con-*quest of Granada *(1670), one of the most popular plays of the day. This was a heroic tragedy, based on a conflict between love and honor, written in heroic couplets and employing elevated if unrealistic poetic diction. In such plays Dryden felt that he was bringing the epic "in little" to the English stage. Although heroic tragedies brought a certain excitement to the theater, they were frequently filled with rant and bombast and exaggerated actions which left them and their authors open to caustic criticism and ridicule.*

Dryden's greatest play, and his first in blank verse, was All for Love *(1678), which he wrote in imitation of Shakespeare and "to please himself." In the same period he adapted for Restoration audiences* Oedipus *and Shakespeare's* Troilus and Cressida, *both in 1679; he had previously altered* The Tempest *in 1667 in collaboration with Sir William Davenant.*

*One of the few great English critics, Dryden was the first to develop a major body of criticism in England; most of this appeared in the form of prefaces. Although he found fault with many of the ancient writers, he held them generally to be the best teachers for the moderns. In the Epi-*logue to the Conquest of Granada *and in the* Defence of the Epilogue *he examined the poets of the preceding age, particularly Jonson, Fletcher, and Shakespeare, and suggested that "the language, wit, and conversation of our age, are improved and refined above the last." In* An Essay of Dramatick Poesy, *the best known of his critical works, Dryden examines, by means of a dialogue, the principal critical tenets of his time. The conversation revolves around the relative merits of the classical, the French neo-classical, the Elizabethan, and the Restoration drama, and sums up much of the literary theory of the period.*

Dryden's contribution to English letters is as great as his range is wide.

He did much to make English prose an instrument of beauty, precision, and efficiency — his essays are models of prose style. His criticism is eclectic, clear, perceptive, and in most instances sound. His own skill demonstrated the value of the rimed couplet as an effective meter for satire and drama. His translations, which occupied his later years, are regarded among the best in English. The king of English letters at his death, Dryden is still ranked among the foremost of English writers. The student of the Restoration will find him in the midst of the intellectual excitement of the age — often the model, often the butt of Restoration wit. Both by statement and by practice he exemplified much that was characteristic of the theater and the intellectual life of the day.

John Dryden. *An Essay of Dramatick Poesy*, in *The Dramatick Works of John Dryden, Esq.* London, 1735. Vol. III.

. . . There are so few who write well in this Age, said *Crites*, that methinks any Praises should be welcome; they neither rise to the Dignity of the last Age, nor to any of the Ancients. . . .

If your Quarrel (said *Eugenius*) to those who now write, be grounded only on your Reverence to Antiquity, there is no Man more ready to adore those great *Greeks* and *Romans* than I am: But on the other side, I cannot think so contemptibly of the Age in which I live, or so dishonourably of my own Country, as not to judge we equal the Ancients in most kinds of Poesy, and in some **page xxxiii /** surpass them; neither know I any reason why I may not be as zealous for the Reputation of our Age, as we find the Ancients themselves were in Reverence to those who lived before them. . . .

But I see I am ingaging in a wide Dispute, where the Arguments are not like to reach close on either side; for Poesy is of so large an Extent, and so many both of the Ancients and Moderns have done well in all Kinds of it, that in citing one against the other, we shall take up more time this Evening, than each Man's Occasions will allow him: Therefore I would ask *Crites* to what Part of Poesy he would confine his Arguments, and whether he would defend the general Cause of the Ancients against the Moderns, or oppose any Age of the Moderns against this of ours.

Crites a little while considering upon this Demand, told *Eugenius* that if he pleased he would limit their Dispute to *Dramatick Poesy;* in which he thought it not difficult to prove, either that the Ancients were superior to the Moderns, or that the last Age to this of ours. **page xxxiv /**

. . . .

Eugenius was going to continue this Discourse, when *Lisideius* told him that it was necessary, before they proceeded further, to take a standing Measure of their Controversy; for how was it possible to be decided who writ the best Plays, before we know what a Play should be? but, this once agreed on by both Parties, each might have Recourse to it, either to prove his own Advantages, or to discover the Failings of his Adversary.

He had no sooner said this, but all desir'd the Favour of him to give the

Definition of a Play; and they were the more importunate, because neither *Aristotle*, nor *Horace*, nor any other, who had writ of that Subject, had ever done it.

Lisideius . . . confess'd he had a rude Notion of it; indeed rather a Description than a Definition. . . : That he conceiv'd a Play ought to be, *A just and lively Image of human Nature, representing its Passions and Humours, and the Changes of Fortune to which it is subject; for the Delight and Instruction of Mankind.*

This Definition (though *Crites* rais'd a Logical Objection against it; that it was only *à genre & fine*, and so   **page xxxv /**   not altogether perfect;) was yet well received by the rest. . . . *Crites*, being desired by the Company to begin, spoke on behalf of the Ancients, in this manner.

If Confidence presage a Victory, *Eugenius*, in his own Opinion, has already triumphed over the Ancients; nothing seems more easy to him, than to over-come those whom it is our greatest Praise to have imitated well: for we do not only build upon their Foundations; but by their Models. . . .   **page xxxvi /**

. . . I must remember you, that all the Rules by which we practice the *Drama* at this Day, (either such as relate to the Justness and Symmetry of the Plot; or the Episodical Ornaments, such as Descriptions, Narrations, and other Beauties, which are not essential to the Play;) were delivered to us from the Observations which *Aristotle* made, of those Poets, who either lived before him or were his Contemporaries: We have added nothing of our own, except we have the Confidence to say our Wit is better; Of which none boast in this our Age, but such as understand not theirs. Of that Book which *Aristotle*   **page xxxvii /** has left us περὶ τῆς Ποιητικῆς, *Horace* his Art of Poetry, is an excellent Com-ment, and, I believe, restores to us that second Book of his concerning Comedy, which is wanting in him.

Out of these two have been extracted the famous Rules which the *French* call, *Des Trois Unitez*, or, The Three Unities, which ought to be observ'd in every regular Play; namely, of Time, Place, and Action.

The Unity of Time they comprehend in twenty four Hours, the compass of a Natural Day; or as near it as can be contriv'd: And the Reason of it is obvious to every one, that the Time of the feigned Action, or Fable of the Play, should be proportion'd as near as can be to the Duration of that Time in which it is represented; since therefore all Plays are acted on the Theatre in a space of Time much within the compass of twenty four Hours, that Play is to be thought the nearest Imitation of Nature, whose Plot or Action is con-fin'd within that Time; and, by the same Rule which concludes this general Proportion of Time, it follows, that all the Parts of it are (as near as may be) to be equally sub-divided; namely, that one Act take not up the suppos'd Time of half a day; which is out of Proportion to the rest; since the other four are then to be straitned within the Compass of the remaining half; for it is un-natural, that one Act, which being spoke or written, is not longer than the rest, should be suppos'd longer by the Audience; 'tis therefore the Poet's Duty, to take care that no Act should be imagin'd to exceed the Time in which it is represented on the Stage; and that the intervals and Inequalities of Time be suppos'd to fall out between the Acts.

This Rule of Time how well it has been observ'd by the Ancients, most of their Plays will witness; you see them in their Tragedies (wherein to follow this Rule, is certainly most difficult) from the very Beginning of their Plays, falling close into that part of the Story which they intend for the Action or principal Object of it: Leaving the former Part to be delivered by Narration: So that they set the Audience, as it were, at the Post where the Race is to be concluded: And saving them the **page xxxviii /** tedious Expectation of seeing the Poet set out and ride the Beginning of the Course, they suffer you not to behold him, till he is in sight of the Goal, and just upon you.

For the Second Unity, which is that of Place, the Ancients meant by it, That the Scene ought to be continued through the Play, in the same Place where it was laid in the Beginning: For the Stage, on which it is represented, being but one and the same Place, it is unnatural to conceive it many; and those far distant from one another. I will not deny, but by the Variation of painted Scenes, the Fancy (which in these Cases will contribute to its own Deceit) may sometimes imagine it several Places, with some Appearance of Probability; yet it still carries the greater likelihood of Truth, if those Places be suppos'd so near each other, as in the same Town or City, which may all be comprehended under the larger Denomination of one Place: For a greater Distance will bear no proportion to the shortness of time, which is allotted in the Acting, to pass from one of them to another. For the Observation of this, next to the Ancients, the *French* are to be most commended. They tye themselves so strictly to the Unity of Place, that you never see in any of their Plays, a Scene chang'd in the middle of an Act: If the Act begins in a Garden, a Street, or Chamber, 'tis ended in the same Place; and that you may know it to be the same, the Stage is so supplied with Persons, that it is never empty all the time: He who enters second has Business with him who was on before; and before the second quits the Stage, a third appears who has Business with him.

This *Corneille* calls *La Liaison des Scenes*, the Continuity or joining of the Scenes; and 'tis a good Mark of a well contriv'd Play, when all the Persons are known to each other, and every one of them has some Affairs with all the rest.

As for the Third Unity, which is that of Action, the Ancients meant no other by it than what the Logicians do by their *Finis*, the End or Scope of any Action: That which is the first in Intention, and last in Execu- **page xxxix /** tion: Now the Poet is to aim at one great and compleat Action, to the carrying on of which all things in his Play, even the very Obstacles, are to be subservient; and the Reason of this is as evident as any of the former.

For two Actions equally labour'd and driven on by the Writer, would destroy the Unity of the Poem; it would be no longer one Play, but two: Not but that there may be many Actions in a Play, as *Ben. Johnson* has observ'd in his *Discoveries*, but they must be all subservient to the great one, which our Language happily expresses in the Name of Under-plots. . . . There ought to be but one Action, says *Corneille*, that is, one compleat Action which leaves the Mind of the Audience in a full Repose: but this cannot be brought to pass, but by many other imperfect Actions which conduce to it, and hold the Audience in a delightful Suspense of what will be.

If by these Rules (to omit any other drawn from the Precepts and Practice of the Ancients) we should judge our modern Plays; 'tis probable, that few of them would endure the Tryal: That which should be the Business of a Day, takes up in some of them an Age; instead of one Action they are the Epitomes of a Man's Life; and for one Spot of Ground (which the Stage should represent) we are sometimes in more Countries than the Map can show us.

But if we will allow the Ancients to have contriv'd well, we must acknowledge them to have written better. . . . **page xl /** . . . I must desire you to take notice, that the greatest Man of the last Age (*Ben. Johnson*) was willing to give place to them in all things: He was not only a profess'd Imitator of *Horace*, but a learned Plagiary of all the others; you track him every where in their Snow. If *Horace, Lucan, Petronius Arbiter, Seneca*, and *Juvenal*, had their own from him, there are few serious Thoughts which are new in him; you will pardon me therefore, if I presume he lov'd their Fashion when he wore their Cloaths. But since I have otherwise a great veneration for him, and you, *Eugenius*, prefer him above all other Poets, I will use no further Arguments to you than his Example: I will produce before you Father *Ben.* dress'd in all the Ornaments and Colours of the Ancients, you will need no other Guide to our Party, if you follow him; and whether you consider the bad Plays of our Age, or regard the good Plays of the last, both the **page xli /** best and worst of the modern Poets, will equally instruct you to admire the Ancients.

Crites had no sooner left speaking, but *Eugenius*, who had waited with some Impatience for it, thus began:

I have observed in your Speech, that the former Part of it is convincing, as to what the Moderns have profited by the Rules of the Ancients; but in the latter you are careful to conceal how much they have excell'd them: We own all the Helps we have from them, and want neither Veneration nor Gratitude, while we acknowledge, that to overcome them we must make use of the Advantages we have received from them; but to these Assistances we have join'd our own Industry; for (had we sat down with a dull Imitation of them) we might then have lost somewhat of the old Perfection, but never acquir'd any that was new. We draw not therefore after their Lines, but those of Nature; and having the Life before us, besides the Experience of all they knew, it is no wonder if we hit some Airs and Features which they have miss'd. I deny not what you urge of Arts and Sciences, that they have flourish'd in some Ages more than others; . . . if Natural Causes be more known now than in the time of *Aristotle*, because more studied, it follows, that Poesy and other Arts may, with the same Pains, arrive still nearer to Perfection; and, that granted, it will rest for you to prove, that they wrought more perfect Images of human Life, than we; which, seeing in your Discourse you have avoided to make good, it shall now be my task to shew you some Part of their Defects, and some few Excellencies of the Moderns. . . . **page xlii /**

Be pleased then, in the first Place, to take notice, that the *Greek* Poesy, which *Crites* has affirm'd to have arriv'd to Perfection in the Reign of the old Comedy, was so far from it, that the Distinction of it into Acts was not known to them; or if it were, it is yet so darkly deliver'd to us, that we cannot make it out.

All we know of it is from the singing of their Chorus, and that too is so uncertain, that in some of their Plays we have reason to conjecture they sung more than five times. *Aristotle* indeed divides the integral Parts of a Play into four: First, the *Protasis*, or Entrance, which gives light only to the Characters of the

Persons, and proceeds very little into any part of the Action: Secondly, the *Epitasis*, or working up of the Plot, where the Play grows warmer: The Design or Action of it is drawing on, and you see something promising that it will come to pass. Thirdly, the *Catastasis*, call'd by the *Romans, Status,* the Height, and full Growth of the Play: We may call it properly the Counter-turn, which destroys that Expectation, imbroils the Action in new Difficulties, and leaves you far distant from that hope in which it found you; as you may have observed in a violent Stream, resisted by a narrow Passage; it runs around to an Eddy, and carries back the Waters with more swiftness than it brought them on. Lastly, the *Catastrophe*, which the *Grecians* call'd λύσις, the *French, le denouement,* and we, the discovery or unravelling of the Plot: There you see all things settling again upon their first Foundations, and the Obstacles which hindred the Design or Action of the Play once remov'd, it ends with that Resemblance of Truth and Nature, that the Audience are satisfied with the Conduct of it. Thus this great Man deliver'd to us the Image of a Play, and I must confess it is so lively, that from thence much light has been deriv'd to the forming it more perfectly into Acts and Scenes; but what Poet first limited to five the Number of the Acts I know not; only we see it so firmly establish'd in the time of *Horace,* that he gives it for a Rule in Comedy; *Neu brevior quinto, neu sit productior actu:* So that you see the *Grecians* cannot be said **page xliii /** to have consummated this Art: writing rather by Entrances, than by Acts; and having rather a general indigested Notion of a Play, than knowing how, and where to bestow the particular Graces of it. . . .

Next, for the Plot, . . . it has already been judiciously observ'd by a late Writer, that in their Tragedies it was only some Tale deriv'd from *Thebes* or *Troy,* or at least some thing that happen'd in those two Ages; which was worn so thread-bare by the Pens of all the Epique Poets, and even by Tradition it self of the Talkative *Greeklings* (as *Ben. Johnson* calls them) that before it came upon the Stage, it was already known to all the Audience: And the People, so soon as ever they heard the Name of *Oedipus,* knew as well as the Poet, that he had kill'd his Father by a Mistake, and committed Incest with his Mother, before the Play; that they were now to hear of a great Plague, an Oracle, and the Ghost of *Laius:* So that they sate with a yawning kind of Expectation, till he was to come with his Eyes pull'd out, and spake a hundred or more Verses in a Tragick Tone, in complaint of his Misfortunes. But one *Oedipus, Hercules,* or *Medea,* had been tolerable; poor People, they scap'd not so good cheap: they had still the *Chapon Bouillé* set before them, till their Appetites were cloy'd with the same Dish, and the Novelty being gone, the Pleasure vanish'd: So that one main End of *Dramatick Poesy* in its Definition, which was to cause Delight, was of consequence destroy'd. **page xliv /**

In their Comedies, The *Romans* generally borrow'd their Plots from the *Greek* Poets; and theirs was commonly a little Girl stollen or wandred from her Parents, brought back unknown to the City, there got with Child by some lewd young Fellow; who, by the help of his Servant, cheats his Father: and when her time comes, to cry *Juno Lucina fer opem;* one or other sees a little Box or Cabinet which was carried away with her, and so discovers her to her Friends, if some God do not prevent it, by coming down in a Machine, and taking the thanks of it to himself.

By the Plot you may guess much of the Characters of the Persons. An old Father, who would willingly before he dies see his Son well married; his debauch'd Son, kind in his Nature to his Mistress, but miserably in want of Money; a Servant or Slave, who has so much Wit to strike in with him, and help to dupe his Father, a Braggadochio Captain, a Parasite, and a Lady of Pleasure.

As for the poor honest Maid, on whom the Story is built, and who ought to be one of the principal Actors in the Play, she is commonly a Mute in it: She has the breeding of the Old *Elizabeth* way, which was for Maids to be seen, and not to be heard, and it is enough you know she is willing to be married, when the Fifth Act requires it.

These are Plots built after the *Italian* Mode of Houses, you see through them all at once; the Characters are indeed the Imitations of Nature, but so narrow as if they had imitated only an Eye or an Hand, and did not dare to venture on the Lines of a Face, or the Proportion of a Body.

But in how straight a compass soever they have bounded their Plots and Characters, we will pass it by, if they have regularly pursued them, and perfectly observ'd those three Unities of Time, Place and Action: the knowledge of which you say is deriv'd to us from them. But in the first Place give me leave to tell you, that the Unity of Place, however it might be practiced by them, was never any of their Rules: We neither   page xlv /   find it in *Aristotle*, *Horace*, or any who have written of it, till in our Age the *French* Poets first made it a Precept of the Stage. The Unity of Time, even *Terence* himself (who was the best and most regular of them) has neglected: His *Heautontimoroumenos* or Self-punisher takes up visibly two Days, says *Scaliger;* the two first Acts concluding the first Day, the three last the Day ensuing; and *Euripides*, in tying himself to one Day, has committed an Absurdity never to be forgiven him: For in one of his Tragedies he has made *Theseus* go from *Athens* to *Thebes*, which was about forty *English* Miles, under the Walls of it to give Battel, and appear Victorious in the next Act; and yet from the time of his Departure to the return of the *Nuntius*, who gives the Relation of his Victory, *AEthra* and the Chorus have but thirty six Verses; which is not for every Mile a Verse.

The like Error is as evident in *Terence* his *Eunuch*, when *Laches*, the old Man, enters by mistake into the House of *Thais*, where betwixt his Exit, and the Entrance of *Pythias*, who comes to give ample Relation of the Disorders he has rais'd within, *Parmeno* who was left upon the Stage, has not above five Lines to speak: *C'est bien employer un temps si court*, says the *French* Poet, who furnish'd me with one of the Observations: And almost all their Tragedies will afford us Examples of the like Nature.

'Tis true, they have kept the Continuity, or as you call'd it, *Liaison des Scenes*, somewhat better: two do not perpetually come in together, talk, and go out together; and other two succeed them, and do the same throughout the Act, which the *English* call by the Name of single Scenes; but the reason is, because they have seldom above two or three Scenes, properly so call'd, in every Act; for it is to be accounted a new Scene, not only every time the Stage is empty, but every Person who enters, tho' to others, makes it so; because he introduces a new Business: Now the Plots of their Plays being narrow, and the Persons few, one of their Acts was written in a less compass than one of our well-wrought **page xlvi /** Scenes, and yet they are often deficient even in this: To go no further than *Terence*, you will find in the *Eunuch*, *Antipho* entring single in the midst of the third Act, after *Chremes* and *Pythias* were gone off: In the same Play you have likewise *Dorias* beginning the fourth Act alone; and after she has made a Relation of what was done at the Soldier's entertainment (which by the way was very inartificial, because she was presum'd to speak directly to the Audience, and to acquaint them with what was Necessary to be known, but yet should have been so contriv'd by the Poet, as to have been told by Persons of the *Drama* to one another, and so by them to have come to the Knowledge of the People) she quits the Stage, and *Phædria* enters next, alone likewise: He also gives you an Account of himself, and of his returning from the Country in *Monologue*, to which unnatural way of Narration *Terence* is subject in all his Plays: In his *Adelphi* or Brothers, *Syrus* and *Demea* enter; after the Scene was broken by the Departure of *Sostrata*, *Geta* and *Canthara;* and indeed you can scarce look into any of his Comedies, where you will not presently discover the same Interruption.

But as they have fail'd both in laying of their Plots, and in the Management, swerving from the Rules of their own Art, by mis-representing Nature to us, in which they have ill satisfied one Intention of a Play, which was Delight; so in the instructive Part they have err'd worse: Instead of punishing Vice, and rewarding Virtue, they have often shewn a prosperous Wickedness, and an unhappy Piety: They have set before us a bloody Image of Revenge in *Medea*, and given her Dragons to convey her safe from Punishment. A *Priam* and *Astyanax* murder'd, and *Cassandra* ravish'd, and the Lust and Murder ending in the Victory of him who acted them. In short, there is no Indecorum in any of our modern Plays, which, if I would excuse, I could not shadow with some Authority from the Ancients.

And one farther Note of them let me leave you: Tragedies and Comedies were not writ then as they are now, promiscuously, by the same Person; but he who **page xlvii /** found his Genius bending to the one, never attempted the other way. This is so plain, that I need not instance to you, that *Aristophanes*, *Plautus*, *Terence*, never any of them writ a Tragedy: *Æschylus*, *Euripides*, *Sophocles* and *Seneca* never meddled with Comedy: The Sock and Buskin were not worn by the same Poet. Having then so much care to excel in one kind, very little is to be pardon'd them if they miscarried in it. . . . **page xlviii /**

. . . *Lisideius*, after he had acknowledg'd himself of *Eugenius* his Opinion concerning the Ancients; yet told him he had forborn, till his Discourse were ended, to ask him, why he preferr'd the *English* Plays above those of other Nations? And whether we ought not to submit our Stage to the Exactness of our next Neighbours?

Tho', said *Eugenius*, I am at all times ready to defend the Honour of my Country against the *French*, and to **page lii /** maintain, we are as well able to vanquish them with our Pens, as our Ancestors have been with their Swords; yet, if you please, added he, looking upon *Neander*, I will commit this Cause to my Friend's management; his Opinion of our Plays is the same with mine: And besides, there is no reason, that *Crites* and I, who have now left the Stage, should re-enter so suddenly upon it; which is against the Laws of Comedy.

If the Question had been stated, replied *Lisideius*, who had writ best, the *French* or *English* forty Years ago, I should have been of your Opinion, and adjudged the Honour to our own Nation; but since that time, (said he, turning toward *Neander*) we have been so long together bad *Englishmen*, that we had no leisure to be good Poets; *Beaumont, Fletcher*, and *Johnson* (who were only capable of bringing us to that degree of Perfection which we have) were just then leaving the World; as if in an Age of so much Horror, Wit and those milder Studies of Humanity had no farther business among us. But the Muses, who ever follow Peace, went to plant in another Country; it was then that the great Cardinal of *Richlieu* began to take them into his Protection; and that, by his Encouragement, *Corneille* and some other *French-men* reform'd their Theatre, (which before was as much below ours, as it now surpasses it and the rest of *Europe*;) But because *Crites*, in his Discourse for the Ancients, has prevented me, by observing many Rules of the Stage, which the Moderns have borrow'd from them; I shall only, in short, demand of you, whether you are not convinc'd that of all Nations the *French* have best observ'd them? in the Unity of Time you find them so scrupulous, that it yet remains a Dispute among their Poets, whether the artificial Day of twelve Hours, more or less, be not meant by *Aristotle*, rather than the natural one of twenty four; and consequently, whether all Plays ought not to be reduc'd into that compass? This I can testify, that in all their *Drama's* writ within these last twenty Years and upwards, I have not observ'd any that have extended the Time to thirty Hours. In the Unity of Place they are full as scrupulous; for many of their Criticks **page liii /** limit it to that very Spot of Ground where the Play is suppos'd to begin; none of them exceed the compass of the same Town or City.

The Unity of Action in all their Plays is yet more conspicuous, for they do not burden them with Under-plots, as the *English* do; which is the reason why many Scenes of our Tragi-comedies carry on a design that is nothing of kin to the main Plot; and that we see two distinct Webs in a Play, like those in ill-wrought Stuffs; and two Actions, that is, two Plays carried on together, to the confounding of the Audience; who, before they are warm in their Concernments for one Part, are diverted to another; and by that means espouse the Interest of neither. From hence likewise it arises, that the one half of our Actors are not known to the other. They keep their distances as if they were *Mountagues* and *Capulets*, and seldom begin an Acquaintance 'till the last Scene of the Fifth Act, when they are all to meet upon the Stage. There is no Theatre in the World has any thing so absurd as the *English* Tragi-comedy, 'tis a *Drama* of our own Invention, and the Fashion of it is enough to proclaim it so; here a Course of Mirth, there another of Sadness and Passion, and a third of Honour and a Duel: Thus in two Hours and a half we run through all the Fits of *Bedlam*. The *French* afford you as much Variety on the same Day, but they do it not so unseasonably, or *mal à propos*, as we: Our Poets present you the Play and the Farce together; and our Stages still retain somewhat of the original civility of the Red Bull. . . .

The End of Tragedies or serious Plays, says *Aristotle*, is to beget Admiration, Compassion, or Concernment; but are not Mirth and Compassion things incompatible? And is it not evident, that the Poet must of necessity destroy the former by intermingling of the latter? That is, he must ruin the sole End and

Object of his Tragedy to introduce somewhat that is forced into it, and is not of the body of it: Would you not think that Physician **page liv /** mad, who having prescribed a Purge, should immediately order you to take Restringents?

But to leave our Plays, and return to theirs, I have noted one great Advantage they have had in the Plotting of their Tragedies; that is, they are always grounded upon some known History . . . ; and in that they have so imitated the Ancients, that they have surpass'd them. For the Ancients, as was observ'd before, took for the foundation of their Plays some Poetical Fiction, such as under that consideration could move but little concernment in the Audience; because they already knew the Event of it. But the *French* goes farther. . . . He so interweaves Truth with probable Fiction, that he puts a pleasing Fallacy upon us, mends the intrigues of Fate, and dispenses with the severity of History, to reward the Virtue which has been render'd to us there unfortunate. Sometimes the Story has left the Success so doubtful, that the Writer is free, by the privilege of a Poet, to take that which of two or more Relations will best suit with his Design: As for Example, In the death of *Cyrus*, whom *Justin* and some others report to have perish'd in the *Scythian* War, but *Xenophon* affirms to have died in his Bed of extream old Age. Nay more, when the Event is past dispute, even then we are willing to be deceiv'd, and the Poet, if he contrives it with appearance of Truth, has all the Audience of his Party; at least during the time his Play is acting: So naturally we are kind to Virtue, when our own Interest is not in Question, that we take it up as the general Concernment of Mankind. On the other side, if you consider the Historical Plays of *Shakespear*, they are rather so many Chronicles of Kings, or the Business many times of thirty or forty Years, crampt into a Representation of two Hours and a half, which is not to imitate or paint Nature, but rather to draw her in miniature, to take **page lv /** her in little; to look upon her through the wrong End of a Perspective, and receive her Images not only much less, but infinitely more imperfect than the Life: This, instead of making a Play delightful, renders it ridiculous. . . .

Another thing in which the *French* differ from us and from the *Spaniards*, is, that they do not embarass or cumber themselves with too much Plot: They only represent so much of a Story as will constitute one whole and great Action sufficient for a Play; we, who undertake more, do but multiply Adventures; which not being produc'd from one another, as Effects from Causes, but barely following, constitute many Actions in the *Drama,* and consequently make it many Plays.

But by pursuing closely one Argument, which is not cloy'd with many Turns, the *French* have gain'd more liberty for Verse, in which they write: They have leisure to dwell on a Subject which deserves it; and to represent the Passions (which we have acknowledg'd to be the Poet's work) without being hurried from one thing to another, as we are in the Plays of *Calderon*, which we have seen lately upon our Theatres, under the name of *Spanish* Plots. I have taken notice but of Tragedy of ours, whose Plot has that uniformity and unity of Design in it, which I have commended in the *French;* and that is *Rollo*, or rather, under the name of *Rollo*, The Story of *Bassianus* and *Geta* in *Herodian;* there indeed the Plot is neither large nor intricate, but just enough to fill the Minds of the Audience, not to cloy them. Besides, you see it founded upon the truth of History, only the time of the Action is not reduceable to the strictness of the Rules; and you see in some places a little Farce mingled, which is below the dignity of the other Parts; and in this all our Poets are extreamly peccant, even *Ben* **page lvi /** *Johnson* himself in *Sejanus* and *Catiline* has given us this Oleo of a Play. . . .

But I return again to the *French* Writers; who, as I have said, do not burden themselves too much with Plot, which has been reproach'd to them by an *ingenious Person* of our Nation as a Fault; for he says they commonly make but one Person considerable in a Play; they dwell on him, and his concernments, while the rest of the Persons are only subservient to set him off. If he intends this by it, that there is one Person in the Play who is of greater Dignity than the rest, he must tax, not only theirs, but those of the Ancients, and, which he would be loth to do, the best of ours, for 'tis impossible but that one Person must be more conspicuous in it than any other, and consequently the greatest share in the Action must devolve on him. We see it so in the management of all Affairs. . . .

But, if he would have us to imagine, that in exalting one Character the rest of them are neglected, and that all of them have not some share or other in the Action of the Play, I desire him to produce any of *Corneille's* Tragedies, wherein every Person (like so many Servants in a well-govern'd Family) has not some Employment, and who is not necessary to the carrying on of the Plot, or at least to your understanding it. **page lvii /**

There are indeed some protatick Persons in the Ancients, whom they make use of in their Plays, either to hear, or give the Relation: But the *French* avoid this with great Address, making their Narrations only to, or by such, who are some way interested in the main Design. And now I am speaking of Relations, I cannot take a fitter Opportunity to add this in favour of the *French*, that they often use them with better judgment and more *à propos* than the *English* do. Not that I commend Narrations in general, but there are two sorts of them: one, of those things which are antecedent to the Play, and are related to make the conduct of it more clear to us; but 'tis a Fault to chuse such Subjects for the Stage as will force us on that Rock; because we see they are seldom listned to by the Audience, and that is many times the ruin of the Play: For, being once let pass without Attention, the Audience can never recover themselves to understand the Plot; and indeed it is somewhat unreasonable, that they should be put to so much trouble, as, that to comprehend what passes in their sight, they must have recourse to what was done, perhaps, ten or twenty Years ago.

But there is another sort of Relations, that is, of things happening in the Action of the Play, and suppos'd to be done behind the Scenes: And this is many times both convenient and beautiful: For, by it the *French* avoid the Tumult, to which we are subject in *England*, by representing Duels, Battels, and the like; which renders our Stage too like the Theaters where they fight Prizes. For what is more ridiculous than to represent an Army with a Drum and five Men behind it; all which, the Heroe of the other side is to drive in before him? or to see a Duel fought, and one slain with two or three thrusts of the Foils, which we know are so blunted, that we might give a Man an Hour to kill another in good earnest with them?

I have observ'd, that in all our Tragedies the Audience cannot forbear laughing when the Actors are to die; 'tis the most comick Part of the whole Play. All *Passions* may be lively represented on the Stage, if to the well- **page lviii /** writing of them the Actor supplies a good commanded Voice, and Limbs that move easily, and without stiffness; but there are many *Actions* which can never be imitated to a just height: Dying especially is a thing which none but a *Roman* Gladiator could naturally perform on the Stage, when he did not imitate or represent, but do it; and therefore it is better to omit the Representation of it.

The Words of a good Writer which describe it lively, will make a deeper Impression of Belief in us, than all the Actor can insinuate into us, when he seems to fall dead before us. . . . When we see Death represented, we are convinc'd it is but Fiction; but when we hear it related, our Eyes (the strongest Witnesses) are wanting, which might have undeceiv'd us; and we are all willing to favour the slight when the Poet does not too grossly impose on us. . . . But it is objected, That if one part of the Play may be related, then why not all? I answer, Some parts of the Action are more fit to be represented, some to be related. *Corneille* says judiciously, that the Poet is not oblig'd to expose to View all particular Actions which conduce to the principal: He ought to select such of them to be seen, which will appear with the greatest **page lix /** Beauty, either by the magnificence of the Show, or the vehemence of Passions which they produce, or some other Charm which they have in them, and let the rest arrive to the Audience by Narration. 'Tis a great mistake in us to believe the *French* present no part of the Action on the Stage: Every alteration or crossing of a Design, every new-sprung Passion, and turn of it, is a part of the Action, and much the noblest, except we conceive nothing to be Action till the Players come to Blows; as if the painting of the Heroe's Mind were not more properly the Poet's Work, than the strength of his Body. . . . Those Actions which by reason of their Cruelty will cause Aversion in us, or by reason of their Impossibility, Unbelief, ought either wholly to be avoided by a Poet, or only deliver'd by Narration. . . . Examples of all these kinds are frequent, not only among all the Ancients, but in the best receiv'd of our *English* Poets. We find *Ben Johnson* using them in his *Magnetick Lady*, where one comes out from Dinner, and **page lx /** relates the Quarrels and Disorders of it to save the undecent appearance of them on the Stage, and to abbreviate the Story: And this in express imitation of *Terence*, who had done the same before him in his *Eunuch*, where *Pythias* makes the like Relation of what had happen'd within at the Soldier's Entertainment. The Relation, likewise, of *Sejanus's* Death, and the Prodigies before it, are remarkable; the one of which was hid from sight to avoid the Horror and Tumult of the Representation; the other to shun the introducing of things impossible to be believ'd. In that excellent Play, *The King and no King, Fletcher* goes yet farther; for the whole unravelling of the Plot is done by Narration in the fifth Act, after the manner of the Ancients; and it moves great Concernment in the Audience, tho' it be only a Relation of what was done many Years before the Play. I could multiply other Instances, but these are sufficient to prove, that there is no Error in chusing a Subject which requires this sort of Narrations; in the ill Management of them, there may. . . . **page lxi /**

. . . I should now speak of the Beauty of their Rhyme, and the just reason I have to prefer that way of writing in Tragedies before ours in Blank-Verse;

but because it is partly receiv'd by us, and therefore not altogether peculiar to them, I will say no more of it in relation to their Plays. For our own, I doubt not but it will exceedingly beautify them, and I can see but one Reason why it should not generally obtain, that is, because our Poets write so ill in it. . . .

Lisideius concluded . . . ; and *Neander* after a little pause thus answer'd him. **page lxii /**

I shall grant *Lisideius*, without much dispute, a great part of what he has urg'd against us; for I acknowledge, that the *French* contrive their Plots more regularly, and observe the Laws of Comedy, and Decorum of the Stage (to speak generally) with more Exactness than the *English*. Farther, I deny not but he has tax'd us justly in some Irregularities of ours which he has mention'd; yet, after all, I am of Opinion, that neither our Faults nor their Virtues are considerable enough to place them above us.

But the lively Imitation of Nature being in the Definition of a Play, those which best fulfil that Law, ought to be esteem'd Superior to the others. 'Tis true, those Beauties of the *French* Poesy are such as will raise Perfection higher where it is, but are not sufficient to give it where it is not: They are indeed the Beauties of a Statue, but not of a Man, because not animated with the Soul of Poesy, which is Imitation of Humour and Passions: And this *Lisideius* himself, or any other, however byass'd to their Party, cannot but acknowledge, if he will either compare the Humours of our Comedies, or the Characters of our serious Plays, with theirs. He who will look upon theirs which have been written 'till these last ten Years or thereabouts, will find it an hard matter to pick out two or three passable Humours amongst them. *Corneille* himself, their Arch-Poet, what has he produc'd, except *The Liar*, and you know how it was cry'd up in *France;* but when it came upon the *English* Stage, though well translated, and that part of *Dorant* acted with so much Advantage as I am confident it never receiv'd in its own Country, the most favourable to it would not put it in Competition with many of *Fletcher's* or *Ben Johnson's*. In the rest of *Corneille's* Comedies you have little Humour; he tells you himself his way is first to shew two Lovers in good Intelligence with each other; in the working up of the Play, to embroil them by some Mistake, and in the latter end to clear it, and reconcile them.

But of late Years *Moliere*, the younger *Corneille, Quinault,* and some others, have been imitating afar off the   **page lxiii /**   quick Turns and Graces of the *English* Stage. They have mix'd their serious Plays with Mirth, like our Tragi-Comedies, since the Death of Cardinal *Richelieu,* which *Lisideius,* and many others, not observing, have commended that in them for a Virtue, which they themselves no longer practise. Most of their new Plays are, like some of ours, derived from the *Spanish* Novels. There is scarce one of them without a Veil, and a trusty *Diego,* who drolls much after the rate of the *Adventures*. But their Humours, if I may grace them with that name, are so thin sown, that never above one of them comes up in any Play: I dare take upon me to find more variety of them in some one Play of *Ben Johnson's*, than in all theirs together: As he who has seen the *Alchymist,* the *Silent Woman,* or *Bartholomew-Fair,* cannot but acknowledge with me.

. . . As for their new Way of mingling Mirth with serious Plot, I do not, with *Lisideius,* condemn the thing, though I cannot approve their manner of doing it:

He tells us, we cannot so speedily recollect our selves after a Scene of great Passion and Concernment, as to pass to another of Mirth and Humour, and to enjoy it with any relish: But why should he imagine the Soul of Man more heavy than his Senses? Does not the Eye pass from an unpleasant Object to a pleasant, in a much shorter time than is required to this? And does not the Unpleasantness of the first commend the Beauty of the latter? The old Rule of Logick, might have convinc'd him, That Contraries when plac'd near, set off each other. A continued Gravity keeps the Spirit too much bent; we must refresh it sometimes, as we bait in a Journey, that we may go on with greater ease. A Scene of Mirth mix'd with Tragedy, has the same effect upon us which our Musick has betwixt the Acts, which we find a Relief to   **page lxiv /**   us from the best Plots and Language of the Stage, if the Discourses have been long. I must therefore have stronger Arguments ere I am convinc'd, that Compassion and Mirth in the same Subject destroy each other; and in the mean time, cannot but conclude, to the Honour of our Nation, that we have invented, increas'd, and perfected a more pleasant way of writing for the Stage, than was ever known to the Ancients or Moderns of any Nation, which is Tragi-Comedy.

And this leads me to wonder why *Lisideius* and many others should cry up the Barrenness of the *French* Plots, above the Variety and Copiousness of the *English*. Their Plots are single, they carry on one Design, which is push'd forward by all the Actors, every Scene in the Play contributing and moving towards it: Our Plays, besides the main Design, have Under-Plots, or By-Concernments, or less considerable Persons, and Intrigues, which are carried on with the Motion of the main Plot: As they say the Orb of the fix'd Stars, and those of the Planets, though they have Motions of their own, are whirl'd about by the Motion of the *primum mobile*, in which they are contain'd: That Similitude expresses much of the English Stage: For if contrary Motions may be found in Nature to agree . . . ; it will not be difficult to imagine how the Under-Plot, which is only different, not contrary to the great Design, may naturally be conducted along with it. . . .   **page lxv /**

As for his other Argument, that by pursuing one single Theme they gain an Advantage to express and work up the Passions, I wish any Example he could bring from them would make it good: for I confess their Verses are to me the coldest I have ever read: Neither indeed is it possible for them, in the way they take, so to express Passion, as that the Effects of it should appear in the Concernment of an Audience, their Speeches being so many Declamations, which tire us with the Length; so that instead of perswading us to grieve for their imaginary Heroes, we are concern'd for our own trouble, as we are in tedious Visits of bad Company; we are in pain till they are gone. . . . To speak generally, it cannot be deny'd, that short Speeches and Replies are more apt to move the Passions, and beget Concernment in us, than the other: For it is unnatural for any one in a Gust of Passion, to speak long together; or for another, in the same Condition, to suffer him without Interruption. . . . **page lxvi /**   As for Comedy, Repartee is one of its chiefest Graces; the greatest Pleasure of the Audience is a Chace of Wit kept up on both sides, and swiftly manag'd. And this our Fore-fathers, if not we, have had in *Fletcher's* Plays, to a much higher Degree of Perfection, than the *French* Poets can, reasonably, hope to reach.

There is another part of *Lisideius* his Discourse, in which he has rather excus'd our Neighbours than commended them; that is, for aiming only to make one Person considerable in their Plays. 'Tis very true what he has urged, That one Character in all Plays, even without the Poet's Care, will have Advantage of all the others; and that the Design of the whole *Drama* will chiefly depend upon it. But this hinders not that there may be more shining Characters in the Play; many Persons of a second Magnitude, nay, some so very near, so almost equal to the first, that Greatness may be oppos'd to Greatness, and all the Persons be made considerable, not only by their Quality, but their Action. 'Tis evident, that the more the Persons are, the greater will be the Variety of the Plot. If then the Parts are managed so regularly, that the Beauty of the whole be kept intire, and that the Variety become not a perplex'd and confus'd Mass of Accidents, you will find it infinitely pleasing to be led in a Labyrinth of Design, where you see some of your way before you; yet discern not the End till you arrive at it. And that all this is practicable, I can produce for Examples many of our *English* Plays: As the *Maids Tragedy*, the *Alchymist*, the *Silent Woman*. . . .   page lxvii /

But to leave this, and pass to the latter part of *Lisideius* his Discourse, which concerns Relations, I must acknowledge with him, that the *French* have reason to hide that part of the Action which would occasion too much Tumult on the Stage, and to chuse rather to have it made known by Narration to the Audience. Farther, I think it very convenient, for the Reasons he has given, that all incredible Actions were remov'd; but, whether Custom has so insinuated it self into our Country-men, or Nature has so form'd them to Fierceness, I know not; but they will scarcely suffer Combats and other Objects of Horror to be taken from them. And indeed, the Indecency of Tumults is all which can be objected against fighting: For why may not our Imagination as well suffer it self to be deluded with the Probability of it, as with any other thing in the Play? For my Part, I can with as great ease persuade my self, that the Blows are given in good earnest, as I can, that they who strike them are Kings or Princes, or those Persons which they represent. For Objects of Incredibility, I would be satisfied from *Lisideius*, whether we have any so remov'd from all appearance of Truth, as are those of *Corneille's Andromede?* A Play which has been frequented the most of any he has writ. If the *Perseus*, or the Son of an Heathen God, the *Pegasus* and the Monster, were not capable to choak a strong Belief, let him blame any Representation of ours hereafter. Those indeed were Objects of Delight; yet the Reason is the same as to the Probability: For he makes it not a Balette or Masque, but a Play, which is to resemble Truth. But for Death, that it ought not to be represented, I have, besides the Arguments alledged by *Lisideius*, the Authority of *Ben Johnson*, who has forborn it in his Tragedies; for both the Death of *Sejanus* and *Catiline* are related: Though in the latter I cannot but observe one Irregularity of that great Poet: He has remov'd the Scene in the same Act,   page lxviii /   from *Rome* to *Catiline's* Army, and from thence again to *Rome;* and besides, has allow'd a very inconsiderable time after *Catiline's* Speech, for the striking of the Battel, and the return of *Petreius*, who is to relate the event of it to the Senate: Which I should not animadvert on him, who was otherwise a painful Observer of . . . the *decorum* of the Stage, if he had not us'd extream Severity in his Judgment on the incomparable *Shake-*

spear for the same fault. To conclude on this Subject of Relations, if we are to be blam'd for shewing too much of the Action, the *French* are as faulty for discovering too little of it: A Mean betwixt both should be observed by every judicious Writer, so as the Audience may neither be left unsatisfied by not seeing what is beautiful, or shock'd by beholding what is either incredible or indecent. I hope I have already prov'd in this Discourse, that though we are not altogether so punctual as the *French*, in observing the Laws of Comedy; yet our Errors are so few, and little, and those things wherein we excel them so considerable, that we ought of right to be preferr'd before them. But what will *Lisideius* say, if they themselves acknowledge they are too strictly bounded by those Laws, for breaking which he has blam'd the *English?* I will alledge *Corneille's* Words, as I find them in the end of his Discourse of the three Unities; *Il est facile aux speculatifs d'estre severes*, &c. " 'Tis easy for speculative Persons to judge severely; but if they would produce to publick View ten or twelve Pieces of this Nature, they would perhaps give more Latitude to the Rules than I have done, when by Experience they had known how much we are limited and constrain'd by them, and how many Beauties of the Stage they banish'd from it.". . . **page lxix /**

. . . .

If they content themselves, as *Corneille* did, with some flat design, which like an ill Riddle, is found out ere it be half propos'd; such Plots we can make every way regular as easily as they: But whene'er they endeavour to rise to any quick turns and counter-turns of Plot, as some of them have attempted, since *Corneille's* Plays have been less in vogue, you see they write as irregularly as we, though they cover it more speciously. Hence the reason is perspicuous, why no *French* Plays, when translated, have, or ever can succeed on the *English* Stage. For, if you consider the Plots, our own are fuller of Variety; if the Writing, ours are more quick and fuller of spirit: and therefore 'tis a strange mistake in those who decry the way of writing Plays in Verse, as if the *English* therein imitated the *French*. We have borrowed nothing from them; our Plots are weav'd in *English* Looms: we endeavour therein to follow the variety and greatness of Characters which are deriv'd to us from *Shakespear* and *Fletcher:* the copiousness and well-knitting of the Intriegues we have from *Johnson;* and for the Verse it self we have *English* Precedents of elder date than any of *Corneille's* Plays: (not to name our old Comedies before *Shakespear*, which were all writ in verse of six feet, of *Alexandrines*, such as the *French* now uses) I can shew in *Shakespear*, many Scenes of Rhyme together, and the like in *Ben Johnson's* Tragedies: In *Catiline* and *Sejanus* sometimes thirty or forty lines; I mean, besides the Chorus, or the Monologues, which by the way, shew'd *Ben* no Enemy to this way of Writing, especially if you read his *Sad Shepherd*, which goes sometimes on Rhyme, sometimes on blank Verse. . . . You find him likewise commending *Fletcher's* Pastoral of the *Faithful Shepherdess;* which is for the most part Rhyme, though **page lxxi /** not refin'd to that Purity to which it hath since been brought: And these Examples are enough to clear us from a servile Imitation of the *French*.

But to return whence I have digress'd, I dare boldly affirm these two things of the *English Drama:* First, That we have many Plays of ours as regular as any of theirs; and which, besides, have more variety of Plot and Characters:

And secondly, that in most of the irregular Plays of *Shakespear* or *Fletcher*, (for *Ben Johnson's* are for the most part regular) there is a more masculine Fancy, and greater Spirit in the writing, than there is in any of the *French*. I could produce even in *Shakespear's* and *Fletcher's* Works, some Plays which are almost exactly form'd; as *The Merry Wives of* Windsor, and *The Scornful Lady:* But, because (generally speaking) *Shakespear*, who writ first, did not perfectly observe the Laws of Comedy, and *Fletcher*, who came nearer to Perfection, yet through Carelessness made many Faults; I will take the Pattern of a perfect Play from *Ben Johnson*, who was a careful and learned Observer of the Dramatick Laws, and from all his Comedies I shall select *The Silent Woman:* of which I will make a short Examen, according to those Rules which the *French* observe.

As *Neander* was beginning to examine *The Silent Woman; Eugenius*, earnestly regarding him, I beseech you, *Neander*, said he, gratify the Company, and me in particular so far as, before you speak of the Play, to give us a Character of the Author; and tell us frankly your Opinion, whether you do not think all Writers, both *French* and *English*, ought to give place to him?

I fear, replied *Neander*, That in obeying your Commands, I shall draw some Envy on my self. Besides, in performing them, it will be first necessary to speak somewhat of *Shakespear* and *Fletcher*, his Rivals in Poesy; and one of them, in my Opinion, at least his Equal, perhaps his Superior.

To begin then with *Shakespear:* he was the Man who of all Modern, and perhaps Ancient Poets, had the largest and most comprehensive Soul. All the Images of Nature were still present to him, and he drew them not   page lxxii / laboriously, but luckily: When he describes any thing, you more than see it, you feel it too. Those who accuse him to have wanted Learning, give him the greater Commendation: he was naturally learn'd: he needed not the Spectacles of Books to read Nature; he look'd inwards, and found her there. I cannot say, he is every where alike; were he so, I should do him injury to compare him with the greatest of Mankind. He is many times flat, and insipid; his Comick Wit degenerating into Clenches, his Serious swelling into Bombast. But he is always great, when some great Occasion is presented to him: No Man can say, he ever had a fit Subject for his Wit, and did not then raise himself as high above the rest of Poets,

Quantum lenta solent inter Viburna Cupressi.

The Consideration of this made Mr. *Hales* of *Eaton* say, That there was no Subject of which any Poet ever writ, but he would produce it much better done in *Shakespear;* and however others are now generally preferr'd before him, yet the Age wherein he liv'd, which had Contemporaries with him, *Fletcher* and *Johnson*, never equall'd them to him in their Esteem: And in the last King's Court, when *Ben's* Reptation was at highest, Sir *John Suckling*, and with him the greater Part of the Courtiers, set our *Shakespear* far above him.

Beaumont and *Fletcher*, of whom I am next to speak, had, with the Advantage of *Shakespear's* Wit, which was their Precedent, great natural Gifts, improv'd by Study. *Beaumont* especially being so accurate a Judge of Plays, that *Ben Johnson* while he liv'd submitted all his Writings to his Censure, and, 'tis thought, us'd his Judgment in correcting, if not contriving all his Plots. What value he had for him appears by the Verses he writ to him; and therefore I need speak no farther of it. The first Play that brought *Fletcher* and him in Esteem, was their *Philaster;* for before that, they had written two or three very unsuccess-fully: As the like is reported of *Ben Johnson,* before he writ *Every Man in his Humour.* page lxxiii /   Their Plots were generally more regular than *Shake-spear's,* especially those which were made before *Beaumont's* Death; and they understood and imitated the Conversation of Gentlemen much better; whose wild Debaucheries, and Quickness of Wit in Repartees, no Poet before them could paint as they have done. Humour, which *Ben Johnson* deriv'd from par-ticular Persons, they made it not their Business to describe: They represented all the Passions very lively, but above all, Love. I am apt to believe the *English* Language in them arriv'd to its highest Perfection; what Words have since been taken in, are rather Superfluous than Ornamental. Their Plays are now the most pleasant and frequent Entertainments of the Stage; two of theirs being acted through the Year for one of *Shakespear's* or *Johnson's:* The Reason is, because there is a certain Gayety in their Comedies, and Pathos in their more serious Plays, which suits generally with all Mens Humours. *Shakespear's* Language is likewise a little obsolete, and *Ben Johnson's* Wit comes short of theirs.

As for *Johnson,* to whose Character I am now arrived, if we look upon him while he was himself, (for his last Plays were but his Dotages) I think him the most learned and judicious Writer which any Theater ever had. He was a most severe Judge of himself as well as others. One cannot say he wanted Wit, but rather that he was frugal of it. In his Works you find little to retrench or alter. Wit and Language, and Humour also in some measure, we had before him; but something of Art was wanting to the *Drama,* 'till he came. He manag'd his Strength to more advantage than any who preceded him, You seldom find him making Love in any of his Scenes, or endeavouring to move the Passions; his Genius was too sullen and Saturnine to do it gracefully, especially when he knew he came after those who had performed both to such an Height. Humour was his proper Sphere, and in that he delighted most to represent Mechanick People. He was deeply conversant in the Ancients, both *Greek* and *Latin,* and he borrow'd boldly from them: There is scarce a Poet or page lxxiv / Historian among the *Roman* Authors of those Times, whom he has not trans-lated in *Sejanus* and *Catiline.* But he has done his Robberies so openly, that one may see he fears not to be taxed by any Law. He invades Authors like a Monarch, and what would be Theft in other Poets, is only Victory in him. With the Spoils of these Writers he so represents old *Rome* to us in its Rites, Ceremonies, and Customs, that if one of their Poets had written either of his Tragedies, we had seen less of it than in him. If there was any Fault in his Language, 'twas, that he weav'd it too closely and laboriously, in his Comedies especially: Perhaps too, he did a little too much Romanize our Tongue, leaving the Words which he translated almost as much *Latin* as he found them: Wherein though he learnedly followed their Language, he did not enough comply with the Idiom of ours. If I would compare him with *Shakespear,* I must acknowl-edge him the more correct Poet, but *Shakespear* the greater Wit. *Shakespear* was the *Homer,* or Father of our Dramatick Poets; *Johnson* was the *Virgil,* the Pattern of elaborate Writing; I admire him, but I love *Shakespear*. To conclude of him, as he has given us the most correct Plays, so in the Precepts which he has laid down in his *Discoveries*, we have as many and profitable Rules for perfecting the Stage, as any wherewith the *French* can furnish us.

Having thus spoken of the Author, I proceed to the Examination of his Comedy, *The Silent Woman.*

Examen of the Silent Woman.

To begin first with the Length of the Action; it is so far from exceeding the Compass of a Natural Day, that it takes not up an Artificial one. 'Tis all included in the Limits of three Hours and an half, which is no more than is required for the Presentment on the Stage. . . . The Scene of it is laid in *London;* the Latitude of Place is almost as little as you can   **page lxxv /**   imagine: For it lies all within the Compass of two Houses, and after the first Act, in one. The Continuity of Scenes is observ'd more than in any of our Plays, except his own *Fox* and *Alchymist.* They are not broken above twice, or thrice at most, in the whole Comedy; and in the two best of *Corneille's* Plays, the *Cid* and *Cinna*, they are interrupted once. The Action of the Play is intirely one; the End or Aim of which is the settling *Morose's* Estate on *Dauphine.* The Intrigue of it is the greatest and most noble of any pure unmix'd Comedy in any Language: You see it in many Persons of various Characters and Humours, and all delightful: As first, *Morose*, or an old Man, to whom all Noise, but his own Talking, is offensive. Some, who would be thought Criticks, say this Humour of his is forc'd: . . . But to convince these People, I need but tell them, that Humour is the ridiculous Extravagance of Conversation, wherein one Man differs from all others. . . .   **page lxxvi /**   The Ancients have little of it in their Comedies. . . . The *French*, tho' they have the word *humeur* among them, yet they have small use of it in their Comedies, or Farces; they being but ill Imitations of the *ridiculum*, or that which stirr'd up Laughter in the old Comedy. But among the *English* 'tis otherwise: Where, by Humour is meant some extravagant Habit, Passion, or Affection, particular (as I said before) to some one Person: By the Oddness of which, he is immediately distinguish'd from the rest of Men; which being lively and naturally represented, most frequently begets that malicious Pleasure in the Audience which is testified by Laughter: As all things which **page lxxvii /**   are Deviations from Customs are ever the aptest to produce it: Though by the way this Laughter is only accidental, as the Person represented is Fantastick or Bizarre; but Pleasure is essential to it, as the Imitation of what is natural. The Description of these Humours, drawn from the Knowledge and Observation of particular Persons, was the peculiar Genius and Talent of *Ben Johnson.* . . .

Besides *Morose*, there are at least, nine or ten different Characters and Humours in the *Silent Woman*, all which Persons have several Concernments of their own, yet all us'd by the Poet, to the conducting of the main Design to Perfection. . . . For the Contrivance of the Plot, 'tis extream elaborate, and yet withal easy; for the . . . untying it, 'tis so admirable, that when it is done, no one of the Audience would think the Poet could have miss'd it; and yet it was conceal'd so much before the last Scene, that any other Way would sooner have enter'd into your Thoughts. . . .   **page lxxviii /**

But our Poet . . . has made use of all Advantages; as he who designs a large Leap, takes his Rise from the highest Ground. One of these Advantages, is that which *Corneille* has laid down as the greatest which can arrive to any Poem, and which himself could never compass above thrice in all his Plays, *viz.* the making Choice of some signal and long-expected Day, whereon the Action of the Play is to depend. This Day was that design'd by *Dauphine,* for the settling of his Uncle's Estate upon him, which to compass he contrives to marry him: That the Marriage had been plotted by him long beforehand, is made evident, by what he tells *True-Wit* in the second Act, that in one Moment he had destroy'd what he had been raising many Months.

There is another Artifice of the Poet, which I cannot here omit, because by the frequent Practice of it in his Comedies, he has left it to us almost as a Rule; that is, when he has any Character or Humour wherein he would shew a *Coup de Maistre,* or his highest Skill; he recommends it to your Observation, by a pleasant Description of it before the Person first appears. Thus, in *Bartholomew-Fair,* he gives you the Pictures of *Numps* and *Cokes,* and in this, those of *Daw, Lafoole, Morose,* and the *Collegiate Ladies;* all which you hear describ'd before you see them. So that before they come upon the Stage you have a longing Expectation of them, which prepares you to receive them favourably; and when they are there, even from their first Appearance you are so far acquainted with them, that nothing of their Humour is lost to you.

I will observe yet one thing further of this admirable Plot; the Business of it rises in every Act. The second is greater than the first; the third than the second, and so forward to the fifth. There too you see, till the very last Scene, new Difficulties arising to obstruct the Action of the Play; and when the Audience is brought into despair that the Business cannot naturally be effected; then, and not before, the Discovery is made. But that the Poet might entertain you with more Variety **page lxxix /** all this while, he reserves some new Characters to show you, which he opens not till the second and third Act. . . . All which he moves afterwards in By-walks, or under-Plots, as Diversions to the main Design, lest it should grow tedious, though they are still naturally join'd with it, and somewhere or other subservient to it. Thus, like a skilful Chess-player, by little and little, he draws out his Men, and makes his Pawns of use to his greater Persons.

If this Comedy, and some others of his, were translated into *French* Prose (which would now be no wonder to them, since *Moliere* has lately given them Plays out of Verse, which have not displeas'd them) I believe the Controversy would soon be decided betwixt the two Nations, even making them the Judges. But we need not call our Heroes to our Aid; Be it spoken to the Honour of the *English,* our Nation can never want in any Age such, who are able to dispute the Empire of Wit with any People in the Universe. And though the Fury of a Civil War, and Power, for twenty Years together, abandon'd to a barbarous Race of Men, Enemies of all good Learning, had buried the Muses under the Ruins of Monarchy; yet with the Restoration of our Happiness, we see reviv'd Poesy lifting up its Head, and already shaking off the Rubbish which lay so heavy on it. We have seen since his Majesty's Return, many Dramatick Poems which yield not to those of any foreign Nation, and which deserve all Laurels but the *English.* . . . **page lxxx /**

This was the Substance of what was then spoke on that Occasion; and

Lisideius, I think, was going to reply, when he was prevented thus by *Crites:* I am confident, said he, that the most material things that can be said, have been already urg'd on either side; if they have not, I must beg of *Lisideius* that he will defer his Answer till another time: for I confess I have a joint Quarrel to you both, because you have concluded, without any Reason given for it, that Rhyme is proper for the Stage. I will not dispute how ancient it hath been among us to write this way; perhaps our Ancestors knew no better till *Shakespeare's* time. I will grant it was not altogether left by him, and that *Fletcher* and *Ben Johnson* us'd it frequently in their Pastorals; and sometimes in other Plays. Farther, I will not argue whether we receiv'd it originally from our own Countrymen, or from the *French*. . . . I have therefore only to affirm, That it is not allowable in serious Plays; for Comedies I find you already concluding with me. To prove this, I might satisfy my self to tell you, how much in vain it is for you to strive against the Stream of the Peoples   page lxxxi /   Inclination; the greatest part of which are prepossess'd so much with those excellent Plays of *Shakespeare, Fletcher,* and *Ben Johnson,* (which have been written out of Rhyme) that except you could bring them such as were written better in it, and those too by Persons of equal Reputation with them, it will be impossible for you to gain your Cause with them, who will still be Judges. . . . But I will not, on this occasion, take the Advantage of the greater Number, but only urge such Reasons against Rhyme, as I find in the Writings of those who have argu'd for the other Way. First then, I am of Opinion, that Rhyme is unnatural in a Play, because Dialogue there is presented as the Effect of sudden Thought. For a Play is the Imitation of Nature, and since no Man, without Premeditation, speaks in Rhyme, neither ought he to do it on the Stage; this hinders not but the Fancy may be there elevated to an higher Pitch of Thought than it is in ordinary Discourse: For there is a Probability that Men of excellent and quick Parts may speak noble things *extempore:* But those Thoughts are never fetter'd with the Numbers or Sound of Verse, without Study; and therefore it cannot be but Unnatural to present the most free way of Speaking, in that which is the most constrain'd. For this Reason, says *Aristotle,* 'Tis best to write Tragedy in that Kind of Verse which is the least such, or which is nearest Prose: And this amongst the Ancients was the Iambique, and with us is Blank Verse, or the Measure of Verse kept exactly, without Rhyme. These Numbers therefore are fittest for a Play. . . . And if it be objected, that neither are Blank Verses made *extempore*,   page lxxxii /   yet as nearest Nature, they are still to be preferr'd. But there are two particular Exceptions which many besides my self have had to Verse; by which it will appear yet more plainly, how improper it is in Plays. And the first of them is grounded on that very Reason for which some have commended Rhyme: They say the Quickness of Repartees in argumentative Scenes receives an Ornament from Verse. Now what is more unreasonable than to imagine, that a Man should not only imagine the Wit, but the Rhyme too upon the sudden? This Nicking of him who spoke before both in Sound and Measure, is so great an Happiness, that you must at least suppose the Persons of your Play to be born Poets. . . . Nor will it serve you to object, that however you manage it, 'tis still known to be a Play; and consequently the Dialogue of two Persons understood to be the Labour of one Poet. For a Play is still an Imitation of Nature; we know we are to be deceiv'd, and we desire to be so; but no Man ever was deceiv'd but with a probability of Truth. . . . page lxxxiii /

Thus, you see, your Rhyme is uncapable of expressing the greatest Thoughts naturally, and the lowest it cannot with any Grace: For what is more unbefitting the Majesty of Verse, than to call a Servant, or bid a Door be shut in Rhyme? And yet you are often forc'd on this miserable Necessity. But Verse, you say, Circumscribes a quick and luxuriant Fancy, which would extend it self too far on every Subject, did not the Labour which is requir'd to well-turn'd and polish'd Rhyme, set Bounds to it. Yet this Argument, if granted, would only prove, that we may write better in Verse, but not more naturally. Neither is it able to evince that; for he who wants Judgment to confine his Fancy in Blank Verse, may want it as much in Rhyme; and he who has it, will avoid Errors in both kinds. . . .

In our own Language we see *Ben Johnson* confining himself to what ought to be said, even in the Liberty of Blank Verse; and yet *Corneille*, the most judicious of the *French* Poets, is still varying the same Sense an hundred ways, and dwelling eternally on the same Subject, though confin'd by Rhyme. Some other Exceptions I have to Verse, but since these I have nam'd are for the most part already publick, I conceive it reasonable they should first be answer'd.

It concerns me less than any, said *Neander*, (seeing he had ended) to reply to this Discourse; because when I should have prov'd, that Verse may be natural in Plays, yet I should always be ready to confess, that those which page lxxxiv / I have written in this kind, come short of that Perfection which is requir'd. Yet since you are pleas'd I should undertake this Province, I will do it, though with all imaginable respect and deference, both to that Person from whom you have borrow'd your strongest Arguments, and to whose Judgment, when I have said all, I finally submit. But before I proceed to answer your Objections, I must first remember you, that I exclude all Comedy from my Defence; and next, that I deny not but Blank Verse may be also us'd, and content my self only to assert, that in serious Plays, where the Subject and Characters are great, and the Plot unmix'd with Mirth, which might allay or divert these Concernments which are produc'd, Rhyme is there as natural, and more effectual than Blank Verse.

And now having laid down this as a Foundation; to begin with *Crites*, I must crave leave to tell him, that some of his Arguments against Rhyme reach no farther than, from the Faults or Defects of ill Rhyme, to conclude against the Use of it in general. May not I conclude against Blank Verse by the same Reason? If the Words of some Poets who write in it, are either ill chosen, or ill placed, (which makes not only Rhyme, but all kind of Verse in any Language unnatural;) Shall I, for their vicious Affectation, condemn those excellent Lines of *Fletcher*, which are written in that kind? Is there any thing in Rhyme more constrain'd than this Line in Blank Verse? *I Heav'n invoke, and strong resistance make;* where you see both the Clauses are plac'd unnaturally; that is, contrary to the common way of Speaking, and that without the Excuse of a Rhyme to cause it: Yet you would think me very ridiculous, if I should accuse the Stubbornness of Blank Verse for this, and not rather the Stiffness of the Poet. Therefore, *Crites*, you must either prove that Words, though well chosen, and duly plac'd, yet render not Rhyme natural in it self; or that however natural and easie the Rhyme may be, yet it is not proper for a Play. If you insist on the former Part, I would ask you what other Conditions are requir'd to make Rhyme natural in it self, besides an E- page lxxxv / lection of apt Words, and a right Disposition of them? For the due Choice of your Words expresses your Sense naturally, and the due Placing them adapts the Rhyme to it. . . . The Necessity of a Rhyme never forces any but bad or lazy Writers to say what they would not otherwise. 'Tis true, there is both Care and Art requir'd to write in Verse; A good Poet never establishes the first Line, till he has sought out such a Rhyme as may fit the Sense, already prepar'd to heighten the second: Many times the Close of the Sense falls into the middle of the next Verse, or farther off, and he may often prevail himself of the same Advantages in *English* which *Virgil* had in *Latin*, he may break off in the *Hemistich*, and begin another Line; Indeed, the not observing these two last things, makes Plays which are writ in Verse, so tedious: For though, most commonly, the Sense is to be confin'd to the Couplet, yet nothing that does *perpetuo tenore fluere*, run in the same Channel, can please always. . . .

If then Verse may be made natural in it self, how becomes it unnatural in a Play? You say the Stage is the Representation of Nature, and no Man in ordinary Conversation speaks in Rhyme. But you foresaw, when you said this, that it might be answer'd; neither does any Man speak in Blank Verse, or in Measure without Rhyme. Therefore you concluded, that which is nearest Nature is still to be preferr'd. But you took no no- page lxxxvi / tice, that Rhyme might be made as natural as Blank Verse, by the well placing of the Words, &c. all the Difference between them, when they are both correct, is the Sound in one, which the other wants; and, if so, the Sweetness of it, and all the Advantage resulting from it, which are handled in the Preface to the *Rival Ladies*, will yet stand good. As for that place of *Aristotle*, where he says Plays should be writ in that kind of Verse, which is nearest Prose; it makes little for you, Blank Verse being properly but measur'd Prose. . . . No Man is tied in Modern Poesie to observe any farther Rule in the Feet of his Verse, but that they be Dissyllables; whether *Spondee*, *Trochee*, or *Iambique*, it matters not; only he is oblig'd to Rhyme. . . . Farther, As to that Quotation of *Aristotle*, our Couplet Verses may be rendred as near Prose as Blank Verse it self, by using those Advan- page lxxxvii / tages I lately nam'd, as Breaks in an Hemistich, or running the Sense into another Line, thereby making Art and Order appear as loose and free as Nature; or not tying our selves to Couplets strictly, we may use the Benefit of the Pindarick way, practis'd in the Siege of *Rhodes;* where the Numbers vary, and the Rhyme is dispos'd carelessly, and far from Chyming. Neither is that other Advantage of the Ancients to be despis'd, of changing the Kind of Verse when they please, with the Change of the Scene, or some new Entrance: For they confine not themselves always to *Iambiques*, but extend their Liberty to all *Lyrique* Numbers, and sometimes even to *Hexameter*. . . .

But perhaps you may tell me I have propos'd such a Way to make Rhyme natural, and consequently proper to Plays, as is unpracticable, and that I shall scarce find six or eight Lines together in any Play, where the Words are so plac'd and chosen as is requir'd to make it natural. I answer, No Poet need constrain himself at all times to it. It is enough he makes it his general Rule; for I deny not but sometimes there may be a Greatness in placing the Words otherwise; and sometimes they may sound better, sometimes also the Variety it self is Excuse enough. But if, for the most part, the Words be plac'd as they are in the Negligence of Prose, it is sufficient to denominate the Way practicable; for we esteem that to be such, which in the Tryal oftner succeeds than misses. And thus far you may find the Practice made good in many Plays; where you do not, remember still, that if you cannot find six natural Rhymes together, it will be as hard for you to produce as many Lines in Blank Verse, even among the greatest of our Poets, against which I cannot make some reasonable Exception.   page lxxxviii /

And this, Sir, calls to my remembrance the beginning of your Discourse, where you told us we should never find the Audience favourable to this Kind of Writing, 'till we could produce as good Plays in Rhyme, as *Ben Johnson*, *Fletcher*, and *Shakespear*, had writ out of it. But it is to raise Envy to the Living, to compare them with the Dead. They are honour'd, and almost adored by us, as they deserve; neither do I know any so presumptuous of themselves as to contend with them. Yet give me leave to say thus much, without Injury to their Ashes, that not only we shall never equal them, but they could never equal themselves, were they to rise and write again. We acknowledge them our Fathers in Wit, but they have ruin'd their Estates themselves before they came to their Childrens Hands. There is scarce an Humour, a Character, or any kind of Plot, which they have not us'd. All comes sullied or wasted to us: And were they to entertain this Age, they could not now make so plenteous Treatments out of such decay'd Fortunes. This therefore will be a good Argument to us either not to write at all, or to attempt some other Way. . . .

This way of writing in Verse, they have only left free to us; our Age is arriv'd to a Perfection in it, which they never knew; and which (if we may guess by what of theirs we have seen in Verse, as the *Faithful Shepherdess*, and *Sad Shepherd:*) 'tis probable they never could have reach'd. For the Genius of every Age is different: And though ours excel in this, I deny not but that to imitate Nature in that Perfection which they did in Prose, is a greater Commendation than to write in Verse exactly. . . .   page lxxxix /

But I come now to the Inference of your first Argument. You said, that the Dialogue of Plays is presented as the Effect of sudden Thought, but no Man speaks suddenly, or *extempore* in Rhyme: And you inferr'd from thence, that Rhyme, which you acknowledge to be proper to Epique Poesy, cannot equally be proper to Dramatick, unless we could suppose all Men born so much more than Poets, that Verses should be made in them, not by them.

It has been fomerly urg'd by you, and confess'd by me, that since no Man spoke any kind of Verse *extempore*, that which was nearest Nature was to be preferr'd. I answer you therefore, by distinguishing betwixt what is nearest to the Nature of Comedy, which is the Imitation of common Persons and ordinary Speaking, and what is nearest the Nature of a serious Play: This last is indeed the Representation of Nature, but 'tis Nature wrought up to a higher Pitch. The Plot, the Characters, the Wit, the Passions, the Descriptions, are all exalted above the Level of common Converse, as high as the Imagination of the Poet can carry them, with proportion to Verisimility. Tragedy we know is wont to image to us the Minds and Fortunes of Noble Persons, and to pourtray these exactly; Heroick Rhyme is nearest Nature, as being the noblest Kind of modern Verse. . . .   page xc /

Blank Verse is acknowledge'd to be too low for a Poem; nay more, for a

Paper of Verses; but if too low for an ordinary Sonnet, how much more for Tragedy, which is by *Aristotle*, in the Dispute betwixt the Epick Poesy and the Dramatick, for many Reasons he there alledges, rank'd above it! . . . . page xci /

. . . You tell us, *Crites*, that Rhyme appears most unnatural in Repartees, or short Replies: When he who answers, (it being presum'd he knew not what the other would say, yet) makes up that part of the Verse which was left incompleat, and supplies both the Sound and Measure of it. This, you say, looks rather like the Confederacy of two, than the Answer of one.

This, I confess, is an Objection which is in every Man's Mouth who loves the Rhyme: But suppose, I beseech you, the Repartee were made only in Blank Verse, might not part of the same Argument be turn'd against you? For the Measure is as often supply'd there as it is in Rhyme. The latter Half of the Hemistich as commonly made up, or a second Line subjoin'd, as a Reply to the former; which any one Leaf in *Johnson's* Plays will sufficiently clear to you. . . . But you tell us, this supplying the last Half of a Verse, or adjoining a whole Second to the former, looks more like the Design of two, than the Answer of one. Suppose we acknowledge it: How comes this Confederacy to be more displeasing to you than in a Dance which is well contriv'd? You see there the united Design of many Persons to make up one Figure: After they have separated themselves in many petty Divisions, they rejoin one by one into a Gross: The Confederacy is plain amongst them; page xcii / for Chance could never produce any thing so beautiful, and yet there is nothing in it that shocks your Sight. I acknowledge the Hand of Art appears in Repartee, as of necessity it must in all kind of Verse. But there is also the quick and poinant Brevity of it (which is an high Imitation of Nature in those sudden Gusts of Passion) to mingle with it: And this, join'd with the Cadency and Sweetness of the Rhyme, leaves nothing in the Soul to the Hearer to desire. . . .

From Replies, which are the most elevated Thoughts of Verse, you pass to those which are most mean, and which are common with the lowest of household Conversation. In these, you say, the Majesty of Verse suffers. You instance in the calling of a Servant, or commanding a Door to be shut, in Rhyme. This, *Crites*, is a good Observation of yours, but no Argument: For it proves no more but that such Thoughts should be wav'd, as often as may be, by the Address of the Poet. But suppose they are necessary in the Places where he uses them, yet there is no need to put them into Rhyme. He may place them in the Beginning of a Verse, and break it off, as unfit, when so debas'd, for any other Use: Or granting the worst, that they require more Room than the Hemistich will allow, yet still there is a Choice to be made of the best Words, and least vulgar (provided they be apt) to express such Thoughts. Many have blam'd Rhyme in general, for this Fault, when the Poet, with a little Care, page xciii / might have redress'd it. But they do it with no more Justice, than if *English* Poesy should be made ridiculous for the sake of the Water-Poet's Rhymes. Our Language is noble, full, and significant; and I know not why he who is Master of it, may not cloath ordinary things in it as decently as the *Latin;* if he use the same Diligence in his Choice of Words. . . .

Thus, *Crites*, I have endeavour'd to answer your Objections; it remains only that I should vindicate an Argument for Verse, which you have gone about to overthrow. It had formerly been said, that the Easiness of Blank Verse renders the Poet too luxuriant; but that the Labour of Rhyme bounds and circumscribes an over-fruitful Fancy. The Scene there being commonly confin'd to the Couplet, and the Words so order'd that the Rhyme page xciv / naturally follows them, not they the Rhyme. To this you answer'd, That it was no Argument to the Question in hand, for the Dispute was not which way a Man may write best; but which is most proper for the Subject on which he writes.

First, give me leave, Sir, to remember you, that the Argument against which you rais'd this Objection, was only secondary: It was built on this *Hypothesis,* that to write in Verse was proper for serious Plays. Which Supposition being granted (as it was briefly made out in that Discourse, by shewing how Verse might be made natural) it asserted, that this way of writing was an help to the Poet's Judgment, by putting Bounds to a wild over-flowing Fancy. I think therefore it will not be hard for me to make good what it was to prove on that Supposition. But you add, that were this let pass, yet he who wants Judgment in the Liberty of his Fancy, may as well shew the Defect of it when he is confin'd to Verse: For he who has Judgment will avoid Errors; and he who has it not, will commit them in all Kinds of Writing.

This Argument, as you have taken it from a most acute Person, so, I confess, it carries much Weight in it. But by using the word *Judgment* here indefinitely, you seem to have put a Fallacy upon us: I grant that he who has Judgment, that is, so profound, so strong, or rather so infallible a Judgment, that he needs no Helps to keep it always pois'd and upright, will commit no Faults either in Rhyme or out of it. And on the other Extream, he who has a Judgment so weak and craz'd, that no Helps can correct or amend it, shall write scurvily out of Rhyme, and worse in it. But the first of these Judgments is no where to be found, and the latter is not fit to write at all. To speak therefore of Judgment as it is in the best Poets: They who have the greatest Proportion of it, want other Helps than from it within. As for Example, who would be loth to say, that he who is indued with a sound Judgment has no need of History, Geography, or Moral Philosophy, to write correctly. Judgment is indeed the Master-workman in a Play: But he requires ma- page xcv / ny subordinate Hands, many Tools to his Assistance. And Verse I affirm to be one of these: 'Tis a Rule and Line by which he keeps his Building compact and even, which otherwise lawless Imagi-nation would raise either irregularly or loosly. At least if the Poet commits Errors with this Help, he would make greater and more without it: 'Tis (in short) a slow and painful, but the surest Kind of Working. *Ovid,* whom you accuse for Luxuriancy in Verse, had perhaps been farther guilty of it, had he writ in Prose. And for your Instance of *Ben Johnson,* who, you say, writ exactly without the Help of Rhyme; you are to remember 'tis only an Aid to a luxuriant Fancy, which his was not: As he did not want Imagination, so none ever said he had much to spare. Neither was Verse then refin'd so much, to be an Help to that Age, as it is to ours. Thus then the second Thoughts being usually the best, as receiving the maturest Digestion from Judgment, and the last and most mature Product of those Thoughts being artfully and labour'd Verse, it may well be inferr'd, that Verse is a great Help to a luxuriant Fancy; and this is what that Argument which you oppos'd, was to evince. . . .
page xcvi /

64

John Dryden

John Dryden. *Epilogue to The Second Part of The Conquest of Granada*, in *The Works of John Dryden*, ed. Sir Walter Scott and George Saintsbury. Edinburgh, 1882–93. Vol. IV.

> They, who have best succeeded on the stage,
> Have still conformed their genius to their age.
> Thus Jonson did mechanic humour show,
> When men were dull, and conversation low.
> Then comedy was faultless, but 'twas coarse:
> Cobb's tankard was a jest, and Otter's horse.
> And, as their comedy, their love was mean;
> Except, by chance, in some one laboured scene,
> Which must atone for an ill-written play,
> They rose, but at their height could seldom stay.
> Fame then was cheap, and the first comer sped;
> And they have kept it since, by being dead.
> But, were they now to write, when critics weigh
> Each line, and every word, throughout a play,
> None of them, no, not Jonson in his height,
> Could pass, without allowing grains for weight.
> Think it not envy, that these truths are told;
> Our poet's not malicious, though he's bold.
> 'Tis not to brand them, that their faults are shown.
> But, by their errors, to excuse his own
> If love and honour now are higher raised,
> 'Tis not the poet, but the age is praised.
> Wit's now arrived to a more high degree;
> Our native language more refined and free.
> Our ladies and our men now speak more wit
> In conversation, than those poets writ.
> Then, one of these is, consequently, true;
> That what this poet writes comes short of you,
> And imitates you ill (which most he fears),
> Or else his writing is not worse than theirs.
> Yet, though you judge (as sure the critics will),
> That some before him writ with greater skill,
> In this one praise he has their fame surpast,
> To please an age more gallant than the last.

page 224 /

John Dryden. *Defence of the Epilogue; or, An Essay on the Dramatic Poetry of the Last Age*, in *The Works of John Dryden*, ed. Sir Walter Scott and George Saintsbury. Edinburgh, 1882–93. Vol. IV.

. . . I have so far engaged my self in a bold epilogue . . . , wherein I have somewhat taxed the former writing, that it was necessary for me either not to print it, or to show that I could defend it. Yet I would so maintain my opinion of the present age, as not to be wanting in my veneration for the past: I would ascribe to dead authors their just praises   **page 225 /**   in those things wherein they have excelled us; and in those wherein we contend with them for the pre-eminence, I would acknowledge our advantages to the age, and claim no victory from our wit. This being what I have proposed to myself, I hope I shall not be thought arrogant when I inquire into their errors; For we live in an age so sceptical, that as it determines little, so it takes nothing from antiquity on trust; and I profess to have no other ambition in this essay, than that poetry may not go backward, when all other arts and sciences are advancing. . . . **page 226 /**

. . . One age learning from another, the last (if we can suppose an equality of wit in the writers) has the advantage of knowing more and better than the former. And this, I think, is the state of the question in dispute. It is therefore my part to make it clear, that the language, wit, and conversation of our age, are improved and refined above the last; and then it will not be difficult to infer, that our plays have received some part of those advantages.

In the first place, therefore, it will be necessary to state, in general, what this refinement is, of which we treat; and that, I think, will not be defined amiss, "An improvement of our Wit, Language, and Conversation; or, an alteration in them for the better."

To begin with Language. That an alteration is lately made in ours, or since the writers of the last age (in which I comprehend Shakespeare, Fletcher, and Jonson), is manifest. Any man who reads those excellent poets, and compares their language with what is now written, will see it almost in every line; but that this is an improvement of the language, or an alteration for the better, will not so easily be granted. For many are of a contrary opinion, that the English tongue was then in the height of its perfection; that from Jonson's time to ours it has been in a continual declination. . . .

But, to show that our language is improved,   **page 227 /**   and that those people have not a just value for the age in which they live, let us consider in what the refinement of a language principally consists: that is, "either in reject-ing such old words, or phrases, which are ill sounding, or improper; or in ad-mitting new, which are more proper, more sounding, and more significant."

The reader will easily take notice, that when I speak of rejecting improper words and phrases, I mention not such as are antiquated by custom only, and, as I may say, without any fault of theirs. For in this case the refinement can be but accidental; that is, when the words and phrases, which are rejected, happen to be improper. Neither would I be understood, when I speak of impropriety of language, either wholly to accuse the last age, or to excuse the present, and least of all myself; for all writers have their imperfections and failings: but I may safely conclude in the general, that our improprieties are less frequent, and less gross than theirs. One testimony of this is undeniable, that we are the first who have observed them; and, certainly, to observe errors is a great step to the correcting of them. But, malice and partiality set apart, let any man, who understands English, read diligently the works of Shakespeare and Fletcher, and I dare undertake, that he will find in every page either some solecism of speech, or some notorious flaw in sense; and yet these men are reverenced, when we are not forgiven. That their wit is great, and many times their expressions noble, envy itself cannot deny. **page 228 /**

. . . But the times were ignorant in which they lived. Poetry was then if not in its infancy among us, at least not arrived to its vigour and maturity: Witness the lameness of their plots; many of which, especially those which they writ first (for even that age refined itself in some measure), were made up of some ridiculous incoherent story, which in one play many times took up the business of an age. I suppose I need not name "Pericles, Prince of Tyre," nor the historical plays of Shakespeare: besides many of the rest, as the "Winter's Tale," "Love's Labour Lost," "Measure for Measure," which were either grounded on impossibilities, or at least so meanly written, that the comedy neither caused your mirth, nor the serious part your concernment. If I would expatiate on this subject, I could easily demonstrate, that our admired Fletcher, who writ after him, neither understood correct plotting, nor that which they call "the decorum of the stage." I would not search in his worst plays for examples: He who will consider his "Philaster," his "Humorous Lieutenant," his "Faithful Shepherdess," and many others which I could name, will find them much below the applause which is now given them. He will see Philaster wounding his mistress, and afterwards his boy, to save himself; not to mention the Clown, who enters immediately, and not only has the advantage of the combat against the hero, **page 229 /** but diverts you from your serious concernment, with his ridiculous and absurd raillery. In his "Humorous Lieutenant," you will find his Demetrius and Leontius staying in the midst of a routed army, to hear the cold mirth of the Lieutenant; and Demetrius afterwards appearing with a pistol in his hand, in the next age to Alexander the Great. And for his Shepherd, he falls twice into the former indecency of wounding women. But these absurdities, which those poets committed, may more properly be called the age's fault than theirs. For, besides the want of education and learning (which was their particular unhappiness), they wanted the benefit of converse: But of that I shall speak hereafter, in a place more proper for it. Their audiences knew no better; and therefore were satisfied with what they brought. Those, who call theirs the golden age of poetry, have only this reason for it, that they were then content with acorns before they knew the use of bread. . . . They had many who admired them, and few who blamed them; and certainly a severe critic is the greatest help to a good wit: he does the office of a friend, while he designs that of an enemy; and his malice keeps a poet within those bounds, which the luxuriancy of his fancy would tempt him to overleap.

But it is not their plots which I meant principally to tax; I was speaking of their sense and language; and I dare almost challenge any man **page 230 /** to show me a page together which is correct in both. As for Ben Jonson, I am loath to name him, because he is a most judicious writer; yet he very often falls into these errors: and I once more beg the reader's pardon for accusing him of them. Only let him consider, that I live in an age where my least faults are severely censured; and that I have no way left to extenuate my failings, but by showing as great in those whom we admire. . . . I cast my eyes but by chance on Catiline; and in the three or four last pages, found enough to conclude that Jonson writ not correctly.

> Let the long-hid seeds
> Of treason, in thee, now shoot forth in deeds
> Ranker than horror.

In reading some bombast speeches of Macbeth, which are not to be understood, he used to say that it was horror; and I am much afraid that this is so.

> Thy parricide late on thy only son,
> After his mother, to make empty way
> For thy last wicked nuptials, worse than they
> That blaze that act of thy incestuous life,
> Which gained thee at once a daughter and a wife

The sense is here extremely perplexed; and I doubt the word *they* is false grammar.

> And be free
> Not heaven itself from thy impiety.

A synchysis, or ill-placing or words, of which Tully so much complains in oratory.

> The waves and dens of beasts could not receive
> The bodies that those souls were frighted *from*.

The preposition in the end of the sentence; a **page 231 /** common fault with him, and which I have but lately observed in my own writings.

> What all the several ills that visit earth,
> Plague, famine, fire, could not reach *unto*,
> The sword, nor surfeits, let thy fury do.

Here are both the former faults: for, besides that the preposition *unto* is placed last in the verse, and at the half period, and is redundant, there is the former synchysis in the words "the sword, nor surfeits," which in construction ought to have been placed before the other.

Catiline says of Cethegus, that for his sake he would

> *Go on upon* the gods, kiss lightning, wrest
> The engine from the Cyclops, and *give fire*
> *At face of a full cloud*, and stand *his ire*.

To "go on upon," is only to go on twice. To "give fire at face of a full cloud," was not understood in his own time; "and stand *his ire*" besides the antiquated word *ire*, there is the article *his*, which makes false construction: and giving fire at the face of a cloud, is a perfect image of shooting, however it came to be known in those days to Catiline.

> Others there are,
> Whom envy to the state draws and pulls on,
> For contumelies received; and such are sure *ones*.

Ones, in the plural number: but that is frequent with him; for he says, not long after,

> Caesar and Crassus, if they be ill men,
> Are mighty *ones*.
> Such men, *they* do not succour more the cause, etc.

They redundant.   **page 232 /**

> Though heaven should speak with all *his* wrath at once,
> We should stand upright and *unfeared*.

His is ill syntax with *heaven;* and by *unfeared* he means *unafraid:* words of a quite contrary signification.

"The ports are open." He perpetually uses ports for gates; which is an affected error in him, to introduce Latin by the loss of the English idiom. . . .

Well-placing of words, for the sweetness of pronunciation, was not known till Mr. Waller introduced it; and, therefore, it is not to be wondered if Ben Jonson has many such lines as these:

"But being bred up in his father's needy fortunes; brought up in's sister's prostitution," etc.

But meanness of expression one would think not to be his error in a tragedy, which ought to be more high and sounding than any other kind of poetry; and yet, amongst others in "Catiline," I find these four lines together:

> So Asia, thou art cruelly even
> With us, for all the blows thee given;
> When we, whose virtues conquered thee,
> Thus by thy vices ruined be.

Be there is false English for *are;* though the rhyme hides it.

But I am willing to close the book, partly out of veneration to the author, partly out of weariness to pursue an argument which is so fruitful in so small a compass. And what correctness, after this, can be expected from Shakespeare or from Fletcher, who wanted that learning and care which Jonson had? I will, therefore, spare   **page 233 /**   my own trouble of inquiring into their faults; who, had they lived now, had doubtless written more correctly. I suppose it will be enough for me to affirm (as I think I safely may), that these, and the like errors, which I taxed in the most correct of the last age, are such into which we do not ordinarily fall. . . .

As for the other part of refining, which consists in receiving new words and phrases, I shall not insist much on it. It is obvious that we have admitted many, some of which we wanted, and therefore our language is the richer for them, as it would be by importation of bullion: Others are rather ornamental than necessary; yet, by their admission, the language is become more courtly, and our thoughts are better drest. . . . They, who have lately written with most care, have, I believe, taken the rule of Horace for their guide; that is, not to be too hasty in receiving of words, but rather to stay till custom has made them familiar to us. . . . For I cannot approve of their way of refining, who corrupt our English idiom by mixing it too much with French: That is a sophistication of language, not an improvement of it; a turning English into French, rather than a refining of   page 234 /   English by French. We meet daily with those fops, who value themselves on their travelling, and pretend they cannot express their meaning in English, because they would put off to us some French phrase of the last edition; without considering, that, for aught they know, we have a better of our own. But these are not the men who are to refine us; their talent is to prescribe fashions, not words. . . .

There is yet another way of improving language, which poets especially have practised in all ages; that is, by applying received words to a new signification. . . . Horace, . . . in this way, . . . had a particular happiness; using all the tropes, and particular metaphors, with that grace which is observable in his Odes, where the beauty of expression is often greater than that of thought. . . .

And therefore, though he innovated little, he may justly be called a great refiner of the Roman tongue. . . .   page 235 /

. . . By this graffing, as I may call it, on old words, has our tongue been beautified by the three fore-mentioned poets, Shakespeare, Fletcher, and Jonson, whose excellencies I can never enough admire. . . .

I should now speak of the refinement of Wit; but I have been so large on the former subject, that I am forced to contract myself in this. I will therefore only observe to you, that the wit of the last age was yet more incorrect than their language. Shakespeare, who many times has written better than any poet, in any language, is yet so far from writing wit always, or expressing that wit according to the dignity of the subject, that he writes, in many places, below the dullest writers of ours, or any precedent age. Never did any author precipitate himself from such height of thought to so low expressions, as he often does. He is the very Janus of poets; he wears almost everywhere two faces; and you have scarce begun to admire the one, ere you despise the other. Neither is the luxuriance of Fletcher, which his friends have taxed in him, a less fault than the carelessness of Shakespeare. He does not well always; and, when he does, he is a true Englishman, — he knows not when to give over. If he wakes in one scene, he commonly slumbers in another; and, if he pleases you in the first three acts, he is frequently so tired with his labour, that he goes heavily in the fourth, and sinks under his burden in the fifth.   page 236 /

For Ben Jonson, the most judicious of poets, he always writ properly, and as the character required; and I will not contest farther with my friends, who call that wit: it being very certain, that even folly itself, well represented, is wit in a larger signification; and that there is fancy, as well as judgment, in it, though not so much or noble: because all poetry being imitation, that of folly is a lower exercise of fancy, though perhaps as difficult as the other; for it is a kind of looking downward in the poet, and representing that part of mankind which is below him.

In these low characters of vice and folly, lay the excellency of that inimitable writer; who, when at any time he aimed at wit in the stricter sense, that is, sharpness of conceit, was forced either to borrow from the ancients, as to my knowledge he did very much from Plautus; or, when he trusted himself alone, often fell into meanness of expression. Nay, he was not free from the lowest and most grovelling kind of wit, which we call clenches, of which "Every Man in his Humour" is infinitely full; and, which is worse, the wittiest persons in the drama speak them. His other comedies are not exempt from them. Will you give me leave to name some few? Asper, in which character he personates himself (and he neither was nor thought himself a fool), exclaiming against the ignorant judges of the age, speaks thus:

> How monstrous and detested is 't, to see
> A fellow, that has neither art nor brain,
> Sit like an *Aristarchus*, or, *stark-ass*,
> Taking men's lines, with a *tobacco face*,
> In *snuff*, etc.   **page 237 /**

And presently after: "I marvel whose wit 'twas to put a prologue in yond Sackbut's mouth. They might well think he would be out of tune, and yet you'd play upon him too." — Will you have another of the same stamp? "O, I cannot abide these limbs of *sattin*, or rather *Satan*."

But, it may be, you will object that this was Asper, Macilente, or Carlo Buffone: you shall, therefore, hear him speak in his own person, and that in the two last lines, or sting of an epigram. It is inscribed to *Fine Grand*, who, he says, was indebted to him for many things which he reckons there; and concludes thus:

> Forty things more, dear *Grand*, which you know true,
> For which, or pay me quickly, or I'll pay you.

This was then the mode of wit, the vice of the age, and not Ben Jonson's; for you see, a little before him, that admirable wit, Sir Philip Sidney, perpetually playing with his words. In his time, I believe, it ascended first into the pulpit, where (if you will give me leave to clench too) it yet finds the benefit of its clergy; for they are commonly the first corrupters of eloquence, and the last reformed from vicious oratory. . . .

But, to conclude with what brevity I can, I will only add this, in defence of our present writers, that, if they reach not some excellencies of Ben Jonson (which no age, I am confident, ever shall), yet, at least, they are above that meanness of thought which I have taxed, and which is frequent in him.   **page 238 /**

That the wit of this age is much more courtly, may easily be proved, by viewing the characters of gentlemen which were written in the last. First, for Jonson: — Truewit, in the "Silent Woman," was his masterpiece; and Truewit was a scholar-like kind of man, a gentleman with an allay of pedantry, a man who seems mortified to the world, by much reading. The best of his discourse is drawn, not from the knowledge of the town, but books; and, in short, he would be a fine gentleman in an university. Shakespeare showed the best of his skill in his Mercutio; and he said himself, that he was forced to kill him in the third act, to prevent being killed by him. But, for my part, I cannot find he was so dangerous a person: I see nothing in him but what was so exceeding harmless, that he might have lived to the end of the play, and died in his bed, without offence to any man.

Fletcher's Don John is our only bugbear; and yet I may affirm, without suspicion of flattery, that he now speaks better, and that his character is maintained with much more vigour in the fourth and fifth acts, than it was by Fletcher in the three former. I have always acknowledged the wit of our predecessors, with all the veneration which becomes me; but, I am sure, their wit was not that of gentlemen; there was ever somewhat that was ill-bred and clownish in it, and which confessed the conversation of the authors.

And this leads me to the last and greatest advantage of our writing, which proceeds from conversation. In the age wherein those poets lived, there was less of gallantry than in ours; neither did they keep the best company of theirs. **page 239 /**   Their fortune has been much like that of Epicurus, in the retirement of his gardens; to live almost unknown, and to be celebrated after their decease. I cannot find that any of them had been conversant in courts, except Ben Jonson; and his genius lay not so much that way, as to make an improvement by it. Greatness was not then so easy of access, nor conversation so free, as now it is. I cannot, therefore, conceive it any insolence to affirm, that, by the knowledge and pattern of their wit who writ before us, and by the advantage of our own conversation, the discourse and raillery of our comedies excel what has been written by them. And this will be denied by none, but some few old fellows who value themselves on their acquaintance with the Black Friars; who, because they saw their plays, would pretend a right to judge ours. The memory of these grave gentlemen is their only plea for being wits. . . . Learning I never saw in any of them; and wit no more than they could remember. In short, **page 240 /**   they were unlucky to have been bred in an unpolished age, and more unlucky to live to a refined one. They have lasted beyond their own, and are cast behind ours; and, not contented to have known little at the age of twenty, they boast of their ignorance at threescore.

Now, if they ask me, whence it is that our conversation is so much refined? I must freely, and without flattery, ascribe it to the court; and, in it, particularly to the king, whose example gives a law to it. His own misfortunes, and the nation's, afforded him an opportunity, which is rarely allowed to sovereign princes, I mean of travelling, and being conversant in the most polished courts of Europe; and, thereby, of cultivating a spirit which was formed by nature to receive the impressions of a gallant and generous education. At his return, he found a nation lost as much in barbarism as in rebellion: And, as the excellency of his nature forgave the one, so the excellency of his manners reformed the other. The desire of imitating so great a pattern first awakened the dull and heavy spirits of the English from their natural reservedness; loosened them from their stiff forms of conversation, and made them easy and pliant to each other in discourse. Thus, insensibly, our way of living became more free; and the fire of the English wit, which was before stifled under a constrained, melancholy way of breeding, began first to display its force, by mixing the solidity of our nation with the air and gaiety of our neighbours. This being **page 241 /**   granted to be true, it would be a wonder if the poets, whose work is imitation, should be the only persons in three kingdoms who should not receive advantage by it; or, if they should not more easily imitate the wit and conversation of the present age than of the past.

Let us therefore admire the beauties and the heights of Shakespeare, without falling after him into a carelessness, and, as I may call it, a lethargy of thought, for whole scenes together. Let us imitate, as we are able, the quickness and easiness of Fletcher, without proposing him as a pattern to us, either in the redundancy of his matter, or the incorrectness of his language. Let us admire his wit and sharpness of conceit; but let us at the same time acknowledge, that it was seldom so fixed, and made proper to his character, as that the same things might not be spoken by any person in the play. Let us applaud his scenes of love; but let us confess, that he understood not either greatness or perfect honour in the parts of any of his women. In fine, let us allow, that he had so much fancy, as when he pleased he could write wit; but that he wanted so much judgment, as seldom to have written humour, or described a pleasant folly. Let us ascribe to Jonson, the height and accuracy of judgment in the ordering of his plots, his choice of characters, and maintaining what he had chosen to the end: But let us not think him a perfect pattern of imitation, except it be in humour; for love, which is the foundation of   **page 242 /**   all comedies in other languages, is scarcely mentioned in any of his plays: And for humour itself, the poets of this age will be more wary than to imitate the meanness of his persons. Gentlemen will now be entertained with the follies of each other; and, though they allow Cobb and Tib to speak properly, yet they are not much pleased with their tankard, or with their rags: And surely their conversation can be no jest to them on the theatre, when they would avoid it in the street.

   To conclude all, let us render to our predecessors what is their due, without confining ourselves to a servile imitation of all they writ; and, without assuming to ourselves the title of better poets, let us ascribe to the gallantry and civility of our age the advantage which we have above them, and, to our knowledge of the customs and manners of it, the happiness we have to please beyond them. **page 243 /**

John Dryden. "The Grounds of Criticism in Tragedy," *Preface to Troilus and Cressida*, in *The Works of John Dryden*, ed. Sir Walter Scott and George Saintsbury. Edinburgh, 1882–93. Vol. VI.

   Tragedy is thus defined by Aristotle. . . . It is an imitation of one entire, great, and probable action; not told, but represented; which, by moving in us fear and pity, is conducive to the purging of those two passions in our minds. More largely thus: Tragedy describes or paints an action, which action must have all the proprieties above named. First, it must be one or single; that is, it must not be a history of one man's life, suppose of Alexander the Great, or Julius Caesar, but one single action of theirs. This condemns all Shakespeare's historical plays, which are rather chronicles represented, than tragedies; and all double action of plays. . . . The natural reason of this rule is plain; for two different independent actions distract the attention and concernment of the audience, and consequently destroy the intention of the poet; if his business be to move terror and pity, and one of his actions be comical, the other tragical, the former will divert the people, and utterly make void his greater purpose. Therefore, as in perspective, so in tragedy, there must be a point of sight in which all the   **page 260 /**   lines terminate; otherwise the eye wanders, and the work is false. This was the practice of the Grecian stage. But Terence made an innovation in the Roman: all his plays have double actions; for it was his custom to translate two Greek comedies, and to weave them into one of his, yet so, that both their actions were comical, and one was principal, the other but secondary or subservient. And this has obtained on the English stage, to give us the pleasure of variety.

As the action ought to be one, it ought, as such, to have order in it; that is, to have a natural beginning, a middle, and an end. A natural beginning, says Aristotle, is that which could not necessarily have been placed after another thing; and so of the rest. This consideration will arraign all plays after the new model of Spanish plots, where accident is heaped upon accident, and that which is first might as reasonably be last; an inconvenience not to be remedied, but by making one accident naturally produce another, otherwise it is a farce and not a play. . . .

The following properties of the action are so easy, that they need not my explaining. It   page 261 /   ought to be great, and to consist of great persons, to distinguish it from comedy, where the action is trivial, and the persons of inferior rank. The last quality of the action is, that it ought to be probable, as well as admirable and great. It is not necessary that there should be historical truth in it; but always necessary that there should be a likeness of truth, something that is more than barely possible; *probable* being that which succeeds, or happens, oftener than it misses. To invent therefore a probability, and to make it wonderful, is the most difficult undertaking in the art of poetry; for that which is not wonderful is not great; and that which is not probable will not delight a reasonable audience. This action, thus described, must be represented and not told, to distinguish dramatic poetry from epic: but I hasten to the end or scope of tragedy, which is, to rectify or purge our passions, fear and pity.

To instruct delightfully is the general end of all poetry. Philosophy instructs, but it performs its work by precept; which is not delightful, or not so delightful as example. To purge the passions by example, is therefore the particular instruction which belongs to tragedy. Rapin, a judicious critic, has observed from Aristotle, that pride and want of commiseration are the most predominant vices in mankind; therefore, to cure us of these two, the inventors of tragedy have chosen to work upon two other passions, which are fear and pity. We are wrought to fear by their setting before our eyes some terrible example of misfortune, which happened to persons of the highest quality; for such an action demonstrates to us that no condition is privileged from the turns of fortune;   page 262 /   this must of necessity cause terror in us, and consequently abate our pride. But when we see that the most virtuous, as well as the greatest, are not exempt from such misfortunes, that consideration moves pity in us, and insensibly works us to be helpful to, and tender over, the distressed; which is the noblest and most godlike of moral virtues. Here it is observable, that it is absolutely necessary to make a man virtuous, if we desire he should be pitied: we lament not, but detest, a wicked man; we are glad when we behold his crimes are punished, and that poetical justice is done upon him. Euripides was censured by the critics of his time for making his chief characters too wicked; for example, Phaedra, though she loved her son-in-law with reluctancy, and that it was a curse upon her family for offending Venus, yet was thought too ill a pattern for the stage. Shall we therefore banish all characters of villainy? I confess I am not of that opinion; but it is necessary that the hero of the play be not a villain; that is, the characters, which should move our pity, ought to have virtuous inclinations, and degrees of moral goodness in them. As for a perfect character of virtue, it never was in nature, and therefore there can be no imitation of it; but there are alloys of frailty to be allowed for the chief persons, yet so that the good which is in them shall outweigh the bad, and consequently leave room for punishment on the one side, and pity on the other.

After all, if any one will ask me, whether a tragedy cannot be made upon any other grounds than those of exciting pity and terror in us; — Bossu, the best of modern critics, answers thus in general: That all excellent arts, and particu-   **page 263 /**   larly that of poetry, have been invented and brought to perfection by men of a transcendent genius; and that, therefore, they, who practise afterwards the same arts, are obliged to tread in their footsteps, and to search in their writings the foundation of them; for it is not just that new rules should destroy the authority of the old. But Rapin writes more particularly thus, that no passions in a story are so proper to move our concernment, as fear and pity; and that it is from our concernment we receive our pleasure, is undoubted. When the soul becomes agitated with fear for one character, or hope for another; then it is that we are pleased in tragedy, by the interest which we take in their adventures.

Here, therefore, the general answer may be given to the first question, how far we ought to imitate Shakespeare and Fletcher in their plots; namely, that we ought to follow them so far only as they have copied the excellences of those who invented and brought to perfection dramatic poetry; those things only excepted, which religion, custom of countries, idioms of languages, etc., have altered in the superstructures, but not in the foundation of the design.

How defective Shakespeare and Fletcher have been in all their plots, Mr. Rymer has discovered in his criticisms. Neither can we, who follow them, be excused from the same, or greater errors; which are the more unpardonable in us, because we want their beauties to countervail our faults. . . .   **page 264 /**

The difference between Shakespeare and Fletcher, in their plottings, seems to be this; that Shakespeare generally moves more terror, and Fletcher more compassion: for the first had a more masculine, a bolder, and more fiery genius; the second, a more soft and womanish. In the mechanic beauties of the plot, which are the observation of the three unities, time, place, and action, they are both deficient; but Shakespeare most. Ben Jonson reformed those errors in his comedies, yet one of Shakespeare's was regular before him; which is, "The Merry Wives of Windsor." For what remains concerning the   **page 265 /**   design, you are to be referred to our English critic. That method which he has prescribed to raise it, from mistake, or ignorance of the crime, is certainly the best, though it is not the only; for amongst all the tragedies of Sophocles, there is but one, "Oedipus," which is wholly built after that model.

After the plot, which is the foundation of the play, the next thing to which we ought to apply our judgment, is the manners; for now the poet comes to work above ground. The groundwork, indeed, is that which is most neces-

.sary, as that upon which depends the firmness of the whole fabric; yet it strikes not the eye so much, as the beauties or imperfections of the manners, the thoughts, and the expressions.

The first rule which Bossu prescribes to the writer of an heroic poem, and which holds too by the same reason in all dramatic poetry, is to make the moral of the work; that is, to lay down to yourself what that precept of morality shall be, which you would insinuate into the people; as, namely, Homer's (which I have copied in my "Conquest of Granada,") was, that union preserves a commonwealth, and discord destroys it; Sophocles, in his "Oedipus," that no man is to be accounted happy before his death. It is the moral that directs the whole action of the play to one centre; and that action or fable is the example built upon the moral, which confirms the truth of it to our experience. When the fable is designed, then, and not before, the persons are to be introduced, with their manners, characters, and passions.

The manners, in a poem, are understood to be those inclinations, whether natural or acquired, which move and carry us to actions, good, bad, **page 266 /** or indifferent, in a play; or which incline the persons to such or such actions. . . . A poet ought not to make the manners perfectly good in his best persons; but neither are they to be more wicked in any of his characters than necessity requires. To produce a villain, without other reason than a natural inclination to villainy, is, in poetry, to produce an effect without a cause; and to make him more a villain than he has just reason to be, is to make an effect which is stronger than the cause.

The manners arise from many causes; and are either distinguished by complexion, as choleric and phlegmatic, or by the differences of age or sex, of climates, or quality of the persons, or their present condition. They are likewise to be gathered from the several virtues, vices, or passions, and many other commonplaces, which a poet must be supposed to have learned from natural philosophy, ethics, and history; of all which, whosoever is ignorant, does not deserve the name of poet.

But as the manners are useful in this art, they may be all comprised under these general heads: First, they must be apparent; that is, in every character of the play, some inclinations of the person must appear; and these are shown in the actions and discourse. Secondly, the manners must be suitable, or agreeing to the persons; that is, to the age, sex, dignity, and other general heads of manners: thus, when a poet has given the dignity of a king to one of his persons, in all his actions and speeches, that person must discover majesty, magnanimity, and jealousy of power, because these are suitable to the general **page 267 /** manners of a king. The third property of manners is resemblance; and this is founded upon the particular characters of men, as we have them delivered to us by relation or history; that is, when a poet has the known character of this or that man before him, he is bound to represent him such, at least not contrary to that which fame has reported him to have been. Thus, it is not a poet's choice to make Ulysses choleric, or Achilles patient, because Homer has described them quite otherwise. Yet this is a rock on which ignorant writers daily split; and the absurdity is as monstrous as if a painter should draw a coward running from a battle, and tell us it was the picture of Alexander the Great.

The last property of manners is, that they be constant and equal, that is, maintained the same through the whole design: thus, when Virgil had once given the name of *pious* to Aeneas, he was bound to show him such, in all his words and actions, through the whole poem. . . . **page 268 /**

From the manners, the characters of persons are derived; for, indeed, the characters are no other than the inclinations, as they appear in the several persons of the poem; a character being thus defined, — that which dis- tinguishes one man from another. . . . A character, or that which distin- guishes one man from all others, cannot be supposed to consist of one par- ticular virtue, or vice, or passion only; but it is a composition of qualities which are not contrary to one another in the same person. Thus, the same man may be liberal and valiant, but not liberal and covetous; so in a comical char- acter, or humour (which is an inclination to this or that particular folly), Falstaff is a liar, and a coward, a glutton, and a buffoon, because all these quali- ties may agree in the same man; yet it is still to be observed, that one virtue, vice, and passion, ought to be shown in every man, as predominant over all the rest; as covetousness in Crassus, love of his country in Brutus; and the same in characters which are feigned.

The chief character or hero in a tragedy, as I have already shown, ought in prudence to be such a man who has so much more of virtue in him than of vice, that he may be left amiable to the audience, which otherwise cannot have any concernment for his sufferings; and it is on this one character, that the pity and terror must be principally, if not wholly, founded: a rule which is extremely necessary, and which none of the **page 269 /** critics, that I know, have fully enough discovered to us. For terror and compassion work but weakly when they are divided into many persons. If Creon had been the chief char- acter in "Oedipus," there had neither been terror nor compassion moved; but only detestation of the man, and joy for his punishment. . . . But making Oedipus the best and bravest person, and even Jocasta but an underpart to him, his virtues, and the punishment of his fatal crime, drew both the pity and the terror to himself.

By what has been said of the manners, it will be easy for a reasonable man to judge whether the characters be truly or falsely drawn in a tragedy; for if there be no manners appearing in the characters, no concernment for the per- sons can be raised; no pity or horror can be moved, but by vice or virtue; therefore, without them, no person can have any business in the play. If the inclinations be obscure, it is a sign the poet is in the dark, and knows not what manner of man he presents to you; and consequently you can have no idea, or very imperfect, of that man; nor can judge what resolutions he ought to take; or what words or actions are proper for him. Most comedies, made up of accidents or adventures, are liable to fall into this error; and tragedies with many turns are subject to it; for the manners can never be evident, where the surprises of fortune take up all the business of the stage; and where the poet is more in pain to tell you what happened to such a man, than what he was. It is one of the excellences of Shakespeare, that the manners of his persons are **page 270 /** generally apparent, and you see their bent and inclinations. Fletcher comes far short of him in this, as indeed he does almost in everything. There are but glimmerings of manners in most of his comedies, which run upon adventures; and in his tragedies, Rollo, Otto, the King and no King, Melantius, and many others of his best, are but pictures shown you in the twilight; you know not whether they resemble vice or virtue, and they are either good, bad, or indifferent, as the present scene requires it. But of all poets, this commendation is to be given to Ben Jonson, that the manners, even of the most inconsiderable persons in his plays, are everywhere apparent.

By considering the second quality of manners, which is, that they be suitable to the age, quality, country, dignity, etc., of the character, we may likewise judge whether a poet has followed nature. In this kind, Sophocles and Euripides have more excelled among the Greeks than Aeschylus; and Terence more than Plautus, among the Romans. . . . Our Shakespeare, having ascribed **page 271 /** to Henry the Fourth the character of a king and of a father, gives him the perfect manners of each relation, when either he transacts with his son or with his subjects. Fletcher, on the other side, gives neither to Arbaces, nor to his king, in "The Maid's Tragedy," the qualities which are suitable to a monarch; though he may be excused a little in the latter, for the king there is not uppermost in the character; it is the lover of Evadne, who is king only in a second consideration; and though he be unjust, and has other faults which shall be nameless, yet he is not the hero of the play. It is true, we find him a lawful prince (though I never heard of any king that was in Rhodes), and therefore Mr. Rymer's criticism stands good, — that he should not be shown in so vicious a character. Sophocles has been more judicious in his "Antigona;" for, though he represents in Creon a bloody prince, yet he makes him not a lawful king, but an usurper, and Antigona herself is the heroine of the tragedy. . . . **page 272 /** To return once more to Shakespeare; no man ever drew so many characters, or generally distinguished them better from one another, excepting only Jonson. I will instance but in one, to show the copiousness of his invention; it is that of Caliban, or the monster, in "The Tempest." He seems there to have created a person which was not in nature, a boldness which, at first sight, would appear intolerable; for he makes him a species of himself, begotten by an incubus on a witch; but this . . . is not wholly beyond the bounds of credibility, at least the vulgar still believe it. We have the separated notions of a spirit, and of a witch. . . ; therefore, as from the distinct apprehensions of a horse, and of a man, imagination has formed a centaur; so, from those of an incubus and a sorceress, Shakespeare has produced his monster. Whether or no his generation can be defended, I leave to philosophy; but of this I am certain, that the poet has most judiciously furnished him with a person, a language, and a character, which will suit him, both by father's and mother's side: he has all the discontents and malice of a witch, and of a devil, besides a convenient proportion of the **page 273 /** deadly sins; gluttony, sloth, and lust, are manifest; the dejectedness of a slave is likewise given him, and the ignorance of one bred up in a desert island. His person is monstrous, and he is the product of unnatural lust; and his language is as hobgoblin as his person; in all things he is distinguished from other mortals. The characters of Fletcher are poor and narrow, in comparison of Shakespeare's. . . ; so that in this part Shakespeare is generally worth our imitation; and to imitate Fletcher is but to copy after him who was a copyer. . . . **page 274 /**

· ·

If Shakespeare be allowed, as I think he must, to have made his characters distinct, it will easily be inferred that he understood the nature of the passions: because it has been proved already that confused passions make undistinguishable   **page 278 /**   characters: yet I cannot deny that he has his failings; but they are not so much in the passions themselves, as in his manner of expression: he often obscures his meaning by his words, and sometimes makes it unintelligible. I will not say of so great a poet, that he distinguished not the blown puffy style from true sublimity; but I may venture to maintain, that the fury of his fancy often transported him beyond the bounds of judgment, either in coining of new words and phrases, or racking words which were in use, into the violence of a catachresis. It is not that I would explode the use of metaphors from passion, for Longinus thinks them necessary to raise it: but to use them at every word, to say nothing without a metaphor, a simile, an image, or description, is, I doubt, to smell a little too strongly of the buskin. . . .   **page 279 /**

.   .   .   .

To speak justly of this whole matter: it is neither height of thought that is discommended, nor pathetic vehemence, nor any nobleness of   **page 281 /**   expression in its proper place; but it is a false measure of all these, something which is like them, and is not them. . . ; it is an extravagant thought, instead of a sublime one; it is roaring madness, instead of vehemence; and a sound of words, instead of sense. If Shakespeare were stripped of all the bombasts in his passions, and dressed in the most vulgar words, we should find the beauties of his thoughts remaining; if his embroideries were burnt down, there would still be silver at the bottom of the melting-pot: but I fear . . . that we, who ape his sounding words, have nothing of his thought, but are all outside; there is not so much as a dwarf within our giant's clothes. Therefore, let not Shakespeare suffer for our sakes; it is our fault, who succeed him in an age which is more refined, if we imitate him so ill, that we copy his failings only, and make a virtue of that in our writings which in his was an imperfection.

For what remains, the excellency of that poet was, as I have said, in the more manly passions; Fletcher's in the softer: Shakespeare writ better betwixt man and man; Fletcher, betwixt man and woman: consequently, the one described friendship better; the other love: yet Shakespeare taught Fletcher to write love: and Juliet and Desdemona are originals. It is true, the scholar had the softer soul; but the master had the kinder. Friendship is both a virtue and a passion essentially; love is a passion only in its nature, and is not a virtue but by accident: good nature makes friendship; but effeminacy love. Shakespeare had an universal mind, which comprehended all characters and passions; Flet-   **page 282 /**   cher a more confined and limited: for though he treated love in perfection, yet honour, ambition, revenge, and generally all the stronger passions, he either touched not, or not masterly. To conclude all, he was a limb of Shakespeare.

. . . The judgment, which is given here, is generally founded upon experience: but because many men are shocked at the name of rules, as if they were a kind of magisterial prescription upon poets, I will conclude with the words of Rapin, in his Reflections on Aristotle's work "Of Poetry:" "If the rules be well considered, we shall find them to be made only to reduce nature into method, to trace her step by step, and not to suffer the least mark of her to escape us: it is only by these, that probability in fiction is maintained, which is the soul of poetry. They are founded upon good sense, and sound reason, rather than on authority; for though Aristotle and Horace are produced, yet no man must argue, that what they write is true, because they writ it; but 'tis evident, by the ridiculous mistakes and gross absurdities which have been made by those poets who have taken their fancy only for their guide, that if this fancy be not regulated, it is a mere caprice, and utterly incapable to produce a reasonable and judicious poem." **page 283 /**

John Dryden. *Preface to Albion and Albanius*, in *The Works of John Dryden*, ed. Sir Walter Scott and George Saintsbury. Edinburgh, 1882–93. Vol. VII.

If wit has truly been defined, "a propriety of thoughts and words," then that definition will extend to all sorts of poetry: and, among the rest, to this present entertainment of an opera. Propriety of thought is that fancy which arises naturally from the subject, or which the poet adapts to it; propriety of words is the clothing of those thoughts with such expressions as are naturally proper to them; and from both these, if they are judiciously performed, the delight of poetry results. An opera is a poetical tale, or fiction, represented by vocal and instrumental music, adorned with scenes, machines, and dancing. The supposed persons of this musical drama are generally supernatural, as **page 228 /** gods, and goddesses, and heroes, which at least are descended from them, and are in due time to be adopted into their number. The subject, therefore, being extended beyond the limits of human nature, admits of that sort of marvellous and surprising conduct, which is rejected in other plays. Human impossibilities are to be received as they are in faith; because, where gods are introduced, a supreme power is to be understood, and second causes are out of doors; yet propriety is to be observed even here. The gods are all to manage their peculiar provinces; and what was attributed by the heathens to one power ought not to be performed by any other. Phoebus must foretell, Mercury must charm with his caduceus, and Juno must reconcile the quarrels of the marriage-bed; to conclude, they must all act according to their distinct and peculiar characters. If the persons represented were to speak upon the stage, it would follow, of necessity, that the expressions should be lofty, figurative, and majestical: but the nature of an opera denies the frequent use of these poetical ornaments; for vocal music, though it often admits a loftiness of sound, yet always exacts an harmonious sweetness; or, to distinguish yet more justly, the recitative part of the opera requires a more masculine beauty of expression and sound. The other, which, for want of a proper English word, I must call the *songish part*, must abound in the softness and variety of numbers; its principal intention being to please hearing rather than to gratify the understanding. It appears, indeed, preposterous at first sight, that rhyme, on any consideration, should take place of reason; but, in order to resolve the problem, this fundamental proposition must be **page 229 /** settled, that the first inventors of any art or science, provided they have brought it to perfection, are, in reason, to give laws to it; and, according to their model, all after-undertakers are to build. Thus, in epic poetry, no man ought to dispute the authority of Homer, who gave the first being to that masterpiece of art, and endued it with that form of perfection in all its parts that nothing was wanting to its excellency. Virgil therefore, and those very few who have succeeded him, endeavoured not to introduce, or innovate, anything in a design already perfected, but imitated the plan of the inventor; and are only so far true heroic poets as they have built on the foundations of Homer. . . . Now, to apply this axiom to our present purpose, whosoever undertakes the writing of an opera, which is a modern invention, though built indeed on the foundation of ethnic worship, is obliged to imitate the design of the Italians, who have not only invented, but brought to perfection, this sort of dramatic musical entertainment. I have not been able, by any search, to get any light, either of the time when it began, or of the first author: but I have probable reasons, which induce me to believe, that some Italians, having curiously observed the gallantries of the Spanish Moors, at their zambras, or royal feasts, where music, songs, and dancing were in perfection, together with their machines, which are usual at their *sortijas*, or running at the ring, and other solemnities, **page 230 /** may possibly have refined upon those Moresque divertisements, and produced this delightful entertainment, by leaving out the warlike part of the carousals, and forming a poetical design for the use of the machines, the songs, and dances. But however it began, . . . we know that, for some centuries, the knowledge of music has flourished principally in Italy, the mother of learning and of arts. . . . **page 231 /**

It is almost needless to speak anything of that noble language, in which this musical drama was first invented and performed. All who are conversant in the Italian cannot but observe that it is the softest, the sweetest, the most harmonious, not only of any modern tongue, but even beyond any of the learned. It seems indeed to have been invented for the sake of poetry and music; the vowels are so abounding in all words, especially in terminations of them, that, excepting some few monosyllables, the whole language ends in them. Then the pronunciation is so manly, and so sonorous, that their very speaking has more of music in it than Dutch poetry and song. It has withal derived so much copiousness and eloquence from the Greek and Latin, in the composition of words, and the formation of them, that if, after all, we must call it barbarous, it is the most beautiful and most learned of any barbarism in modern tongues; and we may at **page 232 /** least as justly praise it, as Pyrrhus did the Roman discipline and martial order, that it was of barbarians, (for so the Greeks called all other nations,) but had nothing in it of barbarity. This language has in a manner been refined and purified from the Gothic ever since the time of Dante, which is above four hundred years ago; and the French, who now cast a longing eye to their country, are not less ambitious to possess their elegance in poetry and music; in both which they labour at impossibilities. It is true, indeed, they have reformed their tongue, and brought both their prose and poetry to a standard; the sweetness, as well as the purity, is much improved, by throwing off the unnecessary consonants, which made their spelling tedious, and their pronunciation harsh: but, after all, as nothing can be improved beyond its own *species*, or further than its original nature will allow; as an ill voice, though ever so thoroughly instructed in the rules of music, can never be brought to sing harmoniously, nor many an honest critic ever arrived to be a good poet; so neither can the natural harshness of the French, or their perpetual ill accent, be ever refined into perfect harmony like the Italian. The English has yet more natural disadvantages than the French; our original Teutonic, consisting most in monosyllables, and those encumbered with consonants, cannot possibly be freed from those inconveniences. The rest of our words, which are derived from the Latin chiefly, and the French, with some small sprinklings of Greek, Italian, and Spanish, are some relief in poetry, and help us to soften our uncouth numbers; which, together with our English genius, incomparably beyond the trifling of the French, in all the nobler parts of verse, will   **page 233 /**   justly give us the pre-eminence. But, on the other hand, the effeminacy of our pro-nunciation, (a defect common to us and to the Danes,) and our scarcity of female rhymes, have left the advantage of musical composition for songs, though not for recitative, to our neighbours.

Through these difficulties I have made a shift to struggle in my part of the performance of this opera; which, as mean as it is, deserves at least a pardon, because it has attempted a discovery beyond any former undertaker of our nation . . . ; so I may thus far be positive, that if I have not succeeded as I desire, yet there is somewhat still remaining to satisfy the curiosity, or itch of sight and hearing. Yet I have no great reason to despair; for I may, without vanity, own some advantages, which are not common to every writer; such as are the knowledge of the Italian and French language, and the being conversant with some of their best performances in this kind; which have furnished me with such variety of measures, as have given the composer, Monsieur Grabut, what occasions he could wish, to show his extraordinary talent in diversifying the recitative, the lyrical part, and the chorus; in all which, not to attribute any-thing to my own opinion, the best judges, and those too of the best quality, who have honoured his rehearsals with their presence, have no less commended the happiness of his genius than his skill. And let me have the liberty to add one thing, that he   **page 234 /**   has so exactly expressed my sense in all places where I intended to move the passions, that he seems to have entered into my thoughts, and to have been the poet as well as the composer. This I say, not to flatter him, but to do him right; because amongst some English musicians, and their scholars, who are sure to judge after them, the imputation of being a Frenchman is enough to make a party, who maliciously endeavour to decry him. But the knowledge of Latin and Italian poets, both which he possesses, besides his skill in music, and his being acquainted wth all the performances of the French operas, adding to these the good sense to which he is born, have raised him to a degree above any man who shall pretend to be his rival upon our stage. . . .   **page 235 /**

. . . It is no easy matter, in our language, to make words so smooth, and numbers so harmonious, that they shall almost set themselves. And yet there are rules for this in nature, and as great a certainty of quantity in our syllables, as either in the Greek or Latin: but let poets and judges understand those first, and then let them begin to study English. When they have chawed a while upon these preliminaries, it may be they will scarce adventure to tax me with want of thought and elevation of fancy in this work; for they will soon be

satisfied, that those are not of the nature of this sort of writing. The necessity
of double rhymes, and ordering of the words and numbers for the sweetness of
the voice, are the main hinges on which an opera must move; and both of
these are without the compass of any art to teach another to perform, unless
Nature, in the first place, has done her part, by enduing the poet with that nicety
of hearing, that the discord of sounds in words shall as much offend him as a
seventh in music would a good composer. I have therefore no need to make
excuses for meanness of thought in many places: the Italians, with all the advantages of their language, are continually forced upon it, or, rather, affect it.
The chief secret is the choice of words; and, by this choice, I do not here
mean elegancy of expression, but propriety of sound, to be varied according to
the nature of the subject. . . .   **page 236 /**

The same reasons which depress thought in an opera have a stronger effect
upon the words, especially in our language; for there is no maintaining the
purity of English in short measures, where the rhyme returns so quick, and is
so often female, or double rhyme, which is not natural to our tongue, because
it consists too much of monosyllables, and those, too, most commonly clogged
with consonants; for which reason I am often forced to coin new words,
revive some that are antiquated, and botch others; as if I had not served out my
time in poetry, but was bound apprentice to some doggrel rhymer, who makes
songs to tunes, and sings them for a livelihood. It is true, I have not been often
put to this drudgery; but where I have, the words will sufficiently show that I
was then a slave to the composition, which I will never be again: it is my part
to invent, and the musician's to humour that invention. . . .

I am now to acquaint my reader with somewhat more particular concerning
this opera, after having begged his pardon for so long a preface to so short
a work. It was originally intended only for a prologue to a play of the nature
of "The Tempest;" which is a tragedy mixed with opera, or a drama, written
in blank verse, adorned with scenes, machines, songs, and   **page 237 /**   dances,
so that the fable of it is all spoken and acted by the best of the comedians; the
other part of the entertainment to be performed by the same singers and
dancers who were introduced in this present opera. It cannot properly be
called a play, because the action of it is supposed to be conducted sometimes
by supernatural means, or magic; nor an opera, because the story of it is not
sung. . . . But some intervening accidents having hitherto deferred the performance of the main design, I proposed to the actors to turn the intended
prologue into an entertainment by itself, as you now see it, by adding two acts
more to what I had already written. The subject of it is wholly allegorical;
and the allegory itself so very obvious, that it will no sooner be read than
understood. It is divided, according to the plain and natural method of every
action, into three parts. For even Aristotle himself is contented to say simply,
that in all actions there is a beginning, a middle, and an end; after which model
all the Spanish plays are built.

The descriptions of the scenes, and other decorations of the stage I had from
Mr. Betterton, who has spared neither for industry, nor cost, to make this
entertainment perfect, nor for invention of the ornaments to beautify it. . . .
page 238 /

. . . The newness of the undertaking is all the hazard. When operas were first set up in France they were not followed over eagerly; but they gained daily upon their hearers, till they grew to that height of reputation which they now enjoy. The English, I confess, are not altogether so musical as the French; and yet they have been pleased already with "The Tempest," and some pieces that followed, which were neither much better written nor so well composed as this. . . . **page 239 /**

Frontispiece

The curtain rises, and a new Frontispiece is seen, joined to the great pilasters, which are on each side of the stage: on the flat of each basis is a shield, adorned with gold; in the middle of the shield, on one side, are two hearts, a small scroll of gold over them, and an imperial crown over the scroll; on the other hand, in the shield, are two quivers full of arrows saltire, etc.; upon each basis stands a figure bigger than the life; one represents Peace, with a palm in one, and an olive branch in the other hand; the other Plenty, holding a cornucopia, and resting on a pillar. Behind these figures are large columns of the Corinthian order, adorned with fruit and flowers: over one of the figures on the trees is the king's cypher; over the other, the queen's: over the capitals, on the cornice, sits a figure on each side; one represents Poetry, crowned with laurel, holding a scroll in one hand, the other with a pen in it, and resting on a book; the other Painting, with a palette and pencils, etc.: on the sweep of the arch lies one of the Muses, playing on a bass-viol; another of the Muses, on the other side, holding a trumpet in one hand, and the other on a harp. Between these figures, in the middle of the sweep of the arch, is a very large panel in a frame of gold; in this panel is painted, on one side, a woman, representing the City of London, leaning her head on her hand in a dejected **page 245 /** posture, showing her sorrow and penitence for her offences; the other hand holds the arms of the city, and a mace lying under it: on the other side is a figure of the Thames, with his legs shackled, and leaning on an empty urn: behind these are two imperial figures; one representing his present majesty; and the other the queen: by the king stands Pallas, (or wisdom and valour,) holding a charter for the city, the king extending his hand, as raising her drooping head, and restoring her to her ancient honour and glory: over the city are the envious devouring Harpies flying from the face of Majesty: by the queen stand the Three Graces, holding garlands of flowers, and at her feet Cupids bound, with their bows and arrows broken, the queen pointing with her sceptre to the river, and commanding the Graces to take off their fetters. Over the king, in a scroll, is this verse of Virgil —

Discite justitiam, moniti, et non temnere divos.

Over the queen, this of the same author —

Non ignara mali, miseris succurrere disco. **page 246 /**

John Dryden. "Epistle the Twelfth. To My Dear Friend Mr. Congreve, on
his Comedy Called The Double Dealer," in *The Works of John Dryden*,
ed. Sir Walter Scott and George Saintsbury. Edinburgh, 1882–93. Vol. XI.

Well, then, the promised hour is come at last,
The present age of wit obscures the past;
Strong were our sires, and as they fought they writ,
Conquering with force of arms, and dint of wit:
Theirs was the giant race, before the flood;
And thus, when Charles returned, our empire stood.
Like Janus, he the stubborn soil manured,
With rules of husbandry the rankness cured;
Tamed us to manners when the stage was rude,
And boisterous English wit with art endued.
Our age was cultivated thus at length;
But what we gained in skill we lost in strength.
Our builders were with wont of genius curst;
The second temple was not like the first;
Till you, the best Vitruvius, come at length,
Our beauties equal, but excel our strength.
Firm Doric pillars found your solid base;
The fair Corinthian crowns the higher space:
Thus all below is strength, and all above is grace.
In easy dialogue is Fletcher's praise;
He moved the mind, but had no power to raise:
Great Jonson did by strength of judgment please;
Yet, doubling Fletcher's force, he wants his ease.
In differing talents both adorned their age;
One for the study, t'other for the stage.
But both to Congreve justly shall submit,
One matched in judgment, both o'ermatched in wit.
In him all beauties of this age we see,
Etherege his courtship, Southerne's purity,
The satire, wit, and strength, of manly Wycherly.
All this in blooming youth you have achieved;
Nor are your foiled contemporaries grieved.
So much the sweetness of your manners move,
We cannot envy you, because we love.
Fabius might joy in Scipio, when he saw
A beardless consul made against the law,
And join his suffrage to the votes of Rome,
Though he with Hannibal was overcome.
Thus old Romano bowed to Raphael's Fame,
And scholar to the youth he taught became.
    O that your brows my laurel had sustained
Well had I been deposed, if you had reigned:
The father had descended for the son;

For only you are lineal to the throne.
Thus, when the state one Edward did depose,
A greater Edward in his room arose:
But now not I, but poetry, is cursed;
For Tom the second reigns like Tom the first.[1]
But let them not mistake my patron's part,
Nor call his charity their own desert.
Yet this I prophesy, — Thou shalt be seen,
(Though with some short parenthesis between,)
High on the throne of wit, and, seated there,
Not mine, — that's little, — but thy laurel wear.
Thy first attempt an early promise made;
That early promise this has more than paid.
So bold, yet so judiciously you dare,
That your least praise is to be regular.
Time, place, and action may with pains be wrought,
But genius must be born, and never can be taught.
This is your portion, this your native store;
Heaven, that but once was prodigal before,
To Shakespeare gave as much, — she could not give him more.
    Maintain your post; that's all the fame you need;
For 'tis impossible you should proceed.
Already I am worn with cares and age,
And just abandoning the ungrateful stage;
Unprofitably kept at Heaven's expense,
I live a rent-charge on His providence:
But you, whom every muse and grace adorn,
Whom I foresee to better fortune born,
Be kind to my remains; and O defend,
Against your judgment, your departed friend!
Let not the insulting foe my fame pursue,
But shade those laurels which descend to you:
And take for tribute what these lines express;
You merit more, nor could my love do less.

John Dryden. *Preface to Fables, Ancient and Modern. Translated into Verse from Homer, Ovid, Boccace, and Chaucer,* in *The Works of John Dryden,* ed. Sir Walter Scott and George Saintsbury. Edinburgh, 1882–93. Vol. XI.

. . . I shall say the less of Mr. Collier, because in many things he has taxed me justly; and I have pleaded guilty to all thoughts and expressions of mine,

[1] Dryden was succeeded, at the Revolution, in his posts of Poet Laureate and Royal Historiographer by Thomas Shadwell. Upon Shadwell's death in 1692, the post of Laureate was bestowed upon Nahum Tate and that of Historiographer upon Thomas Rymer, with whom Dryden was at odds at this time. The reference to the patron is to the Earl of Dorset, who as Lord Chamberlain was required to grant Dryden's offices to persons in greater political favor. [Ed.]

which can be truly argued of obscenity, profaneness, or immorality, and retract them. If he be my enemy, let him triumph; if he be my friend, as I have given him no personal occasion to be otherwise, he will be glad of my repentance. It becomes me not to draw my pen in the defence of a bad cause, when I have so often drawn it for a good one. Yet it were not difficult to prove, that, in many places, he has perverted my meaning by his glosses, and interpreted my words into blasphemy and bawdry, of which they were not guilty; besides, that he is too much given to horse-play in his raillery, and comes to battle like a dictator from the plough. I will not say, "the zeal of God's house has eaten him up;" but I am sure it has devoured some part of his good manners and civility. It might also be doubted, whether it were altogether zeal which prompted him to this rough manner of proceeding; perhaps, it became not one of his function to rake into the rubbish of ancient and modern plays: a divine might have employed his pains to better purpose, than in the nastiness of Plautus and Aristophanes, whose examples, as they excuse not me, so it might be possibly supposed, that he read them not without some pleasure. They who have written commentaries on those poets, or on Horace, Juvenal, and Martial, have explained some vices, which, without their interpretation, had been unknown to modern times. Neither has he judged impartially betwixt the former age and us. There is more bawdry in one play of Fletcher's, called "The Custom of the Country," than in all ours   page 243 /   together. Yet this has been often acted on the stage, in my remembrance. Are the times so much more reformed now, than they were five-and-twenty years ago? If they are, I congratulate the amendment of our morals. But I am not to prejudice the cause of my fellow poets, though I abandon my own defence: they have some of them answered for themselves; and neither they nor I can think Mr. Collier so formidable an enemy, that we should shun him. He has lost ground, at the latter end of the day, by pursuing his point too far, . . . from immoral plays, to no plays, *ab abusu ad usum, non valet consequentia.* But, being a party, I am not to erect myself into a judge. As for the rest of those who have written against me, they are such scoundrels, that they deserve not the least notice to be taken of them. . . . page 244 /

John Evelyn's life (1620–1706) encompassed the tumultuous times of Charles I, the Cromwells, Charles II, James II, and William and Mary. He studied in England and abroad, traveling extensively on the Continent. In a letter to Robert Boyle in 1659 he proposed the establishment of a college where men might devote themselves to "the promotion of experimental knowledge." From this suggestion developed the Royal Society, which made him a fellow at the first meeting after the Restoration. Indicative of the variety of his interests, his publications include translations from Lucretius, essays on architecture, gardening, economic relations among nations, engraving on copper, the smoke menace in London, and forestry. The most important of his writings in his own time was Sylva, or a Discourse of Forest-Trees, and the Propagation of Timber, which was published in 1664 and reached a fourth edition by 1704. He was a recognized authority on architecture and landscape gardening, as well as an active patron of music and art.

Evelyn's Diary, which was not printed until 1818, was not a diary in the usual sense of the word. Although there are day-to-day records, Evelyn seems to have made most of the entries at odd intervals, using notes or writing from memory. The diary is especially interesting for its intimate portraits of leaders of Restoration society and the less frequent comments on the theaters and social life of London.

John Evelyn. *Memoirs of John Evelyn, . . . comprising his Diary, from 1641 to 1705–6,* ed. William Bray. 4 vols. London, 1827.

5 May. I went to visite my Brother in London, and next day to see a new opera,[1] after ye Italian way, in recitative music and sceanes, much inferior to ye Italian composure and magnificence; but it was prodigious that in a time of such publiq consternation such a vanity should be kept up or permitted. I being engag'd with company could not decently resist the going to see it, tho' my heart smote me for it. *1658-9*

25 Jan. After divers yeares since I had seen any play, I went to see acted "The Scornful Lady," at a new theater in Lincoln's Inn Fields. *1660-1*

11 Nov. I was so idle as to go to see a play call'd "Love and Honor"[2]. . . . *1661*
26 Nov. I saw Hamlet Prince of Denmark played, but now the old plays began to disgust this refined age, since his Majestie's being so long abroad.

[1] Probably Sir William Davenant's Opera, in which the cruelty of the Spaniards in Peru was expressed by instrumental and vocal music, and by art of perspective in scenes, 4to, 1658. See the "Biographia Dramatica."
[2] A Tragi-Comedy by Sir William Davenant; the performance appears to have been in the morning.

16 Dec.   I saw a French Comedy acted at White-hall.

1661-2   9 Jan.   I saw acted "The Third Part of the Siege of Rhodes." In this acted ye faire and famous comedian call'd Roxalana from ye part she perform'd; and I think it was the last, she being taken to be the Earle of Oxford's *Misse* (as at this time they began to call lewd women). It was a recitativa musiq.

16 Jan.   . . . This night was·acted before his Ma^ty "The Widow," a lewd play.

11 Feb.   I saw a comedy acted before ye Dutchesse of York at the Cockpit. The King was not at it.

1662   16 Oct.   I saw "Volpone" acted at Court before their Maties.

20 Nov.   Dined w^h the Comptroller, Sir Hugh Pollard; afterwards saw "The Young Admiral"[3] acted before ye King.

27 Nov.   . . . At night saw acted "The Committee," a ridiculous play of Sir R. Howard, where ye mimic Lacy acted the Irish footeman to admiration.

17 Dec.   I saw acted before ye King "The Law against Lovers."[4]

23 Dec.   I went with Sr George Tuke to hear the comedians con and repeate his new comedy, "The Adventures of 5 Hours," a play whose plot was taken out of the famous Spanish poet Calderon.

1662-3   8 Jan.   I went to see my kinsman, Sir Geo. Tuke's comedy acted at ye Duke's theater, which took so universally, that it was acted for some weekes every day, and 'twas believ'd it would be worth to the comedians 4 or £500. The plot was incomparable, but the language stiffe and formal.

5 Feb.   I saw "The Wild Gallant," a comedy;[5] and was at ye greate ball at Court, where his Ma^ty, the Queene, &c. daunced.

1663-4   5 Feb.   I saw "The Indian Queene" acted, a tragedie well written,[6] so beautified with rich scenes as the like had never ben seen here, or haply (except rarely) elsewhere on a mercenary theater.

27 April.   Saw a facetious comedy called "Love in a Tub.". . .

1665   6 April.   In the afternoone I saw acted "Mustapha," a tragedy written by ye Earle of Orrery.

1666   18 Oct.   . . . This night was acted my Lord Broghill's[7] tragedy called "Mustapha" before their Majesties at Court, at which I was present, very seldom going to the publiq theaters for many reasons, now as they were abused to an atheistical liberty, fowle and undecent women now (and never till now) permitted to appeare and act, who inflaming severall young noblemen and gallants, became their misses, and to some their wives;[8] witness ye Earl of Ox-

---

[3] A Tragi-Comedy by James Shirley.

[4] A Tragi-Comedy by Sir William Davenant, taken almost entirely from Shakespeare's "Measure for Measure," and "Much Ado about Nothing," blended together.

[5] By Mr. Dryden. It did not succeed on the first representation, but was considerably altered to the form in which it now appears.

[6] By Sir Robert Howard and Mr. Dryden.

[7] Richard Lord Broghill, created shortly after this Earl of Orrery; he wrote several other plays besides that here noticed.

[8] Mrs. Margaret Hughes, Nell Gwynn, who left the Earl for his Majesty, to whom were added Mrs. Davis and Mrs. Knight.

ford, Sir R. Howard, Prince Rupert, the Earle of Dorset, and another greater person than any of them, who fell into their snares, to ye reproch of their noble families, and ruine of both body and soule. I was invited by my Lo. Chamberlaine to see this tragedy, exceedingly well written, tho' in my mind I did not approve of any such pastime in a time of such judgments and calamities.

14 March. Saw "The Virgin Queene," a play written by Mr. Dryden. *1667*

4 Feb. I saw ye tragedy of "Horace" (written by ye *virtuous* Mrs. Phillips) *1667–8* acted before their Maties. 'Twixt each act a masq and antiq daunce. The excessive gallantry of the ladies was infinite, those especially on that . . . . Castlemaine, esteem'd at £40,000 and more, far outshining ye Queene.

19 June. To a new play with several of my relations, "The Evening Lover,"[9] *1668* a foolish plot, and very prophane; it afflicted me to see how the stage was degenerated and polluted by ye licentious times.

19 Dec. I went to see ye old play of "Cataline" acted, having ben now forgotten almost 40 yeares.

15 Feb. Saw Mrs. Philips's "Horace" acted againe. *1668–9*

9 Feb. I saw the greate ball danc'd by the Queene and distinguished ladies at *1671* White-hall Theater. Next day was acted there the famous play call'd "The Siege of Granada,"[10] two days acted successively; there were indeede very glorious scenes and perspectives, the worke of Mr. Streeter, who well understands it.

14 Dec. Went to see the Duke of Buckingham's ridiculous farce and rhapsody, called "The Recital,"[11] buffooning all plays, yet prophane enough.

5 Jan. I saw an Italian opera in musiq, the first that had ben in England of this *1673–4* kind.

29 Sept. I saw the Italian Scaramucchio act before ye King at Whitehall, *1675* people giving money to come in, which was very scandalous, and never so before at Court diversions. Having seene him act before in Italy, many yeares past, I was not averse from seeing the most excellent of that kind of folly.

John Evelyn. Epistolary Correspondence, in *Memoirs* . . . , ed. William Bray. 4 vols. London, 1827. Vol. IV.

To my Ld Viscount Cornebery.

. . . My L: You are a pious person, and the Lenten abstinence minds me of another incongruity that you Parliament-men will I hope reforme, & that is the frequency of our theatrical pastimes during that indiction. It is not allow'd in any city of Christendom so much as in this one towne of London, where there

---

[9] There is no play extant with this name; it may perhaps be a second title to one; Mr. Evelyn frequently mentions only one name of a play that has two. Or it may be Dryden's comedy of "An Evening's Love, or The Mock Astrologer," which is indeed sufficiently licentious.
[10] "The Conquest of Granada," by Dryden.
[11] This must mean his play of "The Rehearsal."

are more wretched & obscene plays permitted than in all the world besides. At Paris 3 days, at Rome 2 weekely, & at the other cittys of Florence, Venice, &c. but at certaine jolly periods of the yeare, and that not without some considerable emolument to ye publique; whiles our   **page 134 /**   enterludes here are every day alike; so as the ladys & the gallants come reaking from the play late on Saturday night, to their Sonday devotions; the ideas of the farce possesses their fantsies to the infinite prejudice of devotion, besides the advantages it gives to our reprochfull blasphemers. Could not Friday, & Saturday be spar'd; or, if indulg'd, might they not be employ'd for the support of the poore, or as well the maintenance of some worke-house, as a few debauch'd comedians? What if they had an hundred pound p^r ann. lesse com'ing in; this were but policy in them; more than they were borne too, & the onely meanes to consecrate (if I may use the tearme) their scarse allowable impertinences. If my Lord Chancelor would be but instrumental in reforming this one exorbitancy, it would gaine both the King and his Lo^p multitudes of blessings. You know, my L^d, that I (who have written a play[12] & am a scurvy poet too some times) am far from Puritanisme; but I would have no reproch left our adversaries in a thing which may so conveniently be reform'd. Plays are now wth us become a licentious excesse, & a vice, & neede severe censors that should looke as well to their morality, as to their lines and numbers. . . .   **page 135 /**

Y^r &c.

London, 9 Feb. 1664–65.

page 136 /

[12] *Thyrsander,* a tragi-comedy, . . . which he would "write out faire and reforme if he had leasure."

George Farquhar (1678–1707) gave up an acting career after accidentally stabbing a fellow-actor while performing Guyomar in Dryden's Indian Emperor. He is said to have acted well, though his voice was somewhat thin and he suffered from stage fright. Turning to writing comedy, he produced Love and a Bottle *(1699), which was well received at Drury Lane. His second play,* The Constant Couple, or a Trip to the Jubilee *(1700), is said to have been acted fifty-three times in London and twenty-three in Dublin. His most popular plays were* The Recruiting Officer *(1706) and* The Beaux' Stratagem *(1707). His plays represent a transition from the artificial comedy of the Restoration to the comedy of middle-class life in which a more serious note predominates.*

Farquhar's essay on comedy, in the form of a letter to a friend, represents one of the few attempts to offer an analytical treatment of the nature and function of that genre. *He is critical of the theory of the unities, the excessive veneration for antiquity, and the "rules." Advocating that English plays be written for the entertainment and instruction of English audiences, he protests the practice of borrowing from and imitating foreign models.*

The essay is in general a crticism of popular theatrical practices, a statement of an artistic position, and, incidentally, a source of information concerning customs and social conduct in the theater.

George Farquhar. "A Discourse upon Comedy, In Reference to the English Stage. In a Letter to a Friend," in *The Works of the late Ingenious Mr. George Farquhar.* London, 1760. Vol. I.

... *Poetry* alone, and chiefly the *Drama*, lies open to the Insults of all Pretenders; she was one of Nature's eldest Offsprings, whence by her Birthright, and plain Simplicity, she pleads a genuine Likeness to her Mother; born in the Innocence of Time, she provided not against the Assaults of succeeding Ages; and, depending altogether on the generous End of her Invention, neglected those secret Supports and serpen- **page 82 /** tine Devices us'd by other Arts, that wind themselves into Practice for more subtle and politick Designs: Naked she came into the World, and 'tis to be fear'd, like its Professors, will go naked out.

'Tis a wonderful thing, that most Men seem to have a great Veneration for *Poetry*, yet will hardly allow a favourable Word to any Piece of it that they meet; like your *Virtuoso's* in Friendship, that are so ravish'd with the notional Nicety of the Virtue, that they can find no Person worth their intimate Acquaintance. The Favour of being whipt at School for *Martial's Epigrams*, or *Ovid's Epistles*, is sufficient Privilege for turning *Pedagogue*, and lashing all their Successors; and it would seem, by the Fury of their Correction, that the Ends of the Rod were still in their Buttocks. The Scholar calls upon us for *Decorums* and *Oeconomy;* the Courtier cries out for *Wit,* and *Purity of Stile;* the Citizen for *Humour* and *Ridicule;* the Divines threaten us for Immodesty; and the Ladies will have an Intrigue. Now here are a Multitude of Cricks, whereof the twentieth Person only has read *Quae Genus,* and yet every one is a Critick after his own way; that is, such a Play is best, because I like it. A very familiar Argument, methinks, to prove the Excellence of a Play, and to which an Author wou'd be very unwilling to appeal for his Success! Yet such is the unfortunate State of Dramatick Poetry, that it must submit to such Judgments; and by the Censure or Approbation of such Variety, it must either stand or fall. But what *Salvo,* what Redress for this Inconvenience? Why, without all Dispute, an Author must endeavour to pleasure that Part of the Audience, who can lay the best Claim to a judicious and impartial Reflexion. But before he begins, let him well consider to what Division that Claim does most properly belong. The Scholar will be very angry at me for making that the Subject of a Question, which is self-evident without any Dispute; for, says he, who can pretend to understand Poetry better than we, who have read *Homer, Virgil, Horace, Ovid,* &c. at the   page 83 /   University? What Knowledge can out-strip ours that is founded upon the Criticisms of *Aristotle, Scaliger, Vossius,* and the like? We are the better sort, and therefore may claim this as a due Compliment to our Learning; and if a Poet can please us, who are the nice and severe Cricks, he cannot fail to bring in the rest of an inferior Rank.

I should be very proud to own Veneration for Learning, and to acknowledge any Compliment due to the better sort upon that Foundation; but I am afraid the Learning of the better sort is not confin'd to College Studies; for there is such a thing as Reason without Syllogism, Knowledge without *Aristotle,* and Languages besides *Greek* and *Latin:* We shall likewise find in the Court and City several Degrees, superior to those at Commencement. From all which I must beg the Scholar's Pardon, for not paying him the Compliment of the better sort, (as he calls it;) and in the next Place enquire into the Validity of his Title from his Knowledge of *Criticism,* and the Course of his Studies.

I must first beg one Favour of the Graduate — Sir, here is a Pit full of *Covent-Garden* Gentlemen, a Gallery full of Cits, a hundred Ladies of Court-Education, and about two hundred Footmen of nice Morality, who having been unmercifully teaz'd with a Parcel of foolish, impertinent, irregular Plays all this last Winter, make it their humble Request, that you wou'd oblige them with a Comedy of your own making, which they don't question will give them Entertainment. O, Sir, replies the *Square-Cap,* I have long commiserated the Condition of the *English* Audience, that has been forc'd to take up with such wretched Stuff, as lately has crowded the Stage; your *Jubilees* and your *Foppingtons,* and such irregular Impertinence, that no Man of Sense cou'd bear the Perusal of 'em. I have long intended, out of pure Pity to the Stage, to write a perfect Piece of this Nature; and now, since I am honour'd by the page 84 /   Commands of so many, my Intentions shall immediately be put in Practice.

So to work he goes; old *Aristotle, Scaliger,* with their Commentators, are lugg'd down from the high Shelf, and the Moths are dislodg'd from their

Tenement of Years; *Horace, Vossius, Hiensius, Hedelin, Rapin,* with some half a dozen more, are thumb'd and toss'd about, to teach the Gentlemen, forsooth, to write a Comedy; and here he is furnish'd with *Unity of Action, Continuity of Action, Extent of Time, Preparation, of Incidents, Episodes, Narrations, Deliberations, Didacticks, Patheticks, Monologues, Figures, Intervals, Catastrophes, Chorus's, Scenes, Machines, Decorations,* &c. a Stock sufficient to set up any Mountebank in *Christendom:* And if our new Author would take an Opportunity of reading a Lecture upon the Play in these Terms, by the Help of a *Zany* and a Jointstool, his Scenes might go off as well as the Doctor's Packets; but the Misfortune of it is, he scorns all Application to the Vulgar, and will please the better Sort, as he calls his own. Pursuant therefore to his Philosophical Dictates, he first chooses a single Plot, because most agreeable to the Regularity of Criticism; no matter whether it affords Business enough for Diversion or Surprize. He would not for the World introduce a Song or Dance, because his Play must be one entire Action. We must expect no Variety of Incidents, because the Exactness of his three Hours won't give him Time for their Preparation. The Unity of Place admits no Variety of Painting and Prospect, by which Mischance perhaps we shall lose the only good Scenes in the Play. But no matter for that; this Play is a regular Play; this Play has been examin'd and approv'd by such and such Gentlemen, who are staunch Criticks, and Masters of Art; and this Play I will have acted. Look'e Mr. *Rich,* you may venture to lay out a hundred and fifty Pound for dressing this Play, for it was written by a great Scholar, and a Fellow of a College. **page 85 /**

Then a grave dogmatical Prologue is spoken, to instruct the Audience what should please them; that this Play has a new and different Cut from the Farce they see every Day; that this Author writes after the Manner of the *Ancients,* and here is a Piece according to the Model of the *Athenian Drama.* Very well! This goes off *Hum, Drum, so, so.* Then the Players go to work on a Piece of hard knotty Stuff, where they can no more shew their Art, than a Carpenter can upon a Piece of Steel. Here is the Lamp and the Scholar in every Line, but not a Syllable of the Poet; here is elaborate Language, sounding Epithets, Flights of Words that strike the Clouds, whilst the poor Sense lags after, like the Lanthorn in the Tail of a Kite, which appears only like a Star, while the Breadth of the Player's Lungs has Strength to bear it up in the Air.

But the Audience, willing perhaps to discover his ancient Model, and the *Athenian Drama,* are attentive to the first Act or two; but not finding a true Genius of Poetry, nor the natural Air of free Conversation, without any Regard to his Regularity, they betake themselves to other Work; not meeting the Diversion they expected on the Stage, they shift for themselves in the Pit; every one turns about to his Neighbour in a Mask, and for default of Entertainment now, they strike up for more diverting Scenes when the Play is done: And tho' the Play be regular as *Aristotle,* and modest as Mr. *Collier* cou'd wish, yet it promotes more Lewdness in the Consequence, and procures more effectually for Intrigue, than any *Rover, Libertine,* or *Old Batchelor* whatsoever. At last comes the *Epilogue,* which pleases the Audience very well, because it sends them away, and terminates the Fate of the Poet; the *Patentees* rail at him, the Players curse him, the Town damns him, and he may bury his Copy in *Paul's,* for not a Book-seller about it will put it in Print. **page 86 /**

This familiar Account, Sir, I would not have you charge to my Invention, for there are Precedents sufficient in the World to warrant it in every Particular: The Town has been often disappointed in those Critical Plays, and some Gentlemen, that have been admir'd in their speculative Remarks, have been ridicul'd in the Practick. All the Authorities, all the Rules of Antiquity have prov'd too weak to support the Theatre, whilst others, who have dispens'd with the Criticks, and taken a Latitude in the *Oeconomy* of their Plays, have been the chief Supporters of the Stage, and the Ornament of the *Drama*. This is so visibly true, that I need bring in no Instances to enforce it; but you say, Sir, 'tis a Paradox that has often puzzled your Understanding, and you lay your Commands upon me to solve it, if I can. . . .

But in the first Place I must beg you, Sir, to lay aside your superstitious Veneration for Antiquity, and the usual Expressions on that Score; that the present Age is illiterate, or their Taste is vitiated; that we live in the Decay of Time, and the Dotage of the World is fall'n to our Share — 'Tis a Mistake, Sir; the World was never more active or youthful, and true downright Sense was never more universal than at this very Day; 'tis neither confin'd to one Nation in the World, nor to one Party of a City; 'tis remarkable in *England*, as well as *France*, and good genuine Reason is nourish'd as well by the Cold of *Swedeland*, as by the Warmth of *Italy;* 'tis neither   **page 87 /**   abdicated the Court with the late Reigns, nor expell'd the City with the Play-house Bills; you may find it in the *Grand Jury* at *Hick's Hall*, and upon the Bench sometimes among the Justices; then why should we be hamper'd so in our Opinions, as if all the Ruins of Antiquity lay so heartily on the Bones of us, that we cou'd not stir Hand and Foot: No, no, Sir, *ipse dixit* is remov'd long ago, and all the Rubbish of old Philosophy, that in a Manner bury'd the Judgement of Mankind for many Centuries, is now carry'd off; the vast Tomes of *Aristotle* and his Commentators are all taken to pieces, and their Infallibility is lost with all Persons of a free and unprejudic'd Reason.

Then above all Men living, why should the Poets be hoodwink'd at this rate, and by what Authority should *Aristotle's* Rules of Poetry stand so fix'd and immutable? Why, by the Authority of two thousand Years standing, because thro' this long Revolution of Time the World has still continu'd the same — By the Authority of their being receiv'd at *Athens*, a City the very same with *London* in every Particular, their Habits the same, their Humours alike, their publick Transactions and private Societies *Alamode de France;* in short, so very much the same in every Circumstance, that *Aristotle's* Criticisms may give Rules to *Drury-Lane*, the *Areopagus* give Judgment upon a Case in the *King's Bench*, and old *Solon* shall give Laws to the *House of Commons*.

But to examine this Matter a little further: All Arts and Professions are compounded of these two Parts, a speculative Knowledge, and a practical Use; and from an Excellence in both these, any Person is rais'd to Eminence and Authority in his Calling. . . .   **page 88 /**

Is it reasonable, that any Person that has never writ a Distich of Verses in his Life, should set up for a *Dictator* in Poetry; and without the least Practice in his own Performance, must give Laws and Rules to that of others? Upon what Foundation is Poetry made so very cheap and so easy a Task by these Gentlemen? An excellent Poet is the single Production of an Age, when we

have Crowds of Philosophers, Physicians, Lawyers, Divines, every Day, and
all of them competently famous in their Callings. In the two learned Common-
wealths of *Rome* and *Athens*, there was but one *Virgil* and one *Homer*, yet we
have above a hundred *Philosophers* in each, and most part of 'em, forsooth, must
have a touch at Poetry, drawing it into *Divisions, Subdivisions*, &c. when the
Wit of 'em all set together would not amount to one of *Martial's Epigrams*.
page 89 /

Of all these I shall mention only *Aristotle*, the first and great Lawgiver in this
Respect, and upon whom all that follow'd him are only Commentators. Among
all the vast Tracts of this voluminous Author, we don't find any Fragment of
an Epick Poem, or the least Scene of a Play, to authorize his Skill and Excellence in that Art. Let it not be alledg'd, that for aught we know he was an excellent Poet, but his more serious Studies would not let him enter upon Affairs
of this Nature; for every body knows that *Aristotle* was no *Cynick*, but liv'd
in the Splendor and Air of the Court; that he lov'd Riches as much as others
of that Station, and being sufficiently acquainted with his Pupil's Affection to
Poetry, and his Complaint that he wanted an *Homer* to aggrandize his Actions,
he would never have slipt such an Opportunity of further ingratiating himself
in the King's Favour, had he been conscious of any Abilities in himself for such
an Undertaking; and having a more noble and copious Theme in the Exploits
of *Alexander*, than what inspir'd the blind Bard in his Hero *Achilles*. If his
Epistles to *Alexander* were always answer'd with a considerable Present, what
might we have expected from a Work like *Homer's* upon so great a Subject,
dedicated to so mighty a Prince, whose greatest Fault was his vain Glory, and
that he took such Pains to be deify'd among Men? . . . . **page 90 /**

But stay — Without any further Enquiry into the Poetry of *Aristotle*, his
Ability that Way is sufficiently apparent by that excellent Piece he has left
behind him upon that Subject. . . . **page 91 /**

. . . Now if his Rules Of Poetry were drawn from certain and immutable
Principles, and fix'd on the Basis of Nature, why should not his *Ars Poetica* be
as efficacious now, as it was two thousand Years ago? And why should not a
single Plot, with perfect Unity of Time and Place, do as well at *Lincoln's-Inn-
Fields*, as at the Play-house in *Athens*? No, no, Sir, I am to believe that the
Philosopher took no such Pains in Poetry as you imagine; the *Greek* was his
Mother Tongue, and *Homer* was read with as much Veneration among the
School-Boys, as we learn our *Catechism*: Then where was the great Business
for a Person, so expert in Mood and Figure as *Aristotle* was, to range into some
Order a Parcel of Terms of Art, drawn from **page 92 /** his Observations
upon the *Iliads*, and to call these the Model of an *Epick Poem?* Here, Sir, you
may imagine that I am caught, and have all this while been spinning a Thread
to strangle myself: One of my main Objections against *Aristotle's Criticisms*,
is drawn from his Non-performance in Poetry; and now I affirm, that his Rules
are extracted from the greatest Poet that ever liv'd, which gives the utmost
Validity to the Precept, and that is all we contend for.

Look'e, Sir, I lay it down only for a Supposition, that *Aristotle's* Rules for
an *Epick Poem* were extracted from *Homer's Iliads*, and if a Supposition has
weigh'd me down, I have two or three more of an equal Balance to turn the
Scale.

The great Esteem of *Alexander the Great* for the Works of old *Homer*, is sufficiently testify'd by Antiquity, insomuch that he always slept with the *Iliads* under his Pillow: Of this the *Stagyrick* to be sure was not ignorant; and what more proper Way of making his Court could a Man of Letters devise, than by saying something in Commendation of the King's Favourite? A Copy of Commendatory Verses was too mean, and perhaps out of the Element; then something he would do in his own Way, a Book must be made of the Art of Poetry, wherein *Homer* is prov'd a Poet by Mood and Figure, and his Perfection transmitted to Posterity: And if Prince *Arthur* had been in the place of the *Iliads*, we should have had other Rules for *Epick Poetry*, and Doctor B[lackmo]re had carry'd the *Bays* from *Homer*, in Spight of all the Criticks in *Christendom*. But whether *Aristotle* writ those Rules to compliment his Pupil, whether he would made a Stoop at Poetry, to shew that there was no Knowledge beyond the Flight of his Genius, there is no Reason to allow, that *Homer* compil'd his Heroick Poem by those very Rules which *Aristotle* has laid down: For, granting that *Aristotle* might pick such and such Observations from this Piece, they might be mere Accidents resulting casually from the Composition of the Work, and not　page 93 /　any of the essential Principles of the Poem. How usual is it for Criticks to find out Faults, and create Beauties, which the Authors never intend for such; and how frequently do we find Authors run down in those very Parts, which they design for the greatest Ornament? . . . .

Had *Homer* himself, by the same Inspiration that he writ his Poem, left us any Rules for such a Performance, all the World must have own'd it for authentick. But he was too much a Poet to give Rules to that, whose Excellence he knew consisted in a free and unlimited Flight of Imagination; and to describe the Spirit of Poetry, which alone, in the *True Art of Poetry*, he knew to be as impossible, as for Human Reason to teach the Gift of Prophecy by a Definition.

Neither is *Aristotle* to be allow'd any further Knowledge in *Dramatick*, than in *Epick Poetry: Euripides*, whom he seems to compliment by Rules adapted to the Modes of his Plays, was either his Contemporary, or liv'd but a little before him; he was not insensible how much this Author was the Darling of the City, as appear'd by the prodigious Expence disburs'd by the Publick for the Ornament of his Plays; and 'tis probable, he might take this Opportunity of improving his Interest with the People, indulging their Inclination by refining upon the Beauty of what they admir'd. And besides all this, the Severity of *Dramatick* Rage was so fresh in his Memory, in the hard Usage that his Brother *Sophocles* not long before met with upon the Stage, that it was convenient to humour the reigning wit, lest a second *Aristophanes* should　page 94 /　take him to task with as little Mercy, as poor *Socrates* found at the Hands of the first.

I have talk'd so long to lay a Foundation for these following Conclusions: *Aristotle* was no Poet, and consequently not capable of giving Instructions in the Art of Poetry; his *Ars Poetica* are only some Observations drawn from the Works of *Homer* and *Euripides*, which may be mere Accidents resulting casually from the Compositions of the Works, and not any of the essential Principles on which they are compil'd. That without giving himself the Trouble for searching into the Nature of Poetry, he has only complimented the Heroes of

Wit and Valour of his Age, by joining with them in their Approbation; with this Difference, that their Applause was plain, and his more Scholastick.

But to leave these only as Suppositions to be relish'd by every Man at his Pleasure, I shall without complimenting any Author, either Ancient or Modern, inquire into the first Invention of Comedy; what were the true Designs and honest Intentions of that Art; and from a Knowledge of the *End*, seek out the *Means*, without one Quotation of *Aristotle*, or Authority of *Euripides*.

In all Productions, either Divine or Human, the final Cause is the first Mover, because the End or Intention of any rational Action must first be consider'd, before the material or efficient Causes are put in Execution. Now to determine the final Cause of Comedy, we must run back beyond the material and formal Agents, and take it in its very Infancy, or rather in the very first Act of its Generation, when its primary Parent, by proposing such or such an End of his Labour, laid down the first Sketches or Shadows of the Piece. Now as all Arts and Sciences have their first Rise from a final Cause, so 'tis certain that they have grown from very small Beginnings, and that the Current of Time has swell'd them to such a Bulk, that no Body can find the Fountain, by any Proportion between the Head and the Body; this with the Corrup-   **page 95 /**   tion of Time, which has debauch'd things from their primitive Innocence to selfish Designs and Purposes, render it difficult to find the Origin of any Offspring so very unlike its Parent.

This is not only the Case of Comedy, as it stands at present, but the Condition also of the ancient Theatres; when great Men made Shews of this Nature a rising Step to their Ambition, mixing many lewd and lascivious Representations to gain the Favour of the Populace, to whose Taste and Entertainment the Plays were chiefly adapted. We must therefore go higher than either *Aristophanes* or *Menander*, to discover Comedy in its primitive Institution, if we wou'd draw any moral Design of its Invention to warrant and authorize its Continuance.

I have already mention'd the Difficulty of discovering the Invention of any Art, in the different Figure it makes by Succession of Improvements; but there is something in the Nature of Comedy, even in its present Circumstances, that bears so great a Resemblance to the Philosophical *Mythology* of the Ancients, that old *Æsop* must wear the Bays as the first and original Author; and whatever Alterations or Improvements farther Application may have subjoin'd, his *Fables* gave the first Rise and Occasion.

Comedy is no more at present than a *well-fram'd Tale handsomely told, as an agreeable Vehicle for Counsel or Reproof.* This is all we can say for the Credit of its Institution, and is the Stress of its Charter for Liberty and Toleration. Then where shou'd we seek for a Foundation, but in *Æsop's* symbolical Way of moralizing upon Tales and Fables, with this Difference, That his Stories were shorter than ours? He had his Tyrant *Lyon*, his Statesman *Fox*, his Beau *Magpy*, his Coward *Hare*, his Bravo *Ass*, and his Buffoon *Ape*, with all the Characters that crowd our Stages every Day; with this Distinction nevertheless, That *Æsop* made his Beast speak good *Greek*, and our Heroes sometimes can't talk *English*.
page 96 /

But whatever Difference Time has produc'd in the Form, we must in our own Defence stick to the *End* and *Intention* of his *Fables*. *Utile Dulci* was his

Motto, and must be our Business; we have no other Defence against the Presentment of the *Grand Jury*, and for aught I know it might prove a good Means to mollify the Rigour of that Persecution, to inform the Inquisitors, that the great *Æsop* was the first Inventor of these poor Comedies that they are prosecuting with so much Eagerness and Fury; that the first *Laureat* was as just, as prudent, as pious, as reforming, and as ugly as any of themselves. And that the Beasts which are lugg'd upon the Stage by the Horn are not caught in the City, as they suppose, but brought out of *Æsop's* own Forest. We shou'd inform them, besides, that those very Tales and Fables which they apprehend as Obstacles to Reformation, were the main Instruments and Machines us'd by the wise *Æsop* for its Propagation; and as he would improve Men by the Policy of Beasts, so we endeavour to reform Brutes with the Examples of Men. *Fondlewife* and his young Spouse are no more than the *Eagle* and *Cockle;* he wanted Teeth to break the Shell himself, so somebody else run away with the Meat — The Fox in the Play, is the same with the Fox in the Fable, who stuff'd his Guts so full, that he cou'd not get out at the same Hole he came in; so both *Reynards* being Delinquents alike, come to be truss'd up together. Here are Precepts, Admonitions, and Salutary *Innuendo's* for the ordering our Lives and Conversations, couch'd in these *Allegories* and *Allusions.* The Wisdom of the Ancients was wrapt up in Veils and Figures; the *Ægyptian Hieroglyphicks*, and the History of the Heathen Gods are nothing else; but if these Pagan Authorities give Offence to their scrupulous Consciences, let them but consult the Tales and Parables of our *Saviour* in Holy Writ, and they may find this Way of Instruction to be much more Christian than they imagine: *Nathan's* Fable of the poor Man's Lamb had more Influence on   page 97 /   the Conscience of *David*, than any Force of downright Admonition. So that by ancient Practice and modern Example, by the Authority of Pagans, Jews, and Christians, the World is furnish'd with this so sure, so pleasant, and expedient an Art, of schooling Mankind into better Manners. Now here is the primary Design of Comedy illustrated from its Institution; and the same End is equally alledg'd for its daily Practice and Continuance. Then without all Dispute, whatever Means are most proper and expedient for compassing this End and Intention, they must be the *just Rules of Comedy*, and the true *Art of the Stage*.

We must consider then, in the first Place, that our Business lies not with a *French* or a *Spanish* Audience; that our Design is not to hold forth to ancient *Greece*, nor to moralize upon the Vices and Defaults of the *Roman* Commonwealth: No, no; an *English Play* is intended for the Use and Instruction of an *English* audience, a People not only separated from the rest of the World by Situation, but different also from other Nations, as well in the Complexion and Temperament of the Natural Body, as in the Constitution of our Body Politick: As we are a Mixture of many Nations, so we have the most unaccountable Medley of Humours among us of any People upon Earth; these Humours produce Variety of Follies, some of 'em unknown to former Ages; these new Distempers must have new Remedies, which are nothing but new Counsels and Instructions.

Now, Sir, if our *Utile*, which is the End, be different from the Ancients, pray let our *Dulce*, which is the Means, be so too; for you know that to different Towns there are different Ways. . . . I shall gain my Point a nearer Way, and draw it immediately from the first Principle I set down: *That we have the most unac-* page 98 / *countable Medley of Humours among us of any Nation upon Earth;* and this is demonstrable from common Experience: We shall find a *Wildair* in one Corner, and a *Morose* in another; nay, the Space of an Hour or two shall create such Vicissitudes of Temper in the same Person, that he can hardly be taken for the same Man. We shall have a Fellow bestir his Stumps from *Chocolate* to *Coffee-House* with all the Joy and Gaiety imaginable, tho' he wants a Shilling to pay for a Hack; whilst another, drawn about in a Coach and Six, is eaten up with the Spleen, and shall loll in State, with as much Melancholy, Vexation, and Discontent, as if he were making the *Tour* of *Tyburn*. Then what Sort of a *Dulce* (which I take for the Pleasantry of the Tale, or the Plot of the Play) must a Man make use of to engage the Attention of so many different Humours and Inclinations? Will a single Plot satisfy every Body? Will the Turns and Surprizes, that may result naturally from the ancient Limits of Time, be sufficient to rip open the Spleen of some, and physick the Melancholy of others, screw up the Attention of a Rover, and fix him to the Stage, in Spite of his volatile Temper, and the Temptation of a Mask? To make the Moral instructive, you must make the Story diverting: The Splenetick Wit, the Beau Courtier, the heavy Citizen, the fine Lady, and her fine Footman, come all to be instructed, and therefore must all be diverted; and he that can do this best, and with most Applause, writes the best Comedy, let him do it by what Rules he pleases, so they be not offensive to Religion and good Manners.

But *hic labor, hoc opus;* how must this Secret of pleasing so many different Tastes be discover'd? Not by tumbling over Volumes of the Ancients, but by studying the Humour of the Moderns: The Rules of *English* Comedy don't lie in the Compass of *Aristotle*, or his Followers, but in the Pit, Box, and Galleries. And to examine into the Humour of an *English* Audience, let us see by what Means our own *English* Poets have succeeded in this Point. To determine a page 99 / Suit at Law, we don't look into the Archives of *Greece* or *Rome*, but inspect the Reports of our own Lawyers, and the Acts and Statutes of our *Parliaments;* and by the same Rule we have nothing to do with the Models of *Menander* or *Plautus*, but must consult *Shakespear, Johnson, Fletcher,* and others, who by Methods much different from the Ancients have supported the *English* Stage, and made themselves famous to Posterity. We shall find that these Gentlemen have fairly dispensed with the greatest Part of Critical Formalities; the Decorums of Time and Place, so much cry'd up of late, had no Force of Decorum with them, the Oeconomy of their Plays was *ad libitum*, and the Extent of their Plots only limited by the Convenience of Action. I would willingly understand the Regularities of *Hamlet, Macbeth, Harry the Fourth*, and of *Fletcher's* Plays; and yet these have long been the Darlings of the *English* Audience, and are like to continue with the same Applause, in Defiance of all the Criticisms that ever were publish'd in *Greek* and *Latin*.

But are there no Rules, no Decorums to be observ'd in Comedy? Must we make the Condition of the *English* Stage a State of Anarchy? No, Sir — For there are Extreams in Irregularity, as dangerous to an Author, as too scrupulous a Deference to Criticism; and as I have given you an Instance of one, so I shall present you an Example of the other.

There are a Sort of Gentlemen that have had the jaunty Education of Dancing, French, and a Fiddle, who coming to Age before they arrive at Years of Discretion, make a Shift to spend a handsome Patrimony of two or three Thousand Pound, by soaking in the Tavern all Night, lolling a-bed all the Morning, and sauntering away all the Evening between the two Play-houses with their Hands in their Pockets; you shall have a Gentleman of this Size, upon his Knowledge of *Covent-Garden,* and a Knack of witticising in his Cups, set up immediately for a Play-wright. But besides the Gentleman's Wit, and Expe-   page 100 /   rience, here is another Motive: There are a Parcel of saucy impudent Fellows about the Play-house, called Door-keepers, that can't let a Gentleman see a Play in Peace, without jogging, and nudging him every Minute. *Sir, will you please to pay? — Sir, the Act's done, will you please to pay, Sir?* I have broke their Heads all round two or three Times, yet the Puppies will still be troublesome. Before gad, I'll be plagued with 'em no longer; I'll e'en write a Play myself; by which Means, my Character of Wit shall be established, I shall enjoy the Freedom of the House. . . . My own Intrigues are sufficient to found the Plot, and the Devil's in't, if I can't make my Character talk as wittily as those in the *Trip to the Jubilee* — But stay — what shall I call it first? Let me see — *The Rival Theatres* — Very good, by gad, because I reckon the two Houses will have a Contest about this very Play — Thus having found a Name for his Play, in the next Place he makes a Play to his Name, and thus he begins:

ACT I. *Scene* Covent-Garden. *Enter* Portico, Piazza, *and* Turnstile.

Here you must note, that *Portico* being a Compound of practical Rake and speculative Gentleman, is ten to one the Author's own Character, and the leading Card in the Pack *Piazza* is his Mistress, who lives in the Square, and is Daughter to old *Pillariso,* an odd out o'the-way Gentleman, something between the Character of *Alexander the Great* and *Solon,* which must please, because 'tis new.   page 101 /

Turnstile is Maid and Confident to *Piazza,* who, for a Bribe of ten Pieces, lets *Portico* in at the Back-door; so the first Act concludes.

In the second, enter *Spigotoso,* who was Butler perhaps to the *Czar of Muscovy,* and *Fossetana* his Wife. After these Characters are run dry, he brings you in at the third Act *Whinewell* and *Charmarillis* for a Scene of Love to please the Ladies, and so he goes on without Fear or Wit till he comes to a Marriage or two, and then he writes — *Finis.*

'Tis then whisper'd among his Friends at *Will's* and *Hippolito's,* that Mr. *Such-a-one* has writ a very pretty Comedy; and some of 'em, to encourage the young Author, equip him presently with *Prologue* and *Epilogue.* Then the Play is sent to Mr. *Rich,* or Mr. *Betterton,* in a fair legible Hand, with the Recommendation of some Gentleman, that passes for a Man of Parts, and a Critick: In short, the Gentleman's Interest has the Play acted, and the Gentleman's Interest makes a Present to pretty Miss —— she's made his Whore, and the Stage his Cully, that for the Loss of a Month in Rehearsing, and a Hundred Pound in dressing a confounded Play, must give the Liberty of the House to him and his Friends for ever after.

Now such a Play may be written with all the Exactness imaginable, in Respect of Unity in Time and Place; but if you enquire its Character of any

Person, tho' of the meanest Understanding of the whole Audience, he will tell you 'tis intolerable Stuff; and upon your demanding his Reasons, his Answer is, *I don't like it.* His Humour is the only Rule that he can judge a Comedy by, but you find that mere Nature is offended with some Irregularities, and tho' he be not so learn'd in the *Drama*, to give you an Inventory of the Faults, yet I can tell you, that one Part of the Plot had no Dependence upon another, which made this simple Man drop his Attention and Concern for the Event; and so disengaging his Thoughts from the Business of the Action, he sat there very uneasy, thought　page 102 /　the Time very tedious, because he had nothing to do. The Characters were so incoherent in themselves, and compos'd of such Variety of Absurdities, that in his Knowledge of Nature he could find no Original for such a Copy; and being therefore unacquainted with any Folly they reprov'd, or any Virtue that they recommended, their Business was as flat and tiresome to him, as if the Actors had talk'd *Arabick*.

Now these are the material Irregularities of a Play, and these are the Faults which downright Mother-Sense can ensure and be offended at, as much as the most learn'd Critick in the Pit. And altho' the one cannot give me the Reasons of his Approbation or Dislike, yet I will take his Word for the Credit or Disrepute of a Comedy, sooner perhaps than the Opinion of some *Virtuoso's;* for there are some Gentlemen that have fortify'd their Spleen so impregnably with Criticism, and hold out so stiffly against all Attacks of Pleasantry, that the most powerful Efforts of Wit and Humour cannot make the least Impression. What a Misfortune is it to these Gentlemen to be Natives of such an ignorant self-will'd, impertinent Island, where let a Critick and a Scholar find never so many Irregularities in a Play, yet five hundred saucy People will give him the Lie to his Face, and come to see this wicked Play forty or fifty Times in a Year? But this *Vox Populi* is the Devil, tho', in a Place of more Authority than *Aristotle*, it is call'd *Vox Dei.* Here is a Play with a Vengeance (says a Critick) to bring the Transactions of a Year's Time into the Compass of three Hours, to carry the whole Audience with him from one Kingdom to another, by the changing of a Scene. Where's the Probability; nay, the Possibility of all this? The Devil's in the Poet sure, he don't think to put Contradictions upon us.

Look'e, Sir, don't be in a Passion, the Poet does not impose Contradictions upon you, because he has told you no Lie; for that only is a Lie, which is re-　page 103 /　lated with some fallacious Intention that you should believe it for a Truth: Now the Poet expects no more that you should believe the Plot of his Play, than old *Æsop* design'd the World should think his *Eagle* and *Lion* talk'd like you and I; which, I think, was every Jot as improbable as what you quarrel with; and yet the Fables took, and I'll be hang'd if you yourself don't like 'em. But besides, Sir, if you are so inveterate against Improbabilities, you must never come near the Play-house at all; for there are several Improbabilities, nay Impossibilities, that all the Criticisms in Nature cannot correct: As for Instance; in the Part of *Alexander the Great*, to be affected with the Transactions of the Play, we must suppose that we see that great Conqueror, after all his Triumphs, shun'd by the Woman he loves, and importun'd by her he hates; cross'd in his Cups and Jollity by his own Subjects, and at last miserably ending his Life in a raging Madness: We must suppose, that we see the very *Alexander*, the Son of *Philip*, in all these unhappy Circumstances, else we are not touch'd by the Moral, which represents to us the Uneasiness of Human Life in the greatest State, and the Instability of Fortune in Respect of worldly Pomp, yet the whole Audience at the same Time knows, that this is Mr. *Betterton*, who is strutting upon the Stage, and tearing his Lungs for a Livelihood: And that the same Person should be Mr. *Betterton* and *Alexander the Great* at the same Time, is somewhat like an Impossibility in my Mind. Yet you must grant this Impossibility, in Spite of your Teeth, if you ha'n't Power to raise the old Hero from the Grave to act his own Part.

Now for another Impossibility: The less rigid Criticks allow to a Comedy the Space of an artificial Day, or twenty-four Hours; but those of the thorough Reformation will confine it to the natural or solar Day, which is but half the Time. Now admitting this for a Decorum absolutely requisite; this Play begins when it is exactly Six by your Watch, and **page 104 /** ends precisely at Nine, which is the usual time of the Representation. Now is it feasible, *in rerum natura*, that the same Space or Extent of Time can be three Hours by your Watch, and twelve Hours upon the Stage, admitting the same Number of Minutes, or the same Measure of Sand to both? I am afraid, Sir, you must allow this for an Impossibility too; and you may with as much Reason allow the Play the Extent of a whole Year; and if you grant me a Year, you may give me seven, and so to a Thousand. For that a thousand Years should come within the Compass of three Hours, is no more an Impossibility, than that two Minutes should be contain'd in one. . . .

So much for the Decorum of *Time*, now for the Regularity of *Place*. I might make the one a Consequence of t'other, and alledge, that by allowing me any Extent of Time, you must grant me any Change of Place, for the one depends upon t'other; and having five or six Years for the Action of a Play, I may travel from *Constantinople* to *Denmark*, so to *France*, and home to *England*, and rest long enough in each Country besides. But you'll say, How can you carry us with you? Very easily, Sir, if you be willing to go: As for Example; Here is a new Play, the House is throng'd, the Prologue's spoken, and the Curtain drawn represents you the Scene of *Grand Cairo*. Whereabouts are you now, Sir? Were not you the very Minute before in the Pit in the *English* Play-house talking to a Wench, and now *præsto, pass*, you are spirited away to the Banks of the River *Nile*. Surely, Sir, this is a most intolerable Improbability; yet this you must allow me, or else you destroy the very Constitution of Representation: Then in the second Act, with a Flourish of the Fiddles, I change the Scene to *Astrachan*. *O this is intolerable!* Look'e, Sir, 'tis not a jot more intolerable than the other; for you'll find that 'tis much about the same Distance between *Egypt* and *Astrachan*, as it is between *Drury-* **page 105 /**   *Lane* and *Grand Cairo;* and if you please to let your Fancy take Post, it will perform the Journey in the same Moment of Time, without any Disturbance in the World to your Person. You can follow *Quintus Curtius* all over *Asia* in the Train of *Alexander*, and trudge after *Hannibal*, like a *Cadet*, through all *Italy*, *Spain* and *Africa*, in the Space of four or five Hours; yet the Devil a one of you will stir a Step over the Threshold for the best Poet in *Christendom*, tho' he make it his Business to render Heroes more amiable, and to surprize you with more wonderful Accidents and Events.

I am as little a Friend to those rambling Plays as any body, nor have I ever espous'd their Party by my own Practice; yet I could not forbear saying something in Vindication of the great *Shakespear*, whom every little Fellow that can form an *Aoristus primus* will presume to condemn for Indecorums and Absurdities; Sparks that are so spruce upon their *Greek* and *Latin*, that, like our Fops in Travels, they can relish nothing but what is foreign, to let the World know they have been abroad forsooth; but it must be so, because *Aristotle* said it; now I say it must be otherwise, because *Shakespear* said it, and I'm sure that *Shakespear* was the greater Poet of the two. But you'll say, that *Aristotle* was the greater Critick. — That's a Mistake, Sir, for Criticism in Poetry is no more than Judgment in Poetry; which you will find in your Lexicon. Now if *Shakespear* was the better Poet, he must have the most Judgment in his Art; for every body knows that Judgment is an essential Part of Poetry, and without it no Writer is worth a Farthing. But to stoop to the Authority of either, without consulting the Reason of the Consequence, is an Abuse to a Man's Understanding; and neither the Precept of the Philosopher, nor Example of the Poet, should go down with me, without examining the Weight of their Assertions. We can expect no more Decorum or Regularity in any Business, than the Nature of the thing will bear: **page 106 /** now if the Stage cannot subsist without the Strength of Supposition, and Force of Fancy in the Audience, why should a Poet fetter the Business of his Plot, and starve his Action for the Nicety of an Hour, or the Change of a Scene, since the Thought of Man can fly over a thousand Years with the same Ease, and in the same Instant of Time that your Eye glances from the Figure of six or seven on the Dial-Plate; and can glide from the *Cape of Good Hope* to the *Bay of St. Nicolas*, which is quite cross the World, with the same Quickness and Activity, as between *Covent-Garden Church* and *Will's Coffee-House.* Then I must beg of these Gentlemen to let our old *English* Authors alone — If they have left Vice unpunish'd, Virtue unrewarded, Folly unexpos'd, or Prudence unsuccessful, the contrary of which is the *Utile* of Comedy, let them be lash'd to some purpose; if any Part of their Plots have been independent of the rest, or any of their Characters forc'd or unnatural, which destroys the *Dulce* of Plays, let them be hiss'd off the Stage: But if, by a true Decorum in these material Points, they have writ successfully, and answer'd the End of Dramatick Poetry in every Respect, let them rest in Peace, and their Memories enjoy the Encomiums due to their Merit, without any Reflexion for waving those Niceties, which are neither instructive to the World, nor diverting to Mankind; but are like all the rest of the critical Learning, fit only to set People together by the Ears in ridiculous Controversies, that are not one Jot material to the Good of the Publick, whether they be true or false.

And thus you see, Sir, I have concluded a very unnecessary Piece of Work; which is much too long, if you don't like it: But let it happen any way, be assur'd, that I intended to please you, which should partly excuse,

SIR,

Your most humble Servant. **page 106 /**

Charles Gildon (1665–1724) became a hack writer after squandering a family inheritance. He wrote and edited a number of deistic works, and in 1669 published a continuation of Langbaine's account of the English stage. He gained little fame as an author, although by attacking Alexander Pope in print he achieved some notoriety through Pope's unfavorable references to him in the Dunciad and the Epistle to Arbuthnot. Macaulay characterized him as a "bad writer . . . who lived to pester another generation with doggrel and slander. . . ."

Despite such slighting comments, Gildon is worthy of some note because he published an account which comprises a history of the theaters of the late seventeenth century and a life of Betterton.

[Charles Gildon]. *The Life of Mr. Thomas Betterton, The late Eminent Tragedian.* London, 1710.

As it was said of *Brutus* and *Cassius*, that they were the last of the *Romans;* so it may be said of MR. BETTERTON, that he was the last of our *Tragedians.* . . . **page 1 /**

Whether Mr. *Betterton* or *Roscius* make a just Parallel or not in their Meirits as Actors, is difficult to know; but thus far it is certain, that let the Excellence of the *Roman* be never so great, that of the *Briton* was the greatest we had: and tho we shall find, that in *Cicero's* Time the Decorums of the Stage were more exactly observ'd, than in ours, yet we may suppose Mr. *Betterton,* in his own particular Performance, on a Foot with *Roscius,* especially when we consider that our Player excelled in both *Comedy* and *Tragedy,* the *Roman* only in the former, as far as we can discover. . . . **page 2 /**

Mr. *Thomas Betterton* was born in *Tuttlestreet, Westminster;* his Father being Under-Cook to King *Charles the First:* And when he was now come to Years sufficient, his Father bound him Apprentice to one Mr. *Rhodes* a Bookseller, at the Bible at *Charing-Cross,* and he had for his Under-Prentice Mr. *Kynaston.*

But that which prepar'd Mr. *Betterton* and his Fellow-Prentice for the Stage, was that his Master *Rhodes* having formerly been *Wardrobe* Keeper to the King's Company of *Comedians* in the *Black-Fryars,* on General *Monck's* March to *London,* in 1659. with his Army, got a License from the Powers then in being, to set up a Company of Players in the *Cockpit* in *Drury-lane,* and soon made his Company compleat, his Apprentices, Mr. *Betterton* for Mens Parts, and Mr. *Kynaston* for Womens Parts, being at the Head of them.

Mr. Betterton was now about 22 Years of Age, when he got great Applause by acting in the *Loyal Subject,* the *Wildgoose Chase,* the *Spanish Curate,* and many more. But while our young Actor is thus rising under his Master *Rhodes*, Sir *William D'Avenant* getting a Patent of King *Charles* the Second, for erecting a Company under the Name of the Duke of *York's* Servants, took Mr. *Betterton* and all that acted under Mr. *Rhodes* into his Company. And in the Year 1662. open'd his House in *Lincolns-Inn Fields*, with the first and second part of the **page 5 /** *Siege of Rhodes*, having new Scenes, and Decorations of the Stage, which were then first introduc'd into *England*.

Tho this be affirm'd by some, others have laid it to the Charge of Mr. *Betterton* as the first Innovator on our rude Stage, as a Crime; nay, as the Destruction of good Playing; but I think with very little show of Reason, and very little Knowledge of the Stages of *Athens* and *Rome*, where, I am apt to believe, was in their flourishing times as great Actors as ever play'd here before Curtains. For how that which helps the Representation, by assisting the pleasing Delusion of the Mind in regard of the Place, should spoil the Acting, I cannot imagine.

The *Athenian* Stage was so much adorn'd, that the very Ornaments or Decorations cost the State more Money, than their Wars against the *Persians:* and the *Romans*, tho their Dramatic Poets were much inferiour to the *Greeks*, (if we may guess at those, who are perished by those who remain) were yet not behind them in the Magnificence of the Theatre to heighten the Pleasure of the Representation. If this was Mr. *Betterton's* Thought, it was very just; since the Audience must be often puzled to find the Place and Situation of the Scene, which gives great Light to the Play, and helps to deceive us agreeably, while they saw nothing before them but some *Linsy Woolsy* Curtains, or at best some piece of old Tapistry fill'd with awkerd Figures, that would almost fright the Audience. **page 6 /**

This, therefore, I must urge as his Praise, that he endeavour'd to complete that Representation, which before was but imperfect.

Mr. *Betterton* making now the foremost Figure in Sir *William's* Company among the Men, cast his Eyes on Mrs. *Saunderson*, who was no less excellent among the Female Players, and who being bred in the House of the Patentee, improv'd her self daily in her Art; and having by Nature those Gifts which were requir'd to make a perfect Actress, added to them the Beauty of a virtuous Life, maintaining the Character of a good Woman to her old Age. This Lady therefore Mr. *Betterton* made choice of to receive as his Wife; and this preceeding from a Value he had for the Merits of her Mind, as well as Person, produc'd a Happiness in the married State nothing else could ever have given.

But notwithstanding all the Industry of the Patentee and Managers, it seems the *King's House* then carry'd the vogue of the Town; and the *Lincolns-Inn Fields* House being not so commodious, the Players and other Adventurers built a much more magnificent Theatre in *Dorset Gardens;* and fitted it for all the Machines and Decorations the Skill of those times could afford. This likewise proving less effectual than they hop'd, other Arts were employ'd, and the Political Maxim of *Divide and Govern* being put in Practice, the Feuds and Animosities of the King's Company were so well improv'd, as to **page 7 /** produce an Union betwixt the two Patents. . . . **page 8 /**

. . . .

. . . The Union was effected in 1682. and so continu'd till the Year 1695. when the Actors under the united Patents, thinking themselves aggrieved with

Mr. *Betterton* at the head of them, got a new Licence to set up a Play-house once more in *Lincolns-Inn Fields*. But when the Success of that Company began to give way to the Industry of the other, and Mr. *Vanbrugh* had built a new Theatre in the *Hay-Market*, Mr. *Betterton*, weary of the Fatigues and Toil of Government, deliver'd his Company over to the new Licence. But they again giving way to the new Mode of *Opera's*, the Companies were once more united in *Drury-Lane*, and the *Opera's* confin'd to the *Hay-Market*. But Revolutions being so frequent in this *Mimic State*, Mr. *Swinny* got the chief Players over to him and the *Opera* House, among whom was Mr. *Betterton;* who now being very old, and much afflicted with the Gout, acted but seldom; and the Year before he dy'd, the Town paid a **page 10 /** particular Deference to him by making his Day worth 500*l*. . . .

Being now seventy five Years of Age, and long troubled with the Stone and Gout, the latter at last, by repellatory Medicines, was driven into his Stomach, which prov'd so fatal as in a few Days to put an End to his Life. He was bury'd with great Decency at *Westminster-Abby*. . . . **page 11 /**

. . . .

. . . I am of Opinion, (reply'd Mr. *Betterton*) that the Decay of the Stage is in great measure owing to the long Continuance of the **page 14 /** War; yet, I confess, I am afraid, that too much is deriv'd from the Defects of the Stage it self. When I was a young Player under Sir *William Davenant*, we were under a much better Discipline, we were obliged to make our Study our Business, which our young Men do not think it their duty now to do; for they now scarce ever mind a Word of their Parts but only at *Rehearsals*, and come thither too often scarce recovered from their last Night's Debauch; when the Mind is not very capable of considering so calmly and judiciously on what they have to study, as to enter throughly into the Nature of the Part, or to consider the Variation of the Voice, Looks, and Gestures, which should give them their true Beauty, many of them thinking the making a Noise renders them agreeable to the Audience, because a few of the Upper-Gallery clap the loud Efforts of their Lungs, in which their Understanding has no share. They think it a superfluous Trouble to study real Excellence, which might rob them of what they fancy more, Midnight, or indeed whole Nights Debauches, and a lazy Remisness in their Business.

Another Obstacle to the Improvement of our young Players, is, that when they have not been admitted above a Month or two into the Company, tho their Education and former Business were never so foreign to *Acting*, they vainly imagine themselves Masters of that *Art*, which perfectly to attain, requires a studious Application of a Man's whole Life. They take it there- **page 15 /** fore amiss to have the Author give them any Instruction; and tho they know nothing of the Art of Poetry, will give their Censure, and neglect or mind a Part as they think the Author and his Part deserves. Tho in this they are led by Fancy as blind as Ignorance can make it; and so wandring without any certain Rule of Judgment, generally favour the bad, and slight the good. Whereas it has always been mine and Mrs. *Barry's* Practice to consult e'en the most indifferent Poet in any Part we have thought fit to accept of; and I may say it of her, she has often so exerted her self in an indifferent Part, that her Acting has given Success to such Plays, as to read would turn a Man's Stomach;

and tho I could never pretend to do so much Service that way as she has done, yet I have never been wanting in my Endeavours. But while the young Gentlemen will think themselves Masters before they understand any one Point of their Art, and not give themselves Leisure and Time to study the *Graces of* ACTION *and* UTTERANCE, it is impossible that the Stage should flourish, and advance in Perfection. . . . **page 16 /**

Under the . . . Head of Music, I shall presume to say something of *Opera's*, which have of late been dangerous Rivals of the Drama, tho clogg'd with many adventitious or accidental Absurdities more, than the very *Opera* consider'd in it self contains, tho those are so very many and very visible, that they exclude it from the rational Diversions.

I am sensible, that what I am going to say may look like a Condemnation of my own Practice, when I had the Management of the House, and that is in regard of good Dancing. Yet considering, that I was oblig'd, on Account of Self-Defence, to enter into those Measures, I hope what I say here cannot be look'd on as a Deviation from my own Principle; or if it be, I may be allow'd to alter my Opinion in things of this Nature, when we find great Divines do the same every Day in Matters of far greater Importance. **page 142 /**

I know very well, that in this I shall run against the Stream of the Town, I mean of those, who generally make up the Audience; but then I consider, that I am an old Man, and have contracted such a Value for the *Drama*, by so long a Conversation with it, that I would willingly leave for a Legacy to my Successors, a Stage freed from those intolerable Burthens, under which it groans at present by the Depravity of the Taste of the Audience, which as it has risen in Dignity has (I am afraid) fal'n in Purity and Judgment.

About an hundred Years ago, there were about five or six Play-houses at a Time in this Town, tho at that Time much less extended and populous, than at present, all frequented and full; and the Players got Estates, tho the Stage was yet in its Infancy, rude and uncultivated, without Art in the Poet, or in the Decorations, and supported by the *Lower Sort of People*, and yet these LOWER SORT OF PEOPLE discover'd a natural Simplicity and good Taste, when they were pleas'd and diverted with a Drama so naked, and unassisted by any foreign Advantage.

But in our Times (forgive so bold a Truth) the People of Figure, who in Reason might have been expected to be the Guardians and Supporters of the noblest and most rational Diversion, that the Wit of Man can invent, which at once instructs and transports the Soul, were the first, nay, I may say, the only People, who conspir'd its Ruin, by prodigal Subscriptions for **page 143 /** *Squeaking Italians*, and cap'ring Monsieurs; and the more infamously to distinguish their poor and mean Diversions from those more noble of the Public, they would have no Play at all mingled with them, lest the World should think, that they pay'd any Deference to Poetry, Wit, and Sense; or that their Satisfaction and Delight reach'd farther, than their Eyes and Ears. But what was yet worse, their Taste was so far sunk, that they were pleas'd with what shock'd a nice Ear, and what could not divert a curious Eye. For first, the best of *French Dancers* are without Variety; their Steps, their Posture, their Risings are perpetually the *same* Unmeaning *Motion*; a *French Dancer* being at best but a *graceful Mover*, full of a brisk and senseless Activity, unworthy the Eye of a Man of Sense, who can take no Pleasure worth attending, in which the Mind has not a considerable Share. . . .   page 144 /

. . . .

. . . Since there is no Man, who shall accurately consider the several Species of Dances in   page 154 /   use among the Ancients, but will find, that they did not want the Order of Time, Reason, Proportion, and Musical Harmony, and therefore may be apt to think them not unlike the Hobby-Horse Dancing of our Days, which both Men and Women use for the promoting of Lust; but there is no body but may perceive this Difference between theirs and ours, that theirs were employ'd as Exercises often, and conducive to Health, ours after Supper, Feasts, and in the Night Time. Theirs were always directed to express some Passion or Action, or Story of the Gods or Men, ours to nothing but frisking about to shew a useless Activity. And yet how much greater Deference has been paid to *L'Abbe, Ballon, Subligniy,* and the rest, than to *Otway, Shakespear,* or *Johnson?* And while our own Poets were neglected, the *French* Dancers got Estates; and this by the Influence of those, who at the same Expence might have made their own Names and their Country famous for the Encouragement of the politest Arts and Sciences, now neglected to a Degree of Barbarity, greater, than most Nations on this side *Lapland.* . . . page 155 /

It must . . . be allow'd, that Music discovers a wonderful Power, a Power not to be resisted; but I am afraid, that Power acts more on the Body, than the Mind, or by the Body on the Mind; the Ear has a pleasing Sensation at melodious Sounds, and that gratifies the Mind, which cannot naturally be uneasy when the Body is delighted with agreeable Sensations: But this proves Music as transporting, as it is to be but a sensual Pleasure, and deriving no part from Reason, nor directing any part to the Gratification of the rational Soul. But then this Power and Force of *Music* is heighten'd by the Addition of Poetry, which among the Ancients even in Dancing . . . was very seldom left out; for passionate Words give a double Vigour to Harmony, and make for it a surer way to the Heart, than when the Soul is unconcern'd in the bare and solitary Notes. And Vocal Music is agreed by all to be the most noble, and most touching, that Tone being esteem'd the most excellent, which comes nearest to *Vocal Sounds.*   page 157 /

Music therefore ought still, as originally it was, to be mingled with the *Drama,* where it is subservient to Poetry, and comes into the Relief of the Mind, when that has been long intense on some noble Scene of Passion, but ought never to be a separate Entertainment of any Length.

But tho we allow the Vocal the Preheminence of all other sorts of Music, yet we cannot without the greatest Absurdities receive even that on Subjects improper for it, or in a manner unnatural, that is, as it is offer'd to us in our *Opera's,* with which of late the Town (I mean the leading part of the Audience) has been perfectly intoxicated, and in that drunken Fit has thrown away more Thousands of Pounds for their Support, than would have furnish'd us with the best Poetry, and the best Music in the World, without declaring against common Sense. *Opera's* have been said to be the Invention of modern *Italy,* e'er the Return of Learning, and in the midst of that barbarous Ignorance, with which the Inundations of *Vandals, Goths, Huns* and *Lombards* had o'er-whelm'd it; but I think it is pretty plain, that the *Romans* were, before that, sunk as far from their ancient Learning and Sense, as Virtue and Warlike Glory; and *Lucian* puts it beyond Controversy, that the Entertainment, which we now call *Opera's*, was in use in his Time. . . . **page 158 /**

. . . .

. . . I think the Degeneracy of the Age is but too apparent, in the setting up and encouraging so paltry a Diversion, that has nothing in it either manly or noble.

But, says a certain Gentleman, the Business of the Stage is to *please*, and if this Pleasure be found in *Opera's*, what signifie all the objected Absurdities? Tho this be a very ridiculous De- **page 169 /** fence, and will hold of the most scandalous and dullest things in Nature; yet I have heard it urg'd by Men of allow'd Wit, and indeed, who had more of that, than of Reason, and Judgment, which is founded on that. But if this be really a good Argument, *Clinch* of *Barnet, Bartholomew-Fair* Drolls, nay a *Jack-pudding* Entertainment in *Moor-Fields* are noble Entertainments, for all these please, and have as good a Title to the Stage, as *Opera's*, nay, from Reason a better, as not subject to so many Absurdities. But this is consecrated by the Taste of Quality. — If the Taste of Quality sink to that of the *Canaille*, it is not the Persons can give it a Reputation, since their beloved *Cowley* has told us of a *great Vulgar*, as well as *small*.

Would therefore a Man of Sense be for a Diversion, which levels his Under-standing with that of the Refuse of the *Mob?* Yet the following of *Opera's* does this, and insisting in their Vindication, that what-ever pleases deserves Encouragment, since it is a Scandal to be pleas'd with some things, as proving but a weak Capacity, or a very unpolish'd Taste.

There are some Pleasures, which none but Men of fine Sense, and a Gust for the Art, can distinguish, as in Painting, Graving, &c. while the Vulgar look with an equal Eye on the best and the worst. A certain Country Squire of my Acquaintance was drinking in a Country Ale-house, in which seeing several notable Cuts, as of the *Prodigal, Robin Hood* and *Little John*, **page 170 /** and some other scurvy Prints, worse than ever *Overton* sold, he turn'd to the Gentleman, who sate next him, and said, — *Well! this Painting is a noble Art* — And indeed a Graving of old *Vanhove's*, or worse, if any worse can be, would please the *Vulgar*, as well as one of *Edlinch, Audrand*, or any of the *Italian* Cuts; and a piece of a mere Sign-Dauber is as valuable in the Eye of a gross and common Understanding, as one of *Raphael's* or *Thornhill's*. And so in *Music*, a *Taber* and *Pipe*, a *Cymbal* or *Horn-pipe*, will ravish the Mob, more than the admirable Mr. *Shoar* with his incomparable *Lute;* and the Ballad Tune *Lilly Bullero* more, than a fine *Sonato* of *Corelli*. And thus in Poetry, the *Million* will prefer *Bunnyan* and *Quarles* to *Milton* and *Dryden;* yet sure no Gentleman of fine Taste and Genius in all these things, but would be asham'd to urge such an Argument as Pleasing, since all these, which are scandalous, *please* the most in Number.

It is therefore as scandalous to be pleas'd with any thing irrational and absurd on the Stage, in Comparison of the *Drama*, as with *Jack-pudding*, or a *Bartholomew Droll* off it; or to prefer to *Edlinch, Audrand* a *Vanhove*, &c.

or a Consort of Tongs and Keys, or Cymbal and Bagpipe to Mr. *Shoar's* Lute, or the Compositions of *Corelli*.

But, says another, if All that is absurd and irrational should be excluded the Theatre, you must banish a great many of the most celebrated   **page 171 /** Pieces of the Stage; as, *Othello*, which is compos'd of Parts shocking to Reason, and full of Absurdities; the *Maid's Tragedy*, which Mr. *Rhimer* has justly condemn'd, and several others, which no Man has been able to vindicate from Faults equal to those urg'd against *Opera's*. And since our Reason must be shock'd either with *Harmony*, or without it, pray let us have *Opera's*, where the Composer's pleasing Art makes Amends for the Poet's Fooleries. Nay, says another, I will undertake to prove, that there is scarce one Play, that has met tolerable Success, or is very much esteem'd, and call'd a Stock-Play, but what is as absurd, and shocking to Reason, as most *Opera's;* and what is worse, the Authority, which they have obtain'd with the *Many* is so great, that when you attempt to speak against them, both your *Wits* and *Witlings* cry out, *That you're past Shame.*

If indeed, pursues he, you could advance the *British* Stage to the Excellence of that of *Athens*, it would want neither *Reason* nor *Music*, but the happy Mixture would be admirable, and the Diversion divine; but as the Stage is, both in Players and Plays, I cannot discover so mighty a Difference in the Merit of the two Diversions, but that a Man's Sense is as justifiable in the frequenting the one, as the other.

I must confess, this last Objection has too much Weight in it, but then if the Encouragers of this Folly had bestow'd half as much in the Reformation of the Stage, it would have rais'd   **page 172 /** it to an Equality with, if not above that of *Athens* it self, tho that State employ'd immense Sums in the Decorations of it, and the setting out of the Plays; and if any one Man of Power and Interest would heartily engage on the Part of good Sense, Poetry, and the Honour of his Country, we should soon remove this Objection, and discard the Dregs of *Italy* with their harmonious Nonsense.

But there are others, who tell us, that it is the Illness of our present Plays, that excuses their Fondness of *Opera's*. But this is without the least Shadow of Reason or Truth; nor can they in any point prove our Plays to be worse, than those of an hundred Years ago, since it would be too palpable an Instance of their profound Ignorance or extravagant Prejudice, which is below a Man of Sense and Judgment, as may easily be made appear in Tragedy only, of which we are scarce *yet* arriv'd to a just Notion. Nor was there much of Comedy known before the Learned *Ben Johnson*, for no Man can allow any of *Shakespear's* Comedies, except the *Merry Wives of* Windsor. There are indeed excellent Humours scatter'd about, and interwoven in his other Plays; but *Ben Johnson* was the first, that ever gave us one entire Comedy. Since him we have had *Etheridge*, *Wicherly*, *Shadwel*, and *Crown* in some of his Plays, with the Rest of King *Charles* the IId's Reign. Add since the Revolution, Mr. *Congreve* in three Plays has merited great Praise, and very well distinguish'd **page 173 /** his Characters and hit true Humour. Mr. *Vanbrook* too has shewn Abundance of rude, unconducted and unartful Nature; his Dialogue is generally dramatic and easy. Nay, after these our very Farce Writers deserve more Esteem, than the taking Plays of an hundred Years ago, as having as much Nature, more Design and Conduct, and much more Wit.

From hence it appears, that this Objection of the Degeneracy of the present Stage, from what it was formerly, as an Excuse for frequenting *Opera's,* is nothing but a mere groundless Pretence; and that if we met now with as much Encouragement from our dignify'd Audience, as that did from the Vulgar; or if our Judges could distinguish betwixt *good* and *bad* so far, as to encourage the former, and explode the latter, they would soon have Plays more worthy the *English* Genius, and *Opera's* would retire beyond the *Alps.* . . . .   **page 174 /**

Gerard Langbaine (1656–1692) was a critic, historian, and biographer of the English theater. In his first work, Momus Triumphans, or the Plagiaries of the English State exposed . . . (1687), he described himself as a devotee of the theater as well as an omnivorous collector and reader of plays. He noted that he owned nearly a thousand copies of plays, masques, drolls, and interludes. His best-known work is An Account of the English Dramatic Poets, or some Observations and Remarks on the Lives and Writings of all those that have published either Comedies, Tragedies, Tragicomedies, Pastorals, Masques, Interludes, Farces, or Operas, in the English Tongue *(1691). Langbaine is not always an accurate or an objective viewer; for example, as an admirer and personal friend of Shadwell, he is rather severe with Dryden, who in* Mac Flecknoe *had satirized Shadwell as the "true-blue Protestant poet." Still, his biographical, anecdotal, and descriptive accounts of the notable writers and players constitute an invaluable supplement to Downes and Wright.*

Gerard Langbaine. *An Account of the English Dramatick Poets.* Oxford, 1691.

John Dryden, Esq;

A Person whose writings have made him remarkable to all sorts of Men, as being for a long time much read, and in great Vogue. It is no wonder that the Characters given of him, by such as are, or would be thought Wits, are various; since even those, who are generally allow'd to be such, are not yet agreed in their Verdicts. And as their Judgments are different, as to his Writings; so are their Censures no less repugnant to the Managery of his Life, some excusing what these condemn, and some exploding what those commend: So that we can scarce find them agreed in any One thing, save this, That he was Poet Laureat and Historiographer to His late Majesty. For this, and other Reasons, I shall wave all Particularities of his Life; and let pass the Historiographer, that I may keep the closer to the Poet, toward whom I shall use my accustom'd Freedome; and having spoken my Sentiments of his Predecessors Writings, shall venture without partiality, to exercise my slender Judgment in giving a Censure of his Works.

Mr. *Dryden* is the most Voluminous Dramatick Writer of our Age, he having already extant above Twenty Plays of his own writing, as the Title-page of each would perswade the World; tho' some people have been so bold as to call the Truth of this in question, and to   **page 130 /**   propogate in the world another Opinion.

His Genius seems to me to incline to Tragedy and Satyr, rather than Comedy: and methinks he writes much better in *Heroicks*, than in *blank Verse*. His very Enemies must grant that *there* his Numbers are sweet, and flowing; that he has with success practic'd the new way of Versifying introduc'd by his Predecessor Mr. *Waller*, and follow'd since with success, by Sr. *John Denham*, and others. But for Comedy, he is for the most part beholding to French Romances and Plays, not only for his Plots, but even a great part of his Language: tho' at the same time, he has the confidence to prevaricate, if not flatly deny the Accusation, and equivocally to vindicate himself; as in the Preface to the *Mock Astrologer:* where he mentions *Thomas Corneille's le Feint Astrologue* becaus'd 'twas translated, and the Theft prov'd upon him; but never says One word of *Molliere's Depit amoreux*, from whence the greatest part of *Wild-blood* and *Jacinta*, (which he owns are the chiefest parts of the Play) are stollen. I cannot pass by his Vanity[1] in saying, 'That those who have called *Virgil*, *Terence* and *Tasso*, Plagiaries (tho' they much injur'd them) had yet a better Colour for their Accusation: nor his Confidence in sheltring himself under the protection of their great Names, by affirming, 'That he is able to say the same for his Play, that he urges for their Poems; *viz.* That the body of his Play is his own, and so are all the Ornaments of   page 131 / Language, and Elocution in them.' I appeal only to those who are vers'd in the French Tongue, and will take the pains to compare this Comedy with the French Plays above-mention'd; if this be not somewhat more than Mental Reservation, or to use one of his own Expressions,[2] *A Sophisticated Truth, with an allay of Lye in't.*

Nor are his Characters less borrow'd in his Tragedies, and the serious parts of his Tragi-Comedies. . . . It shall suffice me at present, to shew how Magisterially he huffs at, and domineers over, the French in his Preface to the *Conquest of Granada.* 'I shall never (says he) subject my Characters to the *French* Standard; where Love and Honour are to be weigh'd by Drams and Scruples: yet, where I have design'd the patterns of exact Virtue, such as in this Play are the Parts of *Almahide*, of *Ozmyn*, and *Benzaida*, I may safely challenge the best of theirs.' Now the Reader is desir'd to observe that all the Characters of that Play are stollen from the French: so that Mr. *Dryden* took a secure way to Conquest, for having robb'd them of their Weapons, he might safely challenge them and beat them too. . . .   page 132 /

But had he only extended his Conquests over the *French* Poets, I had not medled in this Affair, and he might have taken part with *Achilles*, and *Rinaldo*, against *Cyrus*, and *Oroondates*, without my engaging in this Forreign War: but when I found him flusht with his Victory over the great *Scudery*, and with *Almanzor's* assistance triumphing over the noble Kingdome of *Granada;* and not content with Conquests abroad, like another *Julius Cæsar*, turning his Arms upon his own Country; and as if the proscription of his Contemporaries Reputation, were not sufficient to satiate his implacable thirst after Fame, endeavouring to demolish the Statues and Monuments of his Ancestors, the Works of those his Illustrious Predecessors, *Shakespear, Fletcher*, and *Johnson:* I was resolv'd

---

[1] Preface to *Mock Astrologer.*
[2] *Love in a Nunnery.*

to endeavour the rescue and preservation of those excellent Trophies of Wit, by raising the *Posse-comitatus* upon this Poetick *Almanzor*, to put a stop to his Spoils upon his own Country-men. Therefore I present my self a Champion in the Dead Poets Cause, to vindicate their Fame, with the same Courage, tho' I hope different Integrity than *Almanzor* engag'd in defence of Queen *Almahide*, when he bravely Swore like a *Hero*, that his Cause was right, and She was innocent; **page 133 /** tho' just before the Combat, when alone, he own'd he knew her false:[3]

> *I have out-fac'd my self, and justify'd*
> *What I knew false to all the World beside.*
> *She was as Faithless as her Sex could be;*
> *And now I am alone, she's so to me.*

But to wave this digression, and proceed to the Vindication of the Ancients; which that I may the better perform, for the Readers Diversion, and that Mr. *Dryden* may not tell me, that what I have said, is but *gratis dictum*, I shall set down the Heads of his Depositions against our ancient English Poets, and then endeavour the Defence of those great Men, who certainly deserv'd much better of Posterity, than to be so disrespectively treated as he has used them.

Mr. *Shakespear* as first in Seniority I think ought to lead the Van, and therefore I shall give you his Account of him as follows:[4] '*Shakespear* who many times has written better than any Poet in any Language, is yet so far from writing Wit always, or expressing that Wit according to the dignity of the Subject, that he writes in many places below —— the dullest Writers of ours, or any precedent Age. He is the very *Janus* of Poets; he wears almost every where two Faces; and you have scarce begun to admire the One, e're you despise the other.' Speaking of Mr. *Shakespear's* Plots, he says they were lame,[5] and that **page 134 /** 'many of them were made up of some ridiculous, incoherent Story, which in one Play, many times took up the business of an Age. I suppose (says he) I need not name *Pericles* Prince of *Tyre*, nor the Historical Plays of *Shakespear*; Besides many of the rest, as the *Winters Tale*, *Love's Labour lost*, *Measure for Measure*, which were either grounded on Impossibilities, or at least so meanly written, that the Comedy neither caused your Mirth, nor the serious part your Concernment.' He says further,[6] 'Most of *Shakespear's* Plays, I mean the Stories of them, are to be found in the *Heccatomouthi*, or *Hundred Novels of Cinthio*. I have my self read in his Italian, that of *Romeo* and *Juliet*; *The Moor of Venice*, and many others of them.'

He Characterises Mr. *Fletcher*, who writ after Mr. *Shakespear*,[7] 'As a Person that neither understood correct Plotting, nor that which they call *The Decorum of the Stage*:' of which he gives several Instances out of *Philaster*, *Humourous Lieutenant*, and *Faithful Shepherdess*; which are too long to be here inserted. In another place he speaks of *Fletcher* thus;[8] 'Neither is the Luxuriance of

---

[3] Act 5. Sc. 1.
[5] *Ibid.*
[7] Postscript.

[4] Postscript to *Granada*.
[6] Preface to *Mock Astrologer*.
[8] *Ibid.*

Fletcher a less fault than the Carelessness of *Shakespear*. He does not well always, and when he does, he is a true English-man; he knows not when to give over. If he wakes in one Scene, he commonly slumbers in another: and if he pleases you in the first three Acts, he is fre- **page 135 /** quently so tired with his Labour, that he goes heavily in the Fourth, and sinks under his Burthen in the Fifth.' Speaking of his Plots,[9] he says, '*Beaumont and Fletcher* had most of theirs from *Spanish* Novels: witness *The Chances, The Spanish Curate, Rule a Wife and have a Wife, The little French Lawyer,* and so many others of them as compose the greatest part of their Volume in Folio.'

As to the great *Ben Johnson* he deals not much better with him, though he would be thought to admire him; and if he praise him in one Page, he wipes it out in another: thus tho' he calls him '*The most Judicious of Poets*,[10] and *Inimitable Writer*,' yet, he says, 'his Excellency lay in the low Characters of Vice, and Folly. When at any time (says he) *Ben* aim'd at Wit in the stricter sence, that is sharpness of Conceit, he was forc'd to borrow from the Ancients, (as to my Knowledge he did very much from *Plautus:*) or when he trusted himself alone, often fell into meanness of expression. Nay he was not free from the lowest and most groveling Kind of Wit, which we call *Clenches;* of which *Every Man in his Humour* is infinitely full, and which is worse, the wittiest Persons in the Dramma speak them.'

These are his own Words, and his Judgment of these three Great Men in particular, now take his Opinion of them all in general, which is as follows;[11] 'But Malice and Par- **page 136 /** tiality set apart, let any Man, who understands English, read diligently the Works of *Shakespear* and *Fletcher;* and I dare undertake that he will find in every Page, either some *Solecisme* in Speech, or some notorious flaw in Sence.' In the next Page, speaking of their Sence and Language, he says, 'I dare almost challenge any Man to shew me a Page together which is correct in both. As for *Ben Johnson* I am loath to name him, because he is a most judicious Author, yet he often falls into these Errors.' Speaking of their Wit, he gives it this Character,[12] 'I have always acknowledg'd the Wit of our Predecessors, with all the Veneration that becomes me; but I am sure, their Wit was not that of Gentlemen; there was ever somewhat that was Ill-bred and Clownish in it: and which confest the Conversation of the Authors.' Speaking of the advantage which acrues to our Writing, from Conversation, he says,[13] 'In the Age wherein those Poets liv'd, there was less of Gallantry, than in ours; neither did they keep the best Company of theirs. Their Fortune has been much like that of *Epicurus,* in the Retirement of his Gardens: to live almost unknown, and to be Celebrated after their Decease. I cannot find that any of them were Conversant in Courts, except *Ben Johnson:* and his *Genius* lay not so much that way, as to make an Improvement by it.' He gives this Character of their Audiences;[14] 'They knew no better, and there-fore were satisfied **page 137 /** with what they brought. Those who call theirs *The Golden Age of Poetry,* have only this Reason for it, that they were then content with Acorns, before they knew the use of Bread. . . .'

These are Errors which Mr. *Dryden* has found out in the most Correct

---

[9] Pref. *Astrol.*   [10] Postscript.   [11] Postscript.
[12] *Ibid.*   [13] *Ibid.*   [14] *Ibid.*

Dramatick Poets of the last Age, and says[15] in defence of our present Writers, That if they reach not some of the Excellencies of *Ben Johnson*, yet at least they are above that Meanness of Thought which he has tax'd, and which is so frequent in him.

After this he falls upon the Gentlemen of the last Age in a Character, which (as Bayes says) is sheer point and Satyr throughout;[16] for after having Droll'd upon them, calling them *Old Fellows, Grave Gentlemen*, &c. he summes up his Evidence, and sings an *Io Triumphe;* ascribing his Victory to the Gallantry and Civility of this Age, and to his own Knowledge of the Customs and Manners of it.

I must do Mr. *Dryden* this justice, to acquaint the World, that here, and there in this *Postscript*, he intersperses some faint Praises of these Authors; and beggs the Reader's Pardon for accusing them,[17] 'Desiring him to consider that he lives in Age where his least faults are severely censur'd, and that he has no way left to extenuate his failings, but by shewing as great in those whom he admires.'

Whether this be a sufficient Excuse or no, I leave to the Criticks: but sure I am that this   **page 138 /**   procedure seems exactly agreeable to the Character which an ingenious Person draws of a Malignant Wit,[18] 'Who conscious of his own Vices, and studious to conceal them, endeavours by Detraction to make it appear that others also of greater Estimation in the world, are tainted with the same or greater: as Infamous Women generally excuse their personal Debaucheries, by incriminating upon their whole Sex, callumniating the most Chast and Virtuous, to palliate their own dishonour.'

· ·

page 139 /

. . . It seems he has follow'd *Horace*, whom he boasts to have   **page 140 /** studied,[19] and whom he has imitated in his greatest Weakness, I mean his Ingratitude: if at least that excellent Wit could be guilty of a Crime, so much below his Breeding; for the very suspicion of which, *Scaliger* (who like Mr. *Dryden* seldome spares any man,) has term'd him Barbarous[20]. . . . Mr. *Dryden* having imitated the same Fact, certainly he deserves the same punishment: and if we may not with *Scaliger* call him Barbarous, . . . yet all ingenious Men, that know how he has dealt with *Shakespear*, will count him ungrateful; who by furbishing up an Old Play, witness *The Tempest*, and *Troilus and Cressida*, has got more on the third Day, than its probable, ever *Horace* receiv'd from his Patron for any One Poem in all his Life. The like Debt he stands engag'd for to the *French* for several of the Plays, he has publisht; which if they exceed Mr. *Shakespear* in Oeconomy, and Contrivance, 'tis that Mr. *Dryden's* Plays owe their Advantage to his skill in the French Tongue, or to the Age, rather than his own Conduct, or Performances.

Honest *Shakespear* was not in those days acquainted with those great Wits, *Scudery, Calprenede, Scarron, Corneille*, &c. He was as much a Stranger to

---

[15] *Ibid.*   [16] *Ibid.*   [17] *Ibid.*
[18] Dr. *Charleton's* Different Wits of Men.
[19] Pref. *Relig. Laici.* last Paragraph.
[20] *Poet.* L. 3 C. 97.

French as Latine, (in which, if we believe *Ben Johnson*, he was a very small
page 141 / Proficient;) and yet an humble Story of *Dorastus* and *Fawnia*,
serv'd him for *A Winter's Tale*, as well as *The Grand Cyrus*, or *The Captive
Queen*, could furnish out a Laureat for a *Conquest of Granada*. *Shakespear's
Measure for Measure*, however despis'd by Mr. *Dryden* with his *Much Ado
about Nothing*, were believ'd by Sr. *William Davenant*, (who I presume had as
much judgment as *Sir Positive At-all*[21]) to have Wit enough in them to make
one good Play.

To conclude, if Mr. *Shakespear's* Plots are more irregular than those of Mr.
Dryden's (which by some will not be allow'd) 'tis because he never read
Aristotle, or *Rapin*; . . . . **page 142/**

. . . .

As to Mr. *Fletcher*, should we grant that he understood not the *Decorum*
of the Stage, as Mr. *Dryden*, and Mr. *Flecknoe* before him in his Discourse
on the English Stage, observe; his Errors on that account, are more pardonable
than those of the former, who pretends so well to know it, and yet has offended
against some of its most obvious and established Rules: Witness *Porphirius*[22]
his attempt to kill the Emperor whose Subject he was, and who offer'd to
adopt him his Son, and give him his Daughter in Marriage. *Philocles*[23] joining
with Prince *Lisimantes* in taking the Queen Prisoner, who rais'd him to be her
chief Favourite.[24] If to wound a Woman be an Indecency and contrary to the
Character of Manhood, of which he accuses *Philaster*,[25] and *Perigot*:[26] than Mr.
Dryden has equally offended with Mr. *Fletcher*, since he makes *Abdelmelech*
page 143 / kill *Lyndaraxa*.[27] If it be contrary to the *Decorum* of the Stage
for *Demetrius* and *Leontius* to stay in the midst of a routed Army, to hear the
cold Mirth of *The Humourous Lieutenant*[28] 'tis certainly no less, to stay the
Queen and her Court, to hear the cold Mirth of *Celadon* and *Florimel* about
their Marriage Covenants, whilst the main Action is depending.[29] If Mr.
Fletcher be tax'd by Mr. *Dryden*[30] for introducing *Demetrius* with a Pistol in
his Hand (in the Humourous Lieutenant) in the next Age to *Alexander* the
Great: I think Mr. *Dryden* committed as great a Blunder in his *Zambra Dance*,[31]
where he brought in the *Mahometans* bowing to the Image of *Jupiter*. I
could give you several other Instances, but these are enough to shew, that Mr.
Dryden is no more Infallible than his Predecessors.

As to his failing in the two last Acts, (a fault *Cicero* sometimes alludes to,
and blames in an Idle Poet;) its more to be imputed to his Laziness, than his
want of Judgment. I have either read, or been inform'd, (I know not well
whether) that 'twas generally Mr. *Fletcher's* practice, after he had finish'd
Three Acts of a Play to shew them to the Actors, and when they had agreed
on Terms, he huddled up the two last without that care that behoov'd him;
which gave opportunity to such Friends as Mr. **page 144 /** *Dryden* to

---

[21] See *Sullen Lovers.*
[23] *Maiden Queen.*
[25] *Philaster.*
[27] Conquest of *Granada*, II. Part.
[29] *Maiden Queen.*
[31] Conquest of *Granada*, part I.

[22] *Tyranick Love.*
[24] Postscript.
[26] *Faithful Shepherdess.*
[28] Postscript.
[30] Postscript, *Ibid.*

traduce him. This, tho' no just excuse, yet I believe was known to Mr. *Dryden* before, and therefore ought not as an act of Ignorance, to have been urg'd so fiercely against him.

As to his Plots being borrow'd, 'tis what is allowed by *Scaliger*, and others; and what has been practic'd by Mr. *Dryden*, more than by any Poet that I know: so that *He* of all Men living had no Reason to throw the first Stone at him. . . .

To come lastly to *Ben Johnson*, who (as Mr. *Dryden* affirms,[32]) has borrow'd more from the Ancients than any: I crave leave to say in his behalf, that our late *Laureat* has far out-done him in Thefts, proportionable to his Writings: and therefore he is guilty of the highest Arrogance, to accuse another of a Crime, for which he is most of all men liable to be arraign'd. . . .

I must further alledge that Mr. *Johnson* in borrowing from the Ancients, has only follow'd the Pattern of the great Men of former Ages, *Homer, Virgil, Ovid, Horace, Plautus, Terence, Seneca,* &c. all which have imitated the Example of the industrious Bee, which   **page 145 /**   sucks Honey from all sorts of Flowers, and lays it up in a general Repository. . . .   **page 146 /**

. . . .

Permit me to say farther in his behalf, That if in imitation of these illustrious Examples, and Models of Antiquity, he has borrow'd from them, as they from each other; yet that he attempted, and as some think, happily succeeded in his Endeavours of Surpassing them: insomuch that a certain Person of Quality[33] makes a Question, 'Whether any of the Wit of the Latine Poets be more Terse and Eloquent in their Tongue, than this Great and Learned Poet appears in ours.'

Whether Mr. *Dryden*, who has likewise succeeded to admiration in this way, or Mr. *Johnson* have most improv'd, and best advanc'd   **page 147 /** what they have borrow'd from the Ancients, I shall leave to the decision of the abler Criticks: only this I must say, in behalf of the later, that he has no ways endeavour'd to conceal what he has borrow'd, as the former has generally done. Nay, in his Play call'd *Sejanus* he has printed in the Margent throughout, the places from whence he borrow'd: the same he has practic'd in several of his Masques, (as the Reader may find in his Works;) a Pattern, which Mr. *Dryden* would have done well to have copied, and had thereby sav'd me the trouble of the following Annotations.

There is this difference between the Proceedings of these Poets, that Mr. *Johnson* has by Mr. *Dryden's* Confession[34] *Design'd his Plots himself;* whereas I know not any One Play, whose Plot may be said to be the Product of Mr. *Dryden's* own Brain. When Mr. *Johnson* borrow'd, 'twas from the Treasury of the Ancients, which is so far from any diminution of his Worth, that I think it is to his Honour. . . .   **page 148 /**

On the contrary, tho Mr. *Dryden* has likewise borrow'd from the Greek and Latine Poets, as *Sophocles, Virgil, Horace, Seneca,* &c. which I purposely omit to tax him with, as thinking what he has taken to be lawful prize: yet I cannot but observe withal; that he has plunder'd the chief *Italian, Spanish,* and *French*

---

[32] Pref. *Mock Astrol.*   [33] Poems and Essays, By Mr. *Edw. Howard.*
[34] Pref. *Mock Astrol.*

Wits for Forage, notwithstanding his pretended contempt of them: and not only so, but even his own Countrymen have been forc'd to pay him tribute, or to say better, have not been exempt from being Pillag'd. . . . .Give me leave to say a word, or two, in Defence of Mr. *Johnson's* way of Wit, which Mr. *Dryden* calls *Clenches*.

There have been few great Poets which have not propos'd some Eminent Author for their Pattern. . . . Mr. *Johnson* propos'd *Plautus* for his Model, and not only borrow'd from him, but imitated his way of Wit in English. There are none who have read him, but **page 149 /** are acquainted with his way of playing with Words. . . .

Nor might this be the sole Reason for Mr. *Johnson's* Imitation, for possibly 'twas his Compliance with the Age that induc'd him to this way of writing, it being then as Mr. *Dryden* observes[35] the Mode of Wit, the Vice of the Age, and not *Ben Johnson's:* and besides Mr. *Dryden's* taxing Sir *Philip Sidney* for playing with his Words, I may add that I find it practis'd by several Dramatick Poets, who were Mr. *Johnson's* Cotemporaries: and notwithstanding the advantage which this Age claims over the last, we find Mr. *Dryden* himself as well as Mr. *Johnson,* not only given to Clenches; but sometimes a *Carwichet,* a *Quarter-quibble,* or a bare *Pun* serves his turn, as well as his Friend *Bur* in his *Wild Gallant;* and therefore he might have spar'd this Reflection, if he had given himself the liberty of Thinking. . . . **page 150 /**

For these, and the like Reasons, I shall at present pass by his dis-obliging Reflections on several of his Patrons, as well as the Poets his Cotemporaries; his little Arts to set up himself, and decry others; his dexterity in altering other Mens Thoughts, so as to make them pass for his own; his Tautologies; his Petty-Larcenies, which notwithstanding his stiling of himself *Saturnine,* shew him sufficiently *Mercurial,* at least, if Plagiaries may be accounted under the Government of that Planet. In fine, . . . he resembles Vulgar Painters, who can tolerably copy after a good Original, but either have not judgment, or will not take the pains themselves to design any thing of value. . . . **page 151 /**

John Lacy.

A Comedian whose Abilities in Action were sufficiently known to all that frequented the King's Theatre, where he was for many years an Actor, and perform'd all Parts that he undertook to a miracle: insomuch that I am apt to believe, that as *this* Age never had, so the *next* never will have his *Equal,* at least not his *Superiour.* He was so well approv'd of by King *Charles* the Second, an undeniable Judge in Dramatick Arts, that he caus'd his Picture to be drawn, in three several Figures in the same Table. *viz.* That of *Teague* in the *Committee,* Mr. *Scruple* in *The Cheats,* and *M. Galliard,* in *The Variety:* which piece is still in being in *Windsor-Castle.* Nor did his Talent wholly ly in Acting, he knew both how to judge and write Plays: and if his Comedies are somewhat allied to French Farce, 'tis out of choice, rather than want of Ability to write **page 317 /** true Comedy. . . . **page 318 /**

[35] Postscript to *Granada.*

Nathaniel Lee.

An Author whose Plays have made him sufficiently remarkable to those who call themselves *The Wits;* and One whose Muse deserv'd a better Fate than *Bedlam.* How truly he has verified the Saying of the Philosopher, *Nullum* page 320 / *fit Magnum Ingenium sine mixturâ dementiæ;* even to the Regret and Pity of all that knew him, is manifest: I heartily wish his Madness had not exceeded that *Divine Fury* which *Ovid* mentions, and which usually accompanies the best poet. . . . But alas! his Condition is far worse. as it has been describ'd in a Satyr on the Modern Poets.

> There[1], *in a Den remov'd from human Eyes*
> *Possest with Muse, the Brain-sick-Poet lyes,*
> *Too miserably wretched to be nam'd;*
> *For Plays, for Heroes, and for Passion fam'd.*
> *Thoughtless he raves his sleepless Hours away,*
> *In Chains all Nights, in darkness all the Day.*
> *And if he gets some intervals from pain,*
> *The Fit returns; he foams, and bites his Chain,*
> *His Eye-balls rowl, and he grows mad again.*

However, before this misfortune befel him, he writ several Dramatical Pieces, which gave him a Title to the First Rank of Poets; there being several of his Tragedies, as *Mithridates, Theodosius &c.* which have forc'd Tears from the fairest Eyes in the World: his Muse indeed seem'd destin'd for the Diversion of the Fair Sex; so soft and passionately moving, are his Scenes of Love written. He has publisht Eleven Plays, besides those two, in which he joyn'd with Mr. *Dryden.* . . . page 321 /

Thomas Otway.

An Author who was well known to most Persons of this Age, who are famous for Wit and Breeding. He was formerly (as I have heard) bred for some time in *Christ-Church* Colledge in *Oxford.* From thence he removed to *London,* where he spent some time in Dramatick Poetry; and by degrees writ himself into Reputation with the Court. His Genius in Come- page 395 / dy lay a little too much to Libertinism, but in Tragedy he made it his business for the most part to observe the *Decorum* of the Stage. He was a man of Excellent parts and daily improved in his Writing: but yet sometimes fell into plagiary as well as his Contemporaries, and made use of *Shakespear,* to the advantage of his *Purse,* at least, if not to his Reputation. . . . page 396 /

Mrs. *Katherine Philips.*

A Lady of that admirable Merit, and Reputation, that her Memory will be honour'd of all Men, that are Favourers of Poetry. One, who not only has equall'd all that is reported of the Poetesses of Antiquity, the *Lesbian Sapho,* and the Roman *Sulpitia,* but whose Merit has justly found her Admirers, amongst the greatest Poets of our Age: and though I will not presume to compare our Poets with *Martial,* who writ in praise of *Sulpitia,* or *Horace, Ausonius,*

---

[1] In *Bedlam.*

and *Sydonius*, who commended *Sapho*, least I offend their Modesty who are still living: yet I will be so far bold as to assert, that the Earls of *Orrery* and *Roscommon*, the Incomparable *Cowley*, and the Ingenius *Flatman*, with others (amongst whom I must not forget my much respected Countryman *James Tyrrel* Esq;) would not have employ'd their Pens in praise of the Excellent *Orinda*, had she not justly deserv'd their Elogies, and possibly more than those Ladies of Antiquity: for as Mr. *Cowley* observes, in his third *Stanza* on her Death,

> *Of Female Poets, who had Names of old,*
>   *Nothing is shewn but only told,*
> *And all we hear of them, perhaps may be*
> *Male Flattery only, and Male Poetry;*
> *Few Minutes did their Beauties Lightning waste,*
> *The Thunder of their Voice did longer last,*
>   *But that too soon was past.*
> *The certain proofs of our* Orinda's *Wit,*
> *In her own lasting Characters are writ,*   **page 403 /**
> *And they will long my Praise of them survive,*
>   *Tho' long perhaps that too may live.*
> *The Trade of Glory manag'd by the Pen*
> *Tho' great it be, and every where is found,*
> *Does bring in but small profit to us Men,*
> *'Tis by the numbers of the Sharers drown'd;*
> Orinda, *in the Female Courts of Fame*
> *Engrosses all the Goods of a Poetick Name,*
>   *She doth no Partner with her see;*
> *Does all the business there alone, Which we*
> *Are forc'd to carry on by a whole Company.*

The Occasion of our mention of this Excellent Person in this place, is on the Account of two Dramatick Pieces, which she has translated from the *French* of Monsieur *Corneille;* and that with such exquisite Art and Judgment, that the Copies of each seem to transcend the Original.

Horace, a Tragedy; which I suppose was left imperfect by the untimely Death of the Authress; and the fifth Act was afterwards supply'd by Sir *John Denham*. This Play was acted at Court, by Persons of Quality; the Duke of *Monmouth* speaking the Prologue: Part of which being in Commendation of the Play, I shall transcribe

> *This Martial Story, which thro'* France *did come,*
> *And there was wrought in Great* Corneille's *Loom;*
> Orinda's *Matchless Muse to* Brittain *brought,*
> *And* Forreign *Verse, our* English *Accents taught;*
> *So soft that to our shame, we understand*
> *They could not fall but from a Lady's Hand.*   **page 404 /**
> *Thus while a Woman* Horace *did translate,*
> Horace *did rise above a Roman* Fate.

. . . .

Pompey, a Tragedy, which I have seen acted with great applause, at the Duke's Theatre; and at the End was acted that Farce printed in the fifth Act of *The Play-house to be Let.* This Play was translated at the Request of the Earl of *Orrery*, and published in Obedience to the Commands of the Right Honourable the Countess of *Corse;* to whom it is dedicated. How great an Opinion My L[d] *Orrery* had of this Play, may appear from the following Verses, being part of a Copy addrest to the Authress.

> *You English* Corneille's Pompey *with such Flame,*
> *That you both raise our wonder and his Fame;*
> *If he could read it, he like us would call*
> *The* Copy *greater than the* Original:
> *You cannot mend what is already done,*
> *Unless you'l finish what you have begun:*
> *Who your Translation sees, cannot but say,*
> *That 'tis* Orinda's Work, *and but his* Play.
> *The* French *to learn our Language now will seek,*
> *To hear their* Greatest *Wit* more *nobly speak;*
> Rome *too would grant, were our Tongue to her known,*
> Cæsar *speaks better in't, than in his own.*
> *And all those Wreaths once circled* Pompey's *Brow,*
> *Exalt his Fame, less than your Verses now.* **page 405 /**

Tho. Shadwell, Esq; Poet *Laureat* to their present Majesties.

A Gentleman, whose Dramatick Works are sufficiently known to the World; but espe- **page 442 /** cially his Excellent Comedies; which in the Judgment of some Persons, have very deservedly advanced him to the Honour he now enjoys, under the Title of *Poet Laureat* to their present Majesties. An Advancement which he ingeniously confesses, is chiefly owing to the Patronage of the Noble Earl of *Dorset*, that Great Judge of Wit and Parts; in whose Favour it has been Mr. *Shadwell's* particular Happiness for several Years, to have had an Eminent Share. Mr. *Dryden*, I dare presume, little imagined, when he writ that Satyr of *Mack-Flecknoe*, that the Subject he *there* so much exposes and ridicules, should have ever lived to have succeeded him in wearing the *Bays*.

But I am willing to say the less of Mr. *Shadwell*, because I have publickly profess'd a Friendship for him: and tho' it be not of so long date, as some former Intimacy with others; so neither is it blemished with some unhandsome Dealings, I have met with from Persons, where I least expected it. I shall therefore speak of him with the Impartiality that becomes a Critick; and own I like *His* Comedies better than Mr. *Dryden's;* as having more Variety of Characters, and those drawn from the Life; I mean Men's Converse and Manners, and not from other Mens Ideas, copyed out of their publick Writings: tho' indeed I cannot wholly acquit our *Present Laureat* from borrowing; his Plagiaries being in some places too bold and open to be disguised. . . ; several of them **page 443 /** are observed to my Hand, and in a great measure excused by himself, in the publick Acknowledgment he makes in his several Prefaces, to the Persons to whom he was obliged for what he borrowed.

That Mr. *Shadwell* has propos'd *B. Johnson* for his Model, I am very certain of; and those who will read the Preface to the *Humorists*, may be sufficiently satisfied what a value he has for that Great Man; but how far he has succeeded in his Design, I shall leave to the Reader's Examination. So far only give me leave to premise in our Laureat's Defence, that the Reader is not to measure his Merit by Mr. *Dryden's* Standard; since *Socrates*, never was more persecuted by the Inhumane *Aristophanes*, than Mr. *Shadwell* by Mr. *Dryden's* Pen; and with the same injustice: tho' I think, whoever shall peruse the Modest Defence of the former, in his Epistle to the tenth Satyr of *Juvenal*, will not only acquit him, but love him for his good Humour and gentle Temper, to One who endeavour'd to destroy his *Reputation*, so dear to *All Men*, but the very *Darling* of Poets. . . . **page 444 /**

. . . I hope now, our Author is advanced to a Station, wherein he will endeavour to exert his *Muse;* and having found Encouragement from Majesty it self, aim at writing Dramatick Pieces, equal to those of Antiquity: which however applauded, have been paralleled (I was about to say excelled) by the Comedies of the Admirable *Johnson.*

I must do Mr. *Dryden* so much Justice, as to acknowledge, that in *Epick Poetry*, he far exceeds not only Mr. *Shadwell*, but most, if not all the Poets of our Age: and I could wish our present Laureat, would not give his predecessor such frequent Advantages over him; but rather confine himself within his own Sphere of Comedy. **page 452 /**

William Wytcherley.

A Gentleman, whom I may boldly reckon amongst the Poets of the First Rank: no Man that I know, except the Excellent *Johnson*, having outdone him in Comedy; in which alone he has imploy'd his Pen, but with that Success, that few have before, or will hereafter match him. His Plays are four in Number; *viz.*

Country Wife, a Comedy acted at the Theatre-Royal, and printed 4⁰. *Lond.* 1683. This is reckon'd an Admirable Play.

Gentleman Dancing-Master, a Comedy acted **page 514 /** at the Duke's Theatre; and printed in quarto *Lond.* 1673.

Love in a Wood, or *Saint* James's *Park;* a Comedy, acted at the Theatre-Royal, by His Majesty's Servants; printed 4⁰. *Lond.* 1672. and dedicated to the Dutchess of *Cleveland.*

Plain Dealer, a Comedy acted at the Theatre-Royal, by His Majesty's Servants; printed 4⁰. *Lond.* 1678. and dedicated to Madam B —— Of this Play and its Author, Mr. *Dryden* says thus: 'The Author of the *Plain Dealer*, whom I am proud to call My Friend, has oblig'd all Honest and Virtuous Men, by One of the most Bold, most General, and most Useful Satyrs, which has been presented on the *English* Theatre.' But notwithstanding this Admirable Character, I must take the Freedom to alledge, That our Author has borrow'd his chief Characters of *Manly* and *Olivia*, from *Molliere's Le Misanthrope;* that of Major *Old-fox*, from *Scarron's City Romance;* and that of *Vernish* his seizing *Fidelia*, and discovering her Sex, may possibly be founded on *Silvia Molliere's Memoires.* But notwithstanding all this, the Play is Excellent in its kind; and the Author's Character is justly drawn by Mr. *Evelyn:*

> *As long as Men are false, and Women vain,*
> *While Gold continues to be Virtues bane,*
> *In pointed Satyr* Wycherley *shall Reign.* **page 515 /**

Count Lorenzo Magalotti visited England in 1669 as a member of the entourage of Prince Cosmo III of Tuscany. Magalotti, considered one of the most learned men of the court of Ferdinand II, was secretary to the Academy del Cimento and enjoyed the friendship and esteem of many of the great scholars of Europe, among them Sir Isaac Newton.

Cosmo, although traveling unofficially, was widely received socially in England; he visited most of the major points of interest and attended many of the popular functions of the day. The account of Cosmo's travels recorded by Magalotti is notable for its minute detail and is a valuable contemporary source of information concerning the English scene in the seventeenth century, including the theater.

Conte Lorenzo Magalotti. *Travels of Cosmo the Third, Grand Duke of Tuscany, Through England, During the Reign of King Charles the Second* (1669). London, 1821.

[April 25th]
About mid-day, his highness returned home, and dined as usual. After dinner, he recommenced his visits to the ladies; going towards evening to the King's Theatre, to hear the comedy, in his majesty's box. This theatre is nearly of a circular form, surrounded, in the inside, by boxes separated from each other, and divided into several rows of seats, for the greater accommodation of the ladies and gentlemen, who, in conformity with the freedom of the country, sit together indiscriminately; a large space being left on the ground-floor for the rest of the audience. The scenery is very light, capable of a great page 190 / many changes, and embellished with beautiful landscapes. Before the comedy begins, that the audience may not be tired with waiting, the most delightful symphonies are played; on which account many persons come early to enjoy this agreeable amusement. The comedies which are acted, are in prose; but their plots are confused, neither unity nor regularity being observed; the authors having in view, rather than any thing else, to describe accurately the passions of the mind, the virtues and the vices; and they succeed the better, the more the players themselves, who are excellent, assist them with action, and with the enunciation of their language, which is very well adapted for the purpose, as being a variation, but very much confined and curtailed, of the Teutonic idiom; and enriched with many phrases and words of the most beautiful and expressive description, taken both from ancient and modern languages. From the theatre, his highness returned home, and retiring to his apartment, supped alone. page 191 /

. . . .

. . . His Highness went to the comedy at the Duke of York's theatre, where the music and dancing, after the English manner, were less pleasing than the operas performed by the comedians; because, being in the English language, the only pleasure which we who heard them, can derive from the latter, is that of observing their action, which it cannot be denied, was supereminently excellent. . . . **page 194 /**

. . . .

[Cambridge] Nor was the next college which his highness visited less considerable, called Trinity. . . . **page 228 /** His highness surveyed everything most remarkable in the college. . . . The evening coming on, his highness was introduced into the theatre, a room rather small than spacious, where was represented by the scholars a Latin comedy, which pleased more by the elegance of the dresses, the ease and gracefulness of the actors, than by their elocution, which it was very difficult to understand, without being accustomed to the accent. The story of the comedy was as follows: — A merchant of Nola, whose wife and daughter had been made slaves, sent his son to Constantinople to redeem them; but he falling in love by the way with a certain young lady, instead of prosecuting his journey, returned to his father, bringing the girl along with him, and pretending that she was his sister, and that his mother was dead. Many years afterwards, another merchant arrived at Nola, on his return from Constantinople, with letters **page 229 /** from the wife. The truth having thus come out, the father accomplished their redemption by other means; and when the mother returned to her own country, the son prostrated himself at her feet, and asked pardon for his offence, which she not only granted, but, actuated by maternal tenderness, obtained it also from his father. The comedy concludes, in the midst of rejoicings, with a ball, which was managed with great elegance. **page 230 /**

. . . In the afternoon [June 3rd], his highness left home earlier than usual to make his visits, that he might be at the King's Theatre in time for the comedy, and a ballet set on foot and got up in honor of his highness by my Lord Stafford, uncle of the Duke of Norfolk.

On arriving at the theatre, which was sufficiently lighted on the stage and on the walls to enable the spectators to see the scenes and the performances, his highness seated himself in a front box, where, besides enjoying the pleasure of the spectacle, he passed the evening in conversation with the Venetian ambassador, the Duke of Norfolk, Lord Stafford, and other noblemen.

To the story of Psyche, the daughter of Apollo, which abounded with beautiful incidents, all of them adapted to the performers and calculated to express the force of love, was joined a well-arranged ballet, regulated by the sound of various instruments, with new and fanciful **page 347 /** dances after the English manner, in which different actions were counterfeited, the performers passing gracefully from one to another, so as to render intelligible, by their movements, the acts they were representing.

This spectacle was highly agreeable to his highness from its novelty and ingenuity; and all parts of it were likewise equally praised by the ladies and gentlemen, who crouded in great numbers to the theatre, to fill the boxes, with which it is entirely surrounded, and the pit, and to enjoy the performance, which was protracted to a late hour of the night. . . . **page 348 /**

Samuel Pepys (1633–1703) now occupies an important and distinguished position in English letters. Until the beginning of the nineteenth century, however, he was little known outside the English Admiralty service. Through the influence of a somewhat distant relative, Sir Edward Montagu, he first entered public service. After the Restoration he was appointed Clerk of the Acts for the Navy and later Clerk of the Privy Seal and Secretary to the Admiralty. In these posts he distinguished himself and did much to lay the foundation for the efficiency and fame of the British Navy.

The Diary on which his literary reputation is based, was started on the first of January, 1659–60. It was written for the most part in a shorthand devised about 1630 by Thomas Shelton. In passages of extreme secrecy or delicacy Pepys employed foreign phrases, possibly to prevent his wife, who was exceptionally jealous (often with good cause) or the servants from reading them. Although failing eyesight forced him to cut short his diary in 1669, long before his death, he never destroyed it and ultimately bequeathed it with his books to Magdalene College, Cambridge, where it remained in obscurity until the nineteenth century. It was then transcribed and was published in 1825. Since that date the Diary of Pepys has become one of the best-known works of its kind.

Pepys was an extremely active person who delighted in the conviviality and gossip that went with meeting and knowing influential, interesting people. His wide range of acquaintance included members of the court, actresses and actors, musicians, ladies, and prostitutes — the entire social scale. He enjoyed the court as well as the theater. It is his association with the latter that is of particular interest here, for his regular visits to the playhouses, his often minute descriptions of plays, players, and audiences, his delight in the excitement and the gaiety of theater society — all provide the literary historian with an extremely valuable source of information. Candid, often prejudiced, Pepys is nevertheless a competent judge who provides a reliable guide to the tastes of his time. Moreover, he was enough a man of his age to be torn between his relish for the pleasures of the stage and the discomfort of an uneasy conscience that frequently chided him for such indulgence. Fortunately for the literary historian, Pepys's conscience was easily assuaged, and the pages of the Diary are filled with the record of his devotion to pleasure.

Samuel Pepys. *The Diary of Samuel Pepys*, ed. Henry B. Wheatly. New York, [1900].

1660
Aug.

18th.   This morning I took my wife towards Westminster by water, and landed her at Whitefriars, with £5 to buy her a petticoat, and I to the Privy Seal. By and by comes my wife to tell me that my father has persuaded her to buy a most fine cloth of 26s. a yard, and a rich lace, that the petticoat will come to £5, at which I was somewhat troubled, but she doing it very innocently, I could not be angry. I did give her more money, and sent her away, and I and Creed and Captain Hayward (who is now unkindly put out of the Plymouth to make way for Captain Allen to go to Constantinople, and put into his ship the Dover, which I know will trouble my Lord) went and dined at the Leg in King Street, where Captain Ferrers, my Lord's Cornet, comes to us, who after dinner took me and Creed to the Cockpitt play,[1] the first that I have had time to see since my coming from sea. "The Loyall Subject,"[2] where one Kinaston,[3] a boy, acted the Duke's sister, but made the loveliest lady that ever I saw in my life, only her voice not very good.

11th. . . . Here, in the Park, we met with Mr. Salisbury, who took Mr. Creed _{Oct.} and me to the Cockpitt[4] to see "The Moore of Venice," which was well done. Burt acted the Moore;[5] by the same token, a very pretty lady that sat by me, called out, to see Desdemona smothered.

16th. . . . I did intend to go forth to see a play at the Cockpit this afternoon, but Mr. Moore coming to me, my wife staid at home, and he and I went out together, with whom I called at the upholster's and several other places that I had business with, and so home with him to the Cockpit, where, understanding that "Wit without money"[6] was acted, I would not stay. . . .

30th. . . . In the afternoon, to ease my mind, I went to the Cockpit all alone, and there saw a very fine play called "The Tamer tamed;"[7] very well acted.

20th. . . . To the new Play-house near Lincoln's-Inn-Fields (which was for- _{Nov.} merly Gibbon's tennis-court),[8] where the play of "Beggar's Bush"[9] was newly begun; and so we went in and saw it, it was well acted: and here I saw the first time one Moone,[10] who is said to be the best actor in the world, lately come over with the King, and indeed it is the finest play-house, I believe, that ever was in England. . . .

22d. . . . I to the new playhouse[11] and saw part of the "Traitor,"[12] a very good Tragedy; Mr. Moon did act the Traitor very well.

27th. . . . Soon as dinner was done my wife took her leave, and went . . . to

---

[1] The Cockpit Theatre, situated in Drury Lane, was occupied as a playhouse in the reign of James I. It was occupied by Davenant and his company in 1658, and they remained in it until November 15th, 1660, when they removed to Salisbury Court.

[2] A tragi-comedy by Beaumont and Fletcher. Kynaston's part was Olympia.

[3] Edward Kynaston, engaged by Sir. W. Davenant, in 1660, to perform the principal female characters: he afterwards assumed the male ones in the first parts of tragedy, and continued on the stage till the end of King William's reign. He died in 1712. Who played Archas is unknown; but Betterton, as Downes tells us, was early distinguished for playing in "The Loyal Subject."

[4] The Cockpit theatre in Drury Lane.

[5] Nicholas Burt ranked in the list of good actors after the Restoration. . . .

[6] A comedy by Beaumont and Fletcher, first printed in 1639, and again in 1661.

[7] "The Woman's Prize, or Tamer Tamed," a comedy by John Fletcher, and a sort of sequel to Shakespeare's "Taming of the Shrew," published in the folio edition of Beaumont and Fletcher, 1647.

[8] This was Killigrew's, or the King's House, opened for the first time November 8th, 1660.

[9] The "Beggar's Bush," a comedy by Beaumont and Fletcher, published in the 1647 edition of their plays.

[10] Michael Mohun, or Moone, the celebrated actor. . . .

[11] The King's House, near Lincoln's Inn Fields. . . .

[12] "The Traitor," a tragedy by James Shirley. . . .

a christening of a . . . child . . . , and I to a play, "The Scornfull Lady,"[13] and that being done, I went homewards. . . .

Dec. 5th. . . . I dined at home, and after dinner I went to the new Theatre[14] and there I saw "The Merry Wives of Windsor" acted, the humours of the country gentleman and the French doctor very well done, but the rest but very poorly, and Sir J. Falstaffe[15] as bad as any.

31st. At the office all the morning and after that home, and not staying to dine I went out, and in Paul's Churchyard I bought the play of "Henry the Fourth," and so went to the new Theatre . . . and saw it acted; but my expectation being too great, it did not please me, as otherwise I believe it would; and my having a book, I believe did spoil it a little.

1661
Jan. 3d. . . . To the Theatre, where was acted "Beggars' Bush,"[1] it being very well done; and here the first time that ever I saw women[2] come upon the stage.

7th. . . . To the office, and after that to dinner, where my brother Tom came and dined with me, and after dinner (leaving 12d. with the servants to buy a cake with at night, this day being kept as Twelfth day) Tom and I and my wife to the Theatre, and there saw "The Silent Woman."[3] The first time that ever I did see it, and it is an excellent play. Among other things here, Kinaston, the boy, had the good turn to appear in three shapes: first, as a poor woman in ordinary clothes, to please Morose; then in fine clothes, as a gallant, and in them was clearly the prettiest woman in the whole house, and lastly, as a man; and then likewise did appear the handsomest man in the house. . . .

8th. . . . After dinner I took my Lord Hinchinbroke and Mr. Sidney to the Theatre, and shewed them "The Widdow,"[4] an indifferent good play, but wronged by the women being to seek in their parts.

19th. . . . Went to the Theatre, where I saw "The Lost Lady,"[5] which do not please me much. Here I was troubled to be seen by four of our office clerks, which sat in the half-crown box and I in the 1s. 6d.

28th. . . . To the Theatre, where I saw again "The Lost Lady," which do now please me better than before; and here I sitting behind in a dark place, a lady spit backward upon me by a mistake, not seeing me, but after seeing her to be a very pretty lady, I was not troubled at it at all.

29th. . . . Went to Black-fryers[6] (the first time I ever was there since plays

---

[13] A comedy by Beaumont and Fletcher, first printed in 1616. After the Restoration it was one of the plays acted by Killigrew's company.

[14] Killigrew's house. . . . Pepys sometimes calls it the Theatre and at others the Playhouse.

[15] Falstaff was acted by Cartwright. . . .

[1] A comedy by Beaumont and Fletcher, acted at Whitehall in 1622, and published in 1647. It was revived in November, 1660.

[2] . . . After the Restoration the acting of female characters by women became common. The first English professional actress was Mrs. Coleman, who acted Ianthe in Davenant's "Siege of Rhodes," at Rutland House in 1656.

[3] Ben Jonson's comedy.

[4] "The Widow," a comedy by Ben Jonson, Fletcher, and Middleton, published in 1652.

[5] A tragi-comedy, by Sir William Barclay, published in 1638.

[6] At Apothecaries' Hall, where Davenant produced the first and second parts of "The Siege of Rhodes." Downes says, in his "Roscius Anglicanus," that Davenant's company acted at "Pothecaries Hall" until the building in Lincoln's Inn Fields was ready.

begun), and there after great patience and little expectation, from so poor beginning, I saw three acts of "The Mayd in ye Mill"[7] acted to my great content.

31st. . . . To the Theatre, and there sat in the pit among the company of fine ladys, &c.; and the house was exceeding full, to see Argalus and Parthenia,[8] the first time that it hath been acted: and indeed it is good, though wronged by my over great expectations, as all things else are. . . .

5th. . . . I went by coach to the play-house at the Theatre, our coach in King **Feb.** Street breaking, and so took another. Here we saw Argalus and Parthenia, which I lately saw, but though pleasant for the dancing and singing, I do not find good for any wit or design therein. . . .

9th. . . . To an ordinary to dinner, and then . . . to Whitefriars[9] to the Playhouse, and saw "The Mad Lover,"[10] the first time I ever saw it acted, which I like pretty well, and home.

12th. . . . Thence . . . after a great dispute whither to go, we went by water to Salsbury Court[11] play-house, where not liking to sit, we went out again, and by coach to the Theatre, and there saw "The Scornfull Lady," now done by a woman, which makes the play appear much better than ever it did to me.

16th. I dined . . . and then to the Theatre, where I saw "The Virgin Martyr,"[12] a good but too sober a play for the company.

23rd. . . . Then by water to Whitefriars to the Play-house, and there saw "The Changeling,"[13] the first time it hath been acted these twenty years, and it takes exceedingly. Besides, I see the gallants do begin to be tyred with the vanity and pride of the theatre actors who are indeed grown very proud and rich. . . .

1st. . . . I to Whitefryars, and saw "The Bondman"[14] acted; an excellent play **Mar.** and well done. But above all that ever I saw, Betterton[15] do the Bondman the best.

2d. . . . After dinner I went to the Theatre, where I found so few people (which is strange, and the reason I did not know) that I went out again, and so to Salsbury Court, where the house as full as could be; and it seems it was a new play, "The Queen's Maske,"[16] wherein there are some good humours: among others, a good jeer to the old story of the Siege of Troy, making it to

---

[7] A comedy by Beaumont and Fletcher, first produced in 1623.

[8] A tragi-comedy by Henry Glapthorne, founded on the story of the two lovers in Sidney's "Arcadia," and published in 1639.

[9] Salisbury Court Theatre, which was re-opened in 1660 by Rhodes's company.

[10] A tragi-comedy by Beaumont and Fletcher, printed in the folio of 1647.

[11] Called on the 9th, Whitefriars.

[12] A tragedy by Massinger and Decker, printed in 1622.

[13] A tragedy, by Thomas Middleton, acted before the court at Whitehall, January 4th, 1623–4.

[14] Massinger's play, which was first published in 1624.

[15] Thomas Betterton . . . joined the company of actors formed by Rhodes, bookseller (and formerly wardrobe keeper to the Blackfriars Company), which commenced to act at the Cockpit, in Drury Lane, in 1659. When, after the Restoration, Davenant took over Rhodes's company, Betterton became his principal actor.

[16] "Love's Mistress, or The Queen's Masque," by Thomas Heywood, published in 1636. The plot is borrowed from the "Golden Ass" of Apuleius.

be a common country tale. But above all it was strange to see so little a boy as that was to act Cupid, which is one of the greatest parts in it.

11th. After dinner I went to the theatre, and there saw "Love's Mistress" done by them, which I do not like in some things as well as their acting in Salsbury Court.

14th. . . . To the Theatre, and there saw "King and no King,"[17] well acted.

19th. . . . To White-Fryars, where we saw "The Bondman" acted most excellently, and though I have seen it often, yet I am every time more and more pleased with Betterton's action.

23d. . . . Then out to the Red Bull[18] (where I had not been since plays come up again), but coming too soon I went out again and walked all up and down the Charterhouse yard and Aldersgate street. At last came back again and went in, where I was led by a seaman that knew me, but is here as a servant, up to the tireing-room, where strange the confusion and disorder that there is among them in fitting themselves, especially here, where the clothes are very poor, and the actors but common fellows. At last into the pitt, where I think there was not above ten more than myself, and not one hundred in the whole house. And the play, which is called "All's lost by Lust,"[19] poorly done; and with so much disorder, among others, that in the musique-room the boy that was to sing a song, not singing it right, his master fell about his ears and beat him so, that it put the whole house in an uprore.

25th. . . . To Salisbury Court by water, and saw part of the "Queene's Maske."

26th. After dinner Mrs. Pierce and her husband and I and my wife to Salisbury Court, where coming late he and she light of Col. Boone that made room for them, and I and my wife sat in the pit, and there met with Mr. Lewes and Tom Whitton, and saw "The Bondman" done to admiration.

28th. . . . To the Theatre and saw "Rollo"[20] ill acted.

April 1st. . . . Then to Whitefryars, and there saw part of "Rule a wife and have a wife,"[21] which I never saw before, but do not like it.

2d. . . . And so to White-fryars and saw "The Little Thiefe,"[22] which is a very merry and pretty play, and the little boy do very well.

6th. . . . Then by water . . . to Salisbury Court and there saw "Love's Quarrell"[23] acted the first time, but I do not like the design or words.

20th. . . . To the Cockpitt,[24] . . . and there saw the King and Duke of York and his Duchess. . . . And so saw "The Humersome Lieutenant"[25] acted before

[17] A comedy by Beaumont and Fletcher, acted before the court in 1611 by the King's Players.

[18] The Red Bull was situated in St. John's Street, Clerkenwell.

[19] A tragedy, by W. Rowley.

[20] "Rollo, Duke of Normandy," a tragedy by John Fletcher, published in 1640. It was previously published in 1639 as "The Bloody Brother."

[21] A comedy by John Fletcher, licensed October, 1624.

[22] "The Night Walker, or the Little Thief," a comedy by John Fletcher, acted at court in 1633.

[23] The play is not known otherwise than by this notice.

[24] The Cockpit at Whitehall, the residence of the Duke of Albermarle.

[25] "The Humorous Lieutenant," a tragi-comedy, by Beaumont and Fletcher. Published in the folio of 1647.

the King, but not very well done. But my pleasure was great to see the manner of it, and so many great beauties, but above all Mrs. Palmer, with whom the King do discover a great deal of familiarity.

27th. ... After dinner ... to the Theatre to see "The Chances."[26]

16th. ... Away to the Theatre, and there saw the latter end of "The Mayd's *May* Tragedy,"[27] which I never saw before, and methinks it is too sad and melancholy.

25th. At noon to the Temple, where I staid and looked over a book or two at Playford's, and then to the Theatre, where I saw a piece of "The Silent Woman,"[28] which pleased me. So homewards, and in my way bought "The Bondman" in Paul's Churchyard. ...

4th. ... To the Theatre and saw "Harry the 4th," a good play. *June*

8th. ... I went to the Theatre and there saw Bartholomew Faire,[29] the first time it was acted now-a-days. It is a most admirable play and well acted, but too much prophane and abusive.

16th. ... The afternoon ... I spent in reading "The Spanish Gypsey,"[30] a play not very good, though commended much.

22nd. ... Then to the Theatre, "The Alchymist,"[31] which is a most incomparable play.

2nd. ... Took coach and went to Sir William Davenant's Opera; this being *July* the fourth day that it hath begun, and the first that I have seen it. To-day was acted the second part of "The Siege of Rhodes."[32] We staid a very great while for the King and the Queen of Bohemia. And by the breaking of a board over our heads, we had a great deal of dust fell into the ladies' necks and the men's hair, which made good sport. The King being come, the scene opened; which indeed is very fine and magnificent, and well acted, all but the Eunuch, who was so much out that he was hissed off the stage.

4th. At home all the morning; in the afternoon I went to the Theatre, and there I saw "Claracilla"[33] (the first time I ever saw it), well acted. But strange to see this house, that used to be so thronged, now empty since the Opera begun; and so will continue for a while, I believe.

23rd. ... In the afternoon, finding myself unfit for business, I went to the Theatre, and saw "Brenoralt,"[34] I never saw before. It seemed a good play,

[26] "The Chances," a comedy by Beaumont and Fletcher, published in the folio of 1647. Revived at this time.

[27] By Beaumont and Fletcher. Acted at court in 1613. After the Restoration, Mohun played Melantius; Hart, Amintor; and Mrs. Marshall, Evadne.

[28] Ben Jonson's "Epicene."

[29] A comedy by Ben Jonson; first acted at the Hope theatre, Bankside, October 31st, 1614.

[30] A comedy, by Thomas Middleton and William Rowley, printed 1653, and again in 1661.

[31] Comedy by Ben Jonson, first printed in 1612.

[32] Davenant's opera of the "Siege of Rhodes" was published in 1656. The author afterwards wrote a second part, which Pepys saw. The two parts, as altered, and as acted at Lincoln's Inn Fields, were published in 1663.

[33] A tragi-comedy, by Thomas Killigrew, first published in 1641.

[34] "Brennoralt, or the Discontented Colonel," a tragedy by Sir John Suckling. Written about 1639, and first published in Suckling's Works, 1646.

but ill acted; only I sat before Mrs. Palmer, the King's mistress, and filled my eyes with her, which much pleased me.

25th. . . . Mr. Moore . . . and I to the Theatre, and saw "The Jovial Crew,"[35] the first time I saw it, and indeed it is as merry and the most innocent play that ever I saw, and well performed.

31st. Singing-master came to me this morning; then to the office all the morning. In the afternoon I went to the Theatre, and there I saw "The Tamer Tamed"[36] well done.

August

10th. . . . After dinner took the two young gentlemen and the two ladies and carried them and Captain Ferrers to the Theatre, and shewed them "The merry Devill of Edmunton,"[37] which is a very merry play, the first time I ever saw it, which pleased me well.

14th. . . . After dinner Captain Ferrers and I to the Theatre, and there saw "The Alchymist."

15th. . . . Thence to the Opera, which begins again to-day with "The Witts,"[38] never acted yet with scenes; and the King and Duke and Duchess were there . . . ; and indeed it is a most excellent play, and admirable scenes.

17th. . . . After dinner Captain Ferrers and I to the Opera, and saw "The Witts" again, which I like exceedingly. The Queen of Bohemia was here . . . Troubled in mind that I cannot bring myself to mind my business, but to be so much in love of plays.

23rd. . . . I to W. Joyce's, where by appointment my wife was, and I took her to the Opera, and shewed her "The Witts," which I had seen already twice, and was most highly pleased with it.

24th. . . . Straight to the Opera, and there saw "Hamlet, Prince of Denmark," done with scenes very well, but above all, Betterton[39] did the prince's part beyond imagination.

26th. . . . To the Theatre, and saw the "Antipodes,"[40] wherein there is much mirth, but no great matter else.

27th. . . . My wife and I to the Theatre, and there saw "The Joviall Crew," where the King, Duke and Duchess, and Madame Palmer, were; and my wife, to her great content, had a full sight of them all the while. The play full of mirth.

30th. . . . My wife and I to Drury Lane to the French comedy,[41] which was

[35] "The Jovial Crew, or the Merry Beggars," a comedy, by Richard Brome, acted at the Cockpit, Drury Lane, in 1641.

[36] On October 30th, 1660, Pepys saw this play at the Cockpit theatre.

[37] A comedy acted at the Globe, and first printed in 1608. In the original entry in the Stationers' books it is said to be by T. B., which may stand for Tony or Anthony Brewer. The play has been attributed without authority to Shakespeare and to Drayton.

[38] A comedy, by Sir W. Davenant, licensed in January, 1633–34.

[39] Sir William Davenant introduced the use of scenery. The character of Hamlet was one of Betterton's masterpieces. Downes tells us that he was taught by Davenant how the part was acted by Taylor of the Blackfriars, who was instructed by Shakespeare himself.

[40] A comedy by Richard Brome, first acted at Salisbury Court, 1638, and published in 1640.

[41] The French comedians acted at the Cockpit. The Theatre Royal on the site of the present Drury Lane Theatre was not built till 1663.

so ill done, and the scenes and company and everything else so nasty and out of order and poor, that I was sick all the while in my mind to be there. . . . There being nothing pleasant but the foolery of the farce, we went home.

31st. Thus ends the month. . . . But what is worst, I find myself lately too much given to seeing of plays, and expense, and pleasure, which makes me forget my business, which I must labour to amend.

6th. . . . Much troubled and unfit for business, I went to the Theatre, and *Sept.* saw "Elder Brother"[42] ill acted.

7th. . . . Having appointed the young ladies . . . to go with them to a play to-day, . . . my wife and I took them to the Theatre, where we seated ourselves close by the King, and Duke of York, and Madame Palmer, which was great content; and, indeed, I can never enough admire her beauty. And here was "Bartholomew Fayre," with the puppet-show, acted to-day, which had not been these forty years (it being so satyricall against Puritanism, they durst not till now, which is strange they should already dare to do it, and the King do countenance it), but I do never a whit like it better for the puppets, but rather the worse.

9th. . . . I drank so much wine that I was not fit for business, and therefore at noon I went and walked in Westminster Hall a while, and thence to Salisbury Court play house, where was acted the first time "'Tis pity Shee's a Whore,"[43] a simple play and ill acted, only it was my fortune to sit by a most pretty and most ingenious lady, which pleased me much.

11th. . . . Walking through Lincoln's Inn Fields observed at the Opera a new play, "Twelfth Night,"[44] was acted there, and the King there; so I, against my own mind and resolution, could not forbear to go in, which did make the play seem a burthen to me, and I took no pleasure at all in it; and so after it was done went home with my mind troubled for my going thither, after my swearing to my wife that I would never go to a play without her.

25th. . . . Much against my nature and will, yet such is the power of the Devil over me I could not refuse it, to the Theatre, and saw "The Merry Wives of Windsor," ill done.

26th. . . . Abroad with my wife by coach to the Theatre to shew her "King and no King,"[45] it being very well done.

28th. . . . Dined at home, and then Sir W. Pen and his daughter and I and my wife to the Theatre, and there saw "Father's own Son,"[46] a very good play, and the first time I ever saw it. . . .

2nd. I home and then took my wife out, . . . we went to the Theatre, but *Oct.* coming late, and sitting in an ill place, I never had so little pleasure in a play

42 A comedy, by John Fletcher, acted at the Blackfriars. It was published first in 1637.
43 A tragedy, by John Ford, acted at the Phoenix, Drury Lane, and printed 1633.
44 Pepys seldom liked any play of Shakespeare's, and he sadly blundered when he supposed "Twelfth Night" was a new play.
45 Pepys saw this play acted well on March 14th, 1660–61.
46 The only mention of this piece occurs in a MS. list of plays belonging to Will. Beeston, as governor of the Cockpit, in Drury Lane, preserved in the Lord Chamberlain's office. The list is dated August 10th, 1639. . . .

in my life, yet it was the first time that ever I saw it, "Victoria Corombona."[47] Methinks a very poor play.

4th. . . . Then Captain Ferrers and I to the Theatre, and there came too late, so we staid and saw a bit of "Victoria," which pleased me worse than it did the other day. So we staid not to see it out. . . .

8th. . . . Late after dinner took Mrs. Martha out by coach, and carried her to the Theatre in a frolique, to my great expense, and there shewed her part of the "Beggar's Bush," without much pleasure, but only for a frolique, and so home again.

9th. . . . At home I found Mrs. Pierce la belle, and Madam Clifford, with whom I was forced to stay, and made them the most welcome I could; and I was (God knows) very well pleased with their beautiful company, and after dinner took them to the Theatre, and shewed them "The Chances;" and so saw them both at home. . . .

10th. . . . After dinner Sir W. Pen and my wife and I to the Theatre, . . . where the King came to-day, and there was "The Traytor" most admirably acted; and a most excellent play it is.

21st. . . . Thence to the Wardrobe and dined, and so against my judgment and conscience (which God forgive, for my very heart knows that I offend God in breaking my vows herein) to the Opera, which is now newly begun to act again, after some alteracion of their scene, which do make it very much worse; but the play, "Love and Honour,"[48] being the first time of their acting it, is a very good plot, and well done.

23rd. . . . So back to the Opera, and there I saw again "Love and Honour," and a very good play it is.

25th. After dinner my wife and I to the Opera, and there saw again "Love and Honour," a play so good that it has been acted but three times and I have seen them all, and all in this week; which is too much, and more than I will do again a good while.

26th. . . . So at the office all the morning, and in the afternoon Sir W. Pen, my wife and I to the Theatre, and there saw "The Country Captain,"[49] the first time it hath been acted this twenty-five years, a play of my Lord Newcastle's, but so silly a play as in all my life I never saw, and the first that ever I was weary of in my life.

28th. Hither I sent for Captain Ferrers to me, who comes with a friend of his, and they and I to the Theatre, and there saw "Argalus and Parthenia,"[50] where a woman acted Parthenia, and came afterwards on the stage in men's clothes, and had the best legs that ever I saw, and I was very well pleased with it.

[47] "The White Devil; or, the Tragedie of Paulo Giordano Ursini, Duke of Brachiano, with the Life and Death of Vittoria Corombona, the famous Venetian Courtezan," by John Webster. Acted at the Phoenix, in Drury Lane, and first printed in 1612.

[48] A tragi-comedy by Sir William Davenant. It was originally acted at the Blackfriars, and printed in 1649. . . .

[49] A comedy by the Duke of Newcastle, which was originally played at the Blackfriars, and printed in 1649.

[50] Henry Glapthorne's tragi-comedy.

1st. . . . And so went away to the Theatre, to "The Joviall Crew," and from Nov. hence home. . . .

4th. . . . After dinner . . . to the Opera, where we saw "The Bondman," which of old we both did so doat on, and do still; though to both our thinking not so well acted here (having too great expectations), as formerly at Salisbury-court. But for Betterton[51] he is called by us both the best actor in the world.

12th. . . . My wife and I to "Bartholomew Fayre," with puppets which I had seen once before, and the play without puppets often, but though I love the play as much as ever I did, yet I do not like the puppets at all, but think it be a lessening to it.

15th. . . . To the Opera . . . and there did see the second part of "The Siege of Rhodes" very well done. . . .

18th. . . . After dinner to Mr. Bowers at Westminster for my wife, and brought her to the Theatre to see "Philaster,"[52] which I never saw before, but I found it far short of my expectations. . . .

25th. . . . After dinner Sir W. Pen and I to the Theatre, and there saw "The Country Captain," a dull play, and that being done, I left him . . . and went to the Opera, and saw the last act of "The Bondman. . . .

27th. . . . To the Theatre, and there saw "Hamlett" very well done. . . .

29th. . . . Sir W. Pen and I to the Theatre, but it was so full that we could hardly get any room, so he went up to one of the boxes, and I into the 18*d*. places, and there saw "Love at first sight,"[53] a play of Mr. Killigrew's, and the first time that it hath been acted since before the troubles, and great expectation there was, but I found the play to be a poor thing, and so I perceive every body else do. . . .

2nd. . . . By coach to the Opera, to see "The Mad Lover,"[54] but not much Dec. pleased with the play. . . .

5th. . . . My wife and I to the Opera, and saw "Hamlett" well performed. . . .

16th. . . . After dinner to the Opera, where there was a new play ("Cutter of Coleman Street"),[55] made in the year 1658, with reflections much upon the late times; and it being the first time, the pay was doubled, and so to save money, my wife and I went up into the gallery, and there sat and saw very well; and a very good play it is. It seems of Cowly's making. . . .

---

[51] Thomas Betterton . . . first appeared on the stage at the Cockpit in Drury Lane, in 1659–60. After the Restoration, two distinct companies were established by royal authority: one called the King's Company, under a patent granted to Thomas Killigrew; the other styled the Duke's Company, the patentee of which was Sir William Davenant, who engaged Betterton.

[52] "Philaster; or, Love lies a-bleeding," a tragi-comedy, by Beaumont and Fletcher, acted at court in 1613.

[53] Here, as in so many other instances, Pepys gives the second title only of the play. The correct title is, "The Princesse, or Love at First Sight, a Tragi-Comedy: the scene, Naples and Sicily. Written in Naples by Thomas Killigrew." It was published at London, 1663.

[54] A tragi-comedy by Beaumont and Fletcher, published in the edition of their plays. 1647.

[55] Cutter, an old word for a rough swaggerer: hence the title of Cowley's play. It was originally called "The Guardian," when acted before Prince Charles at Trinity College, Cambridge, on March 12th, 1641.

30th. . . . Home to Sir W. Pen, who with his children and my wife has been at a play to-day and saw "D'Ambois,"[56] which I never saw.

1st. . . . Seeing that the "Spanish Curate"[1] was acted to-day, I . . . sent to young Mr. Pen and his sister to go anon with my wife and I to the Theatre. . . .

5th. . . . At noon Sir W. Pen dined with me, and after dinner he and I and my wife to the Theatre, and went in, but being very early we went out again to the next door, and drank some Rhenish wine and sugar, and so to the House again, and there saw "Rule a Wife and have a Wife" very well done. And here also I did look long upon my Lady Castlemaine, who, notwithstanding her late sickness, continues a great beauty. . . .

18th. . . . Having agreed with Sir Wm. Pen and my wife to meet them at the Opera, and finding by my walking in the streets, which were every where full of brick-battes and tyles flung down by the extraordinary wind the last night (such as hath not been in memory before, unless at the death of the late Protector), that it was dangerous to go out of doors; and hearing how several persons had been killed to-day by the fall of things in the streets, and that the pageant in Fleet-street is most of it blown down, and hath broke down part of several houses, among others Dick Brigden's; and that one Lady Sanderson, a person of quality in Covent Garden, was killed by the fall of the house, in her bed, last night; I sent my boy home to forbid them to go forth. But he bringing me word that they are gone, I went thither and there saw "The Law against Lovers,"[2] a good play and well performed, especially the little girl's (whom I never saw act before) dancing and singing; and were it not for her, the loss of Roxalana[3] would spoil the house. . . .

1st. . . . My wife and I . . . to the Opera, and there saw "Romeo and Juliet," the first time it was ever acted; but it is a play of itself the worst that ever I heard in my life, and the worst acted that ever I saw these people do,[4] and I am resolved to go no more to see the first time of acting, for they were all of them out more or less. . . .

31st. . . . Thence to the play, where coming late, and meeting with Sir W. Pen, who had got room for my wife and his daughter in the pit, he and I into one

---

[56] "Bussy D'Ambois," a tragedy by George Chapman, first published in 1607.

[1] A comedy by Beaumont and Fletcher, acted at court in December, 1622. Pepys saw this play March 16th, 1660–61, at Whitefriars Theatre.

[2] A tragi-comedy, by Sir William Davenant; taken from "Measure for Measure," with the characters of Benedick and Beatrice from "Much Ado about Nothing" added; published in Davenant's Works, 1673.

[3] This actress, so called from the character she played in the "Siege of Rhodes," was Frances or Elizabeth Davenport, who was born March 3rd, 1642. Evelyn saw her on January 9th, 1661–62, she being soon after taken to be "My Lord Oxford's Miss." She was induced to marry Aubrey de Vere, twentieth and last Earl of Oxford, after indignantly refusing to become his mistress, and discovered, when too late, that the nuptial ceremony had been performed by the earl's trumpeter, in the habit of a priest. For more of her history, see "Mémoires de Grammont." . . . Downes ("Roscius Anglicanus," p. 20) places Mrs. Davenport first on the list of the four principal actressess who boarded in Sir William Davenant's house. . . .

[4] Genest gives the cast, on the authority of Downes, as follows ("English Stage," vol. i, p. 42): Romeo — Harris, Mercutio — Betterton, Juliet — Mrs. Saunderson. . . .

of the boxes, and there we sat and heard "The Little Thiefe,"[5] a pretty play and well done. . . .

1st. . . . I and . . . my wife to the playhouse, the Opera, and saw "The Mayde in the Mill," a pretty good play. . . . *April*

2nd. . . . My wife and I by water to the Opera, and there saw "The Bondman" most excellently acted; and though we had seen it so often, yet I never liked it better than to-day, Ianthe[6] acting Cleora's part very well now Roxalana is gone. We are resolved to see no more plays till Whitsuntide, we having been three days together.

9th. Thence to see an Italian puppet play,[7] that is within the rayles there, which is very pretty, the best that ever I saw, and great resort of gallants. *May*

19th. After dinner Sir W. Pen and his daughter, and I and my wife by coach to the Theatre, and there in a box saw "The Little Thief" well done. . . .

20th. . . . My wife and I by coach to the Opera, and there saw the 2nd part of "The Siege of Rhodes," but it is not so well done as when Roxalana was there. . . .

21st. . . . We went to the Theatre to "The French Dancing Master"[8]. . . . The play pleased us very well; but Lacy's part, the Dancing Master, the best in the world. . . .

22d. . . . By coach to the Theatre and saw "Love in a Maze."[9] The play hath little in it but Lacy's part of a country fellow, which he did to admiration. . . . After supper home, and to bed, resolving to make up this week in seeing plays and pleasure. . . .

23rd. . . . After dinner . . . my wife and I slunk away to the Opera, where we saw "Witt in a Constable,"[10] the first time that it is acted; but so silly a play I never saw I think in my life. After it was done, my wife and I to the puppet play in Covent Garden, which I saw the other day, and indeed it is very pleasant. . . .

26th. . . . Thence to take my wife to the Redd Bull,[11] where we saw "Doctor

[5] Pepys had seen Fletcher's play, "The Night-Walker, or the Little Thief," at the Whitefriars Theatre, on April 2nd, 1661.

[6] Mary Saunderson, who married Thomas Betterton, December, 1662, one of Sir William Davenant's company, who acted Ianthe in the "Siege of Rhodes," at Lincoln's Inn Fields. She retired from the stage about 1675, died April, 1712, and was buried in the cloisters of Westminster Abbey on the 13th. The Roxalana here alluded to was Mrs. Davenport.

[7] This appears to have been a predecessor of Powell's more famous puppet-show. An Italian puppet-show was exhibited at Charing Cross in 1666 and 1667.

[8] A droll formed out of the Duke of Newcastle's play of "The Variety," . . . acted by Killigrew's company, March 11th, 1661–62. . . . It is no wonder that Lacy performed his part so well, as he had been brought up as a dancing master. . . .

[9] The second title of Shirley's play of "The Changes." Thumpe, Sir Gervase's man, was one of Lacy's most celebrated parts.

"For his just acting all gave him due praise,
His part in 'The Cheats,' Jony Thumpe, Teg, and Bayes.
In these four excelling; the Court gave him the Bays."

[10] A comedy, by Henry Glapthorne, printed 1640.

[11] The Red Bull Playhouse in Clerkenwell.

Faustus,"[12] but so wretchedly and poorly done, that we were sick of it, and the worse because by a former resolution it is to be the last play we are to see till Michaelmas. . . .

29th. . . . Then to the King's Theatre, where we saw "Midsummer's Night's Dream,"[13] which I had never seen before, nor shall ever again, for it is the most insipid ridiculous play that ever I saw in my life. I saw, I confess, some good dancing and some handsome women, which was all my pleasure. . . .

30th. . . . After dinner we took coach and to the Duke's playhouse, where we saw "The Duchess of Malfy"[14] well performed, but Betterton and Ianthe to admiration. . . . Strange to see how easily my mind do revert to its former practice of loving plays and wine, having given myself a liberty to them but these two days; but this night I have again bound myself to Christmas next, in which I desire God to bless me and preserve me, for under God I find it to be the best course that ever I could take to bring myself to mind my business. . . .

2nd. . . . Hearing that there was a play at the Cockpit . . . , I do go thither, and by very great fortune did follow four or five gentlemen who were carried to a little private door in a wall, and so crept through a narrow place and come into one of the boxes next the King's, but so as I could not see the King or Queene, but many of the fine ladies, who yet are really not so handsome generally as I used to take them to be, but that they are finely dressed. Here we saw "The Cardinall,"[15] a tragedy I had never seen before, nor is there any great matter in it. The company that came in with me into the box, were all Frenchmen that could speak no English, but Lord! what sport they made to ask a pretty lady that they got among them that understood both French and English to make her tell them what the actors said. . . .

20th. . . . And by and by up to the Duke, who was making himself ready; and there among other discourse young Killigrew did so commend "The Villaine,"[16] a new play made by Tom Porter, and acted only on Saturday at the Duke's house, as if there never had been any such play come upon the stage. The same yesterday was told me by Captain Ferrers; and this morning afterwards by Dr. Clerke, who saw it.

22nd. . . . It raining hard, by coach home, being first trimmed here by Benier, who being acquainted with all the players, do tell me that Betterton is not married to Ianthe,[17] as they say; but also that he is a very sober, serious man, and studious and humble, following of his studies, and is rich already with what he gets and saves. . . .

[12] Christopher Marlowe's tragedy, with additional scenes. Printed in 1663.

[13] This seems to be the only mention of the acting of Shakespeare's play at this time, and it does not appear to have been a favourite.

[14] A tragedy by John Webster, first published in 1623. The character of Bosola was taken by Betterton, and that of the Duchess of Malfy by Mary Saunderson, shortly afterwards his wife (Ianthe). The acting is highly praised by Downes.

[15] A tragedy by James Shirley, licensed on November 25th, 1641, and printed in 1652.

[16] A tragedy by T. Porter. "The Villain, a tragedy which I have seen acted at the Duke's Theatre with great applause: the part of Malignii being incomparably played by Mr. Sandford." — *Langbaine*, p. 407. . . .

[17] Mary Saunderson, famous for acting the character of Ianthe in Davenant's "Siege of Rhodes." The marriage license of "Thomas Betterton, bachelor, of Westminster, aged about 30, and Mary Saunderson, of St. Giles, Cripplegate, spinster, about 25," is dated December 24th, 1662. See Chester's "London Marriage Licenses," ed. Foster, 1887, col. 123.

30th. . . . I would not forget two passages . . . at yesterday's dinner. The one, that to the question how it comes to pass that there are no boars seen in London, but many sows and pigs; it was answered, that the constable gets them a-nights. The other, Thos. Killigrew's way of getting to see plays when he was a boy. He would go to the Red Bull, and when the man cried to the boys, "Who will go and be a devil, and he shall see the play for nothing?" then would he go in, and be a devil upon the stage, and so get to see plays.

31st. I thank God I have no crosses, but only much business to trouble my mind with. In all other things as happy a man as any in the world. . . . And all I do impute almost wholly to my late temperance, since my making of my vowes against wine and plays. . . .

10th. . . . Taking my wife up, carried her to Charing Cross, and there showed *Nov.* her the Italian motion, much after the nature of what I showed her a while since in Covent Garden. Their puppets here are somewhat better, but their motions not at all.

15th. . . . So home and to supper, and after reading part of Bussy d'Ambois,[18] a good play I bought to-day, to bed.

17th. . . . My wife and I to the Cockpitt, and we had excellent places, and saw the King, Queen, Duke of Monmouth, his son, and my Lady Castlemaine, and all the fine ladies; and "The Scornfull Lady," well performed. They had done by eleven o'clock. . . .

1st. . . . I to the Cockpitt, with much crowding and waiting, where I saw *December* "The Valiant Cidd"[19] acted, a play I have read with great delight, but is a most dull thing acted, which I never understood before, there being no pleasure in it, though done by Betterton and by Ianthe, and another fine wench that is come in the room of Roxalana;[20] nor did the King or Queen once smile all the whole play, nor any of the company seem to take any pleasure but what was in the greatness and gallantry of the company.

19th. . . . It being cold . . . I did sit all the day till three o'clock by the fire . . . reading a play of Fletcher's, being "A Wife for a Month,"[21] wherein no great wit or language. . . .

26th. . . . To the Duke's house and saw "The Villaine," which I ought not to do without my wife, but that my time is now out that I did undertake it for. But, Lord! to consider how my natural desire is to pleasure, which God be praised that he has given me the power by my late oaths to curb so well as I have done, and will do again after two or three plays more. Here I was better pleased with the play than I was at first, understanding the design better than I did. . . .

27th. . . . After dinner with my wife to the Duke's Theatre, and saw the

---

[18] A tragedy by George Chapman, first published in 1607. The plot is taken from French history of the reign of Henry VIII.

[19] Translated from the "Cid" of Corneille.

[20] Elizabeth Davenport having left the stage, her place was probably taken by Mrs. Norton.

[21] A tragi-comedy, licensed May 27th, 1624, printed in Beaumont and Fletcher's Works, 1647. Pepys does not appear to have seen it acted.

second part of "Rhodes," done with the new Roxalana; which do it rather better in all respects for person, voice, and judgment, than the first Roxalana. . . .

1st. . . . After dinner I . . . took coach, and to the Duke's House,[1] where we saw "The Villaine" again; and the more I see it, the more I am offended at my first undervaluing the play, it being very good and pleasant, and yet a true and allowable tragedy. The house was full of citizens, and so the less pleasant, but that I was willing to make an end of my gaddings, and to set to my business for all the year again to-morrow. Here we saw the old Roxalana[2] in the chief box, in a velvet gown, as the fashion is, and very handsome, at which I was glad. . . .

5th. . . . To the Cockpitt, where we saw "Claracilla," a poor play, done by the King's house (but neither the King nor Queen were there, but only the Duke and Duchess, who did show some impertinent and, methought, unnaturall dalliances there, before the whole world, such as kissing, and leaning upon one another). . . .

6th. . . . After dinner to the Duke's house, and there saw "Twelfth Night" acted well, though it be but a silly play, and not related at all to the name or day. . . .

8th. . . . Dined at home; and there being the famous new play acted the first time to-day, which is called "The Adventures of Five Hours," at the Duke's house, being, they say, made or translated by Colonel Tuke,[3] I did long to see it; and so made my wife to get her ready, though we were forced to send for a smith, to break open her trunk, her mayde Jane being gone forth with the keys, and so we went; and though early, were forced to sit almost out of sight, at the end of one of the lower forms, so full was the house. And the play, in one word, is the best, for the variety and the most excellent continuance of the plot to the very end, that ever I saw, or think ever shall, and all possible, not only to be done in the time, but in most other respects very admittable, and without one word of ribaldry; and the house, by its frequent plaudits, did show their sufficient approbation. So home; with much ado in an hour getting a coach home, and, after writing letters at my office, I went home to supper and to bed, now resolving to set up my rest as to plays till Easter, if not Whitsuntide next, excepting plays at Court.

17th. . . . To the Duke's playhouse, where we did see "The Five Hours" entertainment again, which indeed is a very fine play, though, through my being out of order, it did not seem so good as at first; but I could discern it was not any fault in the play. . . .

February   6th. . . . To Lincoln's Inn Fields; and it being too soon to go to dinner, I

---

[1] Davenant's Company, called from being under the patronage of the Duke of York, the Duke's Company, began to play at Salisbury Court Theatre on November 15th, 1660. The company removed to Portugal Row, Lincoln's Inn Fields, in June, 1661. Davenant's Theatre is usually called the Opera, to distinguish it from the Theatre of the King's Company.
[2] Mrs. Davenport.
[3] Sir Samuel Tuke. . . . His play, "The Adventures of Five Hours," was founded on a play by Calderon, and undertaken on the suggestion of the king, who recommended him to adapt a Spanish play to the English stage. . . .

walked up and down, and looked upon the outside of the new theatre, now a-building in Covent Garden,[4] which will be very fine. . . .

23d. . . . While my wife dressed herself, Creed and I walked out to see what play was acted to-day, and we find it "The Slighted Mayde."[5] . . . By and by took coach, and to the Duke's house, where we saw it well acted, though the play hath little good in it, being most pleased to see the little girl dance in boy's apparel, she having very fine legs, only bends in the hams, as I perceive all women do. The play being done, we took coach and to Court, and there got good places, and saw "The Wilde Gallant,"[6] performed by the King's house, but it was ill acted, and the play so poor a thing as I never saw in my life almost, and so little answering the name, that from beginning to end, I could not, nor can at this time, tell certainly which was the Wild Gallant. The King did not seem pleased at all, all the whole play, nor any body else. . . . It being done, we got a coach and got well home about 12 at night. Now as my mind was but very ill satisfied with these two plays themselves, so was I in the midst of them sad to think of the spending so much money and venturing upon the breach of my vow, which I found myself sorry for, I bless God, though my nature would well be contented to follow the pleasure still. But I did make payment of my forfeiture presently, though I hope to save it back again by forbearing two plays at Court for this one at the Theatre, or else to forbear that to the Theatre which I am to have at Easter. But it being my birthday and my day of liberty regained to me, and lastly, the last play that is likely to be acted at Court before Easter, because of the Lent coming in, I was the easier content to fling away so much money.[7]

22nd. . . . After dinner by coach to the King's Playhouse, where we saw but *April* part of "Witt without mony,"[8] which I do not like much, but coming late put me out of tune, and it costing me four half-crowns for myself and company. . . .

7th. . . . This day the new Theatre Royal[9] begins to act with scenes the *May* Humourous Lieutenant, but I have not time to see it. . . .

8th. . . . To the new playhouse, but could not get in to see it. . . . Took up my wife . . . to the Theatre Royall, being the second day of its being opened. The house is made with extraordinary good contrivance, and yet hath some faults, as the narrowness of the passages in and out of the pitt, and the distance from the stage to the boxes, which I am confident cannot hear; but for all other things it is well, only, above all, the musique being below, and most of it sounding under the very stage, there is no hearing of the bases at all, nor very well of the trebles, which sure must be mended. The play was "The Humerous

[4] The theatre built on the site of the present Drury Lane Theatre for the King's Company under Thomas Killigrew was opened on May 7th. . . , 1663, when the company removed from the Theatre in Vere Street, Clare Market.

[5] A comedy by Sir Robert Stapylton, acted by the Duke's Company in Lincoln's Inn Fields. Betterton and his wife both acted in this play.

[6] Dryden's first play.

[7] The Court theatre was so far public that persons could get in by payment.

[8] A comedy by Beaumont and Fletcher.

[9] This was the first Drury Lane Theatre. . . . The theatre was burned in 1672, and at once rebuilt. It was reopened March 26th, 1674.

Lieutenant,"[10] a play that hath little good in it, nor much in the very part which, by the King's command, Lacy now acts instead of Clun. In the dance, the tall devil's actions was very pretty. The play being done, we home by water, having been a little shamed that my wife and woman were in such a pickle, all the ladies being finer and better dressed in the pitt than they used, I think, to be. To my office to set down this day's passage, and, though my oath against going to plays do not oblige me against this house, because it was not then in being, yet believing that at the time my meaning was against all publique houses, I am resolved to deny myself the liberty of two plays at Court, which are in arreare to me for the months of March and April, which will more than countervail this excess, so that this month of May is the first that I must claim a liberty of going to a Court play according to my oath. . . .

29th. . . . So home to dinner, and out by water to the Royall Theatre, but they not acting today, then to the Duke's house, and there saw "The Slighted Mayde," wherein Gosnell acted Pyramena, a great part, and did it very well, and I believe will do it better and better, and prove a good actor. The play is not very excellent, but is well acted, and in general the actors, in all particulars, are better than at the other house. . . . My mind troubled about my spending my time so badly for these seven or eight days; but I must impute it to the disquiet that my mind has been in of late . . . , and for my going these two days to plays, for which I have paid the due forfeit by money and abating the times of going to plays at Court, which I am now to remember that I have cleared all my times that I am to go to Court plays to the end of this month, and so June is the first time that I am to begin to reckon.

31st (Lord's Day). . . . After dinner up and read part of the new play of "The Five Houres' Adventures," which though I have seen it twice, yet I never did admire or understand it enough, it being a play of the greatest plot that ever I expect to see, and of great vigour quite through the whole play, from beginning to the end. . . .

June　　1st. Begun again to rise betimes by 4 o'clock, and made an end of "The Adventures of Five Houres," and it is a most excellent play. . . .

10th. . . . To the Royal Theatre by water . . . , we saw "Love in a Maze." The play is pretty good, but the life of the play is Lacy's part, the clown, which is most admirable; but for the rest, which are counted such old and excellent actors, in my life I never heard both men and women so ill pronounce their parts, even to my making myself sick therewith. . . .

12th. . . . At noon to the Exchange and so home to dinner, and abroad with my wife by water to the Royall Theatre; and there saw "The Committee,"[11] a merry but indifferent play, only Lacey's part, an Irish footman, is beyond imagination. Here I saw my Lord Falconbridge, and his Lady, my Lady Mary Cromwell, who looks as well as I have known her, and well clad; but when

---

[10] Walter Clun, famous in the character of Iago, acted the part of the Lieutenant at the opening of Drury Lane Theatre, that is, if Downes is to be relied upon, but as he makes the mistake of fixing that occasion on April 8th, he may not be right as to this.

[11] A comedy by Sir Robert Howard, written in ridicule of the Puritans.

the House began to fill she put on her vizard,[12] and so kept it on all the play; which of late is become a great fashion among the ladies, which hides their whole face. So to the Exchange, to buy things with my wife; among others, a vizard for herself. . . .

13th. . . . By water to the Royall Theatre, where I resolve to bid farewell, as shall appear by my oaths to-morrow against all plays either at publique houses or Court till Christmas be over. Here we saw "The Faithfull Sheepheardesse,"[13] a most simple thing, and yet much thronged after, and often shown, but it is only for the scenes' sake, which is very fine indeed and worth seeing; but I am quite out of opinion with any of their actings, but Lacy's, compared with the other house. . . .

22nd. . . . Thence homewards, and in the way first called at Wotton's, the *July* shoemaker's, who tells me the reason of Harris's[14] going from Sir Wm. Davenant's house, that he grew very proud and demanded £20 for himself extraordinary, more than Betterton or any body else, upon every new play, and £10 upon every revive; which with other things Sir W. Davenant would not give him, and so he swore he would never act there more, in expectation of being received in the other House; but the King will not suffer it, upon Sir W. Davenant's desire that he would not, for then he might shut up house, and that is true. He tells me that his going is at present a great loss to the House, and that he fears he hath a stipend from the other House privately. He tells me that the fellow grew very proud of late, the King and every body else crying him up so high, and that above Betterton, he being a more ayery man, as he is indeed. But yet Betterton, he says, they all say do act some parts that none but himself can do. . . .

10th. . . . Calling at Wotton's, my shoemaker's, to-day, he tells me . . . that *December* Harris is come to the Duke's house again; and of a rare play to be acted this week of Sir William Davenant's: the story of Henry the Eighth with all his wives.[15]

22nd. . . . I perceive the King and Duke and all the Court was going to the Duke's playhouse to see "Henry VIII." acted, which is said to be an admirable play. But, Lord! to see how near I was to have broken my oathe, or run the hazard of 20s. losse, so much my nature was hot to have gone thither; but I did not go. . . .

24th. . . . Captain Ferrers to see us, and, among other talke, tells us of the goodness of the new play of "Henry VIII.," which makes me think [it] long

[12] Masks were commonly used by ladies in the reign of Elizabeth, and when their use was revived at the Restoration for respectable women attending the theatre, they became general. They soon, however, became the mark of loose women, and their use was discontinued by women of repute. . . .

[13] A dramatic pastoral by John Fletcher, first acted in 1610.

[14] "Henry Harris, of the city of London, painter," was one of the contracting parties in the agreement for Davenant's Company of November 5th, 1660. He left the company, and expected to be eagerly sought after by Killigrew, but the king prevented his attaching himself to the other house, and he had in the end to rejoin Davenant's company. He acted Romeo when Betterton took Mercutio. . . .

[15] "Henry VIII." was revived at this time with Betterton as the king and Harris as Wolsey, but Pepys's description of the play seems to be a very inaccurate one.

till my time is out; but I hope before I go I shall set myself such a stint as I may not forget myself as I have hitherto done till I was forced for these months last past wholly to forbid myself the seeing of one. . . .

26th. . . . I all the afternoon with my wife to cards, and, God forgive me! to see how the very discourse of plays, which I shall be at liberty to see after New Year's Day next, do set my mind upon them, but I must be forced to stint myself very strictly before I begin, or else I fear I shall spoil all. . . .

1663–64 January

1st. . . . My wife and I . . . went to the Duke's house, the first play I have been at these six months, according to my last vowe, and here saw the so much cried-up play of "Henry the Eighth;" which, though I went with resolution to like it, is so simple a thing made up of a great many patches, that, besides the shows and processions in it, there is nothing in the world good or well done. . . .

2nd. . . . I do find that I am not able to conquer myself as to going to plays till I come to some new vowe concerning it, and that I am now come, that is to say, that I will not see above one in a month at any of the publique theatres till the sum of 50s. be spent, and then none before New Year's Day next, unless that I do become worth £1,000 sooner than then, and then am free to come to some other terms, . . . I . . . to the King's house, . . . and saw "The Usurper,"[1] which is no good play, though better than what I saw yesterday. . . .

27th. . . . My wife and I took coach and to Covent Garden, to buy a maske at the French House, Madame Charett's, for my wife; in the way observing the streete full of coaches at the new play, "The Indian Queene;"[2] which for show, they say, exceeds "Henry the Eighth." . . . .

February

1st. . . . Took my wife out immediately to the King's Theatre, it being a new month, and once a month I may go, and there saw "The Indian Queene" acted; which indeed is a most pleasant show, and beyond my expectation; the play good, but spoiled with the ryme, which breaks the sense. But above my expectation most, the eldest Marshall[3] did do her part most excellently well as I ever heard woman in my life; but her voice not so sweet as Ianthe's;[4] but, however, we came home mightily contented. . . .

March

7th. . . . My wife and I by coach to the Duke's house, where we saw "The Unfortunate Lovers;"[5] but I know not whether I am grown more curious than I was or no, but I was not much pleased with it, though I know not where to lay the fault, unless it was that the house was very empty, by reason of a new play at the other house. . . .

[1] A tragedy by the Hon. Edward Howard, now first acted, but not published until 1668. Oliver Cromwell was alluded to under the name of Damocles the Syracusan, and Hugh Peters is introduced as Hugo de Petra.

[2] "The Indian Queen," a tragedy in heroic verse, by Sir Robert Howard and John Dryden. It was produced with great splendour, with music composed by Purcell.

[3] Anne Marshall, a celebrated actress. . . .

[4] Mrs. Betterton.

[5] A tragedy by Sir William Davenant, first acted at the Blackfriars Theatre, licensed 1635, printed 1643.

8th. . . .We made no long stay at dinner; for "Heraclius"[6] being acted, which my wife and I have a mighty mind to see, we do resolve, though not exactly agreeing with the letter of my vowe, yet altogether with the sense, to see another this month, by going hither instead of that at Court, there having been none conveniently since I made my vowe for us to see there, nor like to be this Lent, and besides we did walk home on purpose to make this going as cheap as that would have been, to have seen one at Court, and my conscience knows that it is only the saving of money and the time also that I intend by my oaths, and this has cost no more of either, so that my conscience before God do after good consultation and resolution of paying my forfeit, did my conscience accuse me of breaking my vowe, I do not find myself in the least apprehensive that I have done any violence to my oaths. The play hath one very good passage well managed in it, about two persons pretending, and yet denying themselves, to be son to the tyrant Phocas, and yet heire of Mauricius to the crowne. The garments like Romans very well. The little girle[7] is come to act very prettily, and spoke the epilogue most admirably. But at the beginning, at the drawing up of the curtaine, there was the finest scene of the Emperor and his people about him, standing in their fixed and different postures in their Roman habitts, above all that ever I yet saw at any of the theatres. . . .

15th. . . . With my wife by coach to the Duke's house, and there saw "The *April* German Princess" acted, by the woman herself; but never was any thing so well done in earnest, worse performed in jest upon the stage; and indeed the whole play, abating the drollery of him that acts her husband, is very simple, unless here and there a witty sprinkle or two. . . .

2nd. . . . Presently by coach to the King's Play-house to see "The Labyrinth,"[8] *May* but, coming too soon, walked to my Lord's to hear how my Lady do, who is pretty well; at least past all fear. There by Captain Ferrers meeting with an opportunity of my Lord's coach, to carry us to the Parke anon, we directed it to come to the play-house door; and so we walked, my wife and I and Mademoiselle. I paid for her going in, and there saw "The Labyrinth," the poorest play, methinks, that ever I saw, there being nothing in it but the odd accidents that fell out, by a lady's being bred up in man's apparel, and a man in a woman's. . . .

1st. . . . I met my wife, . . . and she and I to the King's house, and saw "The *June* Silent Woman;" but methought not so well done or so good a play as I formerly thought it to be, or else I am now-a-days out of humour. Before the play was done, it fell such a storm of hayle, that we in the middle of the pit were fain to rise;[9] and all the house in a disorder, and so my wife and I out and got into a little alehouse, and staid there an hour after the play was done before we could get a coach. . . .

---

[6] "Heraclius; or, the Emperor of the East," translated from the French of Corneille, by Ludovic Carlell. Pepys saw it again, February 4th, 1666-67, at the Duke's Theatre. Carlell's translation (4to, 1664) was, it is said, never acted. The play which Pepys saw was probably never printed. He saw it at the Duke's Theatre.

[7] Her dancing in "The Slighted Maid" is mentioned February 23rd, 1662-63.

[8] Or "The Fatal Embarrassment," taken from Corneille.

[9] The stage was covered in by a tiled roof, but the pit was open to the sky. . . .

20th. . . . Went to a play, only a piece of it, which was at the Duke's house, "Worse and Worse;"[10] just the same manner of play, and writ, I believe, by the same man as "The Adventures of Five Hours;"[11] very pleasant it was, and I begin to admire Harris more than ever. . . .

28th. . . . Seeing "The Bondman"[12] upon the posts, I consulted my oaths and find I may go safely this time without breaking it; I went thither. . . . There I saw it acted. It is true, for want of practice, they had many of them forgot their parts a little; but Betterton and my poor Ianthe outdo all the world. There is nothing more taking in the world with me than that play. . . .

2nd. . . . To the King's play-house, and there saw "Bartholomew Fayre," which do still please me; and is, as it is acted, the best comedy in the world, I believe. I chanced to sit by Tom Killigrew, who tells me that he is setting up a Nursery;[13] that is, is going to build a house in Moorefields, wherein he will have common plays acted. But four operas it shall have in the year, to act six weeks at a time; where we shall have the best scenes and machines, the best musique, and every thing as magnificent as is in Christendome; and to that end hath sent for voices and painters and other persons from Italy. . . .

4th. . . . At noon dined with Sir W. Pen . . . , and he did carry me to a play and pay for me at the King's house, which is "The Rivall Ladys,"[14] a very innocent and most pretty witty play. I was much pleased with it, and it being given me,[15] I look upon it as no breach to my oathe. Here we hear that Clun,[16] one of their best actors, was, the last night, going out of towne (after he had acted the Alchymist, wherein was one of his best parts that he acts) to his countryhouse, set upon and murdered; one of the rogues taken, an Irish fellow. It seems most cruelly butchered and bound. The house will have a great miss of him. . . .

8th. . . . My wife and I abroad to the King's play-house, she giving me her time of the last month, she having not seen any then; so my vowe is not broke at all, it costing me no more money than it would have done upon her, had she gone both her times that were due to her. Here we saw "Flora's Figarys."[17]

---

[10] A comedy adapted from the Spanish by George Digby, Earl of Bristol, which was not printed.

[11] This was not so, as the "Adventures of Five Hours" was by Sir Samuel Tuke, although Downes ("Roscius Anglicanus") says that the Earl of Bristol had a hand in this play.

[12] Massinger's tragedy, first acted before the Court at Whitehall, 1623.

[13] Among the State Papers is the license (dated March, 1664) to William Legg "to erect a nursery for breeding players in London or Westminster under the oversight and approbation of Sir Wm. Davenant and Thos. Killigrew to be disposed of for the supply of the theatres" ("Calendar," Domestic, 1663–64, p. 539).

[14] A tragi-comedy by Dryden, first printed in this year.

[15] His companion paid for him.

[16] A poem upon the death of Walter Clun was published at the time, with the following title: "An Elegy upon the most execrable murder of Mr. Clun, one of the comedians of the Theatre Royal, who was robbed and most inhumanly killed on Tuesday night, being the 2nd of August, 1664, near Tatnam Court, as he was riding to his country house at Kentish Town." Clun was noted for his performance of Iago.

[17] "Flora's Vagaries," a comedy by Richard Rhodes, when a student at Oxford, was first acted by his fellow-students at Christ Church on January 8th, 1663. Sir Henry Herbert records its performance in London on November 3rd, 1663. It was printed in 1670 and 1677. The character of Flora was afterwards played by Nell Gwynn (see October 5th, 1667).

I never saw it before, and by the most ingenuous performance of the young jade Flora, it seemed as pretty a pleasant play as ever I saw in my life. . . .

13th. . . . To the new play, at the Duke's house, of "Henry the Fifth;"[18] a most noble play, writ by my Lord Orrery; wherein Betterton, Harris, and Ianthe's parts are most incomparably wrote and done, and the whole play the most full of height and raptures of wit and sense, that ever I heard; having but one incongruity, or what did not please me in it, that is, that King Harry promises to plead for Tudor to their Mistresse, Princesse Katherine of France, more than when it comes to it he seems to do; and Tudor refused by her with some kind of indignity, not with a difficulty and honour that it ought to have been done in to him. . . .

17th. . . . Thence to Mrs. Pierce's, and with her and my wife to see Mrs. Clarke, where with him and her very merry discoursing of the late play of Henry the 5th, which they conclude the best that ever was made, but confess with me that Tudor's being dismissed in the manner he is is a great blemish to the play. . . .

18th. . . . My wife . . . to see a new play, "The Court Secret."[19] . . . My wife says the play she saw is the worst that ever she saw in her life.

10th. . . . My wife and I . . . to the Duke's house, and there saw "The *September* Rivalls,"[20] which is no excellent play, but good acting in it; especially Gosnell comes and sings and dances finely, but, for all that, fell out of the key, so that the musique could not play to her afterwards, and so did Harris also go out of the tune to agree with her. . . .

28th. . . . To a play, and so we saw, coming late, part of "The Generall," my Lord Orrery's (Broghill)[21] second play; but, Lord! to see how no more either in words, sense, or design, it is to his "Harry the 5th" is not imaginable, and so poorly acted, though in finer clothes, is strange. . . .

4th. . . . After dinner to a play, to see "The Generall;" which is so dull and *October* so ill-acted, that I think it is the worst I ever saw or heard in all my days. I happened to sit near to Sir Charles Sidly;[22] who I find a very witty man, and he did at every line take notice of the dullness of the poet and badness of the action, that most pertinently; which I was mightily taken with; and among others where by Altemire's command Clarimont, the Generall, is commanded to rescue his Rivall, whom she loved, Lucidor, he, after a great deal of demurre,

[18] King Henry was acted by Harris and Owen Tudor by Betterton. Downes says that the "play was spendidly cloath'd. The King in the Duke of York's coronation suit, Owen Tudor in King Charles's, Duke of Burgundy (Smith) in the Lord of Oxford's, and the rest of all new." Mrs. Betterton (Ianthe) acted as Princess Katharine. Mrs. Long was the Queen of France, and Mrs. Davis, Anne of Burgundy.

[19] A tragi-comedy by James Shirley, "written when the stage was interdicted," and first performed after the Restoration. Before the publication of this notice in Pepys, Langbaine's statement was the only evidence that it had ever been acted.

[20] A comedy by Sir William Davenant, first published in 1668. It is an alteration of "The Two Noble Kinsmen." Harris played Theocles; Betterton, Philander. Gosnell is not mentioned in the cast by Downes. The character of Celania was afterwards acted by Mrs. Davis, who captivated Charles II. in this part.

[21] Roger Boyle, Lord Broghill, created Earl of Orrery, 1660. Died October 16th, 1679. A tragi-comedy with the same title has been attributed to Shirley. . . .

[22] The witty Sir Charles Sedley is frequently referred to by Pepys in the Diary.

broke out, "Well, I'le save my Rivall and make her confess, that I deserve, while he do but possesse." "Why, what, pox," says Sir Charles Sydly, "would he have him have more, or what is there more to be had of a woman than the possessing her?" Thence . . . home with my wife . . . , vexed at my losing my time and above 20*s*. in money, and neglecting my business to see so bad a play. Tomorrow they told us should be acted, or the day after, a new play, called "The Parson's Dreame,"[23] acted all by women. . . .

11th. . . . I alone at home at dinner, till by and by Luellin comes and dines with me. He tells me what a bawdy loose play this "Parson's Wedding"[24] is, that is acted by nothing but women at the King's house. . . .

November

5th. . . . With my wife to the Duke's house to a play, "Macbeth,"[25] a pretty good play, but admirably acted. . . .

December

2nd. . . . After dinner with my wife . . . to the Duke's House, and there saw "The Rivalls," which I had seen before; but the play not good, nor anything but the good actings of Betterton and his wife and Harris. . . .

1664–65 January

4th. . . . I to "Love in a Tubb,"[1] which is very merry, but only so by gesture, not wit at all, which methinks is beneath the House. . . .

14th. . . . With my wife to the King's house, there to see "Vulpone,"[2] a most excellent play; the best I think I ever saw, and well acted. . . .

April

3rd. . . . To a play at the Duke's, of my Lord Orrery's, called "Mustapha,"[3] which being not good, made Betterton's part and Ianthe's but ordinary too, so that we were not contented with it at all. . . . All the pleasure of the play was, the King and my Lady Castlemayne were there; and pretty witty Nell,[4] at the King's house, and the younger Marshall[5] sat next us; which pleased me mightily.

17th. . . . We all to a play, "The Ghosts,"[6] at the Duke's house, but a very simple play. . . .

May

15th. . . . After dinner to the King's playhouse, all alone, and saw "Love's Maistresse."[7] Some pretty things and good variety in it, but no or little fancy in it. . . .

1665–66 March

19th. . . . After dinner we walked to the King's play-house, all in dirt, they being altering of the stage to make it wider. But God knows when they will

---

[23] There does not appear to have been any play with this title. It evidently was the "Parson's Wedding," referred to October 11th.

[24] A comedy written by Thomas Killigrew in Switzerland, published in 1663. . . .

[25] This was Sir William Davenant's alteration of Shakespeare's play, which was described by Downes "as being in the nature of an opera." Malone says that it was first acted in 1663. It was not printed until 1763.

[1] "The Comical Revenge, or Love in a Tub," a comedy by Sir George Etherege; licensed for printing, July 8th, 1664, but not published till 1669. It was acted by the Duke's Company, and the Bettertons and Harris were in it.

[2] Ben Johnson's comedy, "Volpone, or the Fox," published 1605.

[3] Now first acted. Betterton took the character of Solyman the Magnificent, and Mrs. Betterton, Roxolana. . . .

[4] Nell Gwynne.   [5] Rebecca Marshall.

[6] A comedy, on the authority of Downes (p. 26) attributed to a Mr. Holden, and probably never printed.

[7] "Loves Maistresse, or The Queen's Masque," by Thomas Heywood, printed 1636, 1640.

begin to act again; but my business here was to see the inside of the stage and all the tiring-rooms and machines; and, indeed, it was a sight worthy seeing. But to see their clothes, and the various sorts, and what a mixture of things there was; here a wooden-leg, there a ruff, here a hobby-horse, there a crown, would make a man split himself to see with laughing; and particularly Lacy's[1] wardrobe, and Shotrell's.[2] But then again, to think how fine they show on the stage by candle-light, and how poor things they are to look now too near hand, is not pleasant at all. The machines are fine, and the paintings very pretty. . . .

29th. . . . Into the new play-house[3] there, the first time I ever was there, and *October* the first play I have seen since before the great plague. . . . By and by the King and Queene, Duke and Duchesse, and all the great ladies of the Court; which, indeed, was a fine sight. But the play being "Love in a Tub,"[4] a silly play, and though done by the Duke's people, yet having neither Betterton nor his wife, and the whole thing done ill, and being ill also, I had no manner of pleasure in the play. Besides, the House, though very fine, yet bad for the voice, for hearing. The sight of the ladies, indeed, was exceeding noble; and above all, my Lady Castlemayne. The play done by ten o'clock. . . .

7th. . . . By water to the Strand, and so to the King's playhouse, where two *December* acts were almost done when I come in; and there I sat with my cloak about my face, and saw the remainder of "The Mayd's Tragedy;" a good play, and well acted, especially by the younger Marshall, who is become a pretty good actor, and is the first play I have seen in either of the houses since before the great plague, they having acted now about fourteen days publickly. . . .

8th. . . . To the King's playhouse, which troubles me since, and hath cost me a forfeit of 10s., which I have paid, and there did see a good part of "The English Monsieur,"[5] which is a mighty pretty play, very witty and pleasant. And the women do very well; but, above all, little Nelly,[6] that I am mightily pleased with the play, and much with the House, more than ever I expected, the women doing better than ever I expected, and very fine women. . . .

27th. . . . In the middle of dinner I rose, and my wife, and by coach to the King's playhouse . . . , and there saw "The Scornfull Lady" well acted; Doll Common[7] doing Abigal most excellently, and Knipp the widow very well, and will be an excellent actor, I think. In other parts the play not so well done as used to be, by the old actors. Anon to White Hall by coach, thinking to have seen a play there to-night, but found it a mistake, so back again. . . .

---

[1] John Lacy, the celebrated comedian.

[2] Robert and William Shotterel both belonged to the King's Company at the opening of their new theatre in 1663. . . . Pepys refers to Robert Shotterel, who, it appears, was living in Playhouse Yard, Drury Lane, 1681–84.

[3] The "Warrant appointing Henry Glover keeper of the Royal Theatre at Whitehall, with the scenes, engines, &c., fee £30 a year from the money allowed for plays, &c.," is dated November 21st, 1666 ("Calendar of State Papers," 1666–67, p. 278).

[4] "The Comical Revenge, or Love in a Tub," a comedy by Sir George Etherege, licensed for printing in 1664, and published in 1669.

[5] A comedy by the Hon. James Howard, son of the Earl of Berkshire, printed in 4to., 1674.

[6] Nell Gwynn played Lady Wealthy, a rich widow. . . .

[7] Mrs. Corey. See January 15th, 1668–69. . . .

28th. . . . To the Duke's house, and there saw "Macbeth" most excellently acted, and a most excellent play for variety. I had sent for my wife to meet me there, who did come, and after the play was done, I out so soon to meet her at the other door that I left my cloake in the playhouse, and while I returned to get it, she was gone out and missed me. . . . I not sorry for it much did go to White Hall, and got my Lord Bellasses to get me into the playhouse; and there, after all staying above an hour for the players, the King and all waiting, which was absurd, saw "Henry the Fifth" well done by the Duke's people, and in most excellent habits, all new vests, being put on but this night. But I sat so high and far off, that I missed most of the words, and sat with a wind coming into my back and neck, which did much trouble me. The play continued till twelve at night. . . .

2nd. . . . Alone to the King's House, and there saw "The Custome of the Country,"[1] the second time of its being acted, wherein Knipp does the Widow well; but, of all the plays that ever I did see, the worst — having neither plot, language, nor anything in the earth that is acceptable. . . . But fully the worst play that ever I saw or I believe shall see. . . .

5th. . . . Away, with my wife, to the Duke's house, and there saw "Mustapha," a most excellent play for words and design as ever I did see. I had seen it before but forgot it, so it was wholly new to me. . . .

7th. . . . To the Duke's house, and saw "Macbeth," which, though I saw it lately, yet appears a most excellent play in all respects, but especially in divertisement, though it be a deep tragedy; which is a strange perfection in a tragedy, it being most proper here, and suitable. . . .

23rd. . . . To the King's house, and there saw "The Humerous Lieutenant:" a silly play, I think; only the Spirit in it that grows very tall, and then sinks again to nothing, having two heads breeding upon one, and then Knipp's singing, did please us. Here, in a box above, we spied Mrs. Pierce; and, going out, they called us, and so we staid for them; and Knipp took us all in, and brought us to Nelly,[2] a most pretty woman, who acted the great part of Cœlia to-day very fine, and did it pretty well: I kissed her, and so did my wife; and a mighty pretty soul she is. We also saw Mrs. Hall,[3] which is my little Roman-nose black girl, that is mighty pretty: she is usually called Betty. Knipp made us stay in a box and see the dancing preparatory to to-morrow for "The Goblins," a play of Suckling's,[4] not acted these twenty-five years; which was pretty; and so away thence, pleased with this sight also, and specially kissing of Nell. . . .

4th. . . . Soon as dined, my wife and I out to the Duke's playhouse, and there saw "Heraclius,"[5] an excellent play, to my extraordinary content; and the

---

[1] This tragi-comedy, which refers to the feudal custom styled the *droit du seigneur*, was acted in 1628, and printed in Beaumont and Fletcher's Works, 1647. Dryden, in the preface to his "Fables," says "there is more indecency in the 'Custom of the Country' than in all our plays together, yet this has been often acted on the stage in my remembrance."

[2] Nell Gwynn.

[3] Betty Hall. . . .

[4] Sir John Suckling's play was first published in 1646, having been acted at the Blackfriars.

[5] See note to March 8th, 1664.

more from the house being very full, and great company; among others, Mrs. Steward, very fine, with her locks done up with puffs, as my wife calls them: and several other great ladies had their hair so, though I do not like it; but my wife do mightily — but it is only because she sees it is the fashion. Here I saw my Lord Rochester and his lady, Mrs. Mallet, who hath after all this ado married him; and, as I hear some say in the pit, it is a great act of charity, for he hath no estate. But it was pleasant to see how every body rose up when my Lord John Butler, the Duke of Ormond's son, come into the pit towards the end of the play, who was a servant to Mrs. Mallet, and now smiled upon her, and she on him. . . .

5th. . . . To the King's house, to show them a play, "The Chances."[6] A good play I find it, and the actors most good in it; and pretty to hear Knipp sing in the play very properly, "All night I weepe;" and sung it admirably. The whole play pleases me well: and most of all, the sight of many fine ladies. . . .

18th. . . . With my wife by coach to the Duke of York's play-house, expecting a new play, and so stayed not no more than other people, but to the King's house, to "The Mayd's Tragedy;" but vexed all the while with two talking ladies and Sir Charles Sedley; yet pleased to hear their discourse, he being a stranger. And one of the ladies would, and did sit with her mask on, all the play, and, being exceeding witty as ever I heard woman, did talk most pleasantly with him; but was, I believe, a virtuous woman, and of quality. He would fain know who she was, but she would not tell; yet did give him many pleasant hints of her knowledge of him, by that means setting his brains at work to find out who she was, but pulling off her mask. He was mighty witty, and she also making sport with him very inoffensively, that a more pleasant rencontre I never heard. But by that means lost the pleasure of the play wholly, to which now and then Sir Charles Sedley's exceptions against both words and pronouncing were very pretty. . . .

1st. . . . I am mighty unjust to her[7] . . . , and had she not been ill . . . and that *March* it were not Friday (on which in Lent there are no plays) I had carried her to a play. . . .

2nd. . . . After dinner, with my wife, to the King's house to see "The Mayden Queene," a new play of Dryden's, mightily commended for the regularity of it, and the strain and wit; and, the truth is, there is a comical part done by Nell, which is Florimell, that I never can hope ever to see the like done again, by man or woman. The King and Duke of York were at the play. But so great performance of a comical part was never, I believe, in the world before as Nell do this, both as a mad girle, then most and best of all when she comes in like a young gallant; and hath the motions and carriage of a spark the most that ever I saw any man have. It makes me, I confess, admire her. . . .

7th. . . . To the Duke's playhouse, . . . and saw "The English Princesse, or Richard the Third;"[8] a most sad, melancholy play, and pretty good; but nothing

[6] A comedy by Beaumont and Fletcher, of which an alteration was produced by the Duke of Buckingham. The play which Pepys saw was probably the duke's revised version, although it was not published until 1682.

[7] [His wife.]

[8] A tragedy by J. Caryl. Betterton acted King Richard; Harris, the Earl of Richmond; and Smith, Sir William Stanley.

eminent in it, as some tragedys are; only little Mis. Davis[9] did dance a jig after the end of the play, and there telling the next day's play; so that it come in by force only to please the company to see her dance in boy's clothes; and, the truth is, there is no comparison between Nell's dancing the other day[10] at the King's house in boy's clothes and this, this being infinitely beyond the other. . . .

21st. . . . I alone out and to the Duke of York's play-house, where unexpectedly I come to see only the young men and women of the house act; they having liberty to act for their own profit on Wednesdays and Fridays this Lent: and the play they did yesterday, being Wednesday, was so well-taken, that they thought fit to venture it publickly to-day; a play of my Lord Falkland's[11] called "The Wedding Night," a kind of a tragedy, and some things very good in it, but the whole together, I thought, not so. I confess I was well enough pleased with my seeing it: and the people did do better, without the great actors, than I did expect, but yet far short of what they do when they are there, which I was glad to find the difference of. . . .

25th. . . . To the King's playhouse. . . . Sir W. Pen and I in the pit, and here saw "The Mayden Queene" again; which indeed the more I see the more I like, and is an excellent play, and so done by Nell, her merry part, as cannot be better done in nature, I think. . . .

30th. . . . Did by coach go see the silly play of my Lady Newcastle's,[12] called "The Humourous Lovers;" the most silly thing that ever come upon a stage. I was sick to see it, but yet would not but have seen it, that I might the better understand her. Here I spied Knipp and Betty,[13] of the King's house, and sent Knipp oranges, but, having little money about me, did not offer to carry them abroad, which otherwise I had, I fear, been tempted to. . . .

April

8th. . . . To the King's house, and saw the latter end of the "Surprisall,"[14] wherein was no great matter, I thought, by what I saw there. . . .

9th. . . . To the King's house . . . , and there we saw "The Tameing of a Shrew," which hath some very good pieces in it, but generally is but a mean play; and the best part, "Sawny,"[15] done by Lacy, hath not half its life, by reason of the words, I suppose, not being understood, at least by me. . . .

11th. . . . I to White Hall, thinking there to have seen the Duchess of New-

[9] Mary Davis, some time a comedian in the Duke of York's troop, and one of those actresses who boarded with Sir W. Davenant, was, according to Pepys, a natural daughter of Thomas Howard, first Earl of Berkshire. She captivated the king by the charming manner in which she sang a ballad beginning, "My lodging it is on the cold ground," when acting Celania, a shepherdess mad for love in the play of "The Rivals." Charles took her off the stage. . . . Miss Davis was also a fine dancer. . . .

[10] As Florimel in "Secret Love, or the Maiden Queen."

[11] Henry Cary, third Viscount Falkland. . . . The title of the play was really "The Marriage Night." It was published in 1664. . . .

[12] Margaret, daughter of Sir Thomas Lucas . . . married William Cavendish, Marquis of Newcastle, created Duke of Newcastle, 1665. The play was written by the husband, and not by the wife.

[13] Betty Hall. See January 23rd, 1666–67.

[14] A comedy by Sir Robert Howard, published in 1665.

[15] This play was entitled "Sawney the Scot, or the Taming of a Shrew," and consisted of an alteration of Shakespeare's play by John Lacy. Although it had long been popular it was not printed until 1698. . . .

castle's coming this night to Court, to make a visit to the Queene, the King having been with her yesterday, to make her a visit since her coming to town. The whole story of this lady is a romance, and all she do is romantick. Her footmen in velvet coats, and herself in an antique dress, as they say; and was the other day at her own play, "The Humourous Lovers;" the most ridiculous thing that ever was wrote, but yet she and her Lord mightily pleased with it; and she, at the end, made her respects to the players from her box, and did give them thanks. . . .

15th. . . . I to the King's house by chance, where a new play: so full as I never saw it; I forced to stand all the while close to the very door till I took cold, and many people went away for want of room. The King, and Queene, and Duke of York and Duchesse there, and all the Court, and Sir W. Coventry. The play called "The Change of Crownes;"[16] a play of Ned Howard's,[17] the best that ever I saw at that house, being a great play and serious; only Lacy did act the country-gentleman come up to Court, who do abuse the Court with all the imaginable wit and plainness about selling of places, and doing every thing for money. The play took very much. . . .

16th. . . . In haste to carry my wife to see the new play I saw yesterday, she not knowing it. But there, contrary to expectation, find "The Silent Woman." However, in; and there Knipp come into the pit. . . . Knipp tells me the King was so angry at the liberty taken by Lacy's part[18] to abuse him to his face, that he commanded they should act no more, till Moone[19] went and got leave for them to act again, but not this play. The King mighty angry; and it was bitter indeed, but very true and witty. I never was more taken with a play than I am with this "Silent Woman," as old as it is, and as often as I have seen it. There is more wit in it than goes to ten new plays. . . .

17th. . . . To the King's playhouse . . . , and saw a piece of "Rollo,"[20] a play I like not much, but much good acting in it: the house very empty. . . .

18th. . . . By coach with my wife to the Duke of York's house, and there saw "The Wits,"[21] a play I formerly loved, and is now corrected and enlarged: but, though I like the acting, yet I like not much in the play now. . . .

19th. . . . So to the playhouse, not much company come, which I impute to the heat of the weather, it being very hot. Here we saw "Macbeth,"[22] which,

[16] This play was entered on the Register of the Stationers' Company, but never printed.

[17] Edward Howard, fifth son of Thomas Howard, first Earl of Berkshire, and brother of Sir Robert Howard, baptized at St. Martin's-in-the-Fields, November 2nd, 1624. His play, the "United Kingdoms," was satirized in "The Rehearsal." Lacy's opinion of his abilities was shared by many of his contemporaries.

[18] In "The Change of Crownes."

[19] [Michael Mohun]

[20] "Rollo, Duke of Normandy," a tragedy by John Fletcher, published in 1640. It was previously published in 1639 under the title of "The Bloody Brother." Hart, Kynaston, Mohun, and Burt all acted in this play.

[21] See August 15th, 1661.

[22] See November 5th, 1664. Downes wrote: "The Tragedy of Macbeth, alter'd by Sir William Davenant; being drest in all it's finery, as new cloaths, new scenes, machines as flyings for the Witches; with all the singing and dancing in it. The first compos'd by Mr. Lock, the other by Mr. Channell and Mr. Joseph Preist; it being all excellently perform'd, being in the nature of an opera, it recompenc'd double the expence; it proves still a lasting play."

though I have seen it often, yet is it one of the best plays for a stage, and variety of dancing and musique, that ever I saw. . . .

20th. . . . At noon dined, and with my wife to the King's house, but there found the bill torn down and no play acted, and so being in the humour to see one, went to the Duke of York's house, and there saw "The Witts" again, which likes me better than it did the other day, having much wit in it. Here met with Mr. Rolt, who tells me the reason of no play to-day at the King's house. That Lacy had been committed to the porter's lodge for his acting his part in the late new play, and that being thence released he come to the King's house, and there met with Ned Howard, the poet of the play, who congratulated his release; upon which Lacy cursed him as that it was the fault of his nonsensical play that was the cause of his ill usage. Mr. Howard did give him some reply; to which Lacy [answered] him, that he was more a fool than a poet; upon which Howard did give him a blow on the face with his glove; on which Lacy, having a cane in his hand, did give him a blow over the pate. Here Rolt and others that discoursed of it in the pit this afternoon did wonder that Howard did not run him through, he being too mean a fellow to fight with. But Howard did not do any thing but complain to the King of it; so the whole house is silenced, and the gentry seem to rejoice much at it, the house being become too insolent. Here were many fine ladies this afternoon at this house as I have at any time seen, and so after the play home . . . , resolving by the grace of God to see no more plays till Whitsuntide, I having now seen a play every day this week till I have neglected my business, and that I am ashamed of, being found so much absent. . . .

May

1st. . . . To the King's playhouse . . . , and saw "Love in a Maze:"[23] but a sorry play: only Lacy's clowne's part, which he did most admirably indeed; and I am glad to find the rogue at liberty again. Here was but little, and that ordinary, company. We sat at the upper bench next the boxes; and I find it do pretty well, and have the advantage of seeing and hearing the great people, which may be pleasant when there is good store. . . . But here was neither Hart, Nell, nor Knipp; therefore, the play was not likely to please me. . . .

21st. . . . I home; but, Lord! how it went against my heart to go away from the very door of the Duke's play-house, and my Lady Castlemayne's coach, and many great coaches there, to see "The Siege of Rhodes." I was very near making a forfeit, but I did command myself. . . .

22nd. . . . To the King's house, where I did give 18*d*., and saw the two last acts of "The Goblins,"[24] a play I could not make any thing of by these two acts, but here Knipp spied me out of the tiring-room, and come to the pit door, and I out to her, and kissed her, she only coming to see me, being in a country-dress, she and others having, it seemed, had a country-dance in the play, but she no other part: so we parted, and I into the pit again till it was done. The house full, but I had no mind to be seen. . . .

24th. . . . My wife and I and Sir W. Pen to the King's play-house, and there saw "The Mayden Queene," which, though I have often seen, yet pleases me

---

[23] The second title of Shirley's play of "The Changes."
[24] See January 23rd, 1666–67.

infinitely, it being impossible, I think, ever to have the Queen's part, which is very good and passionate, and Florimel's part, which is the most comicall that ever was made for woman, ever done better than they two are by young Marshall and Nelly. . . .

22nd. . . . Creed tells me of the fray between the Duke of Buckingham at the *July* Duke's playhouse the last Saturday (and it is the first day I have heard that they have acted at either the King's or Duke's houses this month or six weeks) and Henry Killigrew, whom the Duke of Buckingham did soundly beat and take away his sword, and make a fool of, till the fellow prayed him to spare his life. . . .

1st. . . . I was very merry, and after dinner, upon a motion of the women, I *August* was got to go to the play with them — the first I have seen since before the Dutch coming upon our coast, and so to the King's house, to see "The Custome of the Country." The house mighty empty — more than ever I saw it — and an ill play. . . .

5th. . . . To the Duke of York's house, and there saw "Love Tirckes, or the School of Compliments;"[25] a silly play, only Mis's [Davis's] dancing in a shepherd's clothes did please us mightily. . . .

10th. . . . Several good plays are likely to be abroad soon, as Mustapha and Henry the 5th. . . .

12th. . . . All alone to the King's playhouse, and there did happen to sit just before Mrs. Pierce, and Mrs. Knepp, who pulled me by the hair; and so I addressed myself to them, and talked to them all the intervals of the play, and did give them fruit. The play is "Brenoralt," which I do find but little in, for my part. . . .

13th. . . . To the King's house, and there saw "The Committee," which I went to with some prejudice, not liking it before, but I do now find it a very good play, and a great deal of good invention in it; but Lacy's part is so well performed that it would set off anything. . . .

14th. . . . To the King's play-house, and there saw "The Country Captain," which is a very ordinary play. Methinks I had no pleasure therein at all. . . .

15th. . . . To the Duke's house, where a new play. The King and Court there: the house full, and an act begun. And so went to the King's and there saw "The Merry Wives of Windsor:" which did not please me at all, in no part of it. . . .

16th. . . . After dinner my wife and I to the Duke's playhouse, where we saw the new play acted yesterday, "The Feign Innocence, or Sir Martin Marr-all;" a play made by my Lord Duke of Newcastle, but, as every body says, corrected by Dryden.[26] It is the most entire piece of mirth, a complete farce from one end to the other, that certainly was ever writ. I never laughed so in all my

---

[25] A comedy by James Shirley, apparently acted at the Cock-pit in 1625, but not published till 1667.
[26] Downes says that the Duke gave this comedy to Dryden who adapted it to the stage; but it is entered on the books of the Stationers Company as the production of his grace.

life. I laughed till my head [ached] all the evening and night with the laughing; and at very good wit therein, not fooling. The house full. . . .

17th. . . . To the King's playhouse, where the house extraordinary full; and there was the King and Duke of York to see the new play, "Queen Elizabeth's Troubles, and the History of Eighty Eight."[27] I confess I have sucked in so much of the sad story of Queen Elizabeth, from my cradle, that I was ready to weep for her sometimes; but the play is the most ridiculous that sure ever come upon the stage; and, indeed, is merely a shew, only shews the true garbe of the Queen in those days, just as we see Queen Mary and Queen Elizabeth painted; but the play is merely a puppet play, acted by living puppets. Neither the design nor language better; and one stands by and tells us the meaning of things: only I was pleased to see Knipp dance among the milkmaids, and to hear her sing a song to Queen Elizabeth; and to see her come out in her night-gowne with no lockes on, but her bare face and hair only tied up in a knot behind; which is the comeliest dress that ever I saw her in to her advantage. . . .

19th. . . . Took coach and to the Duke of York's house, all alone, and there saw "Sir Martin Marr-all" again, though I saw him but two days since, and do find it the most comical play that ever I saw in my life. . . .

20th. . . . To the Duke's Playhouse . . . , and there saw "Sir Martin Marr-all" again, which I have now seen three times, and it hath been acted but four times, and still find it a very ingenious play, and full of variety. . . .

22nd. . . . To the King's playhouse, and there saw "The Indian Emperour;" where I find Nell come again, which I am glad of; but was most infinitely displeased with her being put to act the Emperour's daughter; which is a great and serious part,[28] which she do most basely. The rest of the play, though pretty good, was not well acted by most of them, methought; so that I took no great content in it. . . .

23rd. . . . Called my wife, and to the King's house, and saw "The Mayden Queene," which pleases us mightily. . . .

24th. . . . After dinner we to a play, and there saw "The Cardinall" at the King's house, wherewith I am mightily pleased; but, above all, with Becke Marshall. . . . My belly now full with plays, that I do intend to bind myself to see no more till Michaelmas. . . .

26th. . . . I walked to the King's playhouse, there to meet Sir W. Pen, and saw "The Surprizall,"[29] a very mean play, I thought: or else it was because I was out of humour, and but very little company in the house. . . .

September 5th. . . . After dinner . . . , to the Duke of York's house, and there saw Hera-

[27] Pepys here, as elsewhere, took the second title of the piece, as, perhaps, it appeared in the bills of the day. . . .

[28] Nell Gwynn agreed with Pepys that serious parts were unsuited to her. In an Epilogue to the tragedy of the "Duke of Lerma," spoken by her, occur these lines:
> "I know you, in your hearts,
> Hate serious plays, — as I hate serious parts."
and in the Epilogue to "Tyrannical Love":
> "I die
> Out of my calling in a tragedy."

[29] See April 8th, 1667.

clius," which is a good play; but they did so spoil it with their laughing, and being all of them out, and with the noise they made within the theatre, that I was ashamed of it, and resolve not to come thither again a good while, believing that this negligence, which I never observed before, proceeds only from their want of company in the pit, that they have no care how they act. . . .

11th. . . . I by coach to the Duke of York's playhouse, and there saw part of "The Ungratefull Lovers;"[30] and sat by Beck Marshall, who is very handsome near hand. . . .

12th. . . . It was time to go to a play, which I did at the Duke's house, where "Tu Quoque"[31] was the first time acted, with some alterations of Sir W. Davenant's; but the play is a very silly play, methinks; for I, and others that sat by me . . . , were weary of it; but it will please the citizens. . . .

14th. . . . After dinner . . . my wife to the King's playhouse to see "The Northerne Castle,"[32] which I think I never did see before. Knipp acted in it, and did her part very extraordinary well; but the play is but a mean, sorry play; but the house very full of gallants. It seems, it hath not been acted a good while. . . .

16th. . . . Away to the King's play-house, to see the "Scornfull Lady;" but it being now three o'clock, there was not one soul in the pit; whereupon, for shame, we would not go in, but, against our wills, went all to see "Tu Quoque" again, where there is pretty store of company, and going with a prejudice the play appeared better to us. . . . But one of the best parts of our sport was a mighty pretty lady that sat behind us, that did laugh so heartily and constantly, that it did me good to hear her. Thence to the King's house, upon a wager of mine with my wife, that there would be no acting there to-day, there being no company: so I went in and found a pretty good company there, and saw their dance at the end of the play. . . .

20th. . . . By coach to the King's playhouse, and there saw "The Mad Couple,"[33] which I do not remember that I have seen; it is a pretty pleasant play. Thence home, and my wife and I to walk in the garden, she having been at the same play . . . , in the 18*d*. seat. . . .

25th. . . . After dinner I to the King's playhouse, my eyes being so bad since last night's straining of them, that I am hardly able to see, besides the pain which I have in them. The play was a new play; and infinitely full: the King and all the Court almost there. It is "The Storme," a play of Fletcher's;[34] which is but so-so, methinks; only there is a most admirable dance at the end, of the ladies, in a military manner, which indeed did please me mightily. . . .

[30] "The Ungrateful Lovers" is an odd title; and no play of that name has been traced. It probably is intended for Davenant's "Unfortunate Lovers," first published in 1643.
[31] This play, which was called "Greene's Tu Quoque, or the City Gallant," on account of the celebrity of the actor, Thomas Greene, in the part of Bubble, was written by John Cooke, and first printed in 1614, having been edited by the well-known dramatist, Thomas Heywood. . . .
[32] Nothing is known of this play except what is told us by Pepys.
[33] "All Mistaken; or, the Mad Couple," a comedy by the Hon. James Howard, published in 1672. Hart and Nell Gwyn acted Philidor and Mirida, the mad couple.
[34] "The Sea Voyage," a play borrowed from Shakespeare's "Tempest," and first acted in 1622. Published in Beaumont and Fletcher's "Comedies and Tragedies," 1647.

28th. . . . To the Duke of York's playhouse, and there saw a piece of "Sir Martin Marrall," with great delight, though I have seen it so often. . . .

2nd. . . . To the King's house to see "The Traytour," which still I like as a very good play. . . .

5th. . . . To the Duke of York's playhouse, but the house so full, it being a new play, "The Coffee House,"[35] that we could not get in, and so to the King's house: and there, going in, met with Knepp, and she took us up into the tireing-rooms: and to the women's shift, where Nell was dressing herself, and was all unready, and is very pretty, prettier than I thought. And so walked all up and down the house above, and then below into the scene-room, and there sat down, and she gave us fruit: and here I read the questions to Knepp, while she answered me, through all her part of "Flora's Figary's"[36] which was acted to-day. But, Lord! to see how they were both painted would make a man mad, and did make me loath them; and what base company of men comes among them, and how lewdly they talk! and how poor the men are in clothes, and yet what a shew they make on the stage by candle-light, is very observable. But to see how Nell cursed, for having so few people in the pit, was pretty; the other house carrying away all the people at the new play, and is said, now-a-days, to have generally most company, as being better players. By and by into the pit, and there saw the play, which is pretty good, but my belly was full of what I had seen in the house. . . .

14th. . . . To the Duke of York's House, and there went in for nothing into the pit, at the last act, to see Sir Martin Marr-all. . . .

15th. . . . To the Duke of York's house, where, after long stay, the King and Duke of York come, and there saw "The Coffee-house," the most ridiculous, insipid play that ever I saw in my life, and glad we were that Betterton had no part in it. . . .

16th. . . . I away to the Duke of York's house, thinking as we appointed, to meet my wife there, but she was not; and more, I was vexed to see Young (who is but a bad actor at best) act Macbeth in the room of Betterton, who, poor man! is sick: but, Lord, what a prejudice it wrought in me against the whole play, and everybody else agreed in disliking this fellow. Thence home, and there find my wife gone home; because of this fellow's acting of the part, she went out of the house again. . . .

19th. . . . At noon home to a short dinner, being full of my desire of seeing my Lord Orrery's new play this afternoon at the King's house, "The Black Prince,"[37] the first time it is acted; where, though we come by two o'clock, yet there was no room in the pit, but we were forced to go into one of the upper boxes, at 4s. a piece, which is the first time I ever sat in a box in my life. . . . And this pleasure I had, that from this place the scenes do appear very fine indeed, and much better than in the pit. The house infinite full, and the King and

[35] "Tarugo's Wiles, or, The Coffee House," a comedy by Thomas St. Serfe; printed in 1668. Great part of the plot is founded on the Spanish comedy, "No puede ser."

[36] See note, August 8th, 1664.

[37] "The Black Prince," by Roger, Earl of Orrery, is styled a tragedy, although the play ends happily. It was first published in 1669,

Duke of York was there. By and by the play begun, and in it nothing particular but a very fine dance for variety of figures, but a little too long. But, as to the contrivance, and all that was witty (which, indeed, was much, and very witty), was almost the same that had been in his two former plays of "Henry the 5th" and "Mustapha," and the same points and turns of wit in both, and in this very same play often repeated, but in excellent language, and were so excellent that the whole house was mightily pleased with it all along till towards the end he comes to discover the chief of the plot of the play by the reading of a long letter,[38] which was so long and some things (the people being set already to think too long) so unnecessary that they frequently begun to laugh, and to hiss twenty times, that, had it not been for the King's being there, they had certainly hissed it off the stage. But I must confess that, as my Lord Barkeley says behind me, the having of that long letter was a thing so absurd, that he could not imagine how a man of his parts could possibly fall into it; or, if he did, if he had but let any friend read it, the friend would have told him of it; and, I must confess, it is one of the most remarkable instances that ever I did or expect to meet with in my life of a wise man's not being wise at all times, and in all things, for nothing could be more ridiculous than this, though the letter of itself at another time would be thought an excellent letter, and indeed an excellent Romance, but at the end of the play, when every body was weary of sitting, and were already possessed with the effect of the whole letter, to trouble them with a letter a quarter of an hour long, was a most absurd thing. . . .

23rd. . . . To the King's playhouse, and there saw "The Black Prince" again: which is now mightily bettered by that long letter being printed, and so delivered to every body at their going in, and some short reference made to it in heart in the play, which do mighty well; but, when all is done, I think it the worst play of my Lord Orrery's. . . .

24th. . . . To the Duke of York's playhouse; but there Betterton not being yet well, we would not stay, though since I hear that Smith[39] do act his part in "The Villaine," which was then acted, as well or better than he, which I do not believe. . . .

28th. . . . To the King's house, and there saw "The Committee," a play I like well. . . .

1st. . . . Took out my wife, and she and I alone to the King's playhouse, and *November* there saw a silly play and an old one, "The Taming of a Shrew". . . .

2nd. . . . To the King's playhouse, and there saw "Henry the Fourth:" and contrary to expectation, was pleased in nothing more than in Cartwright's[40] speaking of Falstaffe's speech about "What is Honour?" The house full of Parliament-men, it being holyday with them: and it was observable how a gen-

[38] It occurs in the fifth act, and is certainly very long. It was read by Hart, but was afterwards omitted in the acting. . . .

[39] William Smith was an actor with a commanding person. He occupied a prominent position on the stage, and retired between 1684 and 1688. Betterton's part in "The Villain" was Monsieur Brisac; Maligni, the villain, was taken by Sandford.

[40] William Cartwright, actor, who became a bookseller in Turnstile Alley during the period of the Commonwealth. He was after the Restoration one of Killigrew's company, at the original establishment in Drury Lane. . . .

tleman of good habit, sitting just before us, eating of some fruit in the midst of the play, did drop down as dead, being choked; but with much ado Orange Moll did thrust her finger down his throat, and brought him to life again. . . .

7th. . . . At noon resolved with Sir W. Pen to go see "The Tempest," an old play of Shakespeare's, acted, I hear, the first day; and so my wife, and girl, and W. Hewer by themselves, and Sir W. Pen and I afterwards by ourselves; and forced to sit in the side balcone over against the musique-room at the Duke's house, close by my Lady Dorset and a great many great ones. The house mighty full; the King and Court there: and the most innocent play that ever I saw; and a curious piece of musique[41] in an echo of half sentences, the echo repeating the former half, while the man goes on to the latter; which is mighty pretty. The play [has] no great wit, but yet good, above ordinary plays. . . .

11th. . . . After dinner, my wife, and I . . . to the King's play-house, and there saw "The Indian Emperour," a good play, but not so good as people cry it up, I think, though above all things Nell's ill speaking of a great part made me mad. . . .

13th. . . . To the Duke of York's house, and there saw the Tempest again, which is very pleasant, and full of so good variety that I cannot be more pleased almost in a comedy, only the seamen's part a little too tedious. . . .

28th. . . . I away to the King's playhouse, and there sat by my wife, and saw "The Mistaken Beauty,"[42] which I never, I think, saw before, though an old play; and there is much in it that I like, though the name is but improper to it — at least, that name, it being also called "The Lyer," which is proper enough. Here I met with Sir Richard Browne, who wondered to find me there, telling me that I am a man of so much business, which character, I thank God, I have ever got, and have for a long time had and deserved, and yet am now come to be censured in common with the office for a man of negligence. . . .

December

7th. . . . Catelin is likely to be soon acted, which I am glad to hear, but it is at the King's House. But the King's House is at present and hath for some days been silenced upon some difference [between] Hart and Moone. . . .

11th. . . . I met Rolt and Sir John Chichly, and Harris, the player, and there we talked of many things, and particularly of "Catiline," which is to be suddenly acted at the King's house; and there all agree that it cannot be well done at that house, there not being good actors enow: and Burt[43] acts Cicero, which they all conclude he will not be able to do well. The King gives them £500 for robes, there being, as they say, to be sixteen scarlett robes. . . .

12th. . . . I all alone to the Duke of York's house, and saw "The Tempest," which, as often as I have seen it, I do like very well, and the house very full. But I could take little pleasure more than the play, for not being able to look about, for fear of being seen. Here only I saw a French lady in the pit, with a

[41] Evidently the song sung by Ferdinand, wherein Ariel echoes "Go thy way" (act iii., sc. 4), from Davenant's and Dryden's adaptation of the "Tempest," published in 1674. The music was by Banister.

[42] "The Mistaken Beauty; or, the Lyar," a comedy, taken from the "Menteur" of Corneille, printed, in 1661, by its second title only, and without any author's name. Afterwards published as "The Mistaken Beauty" in 1685.

[43] Nicholas Burt.

tunique, just like one of ours, only a handkercher about her neck; but this fashion for a woman did not look decent. . . .

26th. . . . With my wife to the King's playhouse, and there saw "The Surprizall;" which did not please me to-day, the actors not pleasing me; and especially Nell's acting of a serious part, which she spoils. . . .

28th. . . . To the King's house, and there saw "The Mad Couple," which is but an ordinary play; but only Nell's and Hart's mad parts are most excellently done, but especially her's: which makes it a miracle to me to think how ill she do any serious part, as, the other day, just like a fool or changeling; and, in a mad part, do beyond all imitation almost. [It pleased us mightily to see the natural affection of a poor woman, the mother of one of the children brought on the stage: the child crying, she by force got upon the stage, and took up her child and carried it away off of the stage from Hart.] Many fine faces here to-day. . . .

30. . . . With Sir Philip Carteret to the King's playhouse, there to see "Love's Cruelty,"[44] an old play, but which I have not seen before; and in the first act Orange Moll come to me, with one of our porters by my house, to tell me that Mrs. Pierce and Knepp did dine at my house to-day, and that I was desired to come home. So I went out presently, and by coach home, and they were just gone away: so, after a very little stay with my wife, I took coach again, and to the King's playhouse again, and come in the fourth act; and it proves to me a very silly play, and to everybody else, as far as I could judge. . . .

1st. . . . I after dinner to the Duke of York's playhouse, and there saw "Sir Martin Mar-all;" which I have seen so often, and yet am mightily pleased with it, and think it mighty witty, and the fullest of proper matter for mirth that ever was writ; and I do clearly see that they do improve in their acting of it. Here a mighty company of citizens, 'prentices, and others; and it makes me observe, that when I begun first to be able to bestow a play on myself, I do not remember that I saw so many by half of the ordinary 'prentices and mean people in the pit at 2s.6d. a-piece as now; I going for several years no higher than the 12d. and then the 18d. places, though I strained hard to go in then when I did: so much the vanity and prodigality of the age is to be observed in this particular. . . .

January 1667–68

6th. . . . Away to my wife at the Duke of York's house, in the pit, and so left her; and to Mrs. Pierce, and took her and her cozen Corbet, Knepp and little James, and brought them to the Duke's house; and the house being full, was forced to carry them to a box, which did cost me 20s., besides oranges, which troubled me, though their company did please me. Thence, after the play, stayed till Harris was undressed, there being acted "The Tempest," and so he withall, all by coach, home. . . .

7th. . . . I away by coach to the Nursery,[1] where I never was yet, and there to meet my wife and Mercer and Willet as they promised; but the house did

---

[44] A tragedy by James Shirley, first printed in 1640.

[1] There seem to have been, at this time, two distinct "Nurseries for Actors," one in Golden Lane, near the Barbican. . . . The other "Nursery" was in Hatton Garden. . . . The "Nursery" in Barbican appears to have been established by the King's Players under Killigrew, and the one in Hatton Garden for the Duke's Players under Davenant.

not act to-day; and so I was at a loss for them, and therefore to the other two playhouses into the pit, to gaze up and down, to look for them, and there did by this means, for nothing, see an act in "The Schoole of Compliments"[2] at the Duke of York's house, and "Henry the Fourth" at the King's house; but, not finding them, nor liking either of the plays,[3] I took my coach again, and home. . . .

10th. . . . With my wife and Deb. to the King's house, to see "Aglaura," which hath been always mightily cried up; and so I went with mighty expectation, but do find nothing extraordinary in it at all, and but hardly good in any degree. . . .

11th. . . . To the King's house, there to see "The Wild-goose Chase,"[4] which I never saw, but have long longed to see it, being a famous play, but as it was yesterday I do find that where I expect most I find least satisfaction, for in this play I met with nothing extraordinary at all, but very dull inventions and designs. Knepp come and sat by us, and her talk pleased me a little, she telling me how Mis Davis[5] is for certain going away from the Duke's house, the King being in love with her; and a house is taken for her, and furnishing; and she hath a ring given her already worth £600: that the King did send several times for Nelly, and she was with him, but what he did she knows not; this was a good while ago, and she says that the King first spoiled Mrs. Weaver,[6] which is very mean, methinks, in a prince, and I am sorry for it, and can hope for no good to the State from having a Prince so devoted to his pleasure. She told me also of a play shortly coming upon the stage, of Sir Charles Sidly's, which, she thinks, will be called "The Wandering Ladys,"[7] a comedy that, she thinks, will be most pleasant; and also another play, called "The Duke of Lerma;"[8] besides "Catelin," which she thinks, for want of the clothes which the King promised them, will not be acted for a good while. . . .

24th. . . . I to the King's playhouse, to fetch my wife, and there saw the best part of "The Mayden Queene," which, the more I see, the more I love, and think one of the best plays I ever saw, and is certainly the best acted of any thing ever the House did, and particularly Becke Marshall, to admiration. . . .

February 3rd. . . . At noon home to dinner, and thence after dinner to the Duke of York's house, to the play, "The Tempest," which we have often seen, but yet I was pleased again, and shall be again to see it, it is so full of variety, and par-

---

[2] A comedy by James Shirley, first published in 1631. Reproduced in 1667 as "Love's Tricks, or the School of Compliments."

[3] "Whereas we are informed that diverse persons doe rudely presse and with evill language and blowes force their way into the two theatres without paying the prices established," therefore the king declares such proceedings unlawful, "notwithstanding their pretended priviledge by custom of forcing their entrance at the fourth or fifth act without payment." — *Records of the Lord Chamberlain's Office.* . . .

[4] Beaumont and Fletcher's play, first acted in 1632, and published in 1652.

[5] Mary Davis.

[6] Mrs. Weaver was one of the actresses of the King's Company.

[7] Sedley never wrote any play with this title, or, perhaps, the name was altered. The piece here referred to seems to be "The Mulberry Garden", which, on representation, does not seem to have answered Pepys's expectations. It met, however, with success, from the notoriety or fashion of the profligate author.

[8] See February 20th, 1667-68.

ticularly this day I took pleasure to learn the tune of the seaman's dance, which I have much desired to be perfect in, and have made myself so. . . .

6th. . . . I to the Duke of York's playhouse; where a new play of Etherige's,[9] called "She Would if she Could;" and though I was there by two o'clock, there was 1000 people put back that could not have room in the pit: and I at last, because my wife was there, made shift to get into the 18*d.* box, and there saw; but, Lord! how full was the house, and how silly the play, there being nothing in the world good in it, and few people pleased in it. The King was there; but I sat mightily behind, and could see but little, and hear not all. The play being done, I into the pit to look [for] my wife, and it being dark and raining, I to look my wife out, but could not find her; and so staid going between the two doors and through the pit an hour and half, I think, after the play was done; the people staying there till the rain was over, and to talk with one another. And, among the rest, here was the Duke of Buckingham to-day openly sat in the pit; and there I found him with my Lord Buckhurst, and Sidly, and Etherige, the poet; the last of whom I did hear mightily find fault with the actors, that they were out of humour, and had not their parts perfect,[10] and that Harris did do nothing, nor could so much as sing a ketch in it; and so was mightily concerned: while all the rest did, through the whole pit, blame the play as a silly, dull thing, though there was something very roguish and witty; but the design of the play, and end, mighty insipid.

7th. . . . To the King's playhouse, and there saw a piece of "Love in a Maze," a dull, silly play, I think. . . .

11th. . . . To the Duke of York's playhouse, and there saw the last act for nothing, where I never saw such good acting of any creatures as Smith's part of Zanger;[11] and I do also, though it was excellently acted by —, do yet want Betterton mightily. . . .

18th. . . . To the King's house, and there, in one of the upper boxes, saw "Flora's Vagarys," which is a very silly play. . . .

20th. . . . Thence by one o'clock to the King's house: a new play, "The Duke of Lerma," of Sir Robert Howard's: where the King and Court was; and Knepp and Nell spoke the prologue most excellently, especially Knepp, who spoke beyond any creature I ever heard.[12] The play designed to reproach our King with his mistresses, that I was troubled for it, and expected it should be interrupted; but it ended all well, which salved all. The play a well-writ and good play, only its design I did not like of reproaching the King, but altogether a very good and most serious play. . . .

[9] Sir George Etherege, the celebrated wit and man of fashion. He was the author of three comedies, "The Comical Revenge, or Love in a Tub" (1664), "She Would if she Could" (1667), and "The Man of Mode, or Sir Fopling Flutter" (1676).

[10] Shadwell confirms this complaint of Etherege's in the preface to his own "Humourists." He writes: "The last (viz, imperfect action) had like to have destroyed 'She Would if she Could,' which I think (and I have the authority of some of the best judges in England for 't) is the best comedy that has been written since the Restoration of the Stage." Harris played Sir Joslin Jolly. Downes says that it was inferior to "Love in a Tub," but took well.

[11] The play in which Smith acted Zanga was Lord Orrery's "Mustapha.". . .

[12] This prologue, "spoken by Mrs. Ellen and Mrs. Nepp," is prefixed to Sir R. Howard's "Great Favourite, or the Duke of Lerma," 4to, 1688. . . .

22nd. . . . To the Duke's playhouse, and there saw "Albumazar," an old play, this the second time of acting. It is said to have been the ground of B. Jonson's "Alchymist;" but, saving the ridiculousnesse of Angell's part, which is called Trinkilo, I do not see any thing extraordinary in it, but was indeed weary of it before it was done.[13] The King here, and, indeed, all of us, pretty merry at the mimique tricks of Trinkilo. . . .

24th. . . . To the Nursery, where none of us ever were before; where the house is better and the musique better than we looked for, and the acting not much worse, because I expected as bad as could be: and I was not much mistaken, for it was so. However, I was pleased well to see it once, it being worth a man's seeing to discover the different ability and understanding of people, and the different growth of people's abilities by practise. Their play was a bad one, called "Jeronimo is Mad Again,"[14] a tragedy. Here was some good company by us, who did make mighty sport at the folly of their acting, which I could not neither refrain from sometimes, though I was sorry for it. . . . I was prettily served this day at the playhouse-door, where, giving six shillings into the fellow's hand for us three, the fellow by legerdemain did convey one away, and with so much grace faced me down that I did give him but five, that, though I knew the contrary, yet I was overpowered by his so grave and serious demanding the other shilling, that I could not deny him, but was forced by myself to give it him. . . .

25th. . . . To the Nursery, where I was yesterday, and there saw them act a comedy, a pastorall, "The Faythful Shepherd,"[15] having the curiosity to see whether they did a comedy better than a tragedy; but they do it both alike, in the meanest manner, that I was sick of it, but only for to satisfy myself once in seeing the manner of it, but I shall see them no more, I believe. . . .

27th. . . . To the King's House, to see "The Virgin Martyr,"[16] the first time it hath been acted a great while: and it is mighty pleasant; not that the play is worth much, but it is finely acted by Becke Marshal. But that which did please me beyond any thing in the whole world was the wind-musique when the angel comes down, which is so sweet that it ravished me, and indeed, in a word, did wrap up my soul so that it made me really sick, just as I have formerly been when in love with my wife; that neither then, nor all the evening going home, and at home, I was able to think of any thing, but remained all night transported. . . .

March　　2nd. . . . To the King's house to see the "Virgin Martyr" again, which do mightily please me, but above all the musique at the coming down of the angel, which at this hearing the second time, do still commend me as nothing ever did, and the other musique is nothing to it. . . .

5th. . . . After dinner to the King's house, and there saw part of "The Dis-

---

[13] The comedy of "Albumazar" was originally printed in 1615, having been performed before James I. at Trinity College, Cambridge, by the gentlemen of that society, of which John Tomkis, the author of the play, was a member, on March 9th, 1614. . . .

[14] "The Spanish Tragedy, or Hieronymo is mad again," by Thomas Kyd; frequently printed from about 1594. . . .

[15] A pastoral comedy, from the "Pastor Fido" of Guarini, a translation of which, by D. D., Gent., was published in 1633.

[16] A tragedy by Massinger and Decker. See February 16th, 1660–61.

contented Colonel," but could take no great pleasure in it, because of our coming in in the middle of it. . . .

7th. . . . To the King's playhouse, and there saw "The Spanish Gipsys,"[17] the second time of acting, and the first that I saw it. A very silly play, only great variety of dances, and those most excellently done, especially one part by one Hanes,[18] only lately come thither from the Nursery, an understanding fellow, but yet, they say, hath spent £1,000 a-year before he come thither. . . .

25th. . . . With my wife to the King's playhouse to see "The Storme," which we did, but without much pleasure, it being but a mean play compared with "The Tempest," at the Duke of York's house, though Knepp did act her part of grief very well. . . .

26th. . . . To the Duke of York's house, to see the new play, called "The Man is the Master,"[19] where the house was, it being not above one o'clock, very full. But my wife and Deb. being there before, with Mrs. Pierce and Corbet and Betty Turner, whom my wife carried with her, they made me room; and there I sat, it costing me 8s. upon them in oranges, at 6d. a-piece. By and by the King come; and we sat just under him, so that I durst not turn my back all the play. The play is a translation out of French, and the plot Spanish, but not anything extraordinary at all in it, though translated by Sir W. Davenant, and so I found the King and his company did think meanly of it, though there was here and there something pretty: but the most of the mirth was sorry, poor stuffe, of eating of sack posset and slabbering themselves, and mirth fit for clownes; the prologue but poor, and the epilogue little in it but the extraordinariness of it, it being sung by Harris and another[20] in the form of a ballet. . . .

28th. . . . To the King's house, and there saw the "Indian Emperour," a very good play indeed. . . .

1st. . . . In the afternoon out and all alone to the King's house, and there sat *April* in an upper box, to hide myself, and saw "The Black Prince," a very good play; but only the fancy, most of it, the same as in the rest of my Lord Orrey's plays; but the dance very stately. . . .

3rd. . . . To the Duke of York's playhouse, and there saw the latter part of "The Master and the Man." . . .

7th. . . . I by coach to the King's playhouse, and there saw "The English Monsieur;"[21] sitting for privacy sake in an upper box: the play hath much mirth in it as to that particular humour. After the play done, I down to Knipp, and did

---

[17] "The Spanish Gipsie," a comedy by Thomas Middleton and William Rowley, first printed in 1653.

[18] The famous Joseph Haines or Haynes, who was so popular that two biographies of him were printed in 1701, after his death. . . . Haines was a low comedian and a capital dancer. . . . One dramatic piece is attributed to him, "A Fatal Mistake, or the Plot spoiled," 4to, 1692, 1696.

[19] Sir W. Davenant's last play, a comedy published in 1669. The plot is taken from two plays of Scarron — "Jodelet, ou le Maître Valet," and "L'Héritière Ridicule." The scene is laid in Madrid.

[20] Sandford. "This comedy in general was very well perform'd, especially the Master by Mr. Harris; the man by Mr. Underhill. Mr. Harris and Mr. Sandford singing the epilogue like two street Ballad-singers" (Downes, p. 30).

[21] A comedy by the Hon. James Howard. See December 8th, 1666.

stay her undressing herself; and there saw the several players, men and women go by; and pretty to see how strange they are all, one to another, after the play is done. Here I saw a wonderful pretty maid of her own, that come to undress her, and one so pretty that she says she intends not to keep her, for fear of her being undone in her service, by coming to the playhouse. Here I hear Sir W. Davenant is just now dead;[22] and so who will succeed him in the mastership of the house is not yet known. The eldest Davenport[23] is, it seems, gone from this house to be kept by somebody; which I am glad of, she being a very bad actor. . . .

8th. . . . To the Duke of York's playhouse, where we saw "The Unfortunate Lovers,"[24] no extraordinary play, methinks. . . .

9th. . . . Down to the Duke of York's playhouse, there to see, which I did, Sir W. Davenant's corpse carried out[25] towards Westminster, there to be buried. Here were many coaches and six horses, and many hacknies, that made it look, methought, as if it were the buriall of a poor poet. He seemed to have many children, by five or six in the first mourning-coach, all boys. . . .

13th (Monday). . . . With Creed to a play. Little laugh, 4s. . . .

14th (Tuesday). . . . Thence to a play, "Love's Cruelty," . . . and so home. . . . Water, 1s. Porter, 6d. Water, 6d. Dinner, 3s.6d. Play part, 2s. Oranges, 1s. Home coach, 1s. 6d.

15th. . . . To the King's playhouse, into a corner of the 18d. box, and there saw "The Maid's Tragedy," a good play. Coach, 1s.: play and oranges, 2s.6d.

17th (Friday). . . . To the King's house, and saw "The Surprizall," where base singing, only Knepp,[26] who come, after her song in the clouds, to me in the pit, and there, oranges, 2s. . . .

18th (Saturday). . . . I to the King's playhouse, 1s., and to the "Duke of Lerma," 2s.6d., and oranges, 1s.

21st. . . . To the King's house, and saw "The Indian Emperour". . . .

24th. . . . To the King's playhouse, and there saw a piece of Beggar's Bush," which I have not seen some years. . . .

25th. . . . After dinner to the Duke of York's playhouse, and there saw "Sir Martin Marr-all," which, the more I see, the more I like. . . .

27th. . . . I to the King's playhouse, and there saw most of "The Cardinall," a good play. . . .

28th. . . . To the King's house, and there did see "Love in a Maze," wherein very good mirth of Lacy, the clown, and Wintersell,[27] the country-knight, his master. . . .

---

[22] He died the same day, April 7th.
[23] Frances Davenport, the eldest sister of Elizabeth Davenport, the famous Roxalana.
[24] A tragedy by Sir. W. Davenant.   [25] Davenant's house adjoined the theatre.
[26] A comedy by Sir Robert Howard. Mrs. Knepp played Emelia.
[27] William Wintershall, or Wintersell, was one of the original actors under Killigrew, at Drury Lane, and played the king in "The Humorous Lieutenant," at the opening of that theatre. . . . Downes ("Roscius Anglicanus," p. 17) says, "Mr. Wintersell was good in tragedy, as well as in comedy, especially in Cokes, in 'Bartholomew Fair,' that the famous comedian, Nokes, came, in that part, far short of him." . . . One of his best comic parts, to the last, was Master Slender. . . .

29th. ... I to the Duke of York's playhouse, and there saw "Love in a Tubb;" and, after the play done, I stepped up to Harris's dressing-room, where I never was, and there I observe much company come to him, and the Witts, to talk, after the play is done, and to assign meetings. ...

30th. ... Thence I to the Duke of York's playhouse, and there saw "The Tempest," which still pleases me mightily. ...

1st. ... To the King's playhouse, and there saw "The Surprizall:" and a   *May* disorder in the pit by its raining in, from the cupola at top, it being a very foul day, and cold. ...

2nd. ... To the Duke of York's playhouse, at a little past twelve, to get a good place in the pit, against the new play, and there setting a poor man to keep my place, I out, and spent an hour at Martin's, my bookseller's, and so back again, where I find the house quite full. But I had my place, and by and by the King comes and the Duke of York; and then the play begins, called "The Sullen Lovers; or, The Impertinents,"[28] having many good humours in it, but the play tedious, and no design at all in it. But a little boy, for a farce, do dance Polichinelli, the best that ever anything was done in the world, by all men's report: most pleased with that, beyond anything in the world, and much beyond all the play. Thence to the King's house to see Knepp, but the play done. ...

4th. ... Thence to the Duke of York's house, and there saw "The Impertinents" again, and with less pleasure than before, it being but a very contemptible play, though there are many little witty expressions in it; and the pit did generally say that of it. ...

5th. ... At noon home to dinner with Creed and me, and after dinner he and I to the Duke of York's playhouse; and there coming late, he and I up to the balcony-box, where we find my Lady Castlemayne and several great ladies; and there we sat with them, and I saw "The Impertinents" once more, now three times, and the three only days it hath been acted. And to see the folly how the house do this day cry up the play more than yesterday! and I for that reason like it, I find, the better, too; by Sir Positive At-all, I understand, is meant Sir Robert Howard. ...

6th. ... To Westminster Hall, where met with several people, and talked with them, and among other things understand that my Lord St. John is meant by Mr. Woodcocke, in "The Impertinents". ... I back to the King's playhouse and there saw "The Virgin Martyr," and heard the musick that I like so well. ...

7th. ... To the Duke of York's house, and there saw "The Man's the Master," which proves, upon my seeing it again, a very good play. Thence called Knepp from the King's house, where going in for her, the play being done, I did see Beck Marshall come dressed, off of the stage, and looks mighty fine, and pretty, and noble: and also Nell, in her boy's clothes, mighty pretty. But, Lord! their confidence! and how many men do hover about them as soon as they come off the stage, and how confident they are in their talk! Here I did

[28] A comedy by Thomas Shadwell, published in 1668.

kiss the pretty woman newly come, called Pegg, that was Sir Charles Sidly's mistress, a mighty pretty woman, and seems, but is not, modest. . . .

8th. . . . But, Lord! to see how this play[29] of Sir Positive At-all, in abuse of Sir Robert Howard, do take, all the Duke's and every body's talk being of that, and telling more stories of him, of the like nature, that it is now the town and country talk, and, they say, is most exactly true. The Duke of York himself said that of his playing at trap-ball is true, and told several other stories of him. . . .

9th. . . . I into the King's house, and there "The Mayd's Tragedy," a good play. . . .

11th. . . . To the Duke of York's playhouse, and there saw "The Tempest," and between two acts, I went out to Mr. Harris, and got him to repeat to me the words of the Echo, while I writ them down, having tried in the play to have wrote them; but, when I had done it, having done it without looking upon my paper, I find I could not read the blacklead. But now I have got the words clear, and, in going in thither, had the pleasure to see the actors in their several dresses, especially the seamen and monster, which were very droll: so into the play again. But there happened one thing which vexed me, which is, that the orange-woman did come in the pit, and challenge me for twelve oranges, which she delivered by my order at a late play, at night, to give to some ladies in a box, which was wholly untrue, but yet she swore it to be true. But, however, I did deny it, and did not pay her; but, for quiet, did buy 4s. worth of oranges of her, at 6d. a-piece. . . .

14th. . . . To the King's house; but, coming too soon, we out again to the Rose taverne, and there I did give them a tankard of cool drink, the weather being very hot, and then into the playhouse again, and there saw "The Country Captain,"[30] a very dull play, that did give us no content, and besides, little company there, which made it very unpleasing. . . .

15th. . . . I to the King's house, and there saw the last act of "The Committee," thinking to have seen Knepp there, but she did not act. . . .

16th. . . . I did go forth by coach to the King's playhouse, and there saw the best part of "The Sea Voyage,"[31] where Knepp I see do her part of sorrow very well. . . .

18th. . . . To the King's playhouse, where the doors were not then open; but presently they did open; and we in, and find many people already come in, by private ways, into the pit, it being the first day of Sir Charles Sidly's new play, so long expected, "The Mullberry Guarden,"[32] of whom, being so reputed a wit, all the world do expect great matters. I having sat here awhile, and eat nothing to-day, did slip out, getting a boy to keep my place; and to the Rose Tavern, and there got half a breast of mutton, off of the spit, and dined all alone. And so to the play, where the King and Queen, by and by, come, and all the Court; and the house infinitely full. But the play, when it come, though there was, here and there, a pretty saying, and that not very many

[29] "The Impertinents."   [30] The Duke of Newcastle's play. See October 26th, 1661.
[31] A comedy by Fletcher, first acted in 1622. . . .
[32] See note to January 11th, 1667–68.

neither, yet the whole of the play had nothing extraordinary in it, at all, neither of language nor design; insomuch that the King I did not see laugh, nor pleased the whole play from beginning to the end, nor the company; insomuch that I have not been less pleased at a new play in my life, I think. And which made it worse was, that there never was worse musick played. . . .

20th. . . . Walked to the King's playhouse, and saw "The Mulberry-Garden" again, and cannot be reconciled to it, but only to find here and there an independent sentence of wit, and that is all. . . .

22nd. . . . Thence to the Duke of York's house to a play, and saw Sir Martin Marr-all, where the house is full; and though I have seen it, I think, ten times, yet the pleasure I have is yet as great as ever, and is undoubtedly the best comedy ever wrote. . . .

30th. . . . At noon home to dinner, and so to the King's playhouse, and there saw "Philaster;"[33] where it is pretty to see how I could remember almost all along, ever since I was a boy, Arethusa, the part which I was to have acted at Sir Robert Cooke's; and it was very pleasant to me, but more to think what a ridiculous thing it would have been for me to have acted a beautiful woman. . . .

3rd. . . . By coach to the King's house, and there saw good part of "The *June* Scornfull Lady". . . .

19th. . . . Thence home, and by and by comes my wife and Deb. home, have been at the King's playhouse to-day, thinking to spy me there; and saw the new play, "Evening Love,"[34] of Dryden's, which, though the world commends, she likes not. . . .

20th. . . . To the King's house, and there I saw this new play my wife saw yesterday, and do not like it, it being very smutty, and nothing so good as "The Maiden Queen," or "The Indian Emperour," of his making, that I was troubled at it; and my wife tells me wholly (which he confesses a little in the epilogue) taken out of the "Illustre Bassa."

22nd. . . . To the King's playhouse, and saw an act or two of the new play ["Evening's Love"] again, but like it not. Calling this day at Herringman's,[35] he tells me Dryden do himself call it but a fifth-rate play. . . .

24th. . . . To the Duke of York's playhouse, and there saw "The Impertinents," a pretty good play. . . .

27th. . . . To the King's playhouse, and saw "The Indian Queene," but do not doat upon Nan Marshall's acting therein, as the world talks of her excellence therein. . . .

29th. . . . With my wife to the King's playhouse — "The Mulberry Garden," which she had not seen. . . .

---

[33] A tragi-comedy by Beaumont and Fletcher.
[34] A comedy, "Evening's Love, or the Mock Astrologer," not published until 1671. The scene was at Madrid, and the time the last evening of the Carnival in 1665.
[35] H. Herringman, a printer and publisher in the New Exchange.

6th. . . . Walked in the Park. . . . Here comes Harris, and first told us how Betterton is come again upon the stage: whereupon my wife and company to the [Duke's] house to see "Henry the Fifth;" while I to attend the Duke of York. . . . Thence I to the playhouse, and saw a piece of the play, and glad to see Betterton. . . .

11th. . . . After dinner to the King's playhouse, to see an old play of Shirly's called "Hide Parke;" the first day acted; where horses are brought upon the stage: but it is but a very moderate play, only an excellent epilogue spoke by Beck Marshall. . . .

28th. . . . To the Duke of York's playhouse, and there saw "The Slighted Maid,"[36] but a mean play; and thence home, there being little pleasure now in a play, the company being but little. Here we saw Gosnell, who is become very homely, and sings meanly I think, to what I thought she did.

29th. . . . To the King's house, and saw "The Mad Couple,"[37] a mean play altogether. . . .

31st. . . . To the King's house, to see the first day of Lacy's "Monsieur Ragou,"[38] now new acted. The King and Court all there, and mighty merry —a farce. . . .

1st. . . . To the King's house again, coming too late yesterday to hear the prologue, and do like the play better now than before; and, indeed, there is a great deal of true wit in it, more than in the common sort of plays. . . .

5th. . . . Home to dinner, and thence out to the Duke of York's playhouse, and there saw "The Guardian;" formerly the same, I find, that was called "Cutter of Coleman Street;" a silly play. . . .

12th. . . . To the Duke of York's house, and saw "Mackbeth," to our great content. . . .

15th. . . . To the King's playhouse, and there saw "Love's Mistresse"[39] revived, the thing pretty good, but full of variety of divertisement. . . .

17th. . . . To the Duke of York's house, and there saw "Cupid's Revenge,"[40] under the new name of "Love Despised," that hath something very good in it, though I like not the whole body of it. This day the first time acted here. . . .

29th. . . . Carried Harris to his playhouse, where, though four o'clock, so few people there at "The Impertinent's," as I went out; and do believe they did not act, though there was my Lord Arlington and his company there. So I out, and met my wife in a coach, and stopped her going thither to meet me; and took her, and Mercer, and Deb., to Bartholomew Fair, and there did see a ridiculous, obscene little stage-play, called "Marry Andrey;"[41] a foolish thing, but seen by every body. . . .

31st. . . . To the Duke of York's playhouse . . . , and saw "Hamlet," which

---

[36] A comedy by Sir Robert Stapylton.
[37] A comedy by the Hon. James Howard.
[38] "The Old Troop; or, Monsieur Ragou," a comedy by John Lacey, printed in 1672, 4to.
[39] A play by Thomas Heywood.
[40] By Beaumont and Fletcher, and first published in 1615. Downes mentions the revival, but not the change of name.   [41] Merry Andrew.

we have not seen this year before, or more; and mightily pleased with it; but, above all, with Betterton, the best part, I believe, that ever man acted. . . .

4th. . . . To the Fair . . . , but saw no sights, my wife having a mind to see *September* the play "Bartholomew-Fayre," with puppets. Which we did, and it is an excellent play; the more I see it, the more I love the wit of it; only the business of abusing the Puritans begins to grow stale, and of no use, they being the people that, at last, will be found the wisest. . . .

10th. . . . At the Duke's play-house, and there saw "The Maid in the Mill," revived — a pretty, harmless old play. . . .

15th. . . . To the King's playhouse, to see a new play, acted but yesterday, a translation out of French by Dryden, called "The Ladys à la Mode":[42] so mean a thing as, when they come to say it would be acted again to-morrow, both he that said it, Beeson,[43] and the pit fell a-laughing, there being this day not a quarter of the pit full. . . .

17th. . . . To the King's playhouse, and saw "Rollo, Duke of Normandy,"[44] which, for old acquaintance, pleased me pretty well. . . .

18th. . . . To the King's house, and saw a piece of "Henry the Fourth;" at the end of the play, thinking to have gone abroad with Knepp, but it was too late, and she to get her part against to-morrow, in "The Silent Woman". . . .

19th. . . . To the King's playhouse, and there saw "The Silent Woman;" the best comedy, I think, that ever was wrote; and sitting by Shadwell[45] the poet, he was big with admiration of it. . . . Knepp did her part mighty well. . . .

28th. Up betimes, and Knepp's maid comes to me, to tell me that the women's day[46] at the playhouse is to-day, and that therefore I must be there, to encrease their profit. . . . I by coach towards the King's playhouse . . . and there saw "The City Match;"[47] not acted these thirty years, and but a silly play: the King and Court there; the house, for the women's sake, mighty full. . . .

14th. . . . To the King's playhouse, and there saw "The Faythful Shepherdess" *October* again, that we might hear the French Eunuch sing, which we did, to our great content; though I do admire his action as much as his singing, being both beyond all I ever saw or heard. . . .

19th. . . . To the Duke of York's playhouse; and there saw, the first time acted, "The Queene of Arragon,"[48] an old Blackfriars' play, but an admirable one, so good that I am astonished at it, and wonder where it hath lain asleep all this while, that I have never heard of it before. . . .

25th. . . . My wife and I to the Duke of York's house, to see "The Duchesse *November* of Malfy," a sorry play. . . .

[42] No play called "The Ladies à la Mode" has been traced in 1668, or in any earlier or later year. . . .
[43] Probably William Beeston, who had been governor of the Cockpit Theatre.
[44] By John Fletcher.
[45] Thomas Shadwell, the dramatic writer. Died 1692.
[46] Their benefit.
[47] A comedy by Jasper Maine, D.D.
[48] A tragi-comedy by William Habington.

2nd. . . . To the King's playhouse . . . and there saw "The Usurper;" a pretty good play, in all but what is designed to resemble Cromwell and Hugh Peters, which is mighty silly. . . .

3rd. . . . At noon home to dinner, and then abroad again, with my wife, to the Duke of York's playhouse, and saw "The Unfortunate Lovers;" a mean play, I think, but some parts very good, and excellently acted. . . .

8th. . . . Home to dinner, where my wife tells me of my Lord Orrery's new play "Tryphon,"[49] at the Duke of York's house, which, however, I would see, and therefore put a bit of meat in our mouths, and went thither, where, with much ado, at half-past one, we got into a blind hole in the 18*d*. place, above stairs, where we could not hear well, but the house infinite full, but the prologue most silly, and the play, though admirable, yet no pleasure almost in it, because just the very same design, and words, and sense, and plot, as every one of his plays have, any one of which alone would be held admirable, whereas so many of the same design and fancy do but dull one another; and this, I perceive, is the sense of every body else, as well as myself, who therefore showed but little pleasure in it. . . .

9th. . . . With all speed, back to the Duke of York's house, where mighty full again; but we come time enough to have a good place in the pit, and did hear this new play again, where, though I better understood it than before, yet my sense of it and pleasure was just the same as yesterday, and no more, nor any body else's about us. . . .

19th. . . . My wife and I by hackney to the King's playhouse, and there, the pit being full, sat in a box above, and saw "Catiline's Conspiracy,"[50] yesterday being the first day: a play of much good sense and words to read, but that do appear the worst upon the stage, I mean, the least diverting, that ever I saw any, though most fine in clothes; and a fine scene of the Senate, and of a fight, that ever I saw in my life. But the play is only to be read, and therefore home, with no pleasure at all, but only in sitting next to Betty Hall, that did belong to this house. . . .

21st. . . . To the Duke's playhouse, and saw "Macbeth." The King and Court there; and we sat just under them and my Lady Castlemayne, and close to the woman that comes into the pit, a kind of loose gossip, that pretends to be like her, and is so, something. . . . The King and Duke of York minded me, and smiled upon me, at the handsome woman near me: but it vexed me to see Moll Davis, in the box over the King's and my Lady Castlemayne's head, look down upon the King, and he up to her; and so did my Lady Castlemayne once, to see who it was; but when she saw her, she looked like fire; which troubled me. . . .

26th. . . . So home at noon to dinner, and then abroad with my wife to a play, at the Duke of York's house, the house full of ordinary citizens. The play was "Women Pleased,"[51] which we had never seen before; and, though but indifferent, yet there is a good design for a good play. . . .

[49] This tragedy, taken from the first book of Maccabees, was performed with great success. It was first published in 1669. . . .

[50] Ben Jonson's tragedy, first published in 1611. Catiline was taken by Hart, Cethegus by Mohun, Cicero by Burt, and Sempronia by Mrs. Corey.

[51] A tragi-comedy by Fletcher, first published in 1647; well thought of at the time. . . .

30th. . . . After dinner, my wife and I to the Duke's playhouse, and there did see "King Harry the Eighth;" and was mightily pleased, better than I ever expected, with the history, and shows of it. . . .

1st. . . . My wife and I with our coach to the King's playhouse, and there in a box saw "The Mayden Queene."

7th. . . . At noon home to dinner, and thence my wife and I to the King's playhouse, and there saw "The Island Princesse,"[1] the first time I ever saw it; and it is a pretty good play, many good things being in it, and a good scene of a town on fire. We sat in an upper box, and the jade Nell come and sat in the next box; a bold merry slut, who lay laughing there upon people; and with a comrade of hers of the Duke's house, that come in to see the play. . . .

11th. . . . Abroad with my wife to the King's playhouse, and there saw "The Joviall Crew;"[2] but ill acted to what it was heretofore, in Clun's time, and when Lacy could dance. . . .

13th. . . . To the King's playhouse, and there saw, I think, "The Maiden Queene," and so home and to supper. . . .

15th. . . . Up, and by coach to Sir W. Coventry, where with him a good while in his chamber, talking of one thing or another; among others, he told me of the great factions at Court at this day, even to the sober engaging of great persons, and differences, and making the King cheap and ridiculous. It is about my Lady Harvy's being offended at Doll Common's acting of Sempronia,[3] to imitate her; for which she got my Lord Chamberlain, her kinsman, to imprison Doll: when my Lady Castlemayne made the King to release her, and to order her to act it again, worse than ever, the other day, where the King himself was: and since it was acted again, and my Lady Harvy provided people to hiss her and fling oranges at her. . . .

18th. . . . To the Duke of York's playhouse, and there saw "The Witts," a medley of things, but some similes mighty good, though ill mixed. . . .

---

[1] A tragi-comedy by Beaumont and Fletcher; published in 1647, and reprinted in 1669, "as it is acted at the Theatre Royal by His Majesty's servants. With the alterations and new additional scenes."

[2] "The Jovial Crew; or, the Merry Beggars," a comedy by Richard Brome.

[3] The following cast of parts in "The Alchymist," as acted by the King's Company . . . furnishes a clue to the actress described here . . . as "Doll Common":

Subtle	Mr. Clun.
Face	Major Mohun.
Sir E. Mammon	Mr. Cartwright
Surly	Mr. Burt
Ananias	Mr. Lacy
Wholesome	Mr. Bateman
Doll Common	*Mrs. Corey*
Dame Plyant	Mrs. Rutter

The identity, however, is placed beyond doubt by a reference to "Cataline's Conspiracy," where we find Mrs. Corey acting the part of Sempronia, in which "Doll Common," as Pepys styles her, gave offence by imitating Lady Harvey, and consequently was sent to prison. We may add that Mrs. Corey's name stands first in the list of female performers in the King's Company under Killigrew. See "Roscius Anglicanus," 1708.

19th. . . . To the King's house, to see "Horace;"[4] this the third day of its acting — a silly tragedy; but Lacy hath made a farce of several dances — between each act, one: but his words are but silly, and invention not extraordinary, as to the dances; only some Dutchmen come out of the mouth and tail of a Hamburgh sow. Thence, not much pleased with the play. . . .

20th. . . . To the Duke of York's house, and saw "Twelfth Night," as it is now revived; but, I think, one of the weakest plays that ever I saw on the stage. . . .

21st. . . . To the Duke of York's house . . . and there saw "The Tempest;" but it is but ill done by Gosnell, in lieu of Moll Davis. . . .

27th. . . . To the Duke of York's playhouse, and there saw "The Five Hours' Adventure," which hath not been acted a good while before, but once, and is a most excellent play, I must confess. . . .

February

1st. . . . With my wife by coach to the King's playhouse, thinking to have seen "The Heyresse," first acted on Saturday last; but when we come thither, we find no play there; Kinaston, that did act a part therein, in abuse to Sir Charles Sedley, being last night exceedingly beaten with sticks, by two or three that assaulted him, so as he is mightily bruised, and forced to keep his bed.[5] So we to the Duke of York's playhouse, and there saw "She Would if She Could". . . .

2nd. . . . To the King's playhouse, where "The Heyresse," notwithstanding Kinaston's being beaten, is acted: and they say the King is very angry with Sir Charles Sedley for his being beaten, but he do deny it. But his part is done by Beeston, who is fain to read it out of a book all the while, and thereby spoils the part, and almost the play, it being one of the best parts in it; and though the design is, in the first conception of it, pretty good, yet it is but an indifferent play, wrote, they say, by my Lord Newcastle. But it was pleasant to see Beeston come in with others, supposing it to be dark, and yet he is forced to read his part by the light of the candles: and this I observing to a gentleman that sat by me, he was mightily pleased therewith, and spread it up and down. But that, that pleased me most in the play is, the first song that Knepp sings, she singing three or four; and, indeed, it was very finely sung, so as to make the whole house clap her. . . .

6th. . . . After dinner to the King's playhouse, and there . . . did see "The Moor of Venice:" but ill acted in most parts; Mohun, which did a little surprise me, not acting Iago's part by much so well as Clun used to do; nor another Hart's, which was Cassio's; nor, indeed, Burt doing the Moor's so well as I once thought he did. . . .

9th. . . . With my wife to the King's playhouse, and there saw "The Island Princesse," which I like mighty well, as an excellent play: and here we find

---

[4] The "Horace" of P. Corneille, translated by Catherine Phillips, the fifth act being added by Sir John Denham. It was presented at Court by persons of quality, the prologue being spoken by the Duke of Monmouth. See Evelyn's "Diary," under February 5th, 1668–69.

[5] . . . Kinaston was vain of his personal resemblance to Sir C. Sedley, and dressed exactly like him. Sedley, to revenge this insult, hired a bravo to chastise him in St. James's Park, under the pretext that he mistook him for the baronet. According to Pepys, it would seem that the imitation was made in the play of "The Heiress," which is very likely. . . .

Kinaston to be well enough to act again, which he do very well, after his beating by Sir Charles Sedley's appointment. . . .

18th. . . . After dinner my wife and I to the Duke of York's house, to a play, and there saw "The Mad Lover," which do not please me so well as it used to do, only Betterton's part still pleases me. . . .

20th. . . . After dinner out with my wife . . . to the Duke of York's house, and there saw "The Gratefull Servant,"[6] a pretty good play, and which I have forgot that ever I did see. . . .

22nd. . . . In the evening . . . to White Hall, and there did without much trouble get into the playhouse, there in a good place among the Ladies of Honour, and myself also sat in the pit; and there by and by come the King and Queen, and they begun "Bartholomew Fayre." But I like no play here so well as at the common playhouse; besides that, my eyes being very ill since last Sunday and this day se'nnight, with the light of the candles, I was in mighty pain to defend myself now from the light of the candles. . . .

25th. . . . To the Duke of York's house, and there before one, but the house infinite full, where, by and by, the King and Court come, it being a new play, or an old one new vamped, by Shadwell, called "The Royall Shepherdesse;"[7] but the silliest for words and design, and everything, that ever I saw in my whole life, there being nothing in the world pleasing in it, but a good martial dance of pikemen, where Harris and another do handle their pikes in a dance to admiration; but never less satisfied with a play in my life. . . .

26th. . . . I went with my wife and girls to the King's playhouse, to shew them that, and there saw "The Faithfull Shepherdesse." But, Lord! what an empty house, there not being, as I could tell the people, so many as to make up above £10 in the whole house! The being of a new play at the other house, I suppose, being the cause, though it be so silly a play that I wonder how there should be enough people to go thither two days together, and not leave more to fill this house. The emptiness of the house took away our pleasure a great deal, though I liked it the better; for that I plainly discern the musick is the better, by how much the house the emptier. . . .

3rd. . . . To the Duke of York's playhouse, and there saw an old play, the *March* first time acted these forty years, called "The Lady's Tryall,"[8] acted only by the young people of the house; but the house very full. But it is but a sorry play, and the worse by how much my head is out of humour. . . .

8th. . . . After dinner with my wife alone to the King's playhouse, and there saw "The Mocke Astrologer," which I have often seen, and but an ordinary play . . . , and then home, and there my wife to read to me, my eyes being sensibly hurt by the too great lights of the playhouse. . . .

9th. . . . To see "Claricilla," which do not please me almost at all, though there are some good things in it. . . .

---

[6] A comedy by James Shirley, first published in 1630.

[7] A tragi-comedy, altered by Thomas Shadwell from a comedy written by John Fountain, called "The Rewards of Virtue," published in 1661. The "Royal Shepherdess" was published in 1669.

[8] A tragi-comedy by John Ford, published in 1639.

17th. . . . Took my wife by a hackney to the King's playhouse, and saw "The Coxcomb,"[9] the first time acted, but an old play, and a silly one, being acted only by the young people. . . .

April

14th. . . . To the Duke of York's play-house, and there saw "The Impertinents," a play which pleases me well still; but it is with great trouble that I now see a play, because of my eyes, the light of the candles making it very troublesome to me. . . .

16th. . . . My wife . . . abroad . . . to see the new play to-day, at the Duke of York's house, "Guzman" . . . ; I thence presently to the Duke of York's playhouse, and there, in the 18*d.* seat, did get room to see almost three acts of the play; but it seemed to me but very ordinary. After the play done, I into the pit, and . . . here I did meet with Shadwell, the poet, who, to my great wonder, do tell me that my Lord of [Orrery] did write this play, trying what he could do in comedy, since his heroique plays could do no more wonders. This do trouble me; for it is as mean a thing, and so he says, as hath been upon the stage a great while; and Harris, who hath no part in it, did come to me, and told me in discourse that he was glad of it, it being a play that will not take. . . .

17th. . . . Hearing that "The Alchymist" was acted, we did go, . . . to the King's house; and it is still a good play, having not been acted for two or three years before; but I do miss Clun,[10] for the Doctor.[11] But more my eyes will not let me enjoy the pleasure I used to have in a play. . . .

23rd. . . . My wife . . . seeing a play at the New Nursery, which is set up at the house in Lincoln's Inn Fields, which was formerly the King's house. . . . To the King's playhouse, and saw "The Generous Portugalls,"[12] a play that pleases me better and better every time we see it; and, I thank God! it did not trouble my eyes so much as I was afeard it would. . . .

24th. . . . After dinner to the King's house, and there saw "The General"[13] revived — a good play, that pleases me well. . . .

May

12th. . . . After dinner my wife and I to the Duke of York's playhouse, and there, in the side balcony, over against the musick, did hear, but not see, a new play, the first day acted, "The Roman Virgin,"[14] an old play, and but ordinary, I thought; but the trouble of my eyes with the light of the candles did almost kill me. . . .

17th. . . . By coach to the King's playhouse, and saw "The Spanish Curate"[15] revived, which is a pretty good play, but my eyes troubled with seeing it, mightily. . . .

[9] A comedy by Beaumont and Fletcher. . . .
[10] Who had been murdered. See August 4th, 1664.
[11] Subtle, the alchymist.
[12] "The Island Princess," a tragi-comedy by Fletcher, was revived in 1669 as "The Island Princess, or the Generous Portugal." The King of Tidore was acted by Kynaston, and Quisara, the Island Princess, by Mrs. Marshall.
[13] Apparently the play by Lord Orrery, which Pepys first saw acted on September 28th, 1664.
[14] "The Roman Virgin, or Unjust Judge," a tragedy, altered by Thomas Betterton from Webster's "Appius and Virginia." Published in 1679.
[15] "The Spanish Curate," a comedy by Beaumont and Fletcher, was seen by Pepys at the Whitefriars Theatre on March 16th, 1660–61.

Thomas Rymer (1641–1713) was second only to Dryden as a prominent critic of Restoration drama. Of special interest is his criticism of Shakespeare and his conviction that failure to observe classical rules of unity seriously inhibited important drama in England. In The Tragedies of the Last Age consider'd and examin'd by the Practice of the Ancients . . . *(1678), he promised to examine in detail six plays: Fletcher's* Rollo, A King and No King, *and* The Maid's Tragedy; *Shakespeare's* Othello *and* Julius Caesar; *Jonson's* Catiline; *and Milton's* Paradise Lost, *"which some are pleased to call a poem." However, he confined himself to the first three. He returned to attack* Othello *in* A Short View of Tragedy: its Original Excellency and Corruption; with some Reflections on Shakespeare and other practitioners for the Stage. *Conceding Shakespeare's genius in comedy, Rymer denied that he had any capacity for tragedy.*

Although frequently regarded as an advocate of French neo-classical ideas and a champion of French taste, Rymer held in the preface to his translation of Rapin on Aristotle and in A Short View of Tragedy *that the English language had greater potential than other languages. It is striking that in spite of his praise of English literature in general, and of the epic, lyric, and comedy in particular, he is read, remembered, and judged almost entirely for his condemnation of English tragedy. Rymer placed much emphasis on probability, decorum, and the "rules," while exhibiting a lack of sensitivity to the peculiar richness of the Elizabethan drama.*

Thomas Rymer. *A Short View of Tragedy; It's Original, Excellency, and Corruption. With some Reflections on Shakespear, and other Practitioners for the Stage.* London, 1693.

What Reformation may not we expect now, that in *France* they see the necessity of a *Chorus* to their Tragedies? *Boyer,* and *Racine,* both of the Royal Academy, have led the Dance; they have tried the success in the last Plays that were Presented by them. **page 1 /**

The *Chorus* was the root and original, and is certainly always the most necessary part of Tragedy.

The *Spectators* thereby are secured, that their Poet shall not juggle, or put upon them in the matter of *Place,* and *Time,* other than is just and reasonable for the representation.

And the *Poet* has this benefit; the *Chorus* is a goodly *Show,* so that he need not ramble from his Subject out of his Wits for some foreign Toy or Hobbyhorse, to humor the Multitude.

(a) *Aristotle* tells us of *Two Senses* that must be pleas'd, our *Sight,* and our

(a) Poetica.

Ears: And it is vain for a *Poet* (with *Bays* in the Rehearsal) to complain of Injustice, and the wrong Judgment in his *Audience*, unless these *Two senses* be gratified.

The worst on it is, that most People are wholly led by these *Two senses*, and follow them upon content, without ever troubling their Noddle farther.

How many *Plays* owe all their success to a rare *Show?* Even in the days of *Horace*, enter on the Stage a Person in a *Costly strange Habit*, Lord! *What Clapping, what Noise* and Thunder, as Heaven and Earth were coming together! Yet not one word spoken. **page 2 /**

. . . It matters not whether there be any *Plot*, any *Characters*, any *Sense*, or a wise *Word* from one end to the other, provided in our Play we have the *Senate of Rome*, the *Venetian Senate* in their Pontificalibus, or a *Blackamoor* Ruffian, or *Tom Dove*, or other Four-leg'd Hero of the Bear-Garden.

The *Eye* is a quick sense, will be in with our Fancy, and prepossess the Head strangely. Another means whereby the *Eye* misleads our Judgment is the *Action:* We go to see a Play *Acted;* in Tragedy is represented a Memorable *Action;* so the Spectators are always pleas'd to see *Action*, and are not often so ill-natur'd to pry into, and examine whether it be Proper, Just, Natural, in season, or out of season. *Bays* in the Rehearsal well knew this secret: The *Two Kings* are at their *Coranto;* nay, the *Moon and the Earth* dance the *Hey;* any thing in Nature, or against Nature, rather than allow the *Serious Councel*, or other dull business to interrupt, or obstruct *Action*. **page 3 /**

This thing of *Action* finds the blindside of humane-kind an hundred ways. We laugh and weep with those that laugh or weep; we gape, stretch, and are very *dotterels* by example.

.   .   .   .

Many, peradventure, of the Tragical Scenes in *Shakespear*, cry'd up for the *Action*, might do yet better without words: Words are a sort of heavy baggage, that were better out of the way, at the push of *Action;* especially in his *bombast Circumstance*, where the Words and Action are seldom akin, generally are inconsistent, at cross purposes, embarrass or destroy each other; yet to those who take not the words distinctly, there may be something in the buz and sound, that like a drone to a Bagpipe may serve to set off the *Action:* For an instance of the former, Would not a rap at the door better express *Jago's* meaning? than

> *— Call aloud.*
> Jago.   *Do with like timerous accent, and dire yel,* **page 4 /**
> *As when by night and negligence the fire*
> *Is spied in populous Cities.*

For, What Ship? Who is Arrived? The Answer is,

> *'Tis one* Jago, *Auncient to the General,*
> *He has had most Favourable and Happy speed;*
> *Tempests themselves, high Seas, and houling Winds,*
> *The guttered Rocks, and congregated Sands,*
> *Traytors ensteep'd, to clog the guiltless Keel,*

As having senses of Beauty, do omit
Their common Natures, letting go safely by
The divine Desdemona.

Is this the Language of the Exchange, or the Ensuring-Office? Once in a man's life, he might be content at *Bedlam* to hear such a rapture. In a Play one should speak like a man of business . . . ; but by this Gentleman's talk one may well guess he has nothing to do. And he has many Companions, that are

— Hey day!
I know not what to do, nor what to say. (*b*)   **page 5 /**

It was then a strange imagination in *Ben. Johnson*, to go stuff out a Play with *Tully's* Orations. And in *Seneca*, to think his dry Morals, and a tedious strain of Sentences might do feats, or have any wonderful operation in the *Drama*.

Some go to *see*, other to *hear* a Play. The Poet should please both; but be sure that the *Spectators* be satisfied, whatever Entertainment he give his *Audience*.

But if neither the *Show*, nor the *Action* cheats us, there remains still a notable vehicle to carry off nonsense, which is the *Pronunciation*.

By the loud Trumpet, which our Courage aids;
We learn, That sound, as well as sense perswades. (*c*)   **page 6 /**

. . . .

. . . From the Stage, the Bar or the Pulpit, a *good voice* will prepossess our ears, and having seized that Pass, is in a fair way to surprise our Judgment.

Considering then what power the *Shows*, the *Action*, and the *Pronunciation* have over us, it is no wonder that wise men often mistake, and give an hasty Judgment, which upon a review is justly set aside. . . .   **page 7 /**

. . . Amongst the Moderns, never was a Cause canvass'd with so much heat, between the Play-Judges, as that in *France*, about *Corneille's* Tragedy of the *Cid*. The *Majority* were so fond of it, that with them it became a Proverb, (*f*) *Cela est plus beau que la Cid*. On the other side, Cardinal *Richelieu* damn'd it, and said, *All the pudder about it, was only between the ignorant people and the men of judgment*.

Yet this Cardinal with so nice a taste, had not many years before been several times to see acted the Tragedy of Sir *Thomas Moor*, and as often wept at the Representation. Never were known so many people (*g*) crowded to death, as at that Play. . . .

By this Instance we see a man the most sharp, and of the greatest penetration was imposed upon by these cheating Sences, **page 8 /** the Eyes and the Ears, which greedily took in the impression from the *Show*, the *Action*, and from the Emphasis and *Pronunciation;* tho there was no great matter of *Fable*, no *Manners*, no fine *Thoughts*, no *Language;* that is, nothing of a Tragedy, nothing of a Poet all the while.

(*b*) Rehearsal.   (*f*) Pelisson. *Hist. Acad.*
(*c*) Waller.   (*g*) *Parnasse Reform.*

Horace was very angry with these empty *Shows* and Vanity, which the Gentlemen of his time ran like mad after. . . . What would he have said to the *French Opera* of late so much in vogue? There it is for you to bewitch your *eyes*, and to charm your *ears*. There is a Cup of Enchantment, there is Musick and Machine; *Circe* and *Calipso* in conspiracy against Nature and good Sense. 'Tis a Debauch the most insinuating, and the most pernicious; none would think an *Opera* and Civil Reason, should be the growth of one and the same Climate. But shall we wonder at any thing for a Sacrifice to the *Grand Monarch?* such Worship, such Idol. All flattery to him is insipid, unless it be prodigious: Nothing reasonable, or within compass can come near the Matter. All must be monstrous, enormous, and outragious to Nature, to be like him, or give any Eccho on his Appetite. **page 9 /**

Were *Rabelais* alive again, he would look on his *Garagantua* as but a Pygmy.
(*b*) — *The Heroes Race excels the Poets Thought.*

The Academy Royal may pack up their Modes and Methods, & *penses ingenienses;* the *Racines* and the *Corneilles* must all now dance to the Tune of *Baptista.* Here is the *Opera;* here is *Machine* and *Baptista,* farewell *Apollo* and the Muses. . . . **page 10 /**

CHAP. V [II].

From all the Tragedies acted on our English Stage, *Othello* is said to bear the Bell away. The *Subject* is more of a piece, and there is indeed something like, there is, as it were, some phantom of a *Fable.* The *Fable* is always accounted the *Soul* of Tragedy. And it is the *Fable* which is properly the *Poets* part. Because of the other **page 86 /** three parts of Tragedy, to wit, the *Characters* are taken from the Moral Philosopher; the *thoughts,* or sence, from them that teach *Rhetorick:* And the last part, which is the *expression,* we learn from the Grammarians.

This Fable is drawn from a Novel, compos'd in Italian by *Giraldi Cinthio,* who also was a Writer of Tragedies. And to that use employ'd such of his Tales, as he judged proper for the Stage. But with this of the *Moor* he meddl'd no farther.

Shakespear alters it from the Original in several particulars, but always, unfortunately, for the worse. He bestows a name on his *Moor;* and styles him the Moor of *Venice:* a Note of pre-eminence, which neither History nor Heraldry can allow him. *Cinthio,* who knew him best, and whose creature he was, calls him simply a *Moor.* . . . We see no such Cause for the *Moors* preferment to that dignity. And it is an affront to all Chroniclers, and Antiquaries to top upon 'um a *Moor,* with that mark of renown, who yet had never faln within the Sphere of their Cognisance. **page 87 /**

Then is the Moors *Wife,* from a simple Citizen, in *Cinthio,* dress'd up with her Top knots, and rais'd to be *Desdemona,* a Senators Daughter. All this is very strange; And therefore pleases such as reflect not on the improbability. This match might well be without the Parents Consent. . . .

(*b*) Waller.

THE FABLE

Othello, a Blackmoor Captain, by talking of his Prowess and Feats of War, makes Desdemona, *a Senators Daughter to be in love with him; and to be married to him, without her Parents knowledge; And having preferred* Cassio *to be his Lieutenant, (a place which his Ensign* Jago *sued for)* Jago *in revenge, works the Moor into a Jealousy that* Cassio *Cuckolds him: which he effects by stealing and conveying a certain Handkerchief, which had, at the Wedding, been by the Moor presented to his Bride. Hereupon,* Othello *and* Jago *plot the Deaths* **page 88 /** *of* Desdemona *and* Cassio, Othello *Murders her, and soon after is convinced of her Innocence. And as he is about to be carried to Prison, in order to be punish'd for the Murder, He kills himself.*

What ever rubs or difficulty may stick on the Bark, the Moral, sure, of this Fable is very instructive.

First, This may be a caution to all Maidens of Quality how, without their Parents consent, they run away with Blackamoors. . . .

Secondly, This may be a warning to all good Wives, that they look well to their Linnen.

Thirdly, This may be a lesson to Husbands, that before their Jealousie be Tragical, the proofs may be Mathematical.

Cinthio affirms that *She was not overcome by a Womanish Appetite, but by the Vertue of the Moor.* It must be a good-natur'd Reader that takes *Cinthio's* word in this case, tho' in a Novel. *Shakespear,* who is accountable both to the *Eyes,* and to the *Ears,* And to convince the very heart of an Audience, shews that *Desdemona* was **page 89 /** won, by hearing *Othello* talk.

> Othello. — *I spake of most disastrous chances,*
> *of Moving accidents, by flood and field;*
> *of hair-breadth scapes i' th' imminent deadly breach;*
> *of being taken by the insolent foe;*
> *and sold to slavery: of my redemption thence;*
> *and portents in my Travels History:*
> *wherein of Antars vast, and Desarts idle,*
> *rough Quarries, Rocks, and Hills, whose heads touch Heaven,*
> *It was my hint to speak, such was my process:*
> *and of the* Cannibals *that each others eat:*
> *the* Anthropophagi, *and men whose heads*
> *do grow beneath their shoulders —*

This was the Charm, this was the philtre, the love-powder that took the Daughter of this Noble Venetian. This was sufficient to make the Black-amoor White, and reconcile all, tho' there had been a Cloven-foot into the bargain. . . .

Nodes, Cataracts, Tumours, Chilblains, Carnosity, *Shankers,* or any *Cant* in the Bill of an High-German Doctor is as good *fustian Circumstance,* and **page 90 /** as likely to charm a Senators Daughter. But, it seems, the noble Venetians have an other sence of things. The *Doge* himself tells us;

> Doge. *I think this Tale wou'd win my Daughter too. . . .*

Shakespear in this Play calls 'em the *supersubtle venetians*. Yet examine throughout the Tragedy there is nothing in the noble *Desdemona*, that is not below any Countrey Chamber-maid with us. . . .   **page 91 /**

Nothing is more odious in Nature than an improbable lye; And, certainly, never was any Play fraught, like this of *Othello*, with improbabilities.

The *Characters* or Manners, which are the second part in a Tragedy, are not less unnatural and improper, than the Fable was improbable and absurd.

Othello is made a Venetian General. We see nothing done by him, nor related concerning him, that comports with the condition of a General, or, indeed, of a Man, unless the killing himself, to avoid a death the Law was about to inflict upon him. When his Jealousy had wrought him up to a resolution of's taking revenge for the   **page 92 /**   suppos'd injury, He sets *Jago* to the fighting part, to kill *Cassio;* And chuses himself to murder the silly Woman his Wife, that was like to make no resistance.

His Love and his Jealousie are no part of a Souldiers Character, unless for Comedy.

But what is most intolerable is *Jago*. He is no Black-amoor Souldier, so we may be sure he should be like other Souldiers of our acquaintance; yet never in Tragedy, nor in Comedy, nor in Nature was a Souldier with his Character; take it in the Authors own words;

> Em. — *some Eternal Villain,*
> *Some busie, and insinuating Rogue,*
> *Some cogging, couzening Slave, to get some Office.*

. . . .

Shakespear knew his Character of *Jago* was inconsistent. In this very Play he pronounces,

> *If thou dost deliver more or less than Truth,*
> *Thou art no Souldier.* —   **page 93 /**

This he knew, but to entertain the Audience with something new and surprising, against common sense, and Nature, he would pass upon us a close, dissembling, false, insinuating rascal, instead of an open-hearted, frank, plain-dealing Souldier, a character constantly worn by them for some thousands of years in the World. . . .

Nor is our Poet more discreet in his *Desdemona*, He had chosen a Souldier for his Knave: And a Venetian Lady is to be the Fool.

This Senators Daughter runs away to   **page 94 /**   (a Carriers Inn) the *Sagittary*, with a Black-amoor: is no sooner wedded to him, but the very night she Beds him, is importuning and teizing him for a young smock-fac'd Lieutenant, *Cassio*. And tho' she perceives the *Moor* Jealous of *Cassio*, yet will she not forbear, but still rings *Cassio, Cassio* in both his Ears.

Roderigo is the Cully of *Jago*, brought in to be murder'd by *Jago*, that *Jago's* hands might be the more in Blood, and be yet the more abominable Villain: who without that was too wicked on all Conscience; And had more to answer for, than any Tragedy, or Furies could inflict upon him. So there can be nothing in the *characters*, either for the profit, or to delight an Audience.

The third thing to be consider'd is the *Thoughts*. But from such *Characters*, we need not expect many that are either true, or fine, or noble.

And without these, that is, without sense or meaning, the fourth part of Tragedy, which is the *expression* can hardly deserve to be treated on distinctly. The verse rumbling in our Ears are of good use to help off the action.

In the *Neighing* of an Horse, or in the　**page 95 /**　*growling* of a Mastiff, there is a meaning, there is as lively expression, and, may I say, more humanity, than many times in the Tragical flights of *Shakespear*.

Step then amongst the Scenes to observe the Conduct in this Tragedy.

The first we see are *Jago and Roderigo*, by Night in the Streets of *Venice*. After growling a long time together, they resolve to tell *Brabantio* that his Daughter is run away with the Black-a-moor. *Jago* and *Roderigo* were not of quality to be familiar with *Brabantio*, nor had any provocation from him, to deserve a rude thing at their hands. *Brabantio* was a Noble Venetian one of the Sovereign Lords, and principal persons in the Government, Peer to the most Serene *Doge*, one attended with more state, ceremony and punctillio, than any English Duke, or Nobleman in the Government will pretend to. This misfortune in his Daughter is so prodigious, so tender a point, as might puzzle the finest Wit of the most *supersubtle* Venetian to touch upon it, or break the discovery to her Father. See then how delicately *Shakespear* minces the matter:

Rod.　*What ho*, Brabantio, *Signior Brabantio, ho.*　**page 96 /**
Jago.　*Awake, what ho*, Brabantio, *Thieves, thieves, thieves:*
Look to your House, your Daughter, and your Bags
Thieves, thieves.

Brabantio at a Window

Bra.　*What is the reason of this terrible summons?*
What is the matter there?
Rod.　*Signior, is all your Family within?*
Jago.　*Are your Doors lockt?*
Bra.　*Why, wherefore ask you this?*
Jago.　*Sir, you are robb'd, for shame put on your Gown,*
Your Heart is burst, you have lost half your Soul,
Even now, very now, an old black Ram
Is tupping your white Ewe: arise, arise,
Awake the snorting Citizens with the Bell,
Or else the Devil will make a Grandsire of you, arise I said.

Nor have they yet done, amongst other ribaldry, they tell him.

Jago.　*Sir, you are one of those that will not serve God, if the Devil bid you; because we come to do you service, you think us Ruffians, you'le have your Daughter covered with a Barbary Stallion. You'le have your Nephews* **page 97 /** *neigh to you; you'le have Coursers for Cousins, and Gennets for Germans.*
Bra.　*What prophane wretch art thou?*
Jago.　*I am one, Sir, that come to tell you, your Daughter and the Moor, are now making the Beast with two backs.*

In former days there wont to be kept at the Courts of Princes some body in a Fools Coat, that in pure simplicity might let slip something, which made way for the ill news, and blunted the shock, which otherwise might have come too violent upon the party. . . .   page 98 /

But *Shakespear* shews us another sort of address, his manners and good breeding must not be like the rest of the Civil World. *Brabantio* was not in Masquerade, was not *incognito; Jago* well knew his rank and dignity.

> Jago.   *The* Magnifico *is much beloved,*
> *And hath in his effect, a voice potential*
> *As double as the Duke —*

But besides the Manners to a *Magnifico,* humanity cannot bear that an old Gentleman in his misfortune should be insulted over with such a rabble of Skoundrel language, when no cause or provocation. Yet thus it is on our Stage, this is our   page 99 /   School of good manners, and the *Speculum Vitae.*

But our *Magnifico* is here in the dark, nor are yet his Robes on: attend him to the Senate house, and there see the difference, see the effects of Purple.

So, by and by, we find the Duke of *Venice* with his Senators in Councel, at Midnight, upon advice that the Turks, or Ottamites, or both together, were ready in transport Ships, put to Sea, in order to make a Decent upon *Cyprus.* This is the posture, when we see *Brabantio,* and *Othello* join them. By their Conduct and manner of talk, a body must strain hard to fancy the Scene at *Venice;* And not rather in some of our Cinq-ports, where the Baily and his Fisher-men are knocking their heads together on account of some Whale; or some terrible broil upon the Coast. But to show them true Venetians, the Maritime affairs stick not long on their hand; the publick may sink or swim. They will sit up all night to hear a Doctors Commons, Matrimonial, Cause. And have the Merits of the Cause at large laid open to 'em, that they may decide it before they Stir. What can be pleaded to keep awake their attention so wonderfully?   page 100 /

Never, sure, was *form* of *pleading* so tedious and so heavy, as this whole Scene, and midnight entertainment. Take his own words: says the *Respondent.*

> Oth. *Most potent, grave, and reverend Signiors,*
> *My very noble, and approv'd good Masters:*
> *That I have tane away this old mans Daughter;*
> *It is most true: true, I have Married her,*
> *The very front and head of my offending,*
> *Hath this extent, no more: rude I am in my speech.*
> *And little blest with the set phrase of peace,*
> *For since these Arms of mine had seven years pith,*
> *Till now some nine Moons wasted, they have us'd*
> *Their dearest action in the Tented Field:*
> *And little of this great World can I speak,*
> *More than pertains to Broils and Battail,*
> *And therefore little shall I grace my Cause,*
> *In speaking of my self; yet by your gracious patience*
> *I would a round unravish'd Tale deliver,*
> *Of my whole course of love, what drags, what charms*

What Conjuration, and what mighty Magick,
(for such proceedings am I charg'd withal)
I won his Daughter.

All this is but *Preamble,* to tell the Court that He wants words. This was the Elo- **page 101 /** quence which kept them up all Night, and drew their attention, in the midst of their alarms.

One might rather think the novelty, and strangeness of the case prevail'd upon them: no, the Senators do not reckon it strange at all. Instead of starting at the Prodigy, every one is familiar with *Desdemona,* as he were her own natural Father, rejoice in her good fortune, and wish their own several Daughters as hopefully married. Should the Poet have provided such a Husband for an only Daughter of any noble Peer in *England,* the Black-amoor must have chang'd his Skin, to look our House of Lords in the Face. . . . **page 102 /**

A third part in a Tragedy is the *Thoughts:* from Venetians, Noblemen, and Senators, we may expect fine *Thoughts.* Here is a tryal of skill: for a parting blow, the *Duke,* and *Brabantio* Cap *sentences.* Where then shall we seek for the *Thoughts,* if we let slip this occasion? says the Duke:

> Duk. *Let me speak like your self and lay a* Sentence,
> *Which like a greese or step, may help these lovers*
> *Into your favour.*
> *When remedies are past the grief is ended,*
> *By seeing the worst which late on hopes depended,*
> *To mourn a mischief that is past and gone,*
> *Is the next way to draw more mischief on;*
> *What cannot be preserv'd when Fortune takes,*
> *Patience her injury a Mocker makes.*
> *The rob'd that smiles, steals something from a Thief,*
> *He robs himself, that spends an hopeless grief* **page 103 /**
> Bra. *So let the Turk of* Cyprus *us beguile*
> *We lose it not so long as we can smile;*
> *He bears the sentence well, that nothing bears*
> *But the free comfort which from thence he bears,*
> *But he bears both the sentence and the sorrow,*
> *That to pay grief must of poor patience borrow:*
> *These* Sentences *to Sugar, or to Gall,*
> *Being strong on both sides are equivocal.*
> *But words are words, I never yet did hear,*
> *That the bruis'd* Heart *was pierced through the Ear.*
> *Beseech you now to the affairs of State.*

How far wou'd the Queen of *Sheba* have travell'd to hear the Wisdom of our Noble Venetians? . . . . **page 104 /**

For the *Second Act,* our Poet having dispatcht his affairs at *Venice,* shews the Action next (I know not how many leagues off) in the Island of *Cyprus.* The Audience must be there too: And yet our *Bays* had it never in his head, to make any provision of Transport Ships for them. . . .

Come a shoar then, and observe the **page 106 /** Countenance of the People, after the dreadful Storm, and their apprehensions from an Invasion by the Ottomites, their succour and friends scatter'd and tost, no body knew whither. The first that came to Land was *Cassio*, his first Salutation to the Governour, *Montanio*, is:

> Cas. *Thanks to the valiant of this Isle:*
> *That so approve the Moor, and let the Heavens*
> *Give him defence against their Elements,*
> *For I have lost him on the dangerous Sea.*

To him the Governour speaks, indeed, like a Man in his wits.

> Mont. *Is he well Shipt?*

The Lieutenant answers thus.

> Cas. *His Bark is stoutly Tymber'd, and his Pilot*
> *Of very expert, and approv'd allowance,*
> *Therefore my hopes (not surfeited to death)*
> *Stand in bold care.*

The Governours first question was very proper; his next question, in this posture of affairs, is: **page 107 /**

> Mont. *But, good Lieutenant, is our general Wiv'd?*

A question so remote, so impertinent and absurd, so odd and surprising never entered *Bayes's Pericranium*. Only the answer may Tally with it.

> Cas. *Most fortunately, he hath atchiev'd a Maid,*
> *That Parragons description, and wild fame:*
> *One that excels the quirks of blasoning Pens:*
> *And in the essential vesture of Creation,*
> *Does bear an excellency —*

They who like this Authors writing will not be offended to find so much repeated from him. I pretend not here to tax either the *Sense*, or the *Language*; those *Circumstances* had their proper place in the Venetian Senate. What I now cite is to shew how probable, how natural, how reasonable the Conduct is, all along.

I thought it enough that *Cassio* should be acquainted with a Virgin of that rank and consideration in *Venice*, as *Desdemona*. I wondred that in the Senate-house every one should know her so familiarly: yet,   **page 108 /**   here also at *Cyprus*, every body is in a rapture at the name of *Desdemona*: except only *Montanio* who must be ignorant; that *Cassio*, who has an excellent cut in shaping an Answer, may give him the satisfaction:

> Mont. *What is she?*
> Cas. *She that I spoke of: our Captains Captain,*
> *Left in the Conduct of the bold* Jago,
> *Whose footing here anticipates our thoughts*

A Sennets speed: great Jove Othello *guard,*
And swell his Sail with thine own powerful breath,
That he may bless this Bay with his Tall Ship,
And swiftly come to Desdemona's *Arms,*
Give renewed fire to our extincted Spirits,
And bring all Cyprus *comfort:*

Enter Desdemona, &c.

— O behold,
The riches of the Ship is come on shoar.
Ye men of Cyprus, *let us have your Knees:*
Hail to the Lady: and the Grace of Heaven
Before, behind thee, and on every hand.
Enwheel the round — page 109 /

In the name of phrenzy, what means this Souldier? or would he talk thus, if he meant any thing at all? Who can say *Shakespear* is to blame in his *Character* of a Souldier? Has he not here done him reason? When cou'd our *Tramontains* talk at this rate? but our *Jarsey* and *Garnsey* Captains must not speak so fine things, nor compare with the Mediterranean, or Garisons in *Rhodes* and *Cyprus.*

The next thing our Officer does, is to salute *Jago's* wife, with this *Conge* to the Husband,

Cas. *Good Ancient, you are welcome, welcome Mistriss,*
Let it not Gall your Patience, good Jago,
That I extend my Manners, 'tis my Breeding,
That gives me this bold shew of Curtesy.
Jago. *Sir, would she give you so much of her lips,*
As of her tongue she has bestow'd on me,
You'd have enough.
Des. *Alass! she has no speech.*

Now follows a long rabble of Jack-pudden farce betwixt *Jago* and *Desdemona*, that runs on with all the little plays, jingle, page 110 / and trash below the patience of any Countrey Kitchin-maid with her Sweet-heart. The Venetian *Donna* is hard put to't for pastime! And this is all, when they are newly got on shoar, from a dismal Tempest, and when every moment she might expect to hear her Lord (as she calls him) that she runs so mad after, is arriv'd or lost. And moreover.

— In a Town of War,
— The peoples Hearts brimful of fear.

Never in the world had any Pagan Poet his Brains turn'd at this Monstrous rate. . . . page 111 /

But pass we to something of a more serious air and Complexion. *Othello* and his Bride are the first Night, no sooner warm in Bed together, but a Drunken Quarrel happening in the Garison, two Souldiers Fight; And the General rises to part the Fray: He swears.

Othel. *Now by Heaven,*
My blood begins my safer guides to rule,
And passion, having my best judgment cool'd,
Assays to lead the way: if once I stir,
Or do but lift this arm, the best of you
Shall sink in my rebuke: give me to know
How this foul rout began; who set it on,
And he that is approv'd in this offence,
Tho' he had twin'd with me both at a birth,
Should lose me: what, in a Town of War,
Yet wild, the peoples Hearts brimful of fear,
To manage private, and domestick quarrels,
In Night, and on the Court, and guard of safety,
'Tis Monstrous, Jago, *who began?*   page 112 /

In the days of yore, Souldiers did not swear in this fashion. What should a
Souldier say farther, when he swears, unless he blaspheme? action shou'd speak
the rest. . . . He is to rap out an Oath, not Wire-draw and Spin it out: by the
style one might judge that *Shakespears* Souldiers were never bred in a Camp,
but rather had belong'd to some Affidavit-Office. Consider also throughout
this whole Scene, how the Moorish General proceeds in examining into this
Rout; No Justice *Clod-pate* could go on with more Phlegm and deliberation.
The very first night that he lyes with the *Divine Desdemona* to be thus interrupted, might provoke a Mans Christian Patience to swear in another style. . . .
Only his Venetian Bride is a match for him. She understands that the Souldiers
in the Garison are by th' ears together: And presently she, at midnight, is in
amongst them.

Desd. *What's the matter there?*
Othel. *All's well now Sweeting —*
Come away to Bed —   page 113 /

.   .   .   .

In this *Second Act*, the face of affairs could in truth be no other, than

— In a Town of War,
Yet wild, the peoples Hearts brim-ful of fear.

But nothing either in this *Act*, or in the rest that follow, shew any colour
or complexion, any resemblance or proportion to that face and posture it
ought to bear. Should a Painter draw any one *Scene* of this Play, and write
over it, *This is a Town of War;* would any body believe that the Man were in
his senses? . . . .
Cassio having escaped the Storm comes on shoar at *Cyprus*, that night gets
Drunk, Fights, is turn'd out from his Command, grows sober again, takes advice how to be restor'd, is all Repentance and Mortification: yet before he
sleeps, is in the Morning at his Generals door with a noise of Fiddles, page
116 /   and a Droll to introduce him to a little Mouth-speech with the Bride.

Cassio. *Give me advantage of some brief discourse*
With Desdemona *alone.*
Em. *Pray you come in,*
I will bestow you, where you shall have time
To speak your bosom freely.

So, they are put together: And when he had gone on a good while *speaking his bosom, Desdemona* answers him.

Des. *Do not doubt that, before* Emilia *here,*
I give thee warrant of thy place; assure thee,
If I do vow a friendship, I'll perform it,
To the last article —

Then after a ribble rabble of fulsome impertinence, She is at her Husband slap dash:

Desd. *— Good love, call him back.*
Othel. *Not now, sweet* Desdemona, *some other time.*
Desd. *But shall 't shortly?*
Othel. *The sooner, sweet, for you.*
Desd. *Shall 't be to-night at Supper?* page 117 /
Othel. *No, not to night.*
Desd. *To-Morrow Dinner then?*
Othel. *I shall not dine at home,*
I meet the Captains at the Citadel.
Desd. *Why then to morrow night, or Tuesday morn,*
Or night, or Wednesday morn?

After forty lines more, at this rate, they part, and then comes the wonderful Scene, where *Jago* by shrugs, half words, and ambiguous reflections, works *Othello* up to be Jealous. One might think, after what we have seen, that there needs no great cunning, no great poetry and address to make the *Moor* Jealous. Such impatience, such a rout for a handsome young fellow, the very morning after her Marriage must make him either to be jealous, or to take her for a *Changeling*, below his Jealousie. After this *Scene*, it might strain the Poets skill to reconcile the couple, and allay the Jealousie. *Jago* now can only *actum agere*, and vex the audience with a nauseous repetition.

Whence comes it then, that this is the top scene, the Scene that raises *Othello* above all other Tragedies on our Theatres? It is purely from the *Action;* from the page 118 / Mops and the Mows, the Grimace, the Grins and Gesticulation. Such scenes as this have made all the World run after *Harlequin* and *Scaramuccio.* . . . page 119 /

Othello the night of his arrival at *Cyprus*, is to consummate with *Desdemona*, they go to Bed. Both are rais'd and run into the Town amidst the Souldiers that were a fighting: then go to Bed again, that morning he sees *Cassio* with her; She importunes him to restore *Cassio*. *Othello* shews nothing of the Souldiers Mettle: but like a tedious, drawling, tame Goose, is gaping after any paultrey insinuation, labouring to be jealous; And catching at every blown surmize.

Jago. *My Lord, I see you are moved.*
Oth. *No, not much moved.*
Do not think but Desdemona *is honest.*
Jag. *Long live she so, and long live you to think so.*
Oth. *And yet how Nature erring from it self,*
Jag. *I, There's the point: as to be bold with you,*
Not to affect many proposed Matches
Of her own clime, complexion, and degree,
Wherein we see, in all things, Nature tends,
Fye, we may smell in such a will most rank,
Foul disproportion, thoughts unnatural. —

The Poet here is certainly in the right, and by consequence the foundation of the Play   **page 120 /**   must be concluded to be Monstrous; And the constitution, all over, to be *most rank,*

Foul disproportion, thoughts unnatural.

Which instead of moving pity, or any passion Tragical and Reasonable, can produce nothing but horror and aversion, and what is odious and grievous to an Audience. After this fair Mornings work, the Bride enters, drops a Cursey.

Desd. *How now, my dear Othello,*
Your Dinner, and the generous Islanders
By you invited, do attend your presence.
Oth. *I am to blame.*
Desd. *Why is your speech so faint? Are you not well?*
Oth. *I have a pain upon my Fore-head, dear.*

Michael Cassio came not from *Venice* in the Ship with *Desdemona*, nor till this Morning could be suspected of an opportunity with her. And 'tis now but Dinner time; yet the *Moor* complains of his Fore-head. He might have set a Guard on *Cassio*, or have lockt up *Desdemona*, or have observ'd their carriage a day or two longer. He is on other occasions phlegmatick   **page 121 /** enough; this is very hasty.
But after Dinner we have a wonderful flight:

Othel. *What sense had I of her stoln hours of lust?*
I saw 't not, thought it not, it harm'd not me:
I slept the next night well, was free and merry,
I found not Cassio's *kisses on her lips.* —

A little after this, says he,

Oth. *Give me a living reason that she's disloyal.*
Jago. —*I lay with* Cassio *lately,*
And being troubled with a raging Tooth, I could not sleep;
There are a kind of men so loose of Soul,
That in their sleeps will mutter their affairs,
One of this kind is Cassio:

In sleep I heard him say: sweet Desdemona,
Let us be wary, let us hide our loves:
And then, Sir, wou'd he gripe and wring my hand,
Cry out, sweet Creature; and then kiss me hard,
As if he pluckt up kisses by the roots,
That grew upon my lips, then laid his Leg
Over my Thigh, and sigh'd, and kiss'd, and then
Cry'd, cursed fate, that gave thee to the Moor. **page 122 /**

By the Rapture of *Othello*, one might think that he raves, is not of sound Memory, forgets that he has not yet been two nights in the Matrimonial Bed with his *Desdemona*. But we find *Jago*, who should have a better memory, forging his lies after the very same Model. The very night of their Marriage at *Venice*, the Moor, and also *Cassio*, were sent away to *Cyprus*. In the *Second Act*, *Othello* and his Bride go the first time to Bed; The *Third Act* opens the next morning. The parties have been in view to this moment. We saw the opportunity which was given for *Cassio* to *speak his bosom* to her, *once*, indeed, might go a great way with a Venetian. But *once*, will not do the Poets business; The *Audience* must suppose a great many bouts, to make the plot operate. They must deny their senses, to reconcile it to common sense: or make it any way consistent, and hang together.

Nor, for the most part, are the single thoughts more consistent, than is the oeconomy: The Indians do as they ought in painting the Devil White: but says *Othello*:

Oth. *— Her name that was as fresh*
As Dian's *Visage, is now begrim'd and black,*
As mine own face — **page 123 /**

There is not a Monky but understands Nature better; not a Pug in *Barbary* that has not a truer taste of things.

Othello. *— O now for ever*
Farewel the tranquil mind, farewel content;
Farewel the plumed troop, and the big Wars,
That make Ambition Vertue: O farewel,
Farewel the neighing Steed, and the shrill Trump,
The spirit stirring Drum, th' ear-piercing Fief,
The royal Banner, and all quality,
Pride, Pomp, and Circumstance of glorious War,
And O ye Mortal Engines, whose wide throats
Th' immortal Joves great clamours counterfeit,
Farewel, Othello's *occupation's gone.*

These lines are recited here, not for any thing Poetical in them, besides the sound, that pleases. Yet this sort of imagery and amplification is extreamly taking, where it is just and natural. . . . **page 124 /**

Notwithstanding that this Scene had proceeded with fury and bluster sufficient to make the whole Isle ring of his Jealousy, yet is *Desdemona* diverting her self with a paultry buffoon and only solicitous in quest of *Cassio*:

> Desd. *Seek him, bid him come hither, tell him* —
> *Where shou'd I lose that Handkerchief, Emilia?*
> *Believe me I had rather lose my Purse,*
> *Full of Crusado's: And but my noble Moor*
> *Is true of mind, and made of no such baseness,*
> *As Jealous Creatures are; it were enough*
> *To put him to ill thinking.* **page 125 /**
> Em. *Is he not Jealous?*
> Desd. *Who he? I think the Sun, where he was born,*
> *Drew all such humours from him.*

By this manner of speech one wou'd gather the couple had been yoak'd together a competent while, what might she say more, had they cohabited, and had been Man and Wife seven years?

She spies the Moor.

> Desd. *I will not leave him now,*
> *Till* Cassio *is recall'd,*
> *I have sent to bid* Cassio *come speak with you.*
> Othel. — *Lend me thy Handkerchief.*
> Desd. — *This is a trick to put me from my suit.*
> *I pray let* Cassio *be receiv'd agen.*
> Em. — *Is not this man Jealous?*
> — *'Tis not a year or two shews us a man* —

As if for the first year or two, *Othello* had not been jealous? This *third Act* begins in the morning, at noon she drops the Handkerchief, after dinner she misses it, and then follows all this outrage and horrible clutter about it. If we believe a small **page 126 /** Damosel in the last *Scene* of this *Act*, this day is effectually seven days.

> Bianca. — *What keep a week away! seven days, seven nights,*
> *Eightscore eight hours, and lovers absent hours,*
> *More tedious than the Dial eightscore times.*
> *Oh weary reckoning!*

Our poet is at this plunge, that whether this *Act* contains the compass of one day, of seven days, or of seven years, or of all together, the repugnance and absurdity would be the same. For *Othello*, all the while, has nothing to say or to do, but what loudly proclaim him jealous: her friend and confident *Emilia* again and again rounds her in the Ear that *the Man* is Jealous: yet this Venetian dame is neither to see, nor to hear; nor to have any sense or understanding, nor to strike any other note but *Cassio, Cassio.* . . . **page 127 /**

ACT IV.

Enter Jago *and* Othello:

Jago. *Will you think so?*
Othel. *Think so, Jago.*
Jago. *What, to kiss in private?*
Othel. *An unauthorised kiss.*

Jago. *Or to be naked with her friend a-bed,*
An hour or more, not meaning any harm?
Othel. *Naked a-bed,* Jago, *and not mean harm?* —

At this gross rate of trifling, our General and his Auncient March on most heroically; till the Jealous Booby has his Brains turn'd; and falls in a Trance. Would any imagine this to be the Language of Venetians, of Souldiers, and mighty Captains? **page 128 /** no *Bartholomew* Droll cou'd subsist upon such trash. But lo, a Stratagem never presented in Tragedy.

Jago. *Stand you while a part —*
—Incave your self;
And mark the Jeers, the Gibes, and notable scorns,
That dwell in every region of his face,
For I will make him tell the tale a new,
Where, how, how oft, how long ago, and when,
He has, and is again to Cope your Wife:
I say, but mark his gesture. —

With this device *Othello* withdraws. Says *Jago* aside.

Jago. *Now will I question* Cassio *of* Bianca,
A Huswife —
That doats on Cassio —
He when he hears of her cannot refrain
From the excess of Laughter —
As he shall smile, Othello *shall go mad,*
And his unbookish jealousy must conster
Poor Cassio's smiles, gesture, and light behaviour
Quite in the wrong — **page 129 /**

So to work they go: And *Othello* is as wise a commentator, and makes his applications pat, as heart cou'd wish — but I wou'd not expect to find this Scene acted nearer than in *Southwark* Fair. But the *Handkerchief* is brought in at last, to stop all holes, and close the evidence. So now being satisfied with the proof, they come to a resolution, that the offenders shall be murdered. . . .

Jago had some pretence to be discontent with *Othello* and *Cassio:* And what passed hitherto was the operation of revenge. *Desdemona* had never done him harm, always kind to him, and to his Wife; was **page 130 /** his Countrywoman, a Dame of quality: for him to abet her Murder, shews nothing of a Souldier, nothing of a Man, nothing of Nature in it. . . . Can it be any diversion to see a Rogue beyond what the Devil ever finish'd? Or wou'd it be any instruction to an Audience? *Jago* cou'd desire no better than to set *Cassio* and *Othello,* his two Enemies, by the Ears together; so he might have been reveng'd on them both at once: And chusing for his own share, the Murder of *Desdemona,* he had the opportunity to play booty, and save the poor harmless wretch. But the Poet must do every thing by contraries: to surprize the Audience still with something horrible and prodigious, beyond any human imagination. At this rate he must out-do the Devil, to be a Poet in the rank with *Shakespear.*

Soon after this, arrives from *Venice*, *Ludovico*, a noble Cousin of *Desdemona*, presently she is at him also, on the behalf of *Cassio*. . . . **page 131** /

By this time, we are to believe the couple have been a week or two Married: And *Othello's* Jealousie that had rag'd so loudly, and had been so uneasie to himself, must have reach'd her knowledge. The *Audience* have all heard him more plain with her, than was needful to a Venetian capacity: And yet she must still be impertinent in her suit for *Cassio*, well, this *Magnifico* comes from the *Doge*, and Senators, to displace *Othello*. . . . **page 132** /

Of what flesh and blood does our Poet make these noble Venetians? the men without Gall; the Women without either Brains or Sense? A Senators Daughter runs away with this Black-amoor; the Government employs this Moor to defend them against the Turks, so resent not the Moors Marriage at present, but the danger over, her Father gets the Moor Cashier'd, sends his Kinsman, Seignior *Ludovico*, to *Cyprus* with the Commission for a new General; who, at his arrival, finds the Moor calling the Lady his Kinswoman, Whore and Strumpet, and kicking her: what says the *Magnifico*? **page 133** /

> Lud. *My Lord, this would not be believ'd in* Venice,
> *Tho' I shou'd swear I saw't, 'tis very much;*
> *Make her amends: she weeps.*

The Moor has no body to take his part, no body of his Colour: *Ludovico* has the new Governour *Cassio*, and all his Countrymen Venetians about him. What Poet wou'd give a villanous Black-amoor this Ascendant? What Tramontain could fancy the Venetians so low, so despicable, or so patient? this outrage to an injur'd Lady, the *Divine Desdemona*, might in a colder Climate have provoked some body to be her Champion: but the Italians may well conclude we have a strange Genius for Poetry. In the next Scene *Othello* is examining the supposed Bawd; then follows another storm of horrour and outrage against the poor Chicken, his Wife. Some Drayman or drunken Tinker might possibly treat his drab at this sort of rate, and mean no harm by it: but for his excellency, a My lord General, to Serenade a Senator's Daughter with such a volly of scoundrel filthy Language, is sure the most absurd Maggot that ever bred from any Poets addle Brain. **page 134** /

. . . Yet to make all worse, her Murder, and the manner of it, had before been resolv'd upon and concerted. But nothing is to provoke a Venetian; she takes all in good part. . . . With us a Tinkers Trull wou'd be Nettled, wou'd repartee with more spirit, and not appear so void of spleen.

> Desd. *O good* Jago,
> *What shall I do to win my Lord agen?*

No Woman bred out of a Pig-stye, cou'd talk so meanly. Ater this, she is call'd to Supper with *Othello*, *Ludovico*, &c. after that comes a filthy sort of Pastoral Scene, **page 135** /   where the *Wedding Sheets*, and Song of *Willow*, and her Mothers Maid, poor *Barbara*, are not the least moving things in this entertainment. But that we may not be kept too long in the dumps, nor the melancholy Scenes lye too heavy, undigested on our Stomach, this *Act* gives us for a farewell, the *salsa, O picante*, some quibbles, and smart touches. . . .

The last *Act* begins with *Jago* and *Roderigo;* . . .

Roderigo, a Noble Venetian had sought *Desdemona* in Marriage, is troubled to find the Moor had got her from him, advises with *Jago*, who wheadles him to sell his Estate, and go over the Sea to *Cyprus*, in expectation to Cuckold *Othello*, there ha-   **page 136 /**   ving cheated *Roderigo* of all his Money and Jewels, on pretence of presenting them to *Desdemona*, our Gallant grows angry, and would have satisfaction from *Jago;* who sets all right, by telling him *Cassio* is to be Governour, *Othello* is going with *Desdemona*, into *Mauritania;* to prevent this, you are to murder *Cassio*, and then all may be well. . . .

Had *Roderigo* been one of the *Banditi*, he might not much stick at the Murder. But why *Roderigo* should take this for payment, and risque his person where the prospect of advantage is so very uncertain and remote, no body can imagine. It had need be a *super-subtle* Venetian that this Plot will pass upon. Then after a little spurt of villany and Murder, we are brought to the most lamentable, that ever appear'd on any Stage. A noble Venetian Lady is to be murdered by our Poet; in sober sadness, purely for being a Fool. No Pagan Poet but wou'd   **page 137 /**   have found some *Machine* for her deliverance. . . . Has our Christian Poetry no generosity, nor bowels? Ha, Sir *Lancelot!* ha St. *George!* will no Ghost leave the shades for us in extremity, to save a distressed Damosel?

But for our comfort, however felonious is the Heart, hear with what soft language, he does approach her, with a Candle in his Hand:

> Oth. *Put out the light and then put out the light;*
> *If I quench thee, thou flaming Minister,*
> *I can again thy former light restore —*

Who would call him Barbarian, Monster, Savage? Is this a Black-amoor? . . . .

One might think the General should not glory much in this action, but make an hasty work on't, and have turn'd his Eyes away from so unsouldierly   **page 138 /**   an Execution: yet is he all pause and deliberation: handles her as calmly: and is as careful of her Souls health, as it had been her *Father Confessor. Have you prayed to Night*, Desdemona? But the suspence is necessary, that he might have a convenient while so to *roul his Eyes*, and so to *gnaw* his *nether lip* to the spectators. . . .

But hark, a most tragical thing laid to her charge.

> Oth. *That Handkerchief, that I so lov'd, and gave thee,*
> *Thou gav'st to* Cassio.
> Desd. *No by my Life and Soul;*
> *Send for the man and ask him.*
> Oth. *— By Heaven, I saw my Handkerchief in his hand —*
> *—I saw the Handkerchief.*

So much ado, so much stress, so much passion and repetition about an Handkerchief! Why was not this call'd the *Tragedy of the Handkerchief?* . . . **page 139 /**   Had it been *Desdemona's* Garter, the Sagacious Moor might have smelt a Rat: but the Handkerchief is so remote a trifle, no Booby, on this side *Mauritania* cou'd make any consequence from it. . . .   **page 140 /**

. . . We ask here what unnatural crime *Desdemona*, or her Parents had committed, to bring this Judgment down upon her; to Wed a Black-amoor, and innocent to be thus cruelly murder'd by him. What instruction can we make out of this Catastrophe? Or whither must our reflection   page 141 /   lead us? Is not this to envenome and sour our spirits, to make us repine and grumble at Providence; and the government of the World? If this be our end, what boots it to be Vertuous?

Desdemona dropt the Handkerchief, and missed it that very day after her Marriage; it might have been rumpl'd up with her Wedding sheets: And this Night that she lay in her wedding sheets, the *Fairey* Napkin (whilst *Othello* was stifling her) might have started up to disarm his fury, and stop his ungracious mouth. Then might she (in a Traunce for fear) have lain as dead. Then might he, believing her dead, touch'd with remorse, have honestly cut his own Throat, by the good leave, and with the applause of all the Spectators. Who might thereupon have gone home with a quiet mind, admiring the beauty of Providence; fairly and truly represented on the Theatre. . . .   page 142 /

. . . Our Poet, against all Justice and Reason, against all Law, Humanity and Nature, in a barbarous arbitrary way, executes and makes   page 143 /   havock of his subjects, *Hab-nab*, as they come to hand. *Desdemona* dropt her Handkerchief; therefore she must be stifl'd. *Othello*, by law to be broken on the Wheel, by the Poets cunning escapes with cutting his own Throat. *Cassio*, for I know not what, comes off with a broken shin. *Jago* murders his Benefactor *Roderigo*, as this were poetical gratitude. *Jago* is not yet kill'd, because there yet never was such a villain alive. The Devil, if once he brings a man to be dipt in a deadly sin, lets him alone, to take his course: and now when the *Foul Fiend* has done with him, our wise Authors take the sinner into their poetical service; there to accomplish him, and do the Devils drudgery. . . . page 144 /

. . . But the Poet is not, without huge labour and preparation to expose the Monster; and after shew the Divine Vengeance executed upon him. The Poet is not to add wilful Murder to his ingratitude: he has not antidote enough for the Poison: his Hell and Furies are not punishment sufficient for one single crime, of that bulk and aggravation.

> Em.   *O thou dull Moor, that Handkerchief thou speakest on,*
> *I found by Fortune, and did give my Husband:*
> *For often with a solemn earnestness,*
> *(More than indeed belong'd to such a trifle)*
> *He beg'd of me to steal it.*

Here we see the meanest woman in the Play takes this *Handkerchief* for a *trifle* below her Husband to trouble his head about it. Yet we find, it entered into our Poets head, to make a Tragedy of this *Trifle*.

Then for the *unraveling of the Plot*, as they call it, never was old deputy Recor-   page 145 /   der in a Country Town, with his spectacles in summoning up the evidence, at such a puzzle: so blunder'd, and be-doultefied; as is our Poet, to have a good riddance: And get the *Catastrophe* off his hands.

What can remain with the Audience to carry home with them from this sort of Poetry, for their use and edification? how can it work, unless (instead of settling the mind, and purging our passions) to delude our senses, disorder our thoughts, addle our brain, pervert our affections, hair our imaginations, corrupt our appetite, and fill our head with vanity, confusion, *Tintamarre*, and Jingle-jangle, beyond what all the Parish Clarks of *London*, with their *old Testament* farces and interludes, in *Richard* the seconds time cou'd ever pretend to? Our only hopes, for the good of their Souls, can be, that these people go to the Play-house, as they do to Church, to sit still, look on one another, make no reflection, nor mind the Play, more than they would a Sermon.

There is in this Play, some burlesk, some humour, and ramble of Comical Wit, some shew, and some *Mimickry* to divert the spectators: but the tragical part is, plainly none other, than a Bloody Farce, without salt or savour.   **page 146 /**

Thomas Shadwell (1642?–1692), professional dramatist and miscellaneous writer, produced eighteen plays, many of them vividly portraying the manners of the bourgeoisie and the lower classes of English society. Something of this quality is indicated by Sir George Etherege's request from Ratisbon: "Pray let Will Richards send me Mr. Shadwell's [play] when it is printed, that I may learn what follies are now in fashion."

Shadwell's first play, The Sullen Lovers *(1668), based on Molière's Les Fâcheux, played for twelve days, with Shadwell's wife taking the female lead. In the preface he condemned the frivolous wit, the popular disreputable lovers, and the love-honor clichés which had become conventions in Restoration comedy. In addition, he pointed out with some pride that he had "observ'd the three unities, of Time, Place, and Action" and that he had "endeavour'd to represent variety of Humours . . . which was the practice of Ben Johnson."*

A professed disciple of Jonson, whom he thought "all Dramatick Poets ought to imitate, though none are like to come near," Shadwell nevertheless owed much to Etherege, whose play She Would if She Could *(1668) he judged "the best Comedy, that has been written since the Restauration of the Stage."*

Although in The Humourists *(1670) he claimed Dryden as his particular friend, the two poets openly attacked each other when Shadwell replied to Dryden's second satire on Shaftesbury,* The Medal. *Referring to Dryden as an "abandoned rascal" and a "half wit, half fool," Shadwell was in turn characterized by Dryden, in* Mac Flecknoe, *as heir to the realm of Nonsense.*

Shadwell succeeded Dryden as laureate after the Revolution of 1688, but Dryden had perhaps the edge in the exchange, for it has become Shadwell's fate to be remembered less as the poet laureate and more as the butt of Dryden's satire and the victim of his cutting wit:

> The rest to some faint meaning make pretence,
> But Sh —— never deviates into sense.

Thomas Shadwell. Preface to *The Sullen Lovers: or, The Impertinents. A Comedy.* . . . London, 1693.

Preface

Reader,

The success of this Play, as it was much more than it deserv'd, so was much more than I expected: Especially in this very Critical Age, when every man pretends to be a Judge, and some, that never read Three Plays in their lives, and never understood one, are as Positive in their Judgment of Plays, as if they were all *Johnsons*. But had I been us'd with all the severity imaginable, I should patiently have submitted to my Fate; not like the rejected Authors of our Time, who, when their Plays are damn'd, will strut, and huff it out, and laugh at the Ignorance of the Age: Or, like some other of our Modern Fopps, that declare they are resolv'd to Justifie their Plays with their Swords (though perhaps their Courage is as little as their Wit) such as peep through their loop-holes in the Theatre, to see who looks glum upon their Plays: And if they spy a Gentle Squire making Faces, he poor soul must be *Hector'd* till he likes 'em, while the more stubborn *Bully Rock* damn's, and is safe: Such is their discretion in the Choice of their men. Such Gentlemen as these I must confess had need pretend they cannot Err. These will huff, and look big upon the success of an ill Play stuffed full of Songs and Dances, (which have that constraint upon 'em too, that they seldom seem to come in willingly;) when in such Plays the composer and the Dancing Master are the best Poets, and yet the unmerciful Scribler would rob them of all the Honour.

I am so far from valuing my self (as the Phrase is) upon this Play, that perhaps no man is a severer Judge of it than my self; yet if any thing could have made me proud of it, it would have been the great Favour and Counte-nance it receiv'd from His Majesty and their Royal Highnesses.

But I could not perswade my self that they were so favourable to the Play for the Merit of it, but out of a Princely Generosity, to encourage a young beginner, that did what he could to please them, and that otherwise might have been baulk'd for ever: 'Tis to this I owe the success of the Play, and am as far from presumption of my own merits in it, as one ought to be who receives an Alms.

The first hint I receiv'd was from the report of a Play of *Molieres* of three Acts, called *Les Fascheux*, upon which I wrote a great part of this before I read that; and after it came to my hands, I found so little for my use (having before upon that hint design'd the fittest Characters I / could for my pur-pose) that I have made use of but two short Scenes which I inserted afterwards (*viz*) the first Scene in the Second Act between *Stanford* and *Roger*, and *Molieres* story of Piquette, which I have translated into Back-gammon, both of them being so vary'd you would not know them. But I freely confess my Theft, and am asham'd on't, though I have the example of some that never yet wrote Play without stealing most of it; and (like men that lye so long, till they believe themselves) at length, by continual Thieving, reckon their stoln goods their own too: Which is so ignoble a thing, that I cannot but believe that he that makes a common practise of stealing other Mens Wit, would, if he could with the same safety, steal any thing else.

I have in this Play, as near as I could, observ'd the three Unities, of Time, Place, and Action; The time of the Drama does not exceed six hours, the place is in a very narrow Compass, and the Main Action of the Play, upon which all the rest depend, is the Sullen Love betwixt *Stanford* and *Emilia*, which kind of Love is only proper to their Characters: I have here, as often as I could naturally, kept the Scenes unbroken, which (though it be not so much prac-tised, or so well understood, by the *English*) yet among the French Poets is accounted a great Beauty; but after these frivolous excuses the want of Design in the Play has been objected against me: which fault (though I may endeavour a little to extenuate) I dare not absolutely deny: I conceive, with all submission to better Judgments, that no man ought to expect such Intrigues in the little actions of Comedy, as are requir'd in Plays of a higher Nature: But in Plays of Humour, where there are so many Characters as there are in this, there is yet less Design to be expected: For, if after I had form'd three or four forward prating Fopps in the Play, I made it full of Plot, and Business; at the latter end, where the turns ought to be many, and suddenly following one another, I must have let fall the Humour, which I thought wou'd be pleasanter than Intrigues could have been without it; and it would have been easier to me to have made a Plot than to hold up the Humour.

Another Objection, that has been made by some, is, that there is the same thing over and over: Which I do not apprehend, unless they blame the unity of the Action; yet *Horace de Arte Poetica*, says,

Sit quod vis, simplex duntaxit, & unum.

Or whether it be the carrying on of the Humours to the last, which the same Author directs me to do.

Si quid inexpertum Scenae committis, & andes
Personam formare novam, Servetur ad Imum
Qualis ab incepto processerit, & sibi constet.

I have endeavour'd to represent variety of Humours (most of the persons of the Play differing in their characters from one another) which was the practice of *Ben. Johnson*, whom I think all Dramatick Poets ought / to imitate, though none are like to come near; he being the only person that appears to me to have made perfect Representations of Humane Life, Most other Authors that *I* ever read, either have wild Romantick Tales wherein they strain Love and Honour to that Ridiculous height, that it becomes Burlesque; or in their lower Comedies content themselves with one or two Humours at most, and these not near so perfect Characters as the admirable *Johnson* always made, who never wrote Comedy without seven or eight excellent Humours. I never saw one, except that of *Falstaffe*, that was in my judgment comparable to any of *Johnson's* considerable Humours: You will pardon this digression when I tell you he is the man, of all the World, *I* most passionately admire for his Excellency in Dramatick Poetry.

Though I have known some of late so Insolent to say, that *Ben. Johnson* wrote his best Plays without Wit; imagining, that all the Wit in Plays consisted in bringing two persons upon the Stage to break Jests, and to bob one another, which they call Repartie, not considering that there is more Wit and Invention requir'd in the finding out good Humour, and Matter proper for it, than in all their smart Reparties. For in the Writing of a Humour, a Man is confin'd not to swerve from the Character, and oblig'd to say nothing but what is proper to it: But in the Plays which have been wrote of late, there is no such thing as perfect Character, but the two chief persons are most commonly a Swearing, Drinking, Whoring, Ruffian for a Lover, and an impudent ill-bred *Tomrig* for a Mistress, and these are the fine People of the Play; and there is that Latitude in this, that almost any thing is proper for them to say; but their chief Subject is bawdy, and profaneness, which they call *Brisk Writing,* when the most dissolute of Men, that rellish those things well enough in private, are *shock'd* at 'em in publick: And methinks, if there were nothing but the ill Manners of it, it should make Poets avoid that Indecent way of Writing.

But perhaps you may think me as impertinent as any one I represent; that, having so many faults of my own, shou'd take the liberty to judge of others, to impeach my fellow Criminals: I must confess it is very ungenerous to accuse those that modestly confess their own Errours; but Positive Men, that justifie all their faults, are Common Enemies, that no man ought to spare, prejudicial to all Societies they live in, destructive to all Communication, always endeavouring Magisterially to impose upon our Understandings, against the Freedom of Mankind: These ought no more to be suffer'd amongst us than wild beasts: For no correction that can be laid upon 'em are of power to reform 'em; and certainly it was a positive Fool that *Salomon* spoke of, when he said, *Bray him in a Mortar, and yet he will retain his folly.*

But I have troubled you too long with this Discourse, and am to ask your pardon for it, and the many faults you will find in the Play; and / beg you will believe, that whatever I have said of it, was intended not in Justification, but Excuse of it: Look upon it, as it really was, wrote in haste, by a Young Writer, and you will easily pardon it; especially when you know that the best of our Dramatick Writers have wrote very ill Plays at first, nay some of 'em have wrote several before they could get one to be Acted; and their best Plays were made with great expence of labour and time. Nor can you expect a very Correct Play, under a Years pains at the least, from the Wittiest Man of the Nation; It is so difficult a thing to write well in this kind. Men of Quality, that write for their pleasure, will not trouble themselves with exactness in their Plays; and those that write for profit would find too little encouragement for so much pains as a Correct Play would require.

Vale.

Thomas Shadwell. Prologue to *The Sullen Lovers: or, The Impertinents. A Comedy.... London,* 1693.

> *How popular are Poets now adays?*
> *Who can more Men at their first summons raise,*
> *Than many a wealthy home-bred Gentleman,*
> *By all his interest in his Countrey can.*
> *They raise their Friends, but in one day arise*
> *'Gainst one poor Poet, all these Enemies:*
> *For so he has observ'd you always are,*
> *And against all that write maintain a War.*

What shall he give you composition now?
Alas, he knows not what you will allow.
He has no cautionary Song, nor Dance,
That might the Treaty of his Peace advance:
No kind Romantick Lovers in his Play,
To sigh and whine out passion, such as may
Charm waiting-women with Heroick Chime,
And still resolve to live and dye in Rhime;
Such as your ears with Love, and Honour feast,
And Play at Crambo for three hours at least:
That Fight, and Wooe, in Verse in the same breath,
And make Similitudes, and Love in Death:
—— But if you Love a Fool, he bid me say,
He has great choice to shew you in his Play;
(To do you service) I am one to day.
Well Gallants, 'tis his first, Faith, let it go,
Just as old Gamesters by young Bubbles do:
This first and smaller Stake let him but win,
And for a greater Sum you'll draw him in.
Or use our Poet, as you would a Hare,
Which when she's hunted down, for Sport you spare.
At length take up, and damn no more for shame,
For if you only at the Qarrey aime,
This Critick poaching will destroy your Game.

Thomas Shadwell. Preface to *The Humorists; A Comedy.* . . . London, 1691.

Preface

This Play (besides the Errors in the writing of it) came upon the Stage with all the disadvantages imaginable: First, I was forc'd, after I had finish'd it, to blot out the main design of it; finding, that, contrary to my intention, it had given offence. The Second disadvantage was, that notwithstanding I had (to the great prejudice of the Play) given satisfaction to all the exceptions made against it, it Met with the clamorous opposition of a numerous party, bandied against it, and resolved, as much as they could, to damn it, right or wrong, before they had heard or seen a word on't. The last, and not the least, was, That the *Actors* (though since they have done me some right) at first were extremely imperfect in the Action of it. The least of these had been enough to have spoil'd a very good Comedy, much more such a one as mine. The last (*viz.*) imperfect Action, had like to have destroy'd *She would if she could*, which I think (and I have the Authority of some of the best Judges in *England* for't) is the best Comedy that has been written since the Restauration of the Stage: And even that, for the imperfect representation of it at first, received such prejudice, that, had it not been for the favour of the *Court*, in all probability it had never got up again, and it suffers for it; in a great measure to this very day. This of mine, after all these blows, had fall'n beyond Redemption, had it not been revived, after the second day, by her kindness (which I can never enough acknowledge) who, for four days together, beautified it with the most excellent *Dancings* that ever has been seen upon the Stage. This drew my Enemies, as well as Friends, till it was something better Acted, Understood, and Liked, than at first: By this means the poor Play's life was prolonged, and, I hope, will live in spight of Malice; if not upon the Stage, at least in Print.

Yet do not think I will defend all the faults of it: Before it was alter'd, I could better have answer'd for it: yet, as it is, I hope it   /   will not wholly displease you in the Reading. I should not say so much for it, if I did not find so much undeserved Malice against it.

My design was in it, to reprehend some of the Vices and Follies of the Age, which I take to be the most proper, and most useful way of writing Comedy. If I do not perform this well enough, let not my endeavours be blam'd.

Here I must take leave to dissent from those, who seem to insinuate that the ultimate end of a Poet is to delight, without Correction or Instruction: Methinks a Poet should never acknowledge this, for it makes him of as little use to mankind as a Fidler, or Dancing-Master, who delights the Fancy only, without improving the Judgment.

. . . .

I confess, a Poet ought to do all that he can, decently to please, that so he may instruct. To adorn his Images of Virtue so delightfully to affect people with a secret veneration of it in others, and an emulation to practice it in themselves: And to render their Figures of *Vice* and *Folly* so ugly and detestable, to make People hate and despise them, not only in others, but (if it be possible) in their dear selves. And in this latter, I think Comedy more useful than Tragedy; because the Vices and Follies in *Courts* (as they are too tender to be touch'd) so they concern but a few; whereas the Cheats, Villanies, and troublesome Follies, in the common conversation of the World, are of concernment to all the Body of Mankind.

And a Poet can no more justly be censured for ill nature, in detesting such *Knaveries*, and troublesom impertinencies, as are an imposition on all good Men, and a disturbance of Societies in general, than the most vigilant of our Judges can be thought so, for detesting Robbers and Highway-men, who are hanged, not for the sake of the Money they take (for of what value can that be to the life of a Man) but for interrupting common communication, and disturbing Society in general. For the sake of good Men, ill should be punished; and 'tis ill nature to the first, not to punish the last. A Man cannot truly   /   love a good man, that does not hate a bad one; nor a Wise man, that does not hate a Fool; this love and hatred are correlatives, and the one necessarily implies the other. I must confess it were ill nature, and below a man, to fall upon the natural imperfections of men, as of Lunaticks, Ideots, or men born Monstrous. But these can never be made the proper subject of a Satyr, but the affected vanities, and the artificial fopperies of men, which, (sometimes even contrary to their natures) they take pains to acquire, are the proper subject of a Satyr.

And for the Reformation of Fopps and Knaves, I think Comedy most useful, because to render Vices and Fopperies very ridiculous, is much a greater punishment than Tragedy can inflict upon 'em. There we do but subject 'em to hatred, or at worst to death; here we make them live to be dispised and laugh'd at, which certainly makes more impression upon men, than even death can do.

· · · · · · · · · · · · · · · · · · · ·

The rabble of little People, are more pleas'd with *Jack-Puddens* being soundly kick'd, or having a Custard handsomely thrown in his face, than with all the Wit in Plays: and the higher sort of Rabble (as there may be a Rabble of very fine people in this illiterate Age) are more pleased with the extravagant and unnatural actions the trifles, and fripperies of a Play, or the trappings and ornaments of Nonsense, than with all the Wit in the World.

This is one reason why we put our Fopps into extravagant, and unnatural Habits; it being a cheap way of conforming to the understanding of those brisk, gay Sparks, that judge of Wit or Folly by the Habit; that being indeed the only measure they can take in judging of Mankind, who are Criticks in nothing but a Dress.

Extraordinary pleasure was taken of old, in the Habits of the Actors, / without reference to sense, which *Horace* observes, and reprehends in his Epistle to Augustus. . . .

But for a Poet to think (without wit or good humour, under such a Habit) to please men of sense, is a presumption inexcusable. But I challenge the most clamorous and violent of my Enemies (who would have the Town believe that every thing I write, is too nearly reflecting upon persons) to accuse me, with truth, of representing the real Actions, or using the peculiar, affected phrases, or manner of speech of any one particular Man, or Woman living.

I cannot indeed create a new Language, but the Phantastick Phrases, used in any Play of mine, are not appropriate to any one *Fop*, but applicable to many.

Good men, and men of sence, can never be represented but to their advantage, nor can the Characters of Fools, Knaves, Whores, or Cowards (who are the people I deal most with in Comedies) concern any that are not eminently so: Nor will any apply to themselves what I write in this kind, that have but the wit, or honesty, to think tolerably well of themselves.

But it has been objected, that good men, and men of sence enough, may have blind-sides, that are liable to reprehension, and that such men should be represented upon a Stage, is intollerable.

'Tis true, excellent men may have errors, but they are not known by them, but by their excellencies: their prudence overcomes all gross follies, or conceals the less vanities, that are unavoidable Concomitants of human nature; or if some little errors do escape 'em, and are known, they are the least part of those men, and they are not distinguished in the world by them, but by their perfections; so that (if such blind-sides, or errors be represented) they do not reflect upon them, but upon such on whom these are predominant; and that receive such a Bias from 'em, that it turns 'em wholly from the ways of Wisdom or Morality. /

And even this representation, does not reflect upon any particular man, but upon very many of the same kind: For if a man should bring such a humour upon the Stage (if there be such a humour in the world) as only belongs to one, or two persons, it would not be understood by the Audience, but would be thought (for the singularity of it) wholly unnatural, and would be no jest to them neither.

But I have had the fortune to have had a general humour (in a Play of mine) applied to three, or four men (whose persons I never saw, or humours ever heard of) till the Play was acted.

As long as men wrest the Writings of Poets to their own corrupted sense, and with their Clamours prevail too, you must never look for a good Comedy of Humour, for a Humour (being the representation of some extravagance of Mankind) cannot but in some thing resemble some man, or other, or it is monstrous, and unnatural.

After this restraint upon Poets, there is little scope left, unless we retrieve the exploded Barbarisms of Fool, Devil, Giant, or Monster, or translate French Farces, which, with all the wit of the English, added to them, can scarce be made tollerable.

Mr. *Johnson*, I believe, was very unjustly taxed for personating particular men, but it will ever be the fate of them, that write the humours of the *Town*, especially in a foolish, and vicious Age. Pardon me (*Reader*) that I name him in the same Page with my self; who pretend to nothing more, than to joyn with all men of Sense and Learning in admiration of him; which, I think, I do not out of a true understanding of him; and for this I would not value my self. Yet by extolling his way of Writing, I cannot but insinuate to you that I can practise it; though I would if I could, a thousand times sooner than any mans.

And here I must make a little digression, and take liberty to dissent from my particular friend, for whom I have a very great respect, and whose Writings I extreamly admire; and though I will not say his is the best way of Writing, yet, I am sure, his manner of Writing it is much the best that ever was. . . . His Verse is smoother and deeper, his thoughts more quick and surprising, his raptures more mettled and higher. . . . And those Who shall go about to imitate him, will be found / to flutter, and make a noise, but never rise. Yet (after all this) I cannot think it Impudence in him, or any Man to endeavour to imitate Mr. *Johnson*, whom he confesses to have fewer failings than all the English Poets, which implies that he was the most perfect, and best Poet; and why should not we endeavour to imitate him? because we cannot arrive to his excellence? 'Tis true we cannot, but this is no more an argument, than for a Soldier (who considers with himself that he cannot be so great a one as *Julius Caesar*) to run from his Colours, and be none; or to speak of a less thing, why should any man study *Mathematicks* after *Archimedes*, *&c*. This Principle would be an obstruction to the progress of all Learning and knowledge in the world. Men of all Professions ought certainly to follow the best in theirs, and let not endeavours be blamed, if they go as far as they can in the right way, though they be unsuccessful, and attain not their ends. If Mr. *Johnson* be the most faultless Poet, I am so far from thinking it impudence to endeavour to imitate him, that it would rather (in my opinion) seem impudence in me not to do it.

I cannot be of their opinion who think he wanted wit, I am sure, if he did, he was so far from being the most faultless, that he was the most faulty Poet of his time, but it may be answered, that his Writings were correct, though he wanted fire; but I think flat and dull things are as incorrect, and shew as little Judgment in the Author, nay less sprightly and mettled Nonsence does. But I think he had more true Wit than any of his Contemporaries; that other men had sometimes things that seemed more fiery than his, was because they were placed with so many sordid and mean things about them, that they made a greater show. . . .

Nor can I think, to the writing of his humours (which were not only the follies, but vices and subtilties of Men) that Wit was not required, but Judgment; where by the way, they speak as if Judgment were a less thing than Wit. But certainly it was meant otherwise by nature, who subjected wit to the government of judgment, which is the noblest faculty of the mind. Fancy rough-draws, but judgment smooths and finishes; nay judgment does indeed comprehend / Wit, for no Man can have that who has not Wit. In fancy Mad-Men equal, if not excell all others, and one may as well say, that one of those Mad Men is as good a Man, as a temperate Wise Man, as that one of the very Fanciful Plays (admired most by Women) can be so good a Play as one of *Johnson's* Correct, and well-govern'd Comedies.

The reason given by some, why *Johnson* needed not Wit in writing Humor, is because Humor is the effect of Observation, and Observation the effect of Judgment; but Observation is as much necessary in all other Plays, as in Comedies of Humor: For first, even in the highest Tragedies, where the Scene lies in Courts, the Poet must have observed the Customs of Courts, and the manner of conversing there, or he will commit many indecencies, and make his Persons too rough and ill-bred for a Court.

Besides Characters in Plays being Representations of the Virtues or Vices, Passions or Affections of Mankind, since there are no more new Virtues or Vices; Passions or Affections, the Idea's of these can no other way be receiv'd into the imagination of a Poet, but either from the Conversation or Writings of Men. After a Poet has formed a Character (as suppose of an Ambitious Man) his design is certainly to write it naturally, and he has no other rule to guide him in this, but to compare him with other Men of that kind, that either he has heard of, or conversed with in the World, or read of in Books (and even this reading of Books is conversing with Men) nay more; (besides judging of his Character) the Poet can fancy nothing of it, but what must spring from the Observation he has made of Men or Books.

If this argument (that the Enemies of Humor use) be meant in this sense, that a Poet, in the writing of a Fools Character, needs but have a Man sit to him, and have his Words and Actions taken; in this case there is no need of Wit. But 'tis most certain that if we should do so, no one Fool (though the best about the Town) could appear pleasantly upon the Stage, he would be there too dull a Fool, and must be helped out with a great deal of Wit in the Author. I scruple not to call it so, First, because 'tis not your down-right Fool that is a fit Character for a Play, but like Sir *John Dawe* and Sir *Amorous la Foole*, your witty, brisk, airy *Fops* that are *Entreprennants*. Be- / sides Wit in the Writer, (I think, without any Authority for it) may be said to be the invention of remote and pleasant Thoughts of what kind soever; and there is as much occasion for such imaginations in the writing of a curious Coxcomb's part, as in writing the greatest Hero's; and that which may be Folly in the Speaker, may be so remote and pleasant, to require a great deal of Wit in the Writer. The most Excellent *Johnson* put Wit into the Mouths of the meanest of his People, and which, is infinitely difficult, made it proper for 'em. And I once heard a Person, of the greatest Wit and Judgment of the Age, say, That *Bartholomew Fair* (which consists most of low Persons) is one of the wittiest Plays in the World. If there be no Wit required in the rendring Folly ridiculous, or Vice odious, we must accuse *Juvenal* the best Satyrist, and wittiest Man of all the Latine Writers, for want of it.

I should not say so much of Mr. *Johnson* (whose Merit sufficiently justifies him to all Men of Sense) but that I think my self a little obliged to vindicate the Opinion I publickly declared, in my *Epilogue* to this *Play;* which I did upon mature consideration, and with a full satisfaction in my Judgment, and not out of a bare affected vanity of being thought his Admirer.

I have only one word more, to trouble you with, concerning this Trifle of my own, which is, that as it is at present, it is wholly my own, without borrowing a tittle from any Man; which I confess is too bold an attempt for so young a Writer; for (let it seem what it will) a Comedy of Humor (that is not borrowed) is the hardest thing to write well; and a way of Writing, of which a Man can never be certain.

> *Creditur, ex medio quia res accessit, habere*
> *Sudoris minimum, sed habet comoedia tanto*
> *Plus oneris, quanto veniae minus.*

That which (besides judging truly of Mankind) makes Comedy more difficult, is that the faults are naked and bare to most people, but the wit of it understood, or valued, but by few. Wonder not then if a Man of ten times my parts, miscarries in the attempt.

I shall say no more of this of mine, but that the Humours are new (how well chosen I leave to you to judge) and all the words and / actions of the Persons in the Play, are always sutable to the Characters I have given of them; and, in all the Play, I have gone according to that definition of humour, which I have given you in my *Epilogue*, in these words:

> *A Humor is the Biass of the Mind,*
> *By which, with violence, 'tis one way inclin'd:*
> *It makes our Actions lean on one side still;*
> *And, in all Changes, that way bends the Will.*

　　　　　　　　　　　　　　　　　　　　　　　　　　　Vale.

Thomas Shadwell. Epilogue to *The Humorists; A Comedy.* . . . London, 1691.

> *The mighty Prince of Poets, Learned* BEN,
> *Who alone div'd into the Minds of Men:*
> *Saw all their wandrings, all their Follies knew,*
> *And all their vain fantastick Passions drew,*
> *In Images so lively and so true;*
> *That there each Humorist himself might view,*
> *Yet only lash'd the Errors of the Times,*
> *And ne'er expos'd the Persons, but the Crimes:*

And never car'd for private frowns, when he
Did but chastise publick iniquity,
He fear'd no Pimp, no Pick-pocket, or Drab;
He fear'd no Bravo, nor no Ruffian's Stab.
'Twas he alone true Humors understood,
And with great Wit and Judgment made them good.
A Humor is the Byas of the Mind,
By which with violence 'tis one way inclin'd:
It makes our Actions lean on one side still,
And in all Changes that way bends the Will.
This ——
He only knew and represented right.
Thus none but Mighty Johnson *e're could write.*
Expect not then, since that most flourishing Age,
Of BEN, *to see true Humor on the Stage.*
All that have since been writ, if they be scan'd,
Are but faint Copies from that Master's Hand.
Our Poet now, amongst those petty things,
Alas, his too weak trifling Humors brings.
As much beneath the worst in Johnson's *Plays.*
As his great Merit is above our Praise.
For could he imitate that great Author right,
He would with ease all Poets else out-write,
But to out-go all other men, would be
O Noble BEN! *less than to follow thee.*
Gallants you see how hard it is to write,
Forgive all Faults the Poet meant to night:
Since if he Sinn'd, 'twas made for your Delight.
Pray let this find ——
As good success, tho it be very bad,
As any damn'd successful Play e'r had.
Yet if you hiss, he knows not where the harm is,
He'll not defend his Nonsence Vi & Armis.
But this poor Play has been so torn before.
That all, our Cruelty can't wound it more.

                         Finis.

The Frenchman Samuel Sorbière visited England in 1663 and published a record of his visit after his return to Paris in 1664. His work contains a general description of London and of other major points of interest — Canterbury, Dover, Oxford. Although he had many favorable reactions to English and the English people, he found mild fault with English culture. Of particular interest here is his criticism of the English theater, in which he charged that the English dramatists did not appreciate the unities. The work offended many Englishmen; and Louis XIV, in deference to the English, ordered the book suppressed.

Samuel Sorbière. *A Voyage to England, Containing many Things relating to the State of Learning, Religion, And other Curiosities of that Kingdom....* London, 1709.

. . . The Play-house is much more Diverting and Commodious; the best *Play-house* Places are in the Pit, where Men and Women promiscuously sit, every Body with their Company, the Stage is very handsome, being covered with Green Cloth, and the Scenes often change, and you are regaled with new Perspectives. The Musick with which you are entertained diverts your time till the Play begins, and People chuse to go in betimes to hear it. The Actors and Actresses perform their Parts to Admiration, as I have been informed, and so far as I my self could judge of them by their Gestures and Speech. But the Players here wou'd be of little Esteem in *France*, so far short the *English* come of the *French* this Way: The Poets laugh at the Uniformity of the Place, and the Rules of Times: Their Plays contain the Actions of Five and Twenty Years, and after that in the First Act they represent the Marriage of a Prince; they bring in his Son Fighting in the Second, and having Travelled over many Countries: But above all things they set up for Characterizing the Passions, Vertues and Vices of Mankind admirably well; and indeed do not fall much short in the performance. In representing **page 69 /** a Miser, they make him guilty of all the basest Actions that have been practised in several Ages, upon divers Occasions and indifferent Professions: They do not matter tho' it be a Hodch Potch, for they say, they mind only the Parts as they come on one after another, and have no regard to the whole Composition. I understand that all the *English* Eloquence consists in nothing but meer Pedantry, and that *Elegance of the English Language.* their Sermons from the Pulpit, and their pleadings at the Bar, are much of the same Stamp. I can say nothing of my self as to these Particulars, I only tell you what others have assured me to be true. The *English* Books are mostly writ after the same manner, and contain nothing but Rapsodies of things ill enough set together; and yet they are Valued, and the Authors get Reputation by them;

for they frequently never cite the Books from whence they Borrow, and so their Copies are taken for Originals. They are great Admirers of their own Language; and it suits their Effeminacy very well, for it spares them the Labour of moving their Lips: It must needs be very Copious and Adapt; for tho' 'tis a Corruption of the *Teutonick* or *German* which indeed is a very narrow Tongue, yet it openly declares it to be her Business to grow Rich with the Spoils of all dead Languages, and every Day impunedly to appropriate all that is good and proper for her from the living ones: Their Comedies are a kind of Blank Verse, and suit an Ordinary Language better than our Meetre, and make some Melody: They cannot but conceive it to be a troublesome thing to have the Ear continually tickled with the same Cadence; and they say, that to hear Heroick Verses spoken for Two or Three Hours together, and to recoyl back from one to the other, is a Method of Ex- page 70 / pression that is not so natural and diverting: In short, it looks as if the *English* would by no means fall in with the Practices and manner of Representations in other Languages; and the *Italian* Opera's appear more extravagant, and much more disliked by them than ours. But we are not here to enter upon a Dispute about the different Tastes of Men, it's best to leave every one to abound in his own Sence. It's not upon this Occasion only that we may observe, how People many times are much pleased with Trifles; and that one of the greatest Enjoyments they have is to impose upon themselves, or to fill their Heads with some Illusion to Divert them, till another comes on, and so new Airs and Fashions seem always the best and most agreeable to our Fancies. . . .
page 71 /

Prose-
Comedy.

Thomas Sprat. *Observations on Mons. de Sorbiere's Voyage into England.*
London, 1708.

I now pass over to his chief Delight, the *Belles Lettres* of the *English*. He grants *our Stage to be handsome, the Musick tolerable.* . . . But yet he says, that *our Poets laugh at the Rules of Time and Place: That all our Plays contain the Actions of Five and Twenty Years: That we Marry a Prince in the First Act, and bring in his Son fighting in the Second, and his Grandchild in the Third.* But here, Sir, he has committed a greater Disorder of Time than that whereof he accuses our Stage: For he has confounded the Reign of King *Charles* the Second with that of Q. *Elizabeth.* 'Tis true, about an Hundred Years ago the *English* Poets were not very exact in such Decencies; but no more then were the Dramatists of any other Countries. The *English* themselves did laugh away such Absurdities as soon as any; and for these last Fifty Years our Stage has been as regular in those Circumstances as the best in *Europe.* Seeing he thinks fit to upbraid our present Poets with the Errors of which their Predecessors were guilty so long since, I might as justly impute the vile Absurdities that are to be found in *Amadis de Gaul* to *Monsieur de Cornielle, de Scudery, de Chapelaine,* page 166 / *de Voiture,* and the rest of the Famous Modern *French* Wits.

P. 69.
P. 70.
P. 69.

He next blames the *Meanness of Humours which we represent.* And here, P. 69.
because he has thrust this Occasion upon me, I will venture to make a short
Comparison between the *French* Dramatical Poetry and ours. I doubt not,
Sir, but I may do this with the leave of that witty Nation: For as long as I do
not presume to slander their Manners, (from which you see I have carefully
forborn,) I hope they will allow me to examine that which is but Matter of
Wit and Delight: I will not enter into open defiance of them on *Monsieur de
Sorbiere's* Account, but I intreat them to permit me only to try a Civil Turna-
ment with them in his War of Letters. I will therefore make no Scruple to
maintain that the *English* Plays ought to be preferr'd before the *French.* And
to prove this I will not insist on an Argument which is plain to any Observer,
that the greatest Part of their most Excellent Pieces has been taken from the P. 70.
Spaniard; whereas the *English* have for the most part trodden in New Ways
of Invention. From hence I will not draw much Advantage, tho' it may serve
to balance that which he afterwards says of our Books, that *they are generally
stoln out of other Authors;* but I will fetch the Grounds of my Perswasion from
the very Nature and Use of the Stage itself. It is beyond all Dispute, that the
true Intention of such Representations is to give to mankind a Picture of
themselves, and thereby to make Virtue belov'd, Vice abhorr'd, and the little
Irregularities of Mens Tempers, called Humours, expos'd to laughter. The
Two First of these are the proper Subjects of Tragedy, and Trage-Comedy.
And in these I will first try to shew why our Way ought to be preferr'd be-
page 167 /   fore theirs. The *French* for the most part take only One or Two
Great Men, and chiefly insist on some one Remarkable Accident of their Story;
to this End they admit no more Persons than will serve to adorn that: And they
manage all in Rhime, with long Speeches, almost in the Way of Dialogues, in
making high Idea's of Honour, and in speaking Noble things. The *English* on
the other side make their chief Plot to consist of a greater variety of Actions;
and besides the main Design, add many other little Contrivances. By this Means
their Scenes are shorter, their Stage fuller, many more Persons of different
Humours are introduc'd. And in carrying on of this they generally do only
confine themselves to Blank Verse. This is the Difference, and hence the *English* have these Advantages. By the Liberty of Prose they render their Speech
and Pronunciation more Natural, and are never put to make a Contention
between the Rhime and the Sence. By their Underplots they often change the
Minds of their Spectators: Which is a mighty Benefit, seeing one of the greatest
Arts of Wit and Perswasion is the right ordering of Digressions. By their full
Stage they prevent Mens being continually tir'd with the same Objects: And so
they make the Doctrine of the Scene to be more lively and diverting than
the Precepts of Philosophers, or the grave Delight of Heroick Poetry; which
the *French* Tragedies do resemble. Nor is it sufficient to object against this,
that it is undecent to thrust in Men of mean Condition amongst the Actions
of Princes. For why should that misbecome the Stage, which is always
found to be acted on the true Theatre of the World? There being no
Court which only consists of Kings, and Queens, and Counsellors of State.
Upon   **page 168 /**   these Accounts, Sir, in my weak Judgment, the *French
Dramma* ought to give place to the *English* in the Tragical and Lofty Part
of it. And now having obtained this, I suppose they will of their own Ac-

cord resign the other Excellence, and confess that we have far exceeded them in the Representation of the different Humours. The Truth is, the *French* have always seemed almost asham'd of the true Comedy; making it not much more than the Subject of their *Farces:* Whereas the *English* Stage has so much abounded with it, that perhaps there is scarce any Sort of Extravagance of which the Minds of Men are capable but they have in some Measure express'd. It is in Comedies, and not in Solemn Histories, that the *English* use to relate the Speeches of Waggoners, of Fencers, and of Common Soldiers. And this I dare assure *Monsieur de Sorbiere*, that if he had understood our Language, he might have seen himself in all Shapes, as a vain Traveller, an empty Politician, an insolent Pedant, and an idle Pretender to Learning. But though he was not in a Condition of taking Advice from our Stage, for the correcting of his own Vices, yet methinks he might thereby have rectified his Judgment about ours: He might well have concluded, that the *English* Temper *is not so universally heavy and dumpish*, when he beheld their Theatres to be the gayest and merriest in *Europe.* . . . . **page 169 /**

Joseph Spence (1699–1768) is now known chiefly for his collection of anecdotes concerning men of prominence in the late seventeenth and early eighteenth centuries. Dr. Johnson commented: "His learning was not very great, and his mind not very powerful; his criticism, however, was commonly just; what he thought, he thought rightly, and his remarks were recommended by coolness and candour." Despite Johnson's unflattering view of his mental powers and equipment, Spence was generally regarded in his own time as a man of learning and critical perception. An Essay on Pope's Odyssey (1726–27) gained him considerable fame and brought him to the attention of Pope, with whom he developed an intimate friendship. The most notable work published in his own lifetime was Polymetis (1747), a dialogue on Roman poetry and ancient sculpture.

After his meeting with Pope in 1726, Spence began collecting the comments of his friend and other notables of their circle. The collection, not printed in Spence's lifetime, is an important contemporary source of information about public figures of the period and has been used extensively by such biographers as Warburton, Johnson, and Malone. The anecdotes reveal in an engagingly subjective way something of the personal lives and opinions of the men who were such a vital part of the intellectual and social life of their age.

Joseph Spence. *Observations, Anecdotes, and Characters, of Books and Men.* Arranged with Notes by Edmond Malone. London, 1820.

"Rymer, a learned and strict critic?" Ay, that is exactly his character. He is generally right, though rather too severe in his opinion of the particular plays he speaks of; and is, on the whole, one of the best critics we ever had.

page 85 /
— *Mr. Pope.*

Otway has written but two tragedies, out of six, that are pathetic. I believe he did it without much design. . . .

— *Mr. Pope.*

Otway had an intimate friend, one Blakiston, who was shot: the murderer fled towards Dover, and Otway pursued him; in his return he drank water when violently heated, and so got the fever which was the death of him. page 100 /
— *Mr. Dennis,* the Critic.

Nat. Lee was a Fellow of Trinity College in Cambridge. Villiers, Duke of Buck- page 101 / ingham, brought him up to town, where he never

213

did any thing for him; and I verily believe was one occasion of his running mad. He was rather before my time, but I saw him in Bedlam. . . . .

— Lockier.

That Duke of Buckingham (Villiers) was reckoned the most accomplished man of the age in riding, dancing, and fencing. When he came into the presence-chamber, it was impossible for you not to follow him with your eye as he went along, he moved so gracefully. He got the better of his vast estate, and died between two common girls at a little alehouse in Yorkshire.

— Lockier.

It is incredible how much pains he [George Villiers, Duke of Buckingham] took with one of the actors, to teach him to speak some passages in Bayes's part in the Rehearsal, right. The vulgar notion of that   **page 102 /**   play's being hissed off the first night is a mistake.

— Lockier.

The Rehearsal, one of the best pieces of criticism that ever was, and Butler's inimitable poem of Hudibras, must be quite lost to the readers in a century more, if not soon well commented. Tonson has a good key to the former, but refuses to print it, because he had been so much obliged to Dryden.

— Lockier.

In one of Dryden's plays there was this line, which the actress endeavoured to speak in as moving and affecting tone as she could:

"My wound is great — because it is so small."

and then she paused, and looked very distressed. The Duke of Buckingham, who was in one of the boxes, rose immediately from his seat, and added in a loud ridiculing tone of voice —

"Then 'twould be greater, were it none at all."

which had such an effect on the audience, who before were not very well pleased with the play, that they hissed the poor woman off the stage, would never bear her ap-   **page 103 /**   pearance in the rest of her part, and as this was the second time only of its appearance, made Dryden lose his benefit night.

page 104 /
— Lockier.

Dryden has assured me that he got more from the Spanish critics alone than from the Italian and French, and all others put together.

— Lord Bolingbroke.

Even Dryden was very suspicious of rivals. He would compliment Crown, when a play of his failed, but was cold to him if he met with success. He sometimes used to own that Crown had some genius, but   **page 106 /**   then he always added, that his father and Crown's mother were very well acquainted.

— Old Jacob Tonson.

I was about seventeen when I first came to town; an odd looking boy, with short rough hair, and that sort of awkwardness which one always brings up

first out of the country with one. However, in spite of my bashfulness and appearance, I used now and then to thrust myself into Will's, to have the pleasure of seeing the most celebrated wits of that time, who used to resort thither. The second time that ever I was there, Mr. Dryden was speaking of his own things, as he frequently did, especially of such as had been lately published. "If any thing of mine is good," says he, "it is my Mac-Fleckno; and I shall value myself thè more on it, because it is the first piece of ridicule written in heroics." Lockier overhearing this, plucked up his spirit so far as to say in a voice just loud enough to be heard, that Mac-Fleckno was a very fine poem, but that he had not imagined it   page 107 /   to be the first that ever was wrote that way. On this Dryden turned short upon him as surprised at his interposing; asked him how long he had been a dealer in poetry, and added with a smile, "but pray, sir, what is that you did imagine to have been writ so before?" Lockier named Boileau's Lutrin, and Tassoni's Secchia Rapita, which he had read, and knew Dryden had borrowed some strokes from each. "It is true," says Dryden, "I had forgot them." A little after Dryden went out; and in going spoke to Lockier again, and desired him to come to see him the next day. Lockier was highly delighted with the invitation, went to see him accordingly, and was well acquainted with him as long as he lived.   page 108 /
— *Lockier.*

Dryden allowed the Rehearsal to have a great many good strokes in it, "though so   page 109 /   severe (added he) upon myself; but I can't help saying that Smith and Jonson are two of the coolest, most insignificant fellows I ever met with on the stage." This, if it was not spoke out of resentment, betrayed page 110 /   a great want of judgment; for Smith and Jonson are men of sense, and should certainly say but little to such stuff, only enough to make Bayes show on.
— *Lockier.*

I don't think Dryden so bad a dramatic writer as you seem to do. There are many things finely said in his plays as almost by any body. Beside his three best (All for Love, Don Sebastian, and the Spanish Fryar), there are others that are good; as Cleomenes, Sir Martin Mar-all, Limberham, and the Conquest of Mexico. His   page 111 /   Wild Gallant was written while he was a boy, and is very bad. All his plays are printed in the order that they were written.
— *Mr. Pope.*

Dryden lived in Gerrard-street, and used most commonly to write in the ground room next the street.
— *Mr. Pope.*

He had three or four sons; John, Eras-   page 112 /   mus, Charles, and per- haps another. One of them was a priest, and another a captain in the Pope's guards. He left his family estate, which was about 120*l.* a year, to Charles. His historiographer and poet laureat's places were worth to him about 300*l.* a year.
— *Mr. Pope.*

... For some time he wrote a play (at least) every year; but in those days ten broad pieces was the usual highest price for a play; and if they got 50*l.* more in the acting, it was reckoned very well.

— *Mr. Pope.*

It was Dryden who made Will's coffee-house the great resort for the wits of his time. After his death, Addison transferred **page 113 /** it to Button's, who had been a servant of his.

— *Mr. Pope.*

Dryden always uses proper language, lively, natural, and fitted to the subject, it is scarce ever too high or too low; never, perhaps, except in his plays.

— *Mr. Pope.*

Addison was so eager to be the first name, that he and his friend Sir Richard Steele used to run down Dryden's cha- **page 114 /** racter as far as they could. Pope and Congreve used to support it.

— *Tonson.*

The Virtuoso of Shadwell does not maintain his character with equal strength to the end; and this was that writer's general fault. Wycherly used to say of him, that he knew how to start a fool very well, but that he was never able to run him down.

— *Mr. Pope.*

Shadwell's Squire of Alsatia took exceedingly at first, as an occasional play. It discovered the cant terms that were before not generally known, except to the cheats themselves, and was a good deal instrumental toward causing that nest of villains to be regulated by public authority. The story it was built on was a true fact.   **page 115 /**
— *Mr. Dennis,* the Critic.

Sir George Etheridge was as thorough a fop as ever I saw; he was exactly his own Sir Fopling Flutter, and yet he designed Dorimont, the genteel rake of wit, for his own picture!

— *Lockier.*

Wycherly was a very handsome man. His acquaintance with the famous Duchess of Cleaveland commenced oddly enough. One day as he passed that duchess's coach in the Ring, she leaned out of the window, and cried out, loud enough to be heard distinctly by him, "Sir, you're a rascal; **page 116 /** you're a villain." Wycherly from that instant entertained hopes. He did not fail waiting on her next morning; and with a melancholy tone begged to know, how it was possible for him to have so much disobliged her grace? They were very good friends from that time; yet, after all, what did he get by her? He was to have travelled with the young Duke of Richmond. King Charles now and then gave him 100*l.* — not often; and he was an equerry.

— *Mr. Pope.*

Wycherly was fifteen or sixteen when he went to France, and was acquainted there with Madam de Rambouillet, a little after Balzac's death.

— *Mr. Pope.*

He was not unvain of his face. That's a fine one which was engraved for him by Smith, in 1703. He was then about his grand climacteric; but sat for the picture from which it was taken when he was   **page 117 /**   about 28. . . .

                                                        page 118 /
                                                        — *Mr. Pope.*

The chronology of Wycherly's Plays I was well acquainted with, for he has told me over and over. Love in a Wood he wrote when he was but nineteen; the Gentleman Dancing-Master at twenty-one; the Plain Dealer at twenty-five; and the Country Wife at one or two-and-thirty.

                                                        — *Mr. Pope.*

Wycherly must have been born about the year 1638, according to Pope's account; therefore Love in a Wood was written in   **page 125 /**   1659: it, however, was acted for the first time at the Duke's Theatre, in 1672; and it is extremely improbable that he should have had it ten or twelve years by him after the restoration of the theatres, at which time he was certainly in great want of money, living in the Temple, and consorting with such expensive companions as Villiers, Duke of Buckingham, &c. The Gentleman Dancing-Master was first acted in 1673; the Country Wife, in 1675; and the Plain Dealer, in 1677; at which time he was at least thirty-seven, perhaps thirty-nine.

                                                        — *M*[*alone*].

Lord Rochester's character of Wycherly is quite wrong. He was far from being slow in general, and in particular wrote the Plain Dealer in three weeks.

                                                        page 126 /
                                                        — *Mr. Pope.*

None of our writers have a freer, easier way for comedy than Etheridge and Vanbrugh. "Now we have named all the best of them," (after mentioning those two, Wycherly, Congreve, Fletcher, Jonson, and Shakespeare).   **page 142 /**
                                                        — *Mr. Pope.*

I was acquainted with Betterton from a boy.

                                                        — *Mr. Pope.*

Yes, I really think Betterton the best actor I ever saw; but I ought to tell you at the same time, that in Betterton's days   **page 174 /**   the older sort of people talked of Hart's being his superior, just as we do of Betterton's being superior to those now.   **page 175 /**
                                                        — *Mr. Pope.*

James Wright (1643–1713), an antiquary and a miscellaneous writer, is best known today for his Historia Histrionica: an Historical Account of the English Stage, shewing the Ancient Use, Improvement, and Perfection of Dramatick Representations in this Nation. In a Dialogue of Plays and Players. *The history is presented in the form of a dialogue between one Lovewit and an old cavalier. The two, discoursing upon old plays and past actors (such as Lowin; Pollard; Taylor, who was known for his portrayal of Hamlet; and Swanstra, who played Othello "before the wars"), give, in fact, a general outline of the transition of the theater from the Elizabethan age to the Restoration. Written by one who not only loved the stage but knew its history and personalities well, the* Historia *is an extremely valuable contemporary account of the nature of English drama after the closing of the theaters in 1642.*

James Wright. *Historia Histrionica. An Historical Account of the English Stage; showing the Ancient Uses, Improvement, and Perfection of Dramatic Representations, in this Nation. In A Dialogue on Plays and Players* (1699), in *A Select Collection of Old Plays*, Vol. XI. Printed for R. Dodsley, London, 1744.

A Dialogue on Plays and Players

Lovewit, Trueman.

Truem. Ben Johnson! how dare you name Ben Johnson in these times; when we have such a crowd of poets of a quite diffeernt genius; the least of which thinks himself as well able to correct Ben Johnson, as he could a country school-mistress that taught to spell?

Lovew. We have, indeed, poets of a different genius; so are the plays: but in my opinion, they are all of 'em (some few excepted) as much inferior to those of former times, as the actors now in being (generally speaking) are compared to Hart, Mohun, Burt, Lacy, Clun, and Shatterel; for I can reach no farther backward. . . . **page ii /**

Truem. . . . Hart and Clun were bred up boys at the Black-friers, and acted women's parts; Hart was Robinson's boy, or apprentice; he acted the Dutchess in the Tragedy of the Cardinal, which was the first part that gave him reputation. Cartwright and Wintershal belong'd to the private House in Salisbury-Court; Burt was a boy first under Shank at the Black-friers, then under Beeston at the Cock-pit; and Mohun and Shatterel were in the same Condition with him, at the last Place. There Burt used to play the principal womens parts, in par-

218

ticular Clariana, in Love's Cruelty; and at the same time Mo- page iii / hun acted Bellamente, which part he retained after the restoration.

Lovew. That I have seen, and can well remember. I wish they had printed in the last age, (so I call the times before the rebellion) the actors names over against the parts they acted, as they have done since the restoration: and thus one might have guess'd at the action of the men, by the parts which we now read in the old plays.

Truem. It was not the custom and usage of those days, as it hath been since. Yet some few old plays there are that have the names set against the parts, as, the Dutchess of Malfy; the Picture; the Roman Actor; the Deserving Favourite; the Wild-Goose Chase, (at the Black-friers): the Wedding; the Renegado; the Fair Maid of the West; Hannibal and Scipio; King John and Matilda; at the Cock-pit: and Holland's Leaguer, at Salisbury Court.

Lovew. These are but few indeed: but pray, sir, what master-parts can you remember the old Black-friers men to act in Johnson, Shakespear, and Fletcher's plays?

Truem. What I can at present recollect I'll tell you; Shakespear, (who as I have heard was a much better poet than player) Burbage, Hemmings, and others of the page iv / older sort, were dead before I knew the town; but in my time, before the wars, Lowin used to act, with mighty applause, Falstaffe, Morose, Vulpone, and Mammon in the Alchymist; Melancius, in the Maid's Tragedy; and at the same time Amyntor was play'd by Stephen Hammerton, (who was at first a most noted and beautiful woman actor, but afterwards he acted with equal grace and applause, a young lover's part); Taylor acted Hamlet incomparably well, Jago, Truewit in the Silent Woman, and Face in the Alchymist; Swanston us'd to play Othello; Pollard and Robinson were comedians; so was Shank, who us'd to act Sir Roger, in the Scornful Lady: these were of the Black-friers. Those of principal note at the Cock-pit, were, Perkins, Michael Bowyer, Sumner, William Allen, and Bird, eminent actors, and Robins, a comedian. Of the other companies I took little notice.

Lovew. Were there so many companies?

Truem. Before the wars there were in being all these play-houses at the same time. The Black-friers, and Globe on the Bank-side, a winter and summer house, belonging to the same company, called the King's Servants; the Cock-pit or Phænix, in Drury-Lane, called the Queen's Servants; the page v / private house in Salisbury-Court, called the Prince's Servants; the Fortune near White-cross Street; and the Red Bull at the upper end of St. John's Street: the two last were mostly frequented by citizens, and the meaner sort of people. All these companies got money, and liv'd in reputation, especially those of the Black-friers, who were men of grave and sober behaviour.

Lovew. Which I admire at, that the town much less than at present, could then maintain five companies, and yet now two can hardly subsist.

Truem. Do not wonder, but consider, that tho' the town was then, perhaps, not much more than half so populous as now, yet then the prices were small (there being no scenes) and better order kept among the company that came; which made very good people think a play an innocent diversion for an idle hour or two, the plays themselves being then, for the most part, more instructive and moral. Whereas, of late, the play-houses are so extreamly pestered with vizard-masks and their trade, (occasioning continual quarrels and abuses) that many of the more civiliz'd part of the town are uneasy in the company, and shun the Theatre as they would a house of scandal. It is an argument of the worth of   **page vi /**   the plays and actors of the last age, and easily inferred, that they were much beyond ours in this, to consider that they could support themselves merely from their own merit, the weight of the matter, and goodness of the action, without scenes and machines; whereas the present plays with all that shew can hardly draw an audience, unless there be the additional invitation of a Signior Fideli, a Monsieur l'Abbe, or some such foreign regale express'd in the bottom of the bill. . . .   **page vii /**

Lovew. What kind of play-houses had they before the wars?

Truem. The Black-friers, Cockpit, and Salisbury-court, were called private houses, and were very small to what we see now. The Cockpit was standing since the restoration, and Rhode's company acted there for some time.

Lovew. I have seen that.

Truem. Then you have seen the other two, in effect; for they were all three built almost exactly alike, for form and bigness. Here they had pits for the gentry, and acted by candle-light. The Globe, Fortune, and Bull, were large houses, and lay partly open to the weather, and there they always acted by day-light.

Lovew. But pr'ythee, Trueman, what became of these players when the stage was put down, and the rebellion rais'd?

Truem. Most of 'em, except Lowin, Tayler and Pollard (who were superannuated) went into the king's army, and like good men and true, serv'd their old master, tho' in a different, yet more honourable capacity. Robin- **page viii /** son was kill'd at the taking of a place, (I think Basing-house) by Harrison, he that was after hang'd at Charing-cross, who refused him quarter, and shot him in the head when he had laid down his arms. . . . Mohun was a captain. . . . Hart was a lieutenant of horse under sir Thomas Dallison, in prince Rupert's regiment; Burt was cornet in the same troop, and Shatterel quartermaster; Allen of the cockpit was a major, and quarter-master-general at Oxford. I have not heard of one of these players of any note that sided with the other party, but only Swanston, and he profess'd himself a presbyterian, took up the trade of a jeweller . . . ; the rest either lost, or expos'd their lives for their king. When the wars were over, and the royalists totally subdue'd; most of 'em who were left alive gather'd to London, and for a subsistence endeavour'd to revive their old trade privately. They made up one company out of all the scatter'd members of several; and in the winter before the king's murder, 1648, they ventured to act some plays with as much caution and pri- **page ix /** vacy as could be, at the Cockpit. They continued undisturbed for three or four days; but at last, as they were presenting the tragedy of the Bloody Brother (in which Lowin acted Aubrey, Tayler Rollo, Pollard the cook, Burt Latorch, and I think Hart Otto) a party of foot soldiers beset the house, surprized 'em about the middle of the play, and carried 'em away in their habits, not admitting them to shift, to Hatton-house then a prison, where having detain'd them some time, they plundered them of their cloaths, and let 'em loose again. Afterwards, in Oliver's time, they used to act privately, three or four miles or more out of town, now here, now there, sometimes in noblemens houses, in particular

Holland-house at Kensington, where the nobility and gentry who met (but in no great number) used to make a sum for them, each giving a broad piece, or the like. And Alexander Groffe, the woman actor at Blackfriers (who had made himself known to persons of quality) used to be the jackall, and give notice of time and place. At Christmas and Bartholomew-fair, they used to bribe the officer who commanded the guard at Whitehall, and were thereupon connived at to act for a few days, at the Red Bull; but were sometimes notwithstanding disturb'd by soldiers. Some pick'd up a little money by publishing the **page x /** copies of plays never before printed, but kept up in manuscript. For instance, in the year 1652, Beaumont and Fletcher's Wild Goose Chace was printed in folio, for the public use of all the ingenious, as the title-page says, and private benefit of John Lowin and Joseph Tayler, servants to his late majesty; and by them dedicated to the honoured few lovers of dramatick poesy, wherein they modestly intimate their wants; and that with sufficient cause; for whatever they were before the wars, they were after reduced to a necessitous condition. . . .

Lovew. . . . After the restoration, the king's players acted publickly at the Red Bull for some time, and then removed to a new-built playhouse in Vere-street, by Clare- **page xi /** market. There they continued for a year or two, and then removed to the Theatre Royal in Drury-lane, where they first made use of scenes, which had been a little before introduced upon the publick stage by sir William Davenant, at the duke's Old Theatre in Lincolns-inn-fields, but afterwards very much improved, with the addition of curious machines by mr. Betterton at the New Theatre in Dorset-garden, to the great expence and continual charge of the players. This much impaired their profit o'er what it was before; for I have been inform'd by one of 'em, that for several years next after the restoration, every whole sharer in mr. Hart's company, got 1000*l.* per ann. About the same time that scenes first entered upon the stage at London, women were taught to act their own parts; since when, we have seen at both houses several actresses, justly famed as well for beauty, as perfect good action. And some plays, in particular the Parson's Wedding, have been presented all by women, as formerly all by men. Thus it continued for about 20 years, when mr. Hart, and some of the old men began to grow weary, and were minded to leave off; then the two companies thought fit to unite; but of late you see, they have thought it no less fit to divide again, though both companies keep the same **page xii /** name of his majesty's servants. All this while the playhouse musick improved yearly, and is now arrived to greater perfection than ever I knew it. Yet for all these advantages, the reputation of the stage, and peoples affection to it, are much decayed. Some were lately severe against it, and would hardly allow stage-plays fit to be longer permitted. Have you seen mr. Collier's book?

Truem. Yes. . . .

Lovew. And what think you?

Truem. In my mind mr. Collier's reflections are pertinent, and true in the main; the book ingeniously wrote, and well intended; but he has overshot himself in some places. . . . If there be abuses relating to the stage, which I think is too apparent, let the abuse be reformed, and not the use, for that reason only, abolished. . . . **page xiii /**

Lovew. . . . I have been told, that stage-plays are inconsistent with the laws of this kingdom, and players made rogues by statute.

Truem. He that told you so, strain'd a point of truth. I never met with any law wholly to suppress them: sometimes indeed they have been prohibited for a season; as in times of Lent, general mourning, or publick calamities, or upon other occasions, when the government saw fit. Thus by proclamation, 7 of April, in the first year of queen Elizabeth, plays and interludes were forbid till Alhallow-tide next following. Hollinshed, p. 1184. Some statutes have been made for their regulation or reformation, not general suppression. By the stat. 39 Eliz. cap. 4. (which was made for the suppressing of rogues, vagabonds, and sturdy beggars) it is enacted,

S. 2. *"That all persons that be, or utter themselves to be, proctors, procurers, patent gatherers, or collectors for goals, prisons, or hospitals, or fencers, bear-wards, common players of interludes and ministrels, wandring abroad, (other than players of interludes belonging to any baron of this realm, or any other honourable personage of greater degree, to be authoriz'd to play un-* **page xxxv /** *der the hand and seal of arms of such baron or personage) all juglers, tinkers, pedlars, and petty chapmen, wand'ring abroad, all wand'ring persons, &c. able in body, using loytering, and refusing to work for such reasonable wages as is commonly given, &c. These shall be adjudged and deemed rogues, vagabonds, and sturdy beggars, and punished as such."*

Lovew. But this privilege of authorising or licensing, is taken away by the stat. Jac. I. ch. 7. S. 1. and therefore all of them, as mr. Collier says . . . are expressly brought under the aforesaid penalty, without distinction.

Truem. If he means all players, without distinction, 'tis a great mistake. For the force of the queen's statute extends only to wandring players, and not to such as are the king or queen's servants, and establish'd in settled houses, by royal authority. On such, the ill character of vagrant players (or as they are now called, strollers) can cast no more aspersion, than the wandring proctors, in the same statute mentioned, on those of Doctors-Commons. By a stat. made 3 Jac. I. ch. 21. it was enacted, *"That if any person shall in any stage-play, interlude, shew, may-game or pageant, jestingly or profanely speak or use the holy name of God, Christ Jesus, or of the Trinity, he shall forfeit for every such offence* 10l.*"* The stat. 1. **page xxxvi /** Charles I. ch. 1. enacts, *"That no meetings, assemblies, or concourse of people shall be out of their own parishes, on the Lord's-day, for any sports or pastimes whatsoever, nor any bear-baiting, bull-baiting, interludes, common plays, or other unlawful exercises and pastimes, used by any person or persons within their own parishes."* These are all the statutes that I can think of, relating to the stage and players; but nothing to suppress them totally, till the two ordinances of the long parliament, one of the 22d of October 1647, the other of the 11th of Feb. 1647. By which all stage-plays and interludes are absolutely forbid; the stages, seats, galleries, &c. to be pulled down; all players, tho' calling themselves the king or queen's servants, if convicted of acting within two months before such conviction, to be punished as rogues according to law; the money received by them to go to the poor of the parish; and every spectator to pay five shillings to the use of the poor. Also cock-fighting was prohibited by one of Oliver's acts of 31 March, 1644. But I suppose no body pretends these things to be laws. I could say more on this subject, but I must break off here, and leave you, Lovewit; my occasions require it.

Lovew. Farewell, old Cavalier.

Truem. 'Tis properly said; we are almost all of us, now, gone and forgotten.

page xxxvii /

HANDLIST OF SELECTED PLAYS

JOHN BANKS (c. 1652–1706)

The Rival Kings: or The Loves of Oroondates and Statira (1677). T.*
The Destruction of Troy (1678). T.
The Unhappy Favourite: or the Earl of Essex (1681). T.
Vertue Betray'd: or, Anna Bullen (1682). T.
The Island Queens: Or, The Death of Mary, Queen of Scotland (1684, unacted). T.
The Innocent Usurper; or, The Death of the Lady Jane Gray (1694, unacted). T.
Cyrus the Great: or, The Tragedy of Love (1695). T.
The Albion Queens: or the Death of Mary Queen of Scotland (1704). T.

MRS. APHRA BEHN (1640–1689)

The Forc'd Marriage, or The Jealous Bridegroom (1670). T.C.
The Amorous Prince, or, The Curious Husband (1671). C.
The Dutch Lover (1672/73). C.
Abdelazar, or the Moor's Revenge (1676). T.
The Town-Fopp: or Sir Timothy Tawdrey (1676). C.
The Debauchee: or, The Credulous Cuckold (1676/77). C.
The Rover: Or, The Banish't Cavaliers (1676/77). C.
Sir Patient Fancy (1677/78). C.
The Feign'd Curtizans, or, A Night's Intrigue (1678/79). C.
The Young King: or, The Mistake (1679). T.C.
The Second Part of the Rover (1680). C.
The Roundheads, or, The Good Old Cause (1681). C.
The City-Heiress: or, Sir Timothy Treat-all (1681/82). C.
The False Count, or, A New Way to Play an Old Game (1682). C.
The Luckey Chance, or An Alderman's Bargain (1686). C.
The Emperor of the Moon (1686/87). F.
The Widdow Ranter, or, The History of Bacon in Virginia (1689). T.C.
The Younger Brother: or, The Amorous Jilt (1696). C.

THOMAS BETTERTON (1635?–1710)

Appius and Virginia, Acted . . . under the name of The Roman Virgin or Unjust Judge (1669). T.

*	C. Comedy	T. Tragedy
	D.O. Dramatic Opera	T.C. Tragi-comedy
	O. Opera	F. Farce

The Amorous Widow; or, the Wanton Wife (c. 1670). C.
The Revenge: or, A Match in Newgate (1680). C.
The Prophetess: or, the History of Dioclesian (1690). D.O.
King Henry IV with the Humours of Sir John Falstaff (1699). T.C.
The Sequel of Henry the Fourth: With the Humors of Sir John Falstaffe, and Justice Shallow (1719). T.C.

ROGER BOYLE, EARL OF ORRERY (1621–1679)
The History of Henry the Fifth (1664). T.
The General (1664). T.
The Tragedy of Mustapha, Son of Solyman the Magnificent (1665). T.
The Black Prince (1667). T.
Tryphon (1668). T.
Guzman (1669). C.
Mr. Anthony. A Comedy (1671). C.
Herod the Great (1694, unacted). T.

HENRY CAREY, VISCOUNT FALKLAND (d. 1633).
The Marriage Night (1664). C.

JOHN CARYL (1625–1711)
The English Princess, or, The Death of Richard the III (1666/67). T.
Sir Salomon: or, The Cautious Coxcomb (1669). C.

WILLIAM CAVENDISH, DUKE OF NEWCASTLE (1593–1676)
The Humourous Lovers (1667). C.
The Triumphant Widow, or The Medley of Humours (1674). C.

COLLEY CIBBER (1671–1757)
Love's Last Shift; or, The Fool in Fashion (1695/96). C.
Woman's Wit: or, The Lady in Fashion (1696). C.
The Tragical History of King Richard III (1699). T.
Love Makes a Man; or, The Fop's Fortune (1700). C.
She Wou'd and She Wou'd Not; or, the Kind Imposter (1702). C.
The School-Boy: or, The Comical Rivals (1702). F.
The Careless Husband (1704). C.

WILLIAM CONGREVE (1670–1729)
The Old Batchelour (1692/93). C.
The Double Dealer (1693). C.
Love for Love (1695). C.
The Mourning Bride (1697). T.
The Way of the World (1699/1700). C.

ABRAHAM COWLEY (1618–1667)
Cutter of Coleman-Street (1661). C.

JOHN CROWNE (1640–1730?)

Juliana, or, The Princess of Poland (1671). T.

The History of Charles the Eighth of France, or the Invasion of Naples by
the French (1671). T.

Andromache (1674). T.

The Countrey Wit (1675/76). C.

The Destruction of Jerusalem by Titus Vespasian. In Two Parts. (1676/
77). T.

The Ambitious Statesman, or the Loyal Favourite (1678/79). T.

The Misery of Civil-War (1679–80). T.

Henry the Sixth, the First Part. With the Murder of Humphrey Duke of
Glocester (1681). T.

Thyestes (1680/81). T.

City Politiques (1682/83). C.

Sir Courtly Nice: or, It Cannot Be (1685). C.

Darius King of Persia (1688). T.

The English Frier: or, The Town Sparks (1689/90). C.

Regulus (1692). T.

The Married Beau: or, The Curious Impertinent (1694). C.

Caligula (1697/98). T.

SIR WILLIAM DAVENANT (1606–1668)

The First Days Entertainment at Rutland House (1656).

The Siege of Rhodes Made a Representation by the Art of Prospective in
Scenes, And the Story sung in Recitative Musick (1656). O.

The Siege of Rhodes: The First and Second Part (1661). O.

The Cruelty of the Spaniards in Peru. Exprest by Instrumentall and Vocall
Musick, and by the Art of Perspective in Scenes, &c. (1658). O.

The History of Sʳ Francis Drake (1658). O.

The Rivals (1664). C.

The Man's the Master (1667/68). C.

The Tempest, or, The Enchanted Island (1667). C. (Written with
Dryden.)

Macbeth. . . . With all the Alterations, Amendments, Additions, and New
Songs (1672/73). D.O.

JOHN DENNIS (1657–1734)

A Plot, and No Plot (1697). C.

Rinaldo and Armida (1698). T.

Iphigenia (1699). T.

THOMAS DILKE (*fl.* 1696)

The Lover's Luck (1695). C.

The City Lady: or, Folly Reclaim'd (1696/97). C.

The Pretenders: or, The Town Unmaskt (1698). C.

JOHN DRYDEN (1631–1700)

The Wild Gallant (1662/63). C.

The Rival Ladies (1664). T.C.

The Indian Emperour, or, The Conquest of Mexico by the Spaniards. Being the Sequel of the Indian Queen (1665). T. (Indian Queen: *Written with Sir Robert Howard, q.v.*)

The Secret Love, or the Maiden Queen (1666/67). T.C.

Sr Martin Mar-all, or the Feign'd Innocence (1667). C.

An Evening's Love, or the Mock Astrologer (1668). C.

Tyrannick Love, or the Royal Martyr (1669). T.

The Conquest of Granada by the Spaniards: In Two Parts (Pt. I, 1670; Pt. II, 1670/71). T.

Marriage A-la-Mode (1672). C.

The Assignation: or, Love in a Nunnery (1672). C.

Amboyna (1673). T.

Aureng-Zebe (1675). T.

The State of Innocence, and Fall of Man (1677, unacted). O.

All for Love, or, The World well Lost (1677). T.

The Kind Keeper; or, Mr. Limberham (1677/78). C.

Oedipus (1678/79). T. (Written with Nat. Lee.)

Troilus and Cressida, or, Truth found too Late (1679). T.

The Spanish Fryar, or, The Double Discovery (1679/80). C.

The Duke of Guise (1682). T.

Albion and Albanius (1685). D.O.

Don Sebastian, King of Portugal (1689). T.

Amphitryon; or, The Two Socia's (1690). C.

King Arthur: or, The British Worthy (1691). D.O.

Cleomenes, the Spartan Heroe (1692). T.

Love Triumphant; or, Nature will Prevail (1693). T.C.

THOMAS DUFFETT (*fl.* 1678)

The Spanish Rogue (1673). C.

The Mock Tempest (1675). C.

THOMAS D'URFEY (1653–1723)

The Siege of Memphis, or The Ambitious Queen (1676). T.

Madam Fickle: or the Witty False One (1676). C.

The Fool Turn'd Critick (1676). C.

A Fond Husband: or, The Plotting Sisters (1676). C.

Trick for Trick: or, The Debauch'd Hypocrite (1677/78). C.

Squire Oldsapp: or, The Night-Adventurers (1678). C.

The Virtuous Wife; or, Good Luck at last (1679). C.

Sir Barnaby Whigg: or, No Wit like a Womans (1681). C.

The Royalist (1681/82). C.

The Injured Princess, or The Fatal Wager (1681/82). T.C.

A Common-Wealth of Women (1685). C.

The Banditti, or, A Ladies Distress (1685). C.

A Fool's Preferment, or, The Three Dukes of Dunstable (1688). C.

Bussy D'Ambois, or the Husbands Revenge (1690/91). T.

Love for Money: or, the Boarding School (1689). C.

The Marriage-Hater Match'd (1691/92). C.

The Richmond Heiress: or, A Woman Once in the Right (1692/93). C.
The Comical History of Don Quixote (1694). C.
The Comical History of Don Quixote. . . . Part the Second (1694). C.
The Comical History of Don Quixote. The Third Part. With the Mar-
riage of Mary the Buxome (1695). C.
The Intrigues at Versailles: or, A Jilt in all Humours (1696/97). C.
A New Opera, call'd Cinthia and Endimion: or, The Loves of the Deities
(1697). D.O.
The Campaigners: or, The Pleasant Adventures at Brussels (1698). C.
The Famous History of the Rise and Fall of Massaniello. In Two Parts
(1699). T.
The Bath, or, The Western Lass (1701). C.
The Old Mode & the New, or, Country Miss with her Furbeloe (1703). C.
Wonders in the Sun: or, The Kingdom of the Birds (1706). C.O.
The Modern Prophets: or, New Wit for a Husband (1709). C.

SIR GEORGE ETHEREGE (1634?–1691?)
The Comical Revenge; or, Love in a Tub (1664). C.
She Wou'd if She Cou'd (1667/68). C.
The Man of Mode, or, Sᵣ Fopling Flutter (1675/76). C.

GEORGE FARQUHAR (1678–1707)
Love and a Bottle (1699). C.
The Constant Couple; or a Trip to the Jubilee (1699). C.
Sir Harry Wildair: Being the Sequel of the Trip to the Jubilee (1701). C.
The Inconstant: or, The Way to Win Him (1701/02). C.
The Twin-Rivals (1702). C.
The Stage Coach (1703/04). C.
The Recruiting Officer (1706). C.
The Beaux Stratagem (1706/07). C.

RICHARD FLECKNOE (d. 1678?)
Love's Dominion . . . altered and reprinted as Love's Kingdom (1664). T.C.
Erminia. Or, The fair and vertuous Lady (1661, unacted). T.C.
The Damoiselles a la Mode (1668): C.

CHARLES GILDON (1665–1724)
The Roman Bride's Revenge (1697). T.
Phaeton: or, The Fatal Divorce (1698). T.
Measure for Measure, or Beauty the Best Advocate (1699). C.
Love's Victim: or, The Queen of Wales (1701). T.
The Patriot: or, The Italian Conspiracy (1703). T.

GEORGE GRANVILLE, LORD LANSDOWNE (1666–1735)
The She-Gallants (1695). C.
Heroick Love (1697). T.
The Jew of Venice (1701). C.
The British Enchanters: or, No Magick like Love (1706). T.

JOSEPH HARRIS (c. 1650–c. 1715)
 The Mistakes, or, The False Report (1690). T.C.
 The City Bride: or, The Merry Cuckold (1696). C.
 Love's a Lottery, and a Woman the Prize . . . (1698/99). C.

HON. EDWARD HOWARD (1624–c. 1700)
 The Usurper (1663/64). T.
 The Womens Conquest (1670). T.C.
 The Six days Adventure, or the New Utopia (1670). C.
 The Man of Newmarket (1678). C.

SIR ROBERT HOWARD (1626–1698)
 The Committee (1662). C.
 The Surprisal (1662). C.
 The Indian-Queen (1663/64). T.
 The Vestal-Virgin (1664). T.
 The Great Favourite, Or, the Duke of Lerma (1667/68). T.

THOMAS KILLIGREW (1612–1683)
 The Parson's Wedding (1664). C.

JOHN LACEY (c. 1615–1681)
 The Old Troop: or, Monsieur Raggou (1665). C.
 Sauny the Scott: or, The Taming of the Shrew (1667). C.
 The Dumb Lady, or, The Farrier Made Physician (1669). C.
 Sir Hercules Buffoon, or, The Poetical Squire (1684). C.

NATHANIEL LEE (1653?–1692)
 The Tragedy of Nero, Emperour of Rome (1674). T.
 Sophonisba, or Hannibal's Overthrow (1675). T.
 Gloriana, or the Court of Augustus Caesar (1675/76). T.
 The Rival Queens, or the Death of Alexander the Great (1676/77). T.
 Mithridates, King of Pontus (1677/78). T.
 Caesar Borgia: the Son of Pope Alexander the Sixth (1679). T.
 Theodosius; or, The Force of Love (1680). T.
 Lucius Junius Brutus, Father of his Country (1680). T.
 The Princess of Cleve (1681). T.
 Constantine the Great (1683). T.
 The Massacre of Paris (1689). T.

PETER ANTHONY MOTTEUX (1660–1718)
 Love's a Jest (1696). C.
 The Novelty. Every Act a Play (1697). C.
 Beauty in Distress (1698). T.
 The Island Princess, or the Generous Portuguese (1698). O.

Thomas Otway (1652–1685)

Alcibiades (1675). T.

Don Carlos, Prince of Spain (1676). T.

Titus and Berenice. . . . With a Farce call'd the Cheats of Scapin (1676).
T. and F.

Friendship in Fashion (1678). C.

The History and Fall of Caius Marius (1679). T.

The Orphan: or, The Unhappy Marriage (1680). T.

The Souldiers Fortune (1679/80). C.

Venice Preserv'd; or, A Plot Discover'd (1681/82). T.

The Atheist. Or, the Second Part of the Souldiers Fortune (1683). C.

Mrs. Katherine Philips (1631–1664)

Pompey (1662/63). T.

Horace (1667/68). T. (Completed by Sir John Denham.)

Samuel Pordage (1633–1691)

Herod and Marianne (1673). T.

The Siege of Babylon (1677). T.C.

Thomas Porter (1636–1680)

The Villain (1662). T.

A Witty Combat: or, the Female Victor (1664? The German Princess?
See Pepys, April 15, 1664). T.C.

The Carnival (1663). C.

The French Conjurer (1677). C.

Edward Ravenscroft (c. 1650–1697)

The Citizen Turn'd Gentleman (1672). C.

The Careless Lovers (1672/73). C.

The Wrangling Lovers: or, The Invisible Mistress (1676). C.

Scaramouch a Philosopher, Harlequin A School-Boy, Bravo, Merchant, and
Magician. A Comedy After the Italian Manner (1677). F.

King Edgar and Alfreda (1677). T.C.

The English Lawyer (1677). C.

The London Cuckolds (1681). C.

Dame Dobson: or, The Cunning Woman (1683). C.

Titus Andronicus, or the Rape of Lavinia (1686). T.

The Canterbury Guests; or, A Bargain Broken (1694). C.

The Anatomist: or, the Sham Doctor (1697). C.

The Italian Husband (1697). T.

Richard Rhodes (d. 1668)

Flora's Vagaries (1663). C.

SIR CHARLES SEDLEY (1639?–1701)

    The Mulberry-Garden (1668). C.

    Antony and Cleopatra (1676/77). T.

    Bellamira, or the Mistress (1687). C.

ELKANAH SETTLE (1648–1724)

    Cambyses King of Persia (1670/71). T.

    The Empress of Morocco (1673). T.

    Love and Revenge (1674). T.

    The Conquest of China, By the Tartars (1675). T.

    Ibrahim The Illustrious Bassa (1676). T.

    Pastor Fido: or, The Faithful Shepherd (1676). Pastoral.

    Fatal Love: or, The Forc'd Inconstancy (1680). T.

    The Female Prelate: Being the History of the Life and Death of Pope Joan
       (1679). T.

    The Heir of Morocco, with the Death of Gayland (1682). T.

    Distress'd Innocence: or, The Princess of Persia (1690). T.

    The Fairy-Queen (1692). O.

    The New Athenian Comedy (1693, unacted). C.

    The Ambitious Slave: or, a Generous Revenge (1693/94). T.

    Philaster, or Love lies a-bleeding (1695). T.C.

    The World in the Moon (1697). D.O.

    The Virgin Prophetess: or, The Fate of Troy (1701). D.O.

    The City-Ramble: or, A Play-House Wedding (1711). C.

    The Ladys Triumph (1718). D.O.

THOMAS SHADWELL (1642?–1692)

    The Sullen Lovers: Or, the Impertinents (1668). C.

    The Royal Shepherdess (1668/69). T.C.

    The Humorists (1670). C.

    The Miser (1671/72). C.

    Epsom Wells (1672). C.

    The Tempest, or the Enchanted Island (1674). D.O.

    Psyche (1674/75). D.O.

    The Libertine (1675). C.

    The Virtuoso (1676). C.

    The History of Timon of Athens, The Man-Hater. . . . Made into a Play
       (1677/78). T.

    A True Widow (1677/78). C.

    The Woman-Captain (1679). C.

    The Lancashire Witches, And Tegue o Divelly The Irish Priest (1681). C.

    The Squire of Alsatia (1688). C.

    Bury Fair (1689). C.

    The Amorous Bigotte: with the Second Part of Tegue O Divelly
       (1689/90). C.

    The Scowrers (1690). C.

    The Volunteers: or The Stock Jobbers (1692). C.

THOMAS SOUTHERNE (1659–1746)

The Loyal Brother: or, The Persian Prince (1681/82). T.
The Disappointment: or, The Mother in Fashion (1684). T.
Sir Anthony Love: or, The Rambling Lady (1690). C.
The Wives Excuse: or, Cuckolds make themselves (1691). C.
The Maid's Last Prayer: or, Any, rather than Fail (1692/93). C.
The Fatal Marriage: or, The Innocent Adultery (1693/94). T.
Oroonoko (1695). T.
The Fate of Capua (1700). T.
The Spartan Dame (1719). T.
Money the Mistress (1726). T.

SIR ROBERT STAPYLTON (1605?–1669)

The Slighted Maid (1662/63). C.
The Step-mother (1663). T.C.
The Tragedie of Hero and Leander (1669, unacted). T.

NAHUM TATE (1652–1715)

Brutus of Alba: or, The Enchanted Lovers (1678). T.
The Loyal General (1679). T.
The History of King Richard the Second (1680). T.
The History of King Lear (1681). T.
The Ingratitude of a Common-Wealth: Or, the Fall of Caius Martius
    Coriolanus (1681). T.
A Duke and No Duke (1684). F.
Cuckolds-Haven: or, an Alderman No Conjurer. A Farce (1685). F.
The Island-Princess (1687). T.C.
Injur'd Love: or, The Cruel Husband . . . design'd to be acted at the
    Theatre Royal (1707). T.

SIR SAMUEL TUKE (c. 1620–1674)

The Adventures of Five Hours (1662/63). T.C.

SIR JOHN VANBRUGH (1664–1726)

The Relapse: or, Virtue in Danger (1696). C.
The Provok'd Wife (1697). C.
Aesop (Pt. I, 1696; Pt. II, 1696/97). C.
The Country House (1698). F.
The Pilgrim (1700). C.
The False Friend (1701/02). C.
The Confederacy (1705). C.
The Mistake (1705). C.

GEORGE VILLIERS, DUKE OF BUCKINGHAM (1628–1687)

The Rehearsal (1671). C–Burlesque
The Chances (1666/67). C.

JOHN WILMOT, EARL OF ROCHESTER (1648–1680)
 Valentinian (1683/84). T.

WILLIAM WYCHERLEY (1640–1716)
 Love in a Wood, or, St. James's Park (1671). C.
 The Gentleman Dancing-Master (1672). C.
 The Country-Wife (1674/75). C.
 The Plain-Dealer (1676). C.

SUGGESTED TOPICS FOR PAPERS

LIMITED TOPICS

Topics in this list may be used (1) for short papers stressing particular aspects of research technique using only materials in this collection, or (2) for longer papers requiring additional reading in literary or historical sources.

The King's Company
The Duke's Company
Public Condemnation of the Stage
Defense of the Stage
Opera
Restoration Theater: London in Microcosm
Foreign Views of the Restoration Theater
Physical Features of the Restoration Theater
Music and Show (scenic effects) on the Restoration Stage
Stagecraft (costumes, lighting, equipment)
History of the Theaters in the later Seventeenth Century
Pepys and the Theater
The Theater Audience
The Influence of the Audience on the Drama
Women in the Audience
Manners and Conduct of the Audience
The success of particular plays:
  The Adventures of Five Hours
  Hamlet
  The Siege of Rhodes
  The Conquest of Granada
  Sir Martin Mar-all
  The Man of Mode
  and others
Heroic Drama
Types of Comedy
Types of Tragedy

Great Comic Actors
Great Tragedians
Studies of individual actors:
  Thomas Betterton
  Edward Kynaston
  John Lacy
  Michael Mohun
  Elizabeth Barry
  Mrs. Betterton (Mrs. Saunderson)
  and others
Women on the Stage
Men in Women's Parts
Studies of entrepreneurs:
  William Davenant
  Thomas Killigrew
  Colley Cibber
  Thomas Betterton
King Charles II and the Theater
John Dryden:
  Dryden and the Restoration Stage
  Dryden as a Comic Writer
  Dryden as a Tragic Writer
  Dryden and Shakespeare
  Dryden and the Poets of the Last Age
  Dryden and the "Rules"
Ben Jonson and the Restoration Stage
The Plays of Beaumont and Fletcher on the Restoration Stage
The Plays of Shakespeare on the Restoration Stage
Elizabethan, Jacobean, and Caroline Drama on the Restoration Stage
Sources of Plots for Restoration Drama
Sources of Actors for the Stage

235

Definition and Purpose of Drama
Function of Tragedy
Function of Comedy
The Fop on the Stage
The Fop in the Audience

The Court in the Theater
Middle-class Participation in the London
 Theater
Prices of Admission to Stage Plays
Plagiarism

General Topics

Topics in this list may be used for longer papers (1) limited to materials in this collection or (2) supplementing these materials with further reading in literary or historical sources.

The Theater and London Society
Restoration and Elizabethan Stages Contrasted
Restoration Reaction to Elizabethan Romanticism
Social and Moral Issues Related to the Stage
Foreign Influence on Restoration Drama
Theatrical Profits
The Rise of Middle-class Drama
Neoclassical Theory and Restoration Drama
Transition from Jacobean to Restoration Theater
The Residual Effect of the Puritan Rebellion on the Restoration Theater
Restoration Stage Practices Contrasted with Elizabethan
Re-establishment of the Theater after the Rebellion
Aristotle and Restoration Dramatic Theory: the Battle over the Unities
Drama as Statement and Exemplification of Restoration Mores

Heroic Drama: The Epic in Little
Poetry in Drama
Dryden and his Critics
Contemporary Attitudes toward Dryden
Dryden and the French Drama
The Comedy of Humours
The Idea of Decorum
The Idea of Verisimilitude
Dramatic Adaptations for the Restoration Stage
Molière and the Restoration Stage
The Court Theater
English Court Wits and the Theater
Drama as Expression of National Pride
Critical Theories Concerning Drama
The Comedy of Manners
Sentimental Tragedy
Experimentation and the Theater
Drama as a Vehicle for Satire
Patronage of the theater, actors, playwrights
Affectations Revealed through the Theater
Frenchified Englishmen

INDEX